AF505999

Hawthorne, Gender, and Death

Hawthorne, Gender, and Death

Christianity and Its Discontents

Roberta Weldon

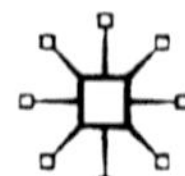

Portions of chapter four were originally published in *ATQ*, Volume 6, No. 1, March 1992. Reprinted by permission of The University of Rhode Island. The author thanks Josie P. Campbell, the editor of *ATQ*, for granting this permission.

First published in 2008 by
PALGRAVE MACMILLAN™
175 Fifth Avenue, New York, N.Y. 10010 and
Houndmills, Basingstoke, Hampshire, England RG21 6XS
Companies and representatives throughout the world.

PALGRAVE MACMILLAN is the global academic imprint of the Palgrave Macmillan division of St. Martin's Press, LLC and of Palgrave Macmillan Ltd. Macmillan® is a registered trademark in the United States, United Kingdom and other countries. Palgrave is a registered trademark in the European Union and other countries.

ISBN-13: 978–0–230–60290–8

Library of Congress Cataloging-in-Publication Data

Weldon, Roberta, 1945–
    Hawthorne, gender, and death : Christianity and its discontents / by Roberta Weldon.
        p. cm.
    Includes bibliographical references and index.
    ISBN 0–230–60290–8
    1. Hawthorne, Nathaniel, 1804–1864—Criticism and interpretation. 2. Death in literature. 3. Mourning customs in literature. 4. Death—Social aspects—United States—History—19th century. 5. Christianity and literature—United States—History—19th century. 6. Sex role in literature. 7. Ethics in literature. I. Title.

PS1892.D35W45 2008
813′.3—dc22   2007035836

A catalogue record for this book is available from the British Library.

Design by Newgen Imaging Systems (P) Ltd., Chennai, India.

First edition: April 2008

10 9 8 7 6 5 4 3 2 1

Printed in the United States of America.

Transferred to Digital Printing in 2008

For Jim, Emily, and Michael

CONTENTS

ACKNOWLEDGMENTS

I have incurred many debts along the way. I thank first my deceased mother and father, Jane and Frank Weldon, for years filled with music, books, and time to play, and my sister, Fran Gelber, for her friendship, for many lively conversations across the miles, and for her example of courage in the face of serious illness. I met my other sister, Marion Griffin, much later in my life but her charm, indefatigable spirit, and kindness only make me regret that I had not known her sooner.

The Sisters of Charity and the Dominican Sisters, women who devoted their lives to providing a free or low cost education to many like me in New York City, are owed a special thanks for their generosity and for inspiring their students with the example of the value of meaningful work.

I am grateful for the encouragement, wisdom, and support I have received throughout the years from friends and colleagues. I wish to thank in particular Lawrence Curry, Patricia Curry, Linda Westervelt, Georgia McInnis, Nancy Ford, Elizabeth Gregory, Elizabeth Brown-Guillory, Pat Pickering, Terrell Dixon, John McNamara, Dorothy Baker, and Thomas Ford. My colleagues and students in the English Department, especially those graduate students who were part of three seminars I directed on Nathaniel Hawthorne, have been special sources of learning and collegiality, and I am in their debt.

I would also like to thank for their support of this project the chair of the Department of English, Wyman Herendeen, and my colleague and the former president of the University of Houston, James Pickering, administrators whose leadership has helped to make the university a fine place to work. I am grateful to the university and to Dean John Antel for granting me a semester Faculty Development Leave to work on the book and to the Houstoun Endowment for a Martha Gano Houstoun Research Grant.

The editors at Palgrave Macmillan, Farideh Koohi-Kamali, Executive Editor, and Julia Cohen, Assistant Editor, deserve thanks for their help and support, as does an anonymous reader for his or her insightful comments and suggestions about the manuscript.

Finally, my deepest gratitude is reserved for my family—Jim, Emily, and Michael. Jim Pipkin, my husband, dear friend, and colleague, has been remarkably loving and supportive for many years. His commitment to his students and his work, and his devotion to his family, have been an inspiration to me. My dear children, Emily and Michael, have grown to become independent, loving, and kind-hearted individuals, and are a source of great joy. All three—Jim, Emily, and Michael—have helped to keep me happy and focused on life, while thinking and writing about death and somber subjects, and I dedicate this book to them with profound thanks and love.

INTRODUCTION

When Emily Dickinson wrote, "All but death can be adjusted," she was referring to the biological death that all human beings experience as part of their contract with nature.[1] This death is fixed and inevitable. But the representation of death is fluid and continually "adjusted" to answer crucial personal and public concerns. It is arbitrary and reflects a particular culture's thinking about last things. It places the corrupting body, the sickness and suffering, the final words, gestures, or silences, the tears, and the mourning in a framework and form that give them meaning. It offers palliatives and consolations, and helps humans maintain their psychological balance in the face of the stark fact of their inevitable dissolution. It is the most necessary of necessary fictions.

This book is about Nathaniel Hawthorne's version of this necessary fiction. It is based on the assumption that the way we imagine death is determined by our culture. More specifically, it argues that death is, as the narrator of Hawthorne's sketch "The Procession of Life" asserts, the organizing "principle" of society (10: 207).[2] Like Michel de Certeau, Hawthorne assumes that culture is born out of the tension between the knowledge of our mortality and the desire to forget, remake, or recover from this knowledge. In *The Writing of History*, Certeau explains that, while "trying to 'get over'" death, we find ourselves fixed on it because it "has organized...the experience of entire civilizations."[3] For both Certeau and Hawthorne, the grave is the center of culture because the way a society "organizes" death shapes its social, moral, and ethical systems. The form of this organization is most apparent in the consolations of dying a culture creates to answer death.

Most mid-nineteenth century middle-class New Englanders sought the answer to death in their Christian beliefs. Faith in God's mercy and Christ's redemptive sacrifice to win immortal life for the dead formed the primary source of consolation. In *Democracy in America*, Alexis de

Tocqueville recognized that religious authority originates in the human dread of annihilation.[4] American Protestantism was particularly suited both to foster and to palliate this dread. Because the Protestant belief system's focus on the individual reading the Bible and interpreting the word shifted religion from a communal centered experience, it might have had the effect of heightening death anxiety by placing so much of the burden for salvation on the individual. From the perspective of middle-class Protestant ideology, not only must believers have the promise of eternal life, they must also have assurance of eternal self. A nineteenth-century Christian commentator sensitive to this desire to maintain a recognizable self into eternity described the afterlife in this way: "As we know ourselves here, so must we there."[5]

But during this period, a confluence of influences—among them, new scientific theory, nascent Darwinian principles, commercialism, and materialism—conspired to arouse less certainty about the orthodox Christian worldview and its power to answer death. The several sects into which Protestantism divided and subdivided and their various permutations of dogmas and creeds could have made belief in general more precarious.[6] Medical and scientific advances raised questions about the nature of death and the threshold between life and death, and stories such as Edgar Allan Poe's "The Facts in the Case of M. Valdemar" entertained the idea that life may not end in eternal transcendence but in a natural dissolution, disturbingly imagined in the tale's final image of the dead body as a "liquid mass of loathsome—of detestable putridity."[7]

The popularity of travel narratives contributed to an awareness, particularly unsettling to those who thought of themselves as citizens of the "hub of the universe," that beliefs were local and arbitrary; there were other cultures and practices surrounding death and dying different from those of Boston. The new taste for Egyptian and Greek funeral monuments showed a willingness to look beyond Christianity to ancient civilizations for commemorative models. Also, there was public discussion in the region during the 1830s and 1840s about the nature and location of cemeteries that set orthodox religious arguments about death and dying alongside naturalistic, secular ones. Jacob Bigelow's treatise on the burial of the dead considers the dead body as both an aesthetic and a public health problem that can be remedied by promoting the location of cemeteries in natural settings where the decomposition of the body can follow the "law of nature" and the useful purpose of replenishing the soil.[8] The very fact that an influential group of citizens advocated moving the graveyard from its location in the center of town, often adjacent to the church, to a nondenominational rural or suburban setting signaled the waning power of the clergy to define the meaning of death.[9]

These examples do not prove that the early nineteenth century in New England was a secular age or, for that matter, even an agnostic or atheistic age, although there were agnostics and atheists. Quite the contrary, it was an age of belief, and Christianity in its many forms was at its center.[10] But, even among Christians, ideas about death and dying, usually remarkably stable over time, were changing.[11] The publications on the founding of Mount Auburn Cemetery illustrate that a variety of responses to death coexisted in the culture. The editor of *The Picturesque Pocket Companion and Visitor's Guide Through Mount Auburn* (1831), for example, included in this single volume writings ranging from Hawthorne's sentimental tale, "The Lily's Quest," to an essay on the graveyards of other cultures, orthodox Christian religious verse, and essays and poems informed by classical stoicism, pantheism, naturalism, and humanism. The selections in this volume seem consistent with the editor's intention to produce neither a "matter-of-fact enquiry" into the subject of death nor a "sentimental history" (5).

When Hawthorne takes up the subject of consolations of dying, he is doing so in a climate that is certainly not univocal in its ideas about death's meaning. In her review of T. Walter Herbert's *Dearest Beloved*, Nina Baym describes the work of art as a "site where cultural energies or messages are received, focused, and sent out again."[12] Hawthorne's novels can be thought of as something similar to force fields of contesting ideas about death where cultural energies are galvanized. Death has a certain power in Hawthorne's fiction. Some of the most affecting scenes are those imagining the dead or dying: Dimmesdale's death in *The Scarlet Letter*, the taunting of Judge Pyncheon's dead body in *The House of the Seven Gables*, the recovery of drowned Zenobia in *The Blithedale Romance*, and the death and funeral ritual of the Model in *The Marble Faun*. Since death is the only event that is impossible to experience before transforming it into art, it is "always only represented" and, in that regard, unusually sensitive to the cultural currents which run through that literary force field.[13] Moving into the imaginary space of death, then, means occupying a writerly territory that is both peculiarly culture bound and unbounded, beyond the cultural center and yet firmly determined by it.[14]

It is in this space that Hawthorne's fiction invites reassessment of nineteenth-century New England's consolations of dying and exposes their contradictions and their failings. Whether it is the orthodox

Christian idea of eternal life, the concept of "familial immortality," utopian schemes, or a belief in the transcendent possibilities of love or art, the novels suggest their inadequacy as answers to death. They especially betray uncertainty about the power of these consolations to shore up the male's sense of himself as powerful or assuage his fear of personal annihilation. Viewing life *sub specie mortis*, from the perspective of the grave, which is frequently the perspective of Hawthorne's fiction, creates unease about the wisdom and cost of following conventional paths to immortality. It requires that death's finality be taken into account when deciding about the nature of happiness, human aspiration, and life's meaning. It involves traversing dangerous psychological terrain, acknowledging that there are ends without beginnings, and accepting failure. To embrace death as a fact of life often provokes doubt about the old certainties of religious, moral, and ethical thought, rather than inspires belief.

In Hawthorne's fiction, death denial is primarily male work.[15] To make death yield meaning, the male protagonist is frequently willing to overlook, reject, and sacrifice women. More often than not, the male protagonist's fear is not that he will be parted from his lover but that their union will drag him down to the grave. To forestall this, he writes the text of his immortality narrative on the female body. This is not an unfamiliar pattern in American fiction; what is unusual is the extent to which Hawthorne's fiction reveals that this kind of behavior reflects cultural values, and particularly its assumptions about death and dying.

The male desire to "feel…immortal," as Hawthorne expresses it in *The Marble Faun*, is a compelling, if destructive, psychological need rarely accompanied by the vision to realize it justly or rightly (4: 194). Hawthorne's males are captive to cultural assumptions about death that can ruin the relationships between men and women and often place women in the role of self-sacrificing sufferer and men in the role of sovereign self. Hawthorne's fiction asks us to consider the condition of women, women hurt and pained by men, oftentimes dead women. The suffering of these women is so intense and unjust that it forces analysis of its cause and cure, and prompts us to ask, "To what purpose?" Inspiring this kind of question makes Hawthorne difficult to categorize as a misogynistic or antifeminist writer. His novels assert the dominance of the male order at the same time that they invite a dialogue with suffering and dead women.

In *Political Theory for Mortals: Shades of Justice, Images of Death*, John E. Seery explains that the basis for a new social order could be acknowledging the claims of the dead, particularly those wronged in the past, and he calls this acknowledgment "Plutonic justice."[16] Hawthorne's novels, often centered around graves, ghosts, and dead women, invite opening this sort of dialogue with the dead. The suffering or dead body of a woman has the potential to become a political site, the focal point or the organizing "principle" of society. It exposes the frailty of the system's consolations of dying—ideas that preserve men from knowledge of the self's ephemerality but at the cost of creating a culture in mourning.

What may bother the twenty-first century reader is that the women's question is often not the primary or the most urgent one in Hawthorne's novels. It is a point made along the way, secondary but related to the questions of why men are so unhappy and what could make them happy. Hawthorne's fiction rests on some basic assumptions. The misery of men is related to the culture's ideas about death and dying. The condition of men will not change until these ideas are changed. The suffering of women, while it may be different from that of men, is related to, and perhaps even contingent upon, male suffering, and it will also not be relieved until men change their assumptions.

If the nineteenth-century Protestant church was turning away from the image of a militant Christ but still sought a Christ triumphant, it created out of the tension between these two desires a Christ who confirmed his omnipotence through self-abnegation and sacrifice. Hawthorne consistently writes his male protagonist's story in the folds of this paradox as a struggle against narcissism yet for identity and everlasting power. Because nineteenth-century New England society is so markedly defined by its Christian culture, it comes as no surprise that Hawthorne's *The Scarlet Letter* would turn first to consider the Christian consolation of dying—eternal life—by exploring a Christian minister's response to his own mortality. Chapter one, "Unholy Dying in *The Scarlet Letter*," considers the way this novel works with and against the patterns of the Renaissance *ars moriendi* tradition and the popular nineteenth-century ministerial biography to create its portrait of a dying minister. Both a psychological and a social dynamic direct Dimmesdale's performance of death. His male death fantasy of autonomy, self-perpetuation, and sacrifice, a fantasy so culturally viable that the community is complicit in its performance, inspires skepticism about the Christian scheme of immortality.

To understand Hester's involvement in Dimmesdale's story is to appreciate the logic behind Hélène Cixous's thesis that men "need femininity to be associated with death."[17] Despite Hester's belief that love has a holy "consecration," Dimmesdale's condition, reduplicated and made assailable in Chillingworth's, tests this assumption. In the society of Boston, something like Cixous's version of the male "need" defines the terms of the heterosexual couple relationship and writes the script of the consolations of dying. Hester's diagnosis of Dimmesdale's ailment and her alternative remedy for the problem of death prove susceptible to the same scrutiny as Dimmesdale's. Her perspective on death appears to be modern in its secular logic, but, at base, is equally conservative in its preservation of the primacy of the male social order.

Placing male death anxiety at the center of *The Scarlet Letter* also makes more apparent that, while Hawthorne was mourning the death of his mother, the Hawthorne-Narrator he created in "The Custom-House" sketch is struggling with the fear of annihilation. In his fiction, Hawthorne was consistently unwilling to counter this anxiety with heroic apotheosis. Apotheotic aspirations prove hollow or misguided, and a sure road to mortal failure. Like many of his contemporaries, Hawthorne was not particularly susceptible to hero worship. When he decided on a minister as his central protagonist in his first major novel, he chose one of a very small class of men who might qualify for this status in his culture. In chapter two, " 'The Custom-House,' the Secular Pilgrim, and the Happy Death," I consider Hawthorne's adoption of the persona of the anxious secular man of his time who struggles to live without the psychological consolation offered by a Christian belief in personal immortality and seeks consolation in heroic apotheosis. Beset by a desire to achieve happiness and meaning, this secular man tames his fears about death by tapping into the Christian mythology of death and resurrection. In his portrait of the artist as persecuted bureaucrat, Hawthorne imagines himself aspiring to the "rapt height" to which Melville later elevated him in "Hawthorne and His Mosses" and winning an eternal reward by triumphing in his struggle against the repressive forces in his community.[18] But ultimately "The Custom-House" sketch undercuts these immortalizing hopes. Deriding his aspirations for apotheosis (and perilously close to mocking the Christian doctrines of resurrection and ascension), Hawthorne imagines himself at rest not in the company of Shakespeare in the heaven of literary immortality but at the site of the town-pump as the subject of local gossip and limited fame.

The chapter concludes with a discussion of Hawthorne's response to the death of his mother recorded in his journals. I speculate on the nature of Hawthorne's psychological condition that determines his form of mourning, using Freud and the contemporary psychologist John Bowlby's theories about death.

In a lecture delivered to the senior class of the Harvard Divinity College in 1838, Ralph Waldo Emerson expressed concern that "when men die we do not mention them." In characterizing his contemporaries in this way, Emerson may have been one of the earliest to recognize what some cultural historians identify as an emerging pattern in nineteenth-century middle-class society—the evasion of death. In chapter three, "'Familial Immortality' and the 'Dying of Death' in *The House of the Seven Gables*," I approach Hawthorne's second novel as a study of his contemporaries' complex attitudes about the dying of death and the way their attitudes affected male notions about the autonomy and permanence of the self.

In this novel, Hawthorne imagines a secular world in which the Christian idea of eternal life no longer constitutes the single, standard answer to death, and "familial immortality" has a wide appeal.[19] *The House of the Seven Gables* places this middle-class answer to death under intense scrutiny and exposes it as a source of some of the intolerable contradictions that beset family life. In his tragi-comic version of his contemporaries' way of dying, Hawthorne presents not a paean to middle-class family life, but a domestic Gothic horror story.

Read through the lens of Freud's theory of the death wish and Luce Irigaray's response to it in *Sexes and Genealogies*, Holgrave's relationship with Phoebe in the novel illustrates the male need to forestall a recognition of mortality by displacing death anxiety in the female partner and exerting control over her. But at the same time that this tactic creates the illusion of male immortality, it also reconfirms a link with the dead father, a connection which the reference to Aeneas's journey to the underworld at the novel's conclusion recalls. The macabre scene in which the novel's narrator berates the dead Judge Pyncheon—a scene that comes closest in Hawthorne's fiction to representing an unmediated confrontation with death—illustrates the bitter wages of adopting ancestor worship and progeny as a moral answer to death anxiety. Portraying death in a visual image at the novel's conclusion in the form of the ghost of Alice Pyncheon sustains the distinctions inherent in the novel's plot. The nineteenth-century family is constructed to facilitate male death denial by promoting the illusion of family permanence, but in promoting this fiction it invariably creates its own hauntings. The ghost of Alice Pyncheon invites a dialogue with the dead that could form the basis of a new social order established on the ethical principle of "Plutonic Justice."

Luce Irigaray argues that the murder of the mother is the "founding act" of the social order.[20] In *The Blithedale Romance*, Coverdale writes his version of this "original matricide," but Hawthorne insinuates into the narrative a somewhat different and more complex point of view.[21] Chapter four, "From Melancholy to Mourning: Death and Politics in *The Blithedale Romance*," considers the way Coverdale revises for his contemporaries the accused queen narrative of folk and medieval literature. Coverdale's identity as melancholy male in the tradition of Shakespeare's Jacques and Hamlet determines his misogynistic reading of Zenobia and her death.

In *The Blithedale Romance*, Hawthorne establishes a relationship between the dead body of a woman and the body politic in the emerging "new" secular state. Since the death of Zenobia is the central fact and the compelling event of the narrative, her body becomes a site of political contestation. But the novel ultimately questions whether the dead body of a woman can be a revolutionary force that galvanizes a society for social reform. Can there be "Plutonic Justice" for dead Zenobia?

The Marble Faun includes the most complete exploration of the patriarchal system in Hawthorne's fiction. Victor Turner's ideas about cultural systems provide an illuminating model for reading the social drama played out in the novel, as they do in "The Custom-House" sketch. In chapter five, " 'Intimate Equality': Sacrifice and Death in *The Marble Faun*," I argue that Donatello's allegiance to Miriam disrupts the patriarchal system and reconfigures alliances. New allegiances form that cross conventional gender lines. Donatello's actions are so threatening that they ripple through the patriarchal system and necessitate his reeducation so that he accepts culturally regnant ideas about women and death. In its portrayal of Donatello's acculturation to these ideas about the male–female relationship under the tutelage of Kenyon, the novel exposes the logic of these moral and ethical systems: how they are inscribed, how they are stabilized, and why it is so difficult for them to be transformed.

But the novel also uncovers a symptom of the system's disintegration. Death has to have meaning to sustain a cultural system, and Christianity's strategies for denying death seem unable to offer the proper consolations. In this way, Hawthorne's last completed novel provides a glimpse of the nineteenth-century's flirtation with annihilationism. The "abyss" threatens the four central protagonists in this novel, and Miriam's worry that Rome will "inevitably sink" because it was built over a vast "chasm" is a hypothesis awaiting verification.[22] The novel seems to be hovering on the edge of the precipice, teetering between belief in the moral and ethical system which will provide safe conduct across to "home" and doubt or disbelief which can cause a plummet to the grave.

The final chapter returns to *The Marble Faun* to understand how it unfolds the differences between the matriarchal and patriarchal myths and how these differences are complicated by issues of race. By setting at odds matriarchal "heathenism" and patriarchal Christianity, and aligning these belief systems with racial and gender differences, Hawthorne makes it difficult to resolve in a hopeful way the questions the novel raises. The fates of the two couples in the novel suggest that they are captive to their racial and gender identities, and, granted Hawthorne's historical and political situation, their competing "systems" seem to portend strife and conflict.

Hawthorne included more direct references to classical mythology in his final novel than he had in all his other fiction combined. By confining these myths to fragmentary allusions, he denies their power to answer death. In the same way, he also compromises and limits the power of the central transformative myth of the Christian culture: the sacrifice of Jesus Christ. Sacrifice is Kenyon's answer to death—an answer that reflects the dominant ideology of the New England middle class—but the novel raises questions about the ethics of sacrifice. If a culture writes its immortality narrative in the suffering of those without power, then the Christian system at its core is vulnerable to criticism.

Hawthorne's personal dilemma in working through the conundrum writing this final novel posed was closely related to the one he imagined Melville was experiencing when he met him at Redcar in November of 1856: If he could not "believe," could he be "comfortable," that is, happy, "in his unbelief"?[23] Could he relinquish his aspirations for limitless self, perhaps connected with his hopes for personal and literary immortality, and accept an ethical system bounded by limits, failure, and death? In the last section of the chapter, "The Death of the 'Cultural Structure of a Lifetime,'" I speculate about the personal experiences and preoccupations that brought Hawthorne to the final vision he articulated in this novel. In an essay about Thomas Mann's *Death in Venice*, Heinz Kohut considered the possibility that at the time of writing the novel Mann was becoming consciously aware of the issue of sexual repression, its connection to repetition (or "copying"), loss of creative power, and death.[24] Hawthorne might also have reached a similar crisis point, and, like Mann, might well have been working through the consequences of the death of the "cultural structure of a lifetime."[25] Having undermined and dismantled in his fiction the cultural system which made it possible for him and his contemporaries to "get over" death, he was left to rely totally on the self as the source of value, order, and meaning—a liberating yet terrifying prospect.

A disturbing question, evoked by Cixous, hovers over this project: Why do men need femininity to be associated with death?[26] This question has a particular urgency for women who witness the atrocious acts of violence men commit against women in our culture.[27] Because in my career as a teacher and scholar the male writer I most often study and teach is Nathaniel Hawthorne, I took as one of my tasks when writing this book to try to see if I could understand the reasons he so often associated femininity with death, if not in life then as imagined in his art.

There are those who might consider it wrong-headed to try to explore the implications of this question by considering literature of any kind, and particularly literature written by a nineteenth-century canonical male writer.[28] I actually began this project planning to consider Hawthorne and his writings as part of a discussion of a group of female and male writers of various ethnicities to understand the ways in which they represented death and dying. The focus evolved, though, as I began to recognize the cluster of related issues that was emerging and the economy Hawthorne offered as a writer who shared his gender's construction of reality while simultaneously questioning it. Once my center shifted from one dealing exclusively with representations of death and dying to one focused on consolations of dying, my subject became more complex and my approach to it more unorthodox, leading me to excursions into psychoanalysis, philosophy, cultural anthropology, and feminist theory. The psychoanalytic theories of Freud and Kohut proved an adequate starting point because they began to explain, from a male-centered perspective, the "disintegration anxiety" at the core of death denial, but this psychoanalytic approach needed to be contextualized. William Beers's *Women and Sacrifice*, a study which established and explored the connection between violence toward women and male "disintegration anxiety," caused me to begin to appreciate how deeply this question touched on the construction of the male identity and the system of beliefs and meaning which underpins it. Death denial may be an individual or intersubjective act, but the form it takes is largely culturally determined and a significant indicator of the male symbolic order. To understand this order meant thinking about the way male theorists speak about loss and mourning and its manifestation in the complex reciprocities of the male-female relationship.

I came to Hawthorne's writing, then, wanting to understand how this discourse of death denial and its compensatory consolations can be translated into literary narratives and how these narratives reflect cultural positions and values. So rather than being a chapter in a larger study of death and dying, Hawthorne and his fiction became the test case under study, and the book expanded horizontally with references to other writers of the male classic tradition, such as Virgil and Homer, and to nineteenth-century writers of Hawthorne's circle, as I tried to recuperate a sense of the male tradition of consolations of dying Hawthorne was working in and perhaps developing or contesting.

The writings of the French feminists Luce Irigaray and Hélène Cixous proved to be invaluable in a number of ways. Their writings about traditional beliefs sometimes expose ruptures in the systems of meaning that hint at the possibility of shifting the perspective and changing the order of meaning by asking different questions posited on different assumptions. They remind us that literature, as a form of myth-making, is not simply representational but imaginative. While it may portray the way things are, or even explain why things are the way they are, it also can subtly invite revision—new myths differently imagined. In this way, it seems possible that literature can slip the yoke of cultural determinism.

Saying this does not mean denying the local cultural concerns that surround this subject. An exclusively psychoanalytic or French feminist approach to the questions might infer that male death denial is experienced in the same way transculturally, and while there are admittedly certain constants in the responses to death, I have also tried to be attentive to how they are articulated in a cultural context and continually "adjusted" to suit the circumstances of a particular time and place.

Of course, one of the particular circumstances of Hawthorne's day was the conflict surrounding the issue of slavery and race. For the most part, the parameters I have set for my investigation have excluded this issue. While there are numerous references in Hawthorne's fiction to blackness and to mental enslavement, I tend to agree with Dennis Berthold, who argues cogently that "substituting metaphors and generic codings for direct discourse valuably extends racial themes in literature, but it risks robbing them of their political urgency and historical force."[29] But in *The Marble Faun* when Hawthorne introduces two possibly racially different individuals into his four central character ensemble, the problem of race intersects with that of gender and provides a special urgency to the question of the social reality of a system's oppression.

Acknowledging the complexities of Hawthorne's historical and cultural situation meant revising my initial question. For the purposes of this study asking "Why do men need femininity to be associated with death?" meant assessing "Why do nineteenth-century New England men need femininity to be associated with death?" and "Why did

Nathaniel Hawthorne in his fictions need femininity to be associated with death?" And even this question needed further modification when *The Marble Faun* brought this discussion into the terrain of race and slavery. This book began with my interest in answering a question that required understanding how individuals and cultures come to terms with death. But it ended with appreciating the ways consolations of dying reflect imperatives of living and have significant ethical and moral implications.

C H A P T E R   O N E

Unholy Dying in The Scarlet Letter

In a notebook entry of 1836, Nathaniel Hawthorne imagines death not in the more conventional images of the grim reaper or the devil but as "a great parent" that "comes and sweeps them all through one darksome portal,—all his children" (8: 22–23). What is most fearsome about death is its power to annihilate the self, to sweep those in its wake into a "darksome portal" from which there is no return. Mortality is at the service, not of an inexorable natural force, but of a tyrannical father who imposes his will with a social and political authority. The human family is linked primarily by their responses to this grim paternal sweeper. Formulating these responses to evade the fact of personal annihilation or to "get over" death is the work of culture, and for this reason Michel de Certeau assumes that death "organizes" civilization.[1] The dynamic equilibrium of a culture can be measured by the way it allays the terror of annihilationism and answers death.

In *The Scarlet Letter*, Hawthorne tests this assumption by writing a pseudo-history of a culture whose males are obsessed with "last things" and their own ephemerality. They reconstitute their nature, perhaps unconsciously, on the basis of their measure of what will sustain the illusion of the infinity of the self. Dimmesdale dissociates himself from death at the cost of his relationship with Hester. But what is remarkable is that in telling Dimmesdale's story Hawthorne does not present his fantasy as some unique expression of a peculiar inner life. Dimmesdale may be perverse but his fantasy is the logical extension of his culture's assumptions about holy living and holy dying. Dimmesdale's male death fantasy of autonomy and self-perpetuation, a fantasy that is presented as so culturally viable that the community is complicit in its performance, is at the center of the Christian scheme of immortality.

The conjunction of redemption, narcissism, and misogyny that this fantasy perpetuates is responsible for much of what is antithetical to life and happiness in Hawthorne's portrayal of Puritan Boston. This system of holy living and holy dying discloses that Christianity has embedded in its theological core a disturbing constellation of virility, immortality, and management of women. In more general terms, *The Scarlet Letter* reveals the reasons that a Christian culture like Puritan Boston fosters attitudes that allow some men to do violence to women.

The Scarlet Letter presents Hawthorne's version of the cost exacted on women and on men by this conception of immortality played out by the males of Puritan Boston and explores its personal and social consequences. The novel hints at the failure of the culture's construction, specifically as it is shaped by Christian rituals, for answering its need for power over death. At the same time, it projects an alternative solution to the problem of death—one invested in Hester—that appears to be modern in its secular logic, but, at base, is equally conservative in its preservation of the primacy of the male order.

The Art of Dying

The ambivalent response of the novel's contemporary reviewers to Dimmesdale was determined, in part, by the ways Hawthorne draws upon the Christian tradition to transcribe a myth of Christian living and dying which would seem historically accurate. Hawthorne needed to create a portrait that was compatible in some respects with his contemporaries' most popular ideas about Christianity. In short, the Christianity of Puritan Boston had to be recognizable to his contemporaries as Christianity. At the same time, I suspect that Hawthorne wanted his account to be sufficiently different so that critiquing Christianity would not remove the author from the safety of his characteristic "neutral territory" perspective (1: 36).[2] As a result, the novel resonates with references to the most popular Christian texts of his day, including the Bible, Milton's *Paradise Lost*, Bunyan's *Pilgrim's Progress*, Renaissance devotional literature, and the ministerial biography, but the allusions are infused with variations that counterbalance, undermine, and complicate a conventional Christian reading.[3]

Hawthorne's portrait of Dimmesdale depends on a shorthand of allusions to Christian texts that successfully evoke a conventional Christian worldview. By creating the impression of orthodoxy, Hawthorne encourages his contemporary Christian readers to believe throughout most of the novel that they know how to assess this minister. Dimmesdale's primary sin would have been readily identifiable to them from a biblical perspective. He had violated the divine injunction against adultery, and death was the customary wages the Bible prescribed for lustful desire: "Then when lust hath conceived, it bringeth forth sin: and sin, when it is finished, bringeth forth death" (James 1:15). Many of Hawthorne's contemporaries were also intimately familiar with the text of Bunyan's *Pilgrim's Progress* and would have understood Dimmesdale's capitulation to hypocrisy and vainglory as serious wrongs which often led to the slough of despair.

The pattern of Dimmesdale's life as a journey to death also conforms to the conventions found in many Christian precedents. Hawthorne knew the classic text of Renaissance devotional literature—Jeremy Taylor's *Holy Living and Holy Dying*—and was well aware of its popularity among his contemporaries as a book of family devotion that set forth the proper way for the Christian to live and die.[4] Taylor reminds his readers that life is a journey to death: "while we think a thought, we die; and the clock strikes, and reckons on our portion of Eternity: we form our words with the breath of our nostrils, we have the lesse to live upon, for every word we speak."[5] Milton's *Paradise Lost* also describes life as a "long day's dying to augment our pain" (X: 964).[6]

The plot trajectory of Dimmesdale's life story follows that of several popular ministerial biographies of nineteenth-century New England. The novel and the ministerial biographies share the assumption that life is "a long day's dying" as they trace the progress of their sickly minister subjects to death.[7] For example, Horace Bushnell, a contemporary of Hawthorne's, referred to his death throughout his adult life as if it were imminent. On April 14, 1855 when he was fifty-three years old, he wrote in a letter to his wife, "Shall I ever see another birthday, or is this the last?"[8] Also, William Peabody, a popular and charismatic minister, spent most of his life preparing for death. Like so many other ministers who were the subjects of biographies, he had a "delicate" frame, a "sensitive" mind, suffered from a protracted illness of a mysterious nature, and grew more effective and honored as a preacher as he grew more sickly.[9] In fact, in the ministerial biography sickness is frequently a sign of saintedness; the grievously ill minister serves as a moral exemplum who can uplift the public spirit.

Dimmesdale is sickly, but not sainted; his "long day's" journey has made him an unlikely candidate for an inspiring or model death. Hawthorne disrupts conventional expectations with the way he presents the scene of Dimmesdale's dying. One of the primary signs of a good life was a good death. Many seventeenth-century Puritan Christians and Christians of nineteenth-century New England believed that life's last act was the time of the final battle between good and evil for the soul of the dying. This belief is apparent in both the art and literature of the Renaissance *ars moriendi* tradition and the ministerial biography that this tradition influenced, and Dimmesdale's death scene dramatizes many of its expected features and conventions.[10] Key details, however, complicate the scene and make Dimmesdale's dying so perplexing that it is virtually uninterpretable.

Hawthorne captures the essence of the *ars moriendi* tradition when he gathers together in an intensely visual final scene many of the significant images of a Renaissance death scene: the dying or *moriens*, the deathbed, the physician, the minister, the witnesses (usually, the family and friends of the *moriens*), and the will.[11] In some respects, Dimmesdale's dying appears to be conventional. Chillingworth, the personification of the evil tempter, tries to hold him back from the public confession necessary to open him to God's mercy and grace. Similarly, Pearl, who in this scene plays the role of the good angel, protects him from despair with a healing kiss. From the perspective of the *ars moriendi*, Dimmesdale also says some of the right things in his final moments. What some might take as cruel rejection of Hester, the *ars moriendi* tradition could explain as the necessary disengagement from worldly attachments before dying.

But Hawthorne complicates Dimmesdale's dying in several ways. While he includes many of the conventional props and character types of the Renaissance *ars moriendi* tradition and of contemporary deathbed scenes in ministerial biographies, these inclusions defy easy categorization. The minister is present, but this minister is also the dying reprobate Christian. The physician, who traditionally plays the role of healer and consoler, becomes the tempter figure. Even a small detail such as the will, which is frequently mentioned as an important part of the death scene, becomes a source of puzzlement. Writing a will signified that the dying man left his worldly affairs in order, particularly mindful of his responsibility to provide for his widow and other dependents. Dimmesdale, Pearl's father, leaves no will, while Chillingworth, the childless and cuckolded husband, makes financial provisions for his wife's daughter by another man.

Hawthorne also defies popular taste with his decision to move the minister's death from the bedroom, with its associations with the private and the female, to the scaffold, the gendered space of the male order and the public world. This change suggests Hawthorne's resistance to presenting a sentimental dying, although what he forfeits in sentimentality he compensates for with sensation. To readers brought up on tears, visions, and rapture as the meat of a minister's dying moments, Dimmesdale's exit must have seemed both more and less than what they wanted: grand and apotheotic, but, at the same time, suspect and not completely satisfying.

Hawthorne's contemporaries would have believed it was important for Dimmesdale to die properly, not just for himself, but for those who witnessed his death.[12] As Eliza Lee Cabot Follen explains in *The Life of Charles Follen*, the death of a minister, like his life as a whole, had as its "higher purpose" ensuring that "many hearts might be elevated, many souls quickened and blessed, by the contemplation of the life and character of such a being."[13] In a moment of reflection, Dimmesdale entertains a similar perspective on the elevating effect of witnessing the death of a good minister. In the night scaffold scene, he sees Reverend Wilson returning from ministering at the deathbed of John Winthrop and imagines him transfigured "like the saint-like personages of olden time" because of the holy dying he has witnessed (1: 150).[14] In both the *ars moriendi* tradition and the ministerial biography, the dying person is considered to be a type of Christ, and by being present at the death the witnesses participate in Christ's redemption. The response of the witnesses to the death scene and the departing words or directives validate the state of the dying Christian's soul and signify the ongoing vitality of the Christian faith. Consoling and meaningful final words and gestures confirm the "goodness" of the death and the worthiness of the dying for eternal life, as well as renew the witnesses and the entire Christian community.

What would have been sorely missed in this scene, judging from the popular ministerial biographies, is the absence of assurances of eternal life for the dying. The responses of the witnesses to Dimmesdale's dying are problematic. Chillingworth is angry because he believes he has been thwarted, Hester is perplexed, and Pearl is saddened. The crowd utters "a strange, deep voice of awe and wonder," a reaction that is difficult to interpret (1: 257). If *Paradise Lost* can provide some direction, "awe" can be an expression of ignorance and susceptibility to sin, a condition similar to Eve's when Satan exhorts her to eat the fruit. He tells her that her "fear itself of Death removes the fear. / Why then was this forbid? Why but to awe, / Why but to keep ye low and ignorant" (9: 702–4).[15] The minister's death should reaffirm the faith of the witnesses, but Dimmesdale's death inspires a crisis of legitimation which threatens the whole civil order. As Sarah Webster Goodwin and Elisabeth Bronfen explain in *Death and Representation*, "political systems inaugurate their power by using ritual representations of death. A recourse to death often serves as antidote to a crisis in belief, as confirmation of moral and social values."[16] Hawthorne may have used Dimmesdale's death to inspire rather than dispel a "crisis in belief" because it is a public act with a curiously private meaning, the secret of which Dimmesdale takes with him to the grave. Diverging so radically from the conventional script of dying may be Hawthorne's indirect way of reflecting uncertainty about personal immortality and the ideas about the afterlife Christianity encourages.

Every culture offers ways of explaining and coping with death or, as they are described in the Christian tradition, consolations of dying. Puritan Christians and nineteenth-century New England Christians shared a conviction that the chief consolation was eternal life. But the responses of the witnesses reverberate in the reader and force a reappraisal of Dimmesdale's beliefs, in particular his assurance of an afterlife. They also raise questions about the Christian philosophy which informs his faith and causes him to believe that his choice is between God and eternal life or women and death. At base, Dimmesdale's death scene gathers to a point all of the doubts and questions that the novel has raised about the conventional Christian way of living and dying. More specifically, for the purposes of my argument, it calls for a reappraisal of the traditional Christian association of women and death, revealing that this conjunction is the source of violence against women and a justification for the destructive ethic of sacrifice and self-sacrifice.

"Blameworthy Desire"

The Scarlet Letter has been described as a love story, but, in fact, it is a story that explains the reasons that men deny women, do violence to and punish them, and keep themselves apart from them.[17] Relationships between men and women in this novel are minimal. The sexes are segregated; women converse with women at the scaffold, men with men at the governor's hall. The facts of actual Puritan society may cause the reader to think of family units or married couples even though in the novel none exist, except for Hester and Chillingworth, whose marriage failed, and Hester and Dimmesdale, who rarely meet privately and reside together only in the grave. Men separate themselves from women and ultimately reject them because they believe they must to save themselves or, more precisely, to save their souls, escape death, and achieve immortality. And what they do is a logical, if extreme, extension of the behavior that is implicitly called for and justified by Christian thinking about the nature of women.

The philosophical principle underlying Dimmesdale's and his culture's conception of women is the orthodox Christian idea that within a human being reside two principles: the soul, the higher principle, the means to transcendence and eternal life, and the body, which is associated with corruption and death. In the *Phaedo*, Socrates explains that to follow the promptings of the corporeal or bodily impulses, "the human, and mortal, and unintellectual, and multiform, and dissoluble, and changeable," is to render oneself vulnerable to a physical death that brings only corruption.[18] Augustine rearticulates this principle as an important tenet of Christian philosophy when he writes that "blameworthy desire called passion" is the "love of things which each one can lose against his will," and he warns that if one does love in this way the soul will not be freed from the prison of the body and from death.[19] From this perspective men should avoid investing their love in the perishable object of woman.[20]

In *Women and Death: Linkages in Western Thought and Literature*, Beth Ann Bassein points out that Western Christian thought associates women with the body, regarding them as "fleshly creature[s]," whose "efforts to achieve immortality were therefore made more difficult," as, of course, were the efforts of those men who invested their love in these perishable beings.[21] The biblical story of Eve, a prototype of Hester, identifies women as the cause of sin and death and explains the need for redemption by a male Christ. Seen in light of this tradition, Dimmesdale's love for Hester is rooted, as Chillingworth asserts, in his "animal nature," which is associated with corruption and death. After his sin with Hester, Dimmesdale undertakes rigorous study, fasts and vigils, and daily self-scourging "to keep the grossness of this earthly state from clogging and obscuring his spiritual lamp" (1: 120). While granting Dimmesdale his spiritual nature despite his moral failings, the novel resists spiritualizing Hester and links her instead to the counter qualities the Christian culture associates with women. As a creative individual and a freethinker given to intellectual speculation, Hester, arguably, lives the life of the mind, and yet it is the body, the physical being, which defines her. When the narrator describes her for the first time after she emerges from the prison door, he lingers over her body. He carefully notes her shoulders, her bosom, her arms, her hair, her blush, her stature, and her clothes. The word "spirit" is seldom used in connection with Hester.

Hester is closely aligned with the mortal, dissoluble, earthly, material, and temporal—all that Christian philosophy sees as baser principles and impediments to "rising above" death. Her world revolves around children, work, clothes, the sick, and the dying. She creates new life, giving birth to Pearl, but she also plays a role in the passage to death. When the narrator comments that Hester is returning from the sickbed of Winthrop, the nineteenth-century reader still familiar with the role women in the community played tending the dying or preparing the dead body probably would have assumed that Hester had been occupied with these duties; or, granted her skill as a seamstress, readily accepted that she could have been measuring the corpse for its shroud or robe. When Hester visits Governor Bellingham, she delivers a pair of gloves, an article of clothing that Hawthorne's contemporaries knew were used as invitations to funerals and as commemorative objects.[22] After Dimmesdale's meeting with Hester in the night scaffold scene, the glove that he leaves behind betrays both his intimacy with Hester and his continuing vulnerability to death.

These associations help to explain the reasons that Hester is linked with the Medusa.[23] In *The Scarlet Letter*, Hawthorne retained the important kernel of the myth: the metaphor of gazing, particularly gazing that attempts to exert "influence from afar."[24] The "magnetic power" of Hester's gaze connects her to the Medusa and defines her as the fascinator, the threat that sometimes becomes the focus of a community's violence (1: 197). Like the Medusa, the fascinator is believed to possess "the evil eye," a metonym for these special or different powers that the community fears and that require her marginalization.[25] As iconoclast, outcast, and visionary, the fascinator thinks what cannot be thought, and represents for the community what they strive to deny. Hester has been given the scarlet letter and placed on the margins because she represents the body and sexuality, forces that her community has attempted to repress because they believe that in controlling them they can contain death.

From this standpoint, Dimmesdale's rejection of Hester is both inevitable and enlightening.[26] Assuming that it is a reflection of cultural attitudes, Dimmesdale's fantasy of death and dying portends the inevitable failure of the male-female relationship in Puritan Boston. It is a key manifestation of one of the defining ideas of this cultural system, a point so basic that it may qualify as the principle determining the "very nature of the opposite sex" which, as the narrator explains,

Hester knows must be "modified" before the status of women can improve (1: 165).

Male Narcissism, Women, and Sacrifice

Hélène Cixous believes that men associate women with the Medusa because "they need femininity to be associated with death."[27] What is unusual about *The Scarlet Letter* is not the association per se. Hawthorne's significant contribution is that *The Scarlet Letter* offers an explanation of the psychological and cultural basis of this association, one that implicates Christianity.

To explain the way the novel comments on the "need" that drives this association, I approach it from the perspective of William Beers's anthropological study of women, gender, and sacrifice set forth in his book *Women and Sacrifice: Male Narcissism and the Psychology of Religion.* Beers undertakes a psychological and cultural investigation and explanation of the violent and destructive way that men sometimes relate to women and offers a thesis helpful in understanding the novel.

Beers's perspective is incisive as well as compatible with the novel's construction of gender relations in two key respects. The point of view is male-centered, as is that of the novel, and the assumptions are those of Christian philosophy even though Beers critiques them, as I see Hawthorne doing as well in his novel. In his book, Beers examines the dynamic of "contradiction, gender, and power," particularly as it is expressed in the male ritual of blood sacrifice.[28] His study is strongly influenced by the research of cultural anthropologist Clifford Geertz, who proposes a psychological reading of the sociocultural phenomenon of sacrifice, and by the work of psychoanalyst Heinz Kohut, particularly his theories of narcissism and idealized self-objects formulated from a male-centered perspective.

To understand the meaning of sacrifice, Beers investigates the way a patriliny controls the rituals and symbols of a culture. While there is no blood sacrifice in *The Scarlet Letter,* the psychological and cultural contexts in which blood sacrifice occurs mirror those of the novel. In blood sacrifice, the "psychological motivation of men is to control the male-perceived power of women" as part of a strategy of preserving lines of patriarchal power in the social order.[29] Consequently, the psychological condition of males leads to the creation of a social order that is dominated by male power and frequently hostile and destructive to women. Using Beers's ideas and those of Kohut and Geertz makes it more apparent that Hawthorne creates such a social order in Puritan Boston. *The Scarlet Letter* can be read as a novel that explains the male mind and the cultural systems, symbols, and rituals that it generates. It exposes the patrilineal social order as one that links women and death and presents the view that the only way for a male to ensure a Christian life that culminates in a Christian death and the eternal happiness of heaven is to reject women.

Wedding the psychoanalytic theory of Kohut to the anthropological theory of Geertz allows Beers to argue that the male "fear of disintegration" caused by "faulty mirroring," which is a form of "narcissistic injury," provides the basis for a social theory of sacrifice.[30] According to Kohut, crucial to the male child's concept of self is his experience of the relation between the self and self-objects.[31] The appropriate response of the "mirroring self-object," usually identified as the mother, is crucial to the development of a "creative" and "productive" self.[32] If there is an "insufficiency of the responses from the side of the earliest mirroring self-object," the male child may respond with disappointment, hurt, and, even in some cases, violence and rage because the "object loss" causes him to feel abandoned and betrayed.[33] Because the "mirroring self-object" does not fulfill the male child's expectations, he creates an "idealized parent imago," and, as Kohut explains in "Forms and Transformations of Narcissism," "every shortcoming detected in the idealized parent leads to a corresponding internal preservation of the externally lost quality of the object."[34] It is out of the complex interplay between the "idealized parent imago," the "grandiose self" (an expression of the "grandiose and exhibitionistic image of the self"), and the responses of the "mirroring self-object" that the individual creates the "nuclear self."[35] When this process is not successful, the self experiences fragmentation, dissolution, and an accompanying anxiety.[36] In *The Analysis of the Self*, Kohut argues that the "symptomatic results" of "narcissistic personality disorders" are manifested in several specific ways.[37] Because so many of them help to conceptualize Dimmesdale's condition, I will cite Kohut's entire list of symptoms: "fear of loss of the reality self through ecstatic merger with the idealized parent imago, or through the quasi-religious regressions toward a merger with God or with the universe; fear of loss of control with reality and fear of permanent isolation through the experience of unrealistic grandiosity; frightening experiences of shame and self-consciousness through the intrusion of exhibitionistic libido; and hypochondriacal worries about physical or mental illness due to hypocathexis of disconnected aspects of the body and the mind."[38] "Faulty" or "insufficient" mirroring by self-objects, then, is the source of pain, deep and insatiable longing (which could be conceived as a form of mourning), and the most griev-ous narcissistic injury to the male self—fear of the "permanent disinte-gration of the self."[39]

Kohut's theory provides an explanation of the logic and operation of male narcissism, but his explanation focuses on the individual rather than society, although some aspects of the theory have social implica-tions. Beers points out that Geertz's approach explains the "psychody-namics" of the social construct of ritual, as well as the way "ritual helps create, express, and conceal the anxiety" associated with male fear of "disintegration."[40] Geertz's approach also provides the basis for positing a correlation between individual anxiety and social tension, a thesis that would explain Dimmesdale's problems as manifestations of a social and cultural dynamic. Consequently, Beers argues that male "narcissistic disintegration anxiety," its attendant fear and rejection of women, and its frequent eruption as violence are expressed in the "religious symbols and rituals that address that anxiety."[41]

Beers's thesis helps us to understand the violence against Hester enacted by society, Dimmesdale's rejection of Hester, and his last acts on the scaffold. In the first scaffold scene, the male society's ritual enacts its power over Hester by marking her with the "A," placing her on the scaffold, and summoning the community to witness. The gaze of the society reconfirms her identity as material, physical, the body. In this culture, she represents everything that must be resisted to avoid death. When Dimmesdale mounts the scaffold in the final scene, his actions symbolize a reenactment of the first scaffold scene and its ritual of punishment. His adultery with Hester has been a grievous threat to his experience of the continuity of the self, and it is respon-sible for many of the symptoms of "narcissistic disintegration anxiety" that Kohut describes in his essay. At times, Dimmesdale experiences himself as unreal. In his anguish he asks, "Then, what was he?—a substance?—or the dimmest of all shadows?" (1: 143). He seeks self-punishment because only pain confirms his existence. He feels utterly isolated and yet even in his sin he maintains his sense of grandiosity, for he is "the one sinner of the world!" (1: 254). He wants to be shamed, self-consciously displaying himself and "confessing" in the darkness of night. He morbidly interprets the comet as a private revelation to him alone, even though the community understands it as a providential sign for the whole society. At the same time, fear of exposure motivates him and causes him to experience "hypochondriacal" symptoms. In the forest, under the influence of Hester, Dimmesdale agrees to leave with her for Europe. But later this decision seems only to harm further the negotiations between his "grandiose self" and the "idealized self objects," and to exacerbate his symptoms and leave him near disintegration. It is in this condition that the Christian Pilgrim, Dimmesdale, undertakes his final journey to the scaffold and addresses his anxiety by enacting a form of ritual which involves choosing God, not Hester.

From Dimmesdale's—and the Puritan community's—perspective, the choice is absolutely necessary. In the last scenes of the novel, although Hester gazes "stedfastly" at Dimmesdale, hoping for some acknowledgment from him, he has become "remote from her own sphere, and utterly beyond her reach" (1: 239). The power of her gaze has been displaced by the gaze of "God's eye" (1: 255). As he understands it, the choice is woman, the body, and death or God, the spirit, and eternal life. In Kohut's terms, Dimmesdale has substituted the "omnipotent self-object," God, for a "self-object," Hester, because he has come to see her as an object that confirms his vulnerability to death. The only way for Dimmesdale to escape the gravest narcissistic wound, the recognition of his mortality and the fact of his self-annihilation in death, is by abandoning Hester and identifying with the omnipotence of God.

Hester is sacrificed so that the idea of a permanent self that Dimmesdale cherishes can live. He does feel a strong need and desire for Hester, a longing, but it is not sufficiently strong to overcome his accompanying dread. No earthly woman could satisfy his deeper craving for the narcissistic power to be found in the experience of an enhanced, limitless self. Perhaps David Bakan in *Disease, Pain, and Sacrifice* explains the internal logic of sacrifice most succinctly when he describes it as a process "in which that which is 'me' is made into something which is 'not-me,' and in which that 'not-me' is sacrificed in order that 'I' might continue to live."[42] As psychoanalytic theory predicts, Dimmesdale sacrifices Hester to ensure that the "I" might live. The impulse that he follows is narcissistic, but difficult for the acculturated Christian male to deny. In a sense, Dimmesdale's dying is the only way he can imagine living.

His choice sets in motion their personal tragedy and has disastrous implications for both Hester and himself. Less dramatically obvious are the compelling social and cultural dimensions of the tragedy. As Beers's thesis suggests, Dimmesdale's decision is so significant because it emphasizes the fault line in popular Christian ideology—the rupture which exposes the underside of the male project for immortality. Achieving transcendence requires sacrificing women. Read in retrospect from the final scaffold scene, Hester's earlier thoughts about "the very nature of the opposite sex" seem prescient (1: 165). If crucial aspects of cultural systems are configured around the need to explain death, Dimmesdale's convictions about what he must do to evade any recognition of his personal mortality are so engrained that they would seem "like nature" (1: 165). Since, from the perspective of the patriliny, love of God, not love of woman, offers the surest possibility of personal salvation, Dimmesdale seems both psychologically and culturally pre-determined to play his final scene as he does.

Death Without Christian Consolation

Chillingworth's fate proves the same point, but in a different way. As the counterpoint to Dimmesdale, Chillingworth represents the man who endures the death of the non-Christian or, more accurately, pre-Christian man. Hawthorne's conceptualization of Chillingworth allows him to depict his culture's view of a death that is unmediated by Christian theology and philosophy. Unmediated confrontation with the fact of personal mortality brings an irreparable sense of loss, rage, and mourning. When the perspective on death lacks the construction provided by a belief in transcendence, death means corruption, dissolution, and the disintegration of the self. Chillingworth experiences this kind of unmediated death.[43]

Chillingworth seems to nurture no conventional Christian beliefs nor to follow any system of Christian morals. He responds to Hester and Dimmesdale from a different cultural construction—one that recalls classical rather than Christian values. When Chillingworth learns that Hester has betrayed him, he suffers what Kohut would describe as a dire narcissistic wound caused by the investment he has made in this "primary self-object." He responds to this wound with what Henry Staten calls "vengeful automourning" (21).[44] Staten uses this term to describe the response of Achilles in the *Iliad* to the loss of Briseis and sees its parallel expression in the whole Greek society's decision to wage the Trojan War to avenge the loss of Helen.

In certain ways, Chillingworth's history with Hester replays this classical narrative. Hester, like Helen, has come from across the waters, and what has motivated her departure without her husband is not totally clear. But what is clear is that this unconventional, and per-haps unsanctioned, journey has had serious consequences because, like Helen's journey, it has led to wounds to the "honor" of her husband.[45] He has responded to this wounding with a vengeful fury, a form of "narcissistic rage." Like Achilles, Chillingworth seems to believe that no reparation can be great enough to compensate for his loss and suffering. Nonetheless, because it is compensation for his loss that drives him, Chillingworth never manifests any real interest in Hester herself, as the scene when he visits her and Pearl in prison in Chapter Four illustrates. He does not seem to love her and has no desire to win her back. She exists for him only as a prize or possession, and, once she has been stolen or damaged, all that remains is vengeance on the man who has humiliated him.

Chillingworth leads his life and lays the grounds for his death without the construction provided by Christian theology and its consolations for death. He finds little to value apart from honor and creating respect for the self. His primary good is self-protection. He does not alleviate Hester or Pearl's pain out of a sense of altruism or kindness, but as part of a plan to save himself from public humiliation and enact revenge. In keeping with his pre-Christian values, erotic passion, implication with the body of woman, for him clearly leads to wounding, narcissistic rage, disintegration, and death. No one, certainly not Hester, can dissuade him from his fate because he believes that there is no freedom of the will and no mercy, only a "dark necessity" that feeds the logic of morbid vengeance (1: 174).

His vital principle is not the Christian soul or spirit, but "strength and energy—all his vital and intellectual force" (1: 260). His death is very much a death of a natural or material creature. This is the alternative to Dimmesdale's death. It is death without palliatives and consolations. Chillingworth simply "shrivelled away" and died "like an uprooted weed that lies wilting in the sun" (1: 260). From the Christian perspective, his death is the gruesome and proper fate of the man whose earthly or material concerns have controlled him.

It is this sense of absolute, final self-annihilation that Dimmesdale wants to avoid by choosing God rather than Hester. Chillingworth's life makes apparent the fate of the man who lives by the material and earthly. But if his life has been unhappy, so has the life of Dimmesdale, the man who sacrificed all for God and spirit.

A Widow's Work

Everyone in *The Scarlet Letter* suffers. The difficulty lies in explaining inefficacious suffering—suffering that becomes destructive or masochistic, suffering whose economy is questionable. While my students accept the suffering of Chillingworth and Dimmesdale as deserved, they are less sanguine about Hester's pain and sometimes ask, "Why doesn't Hester leave Boston? Why doesn't she put aside her sorrow and grief?" It seems clear to them that Hester has expended too much of the capital of suffering on Dimmesdale. Despite any radical proto-feminist ideas that Hester entertains, the narrator is straightforward about one point: Dimmesdale comes first for Hester. Her motive for staying in Boston is the hope that she can have a relationship with him. For him, she is willing to allow both herself and her daughter to suffer.

Hester's vision of holy living and dying is radically different from Dimmesdale's. As Hawthorne imagines her, she practices the secular religion of romantic love. In the forest scene, she offers Dimmesdale an alternative version of self-perpetuation, resurrection based on the romantic fantasy of "'merger,' symbiosis" with the beloved as a means to extend the power of the self.[46] After Dimmesdale's plea that she "resolve for me," she proposes triumphant passion as the means of apotheosis. The "old" conventional Arthur Dimmesdale will die, and another Arthur Dimmesdale will have "risen up all made anew" (1: 202). Their erotic union can transform the "poor pilgrim" who never moved "beyond the scope of generally received laws" into a man who believes that escape is the path to a "new life" (1: 200).

The tension between Hester's "secular" and Dimmesdale's "theological" strategies for evading death is apparent in the novel's concluding scenes.[47] When Dimmesdale asks, "Is not this better," as he looks ahead to a transcendent union with God instead of escape to Europe with Hester, she seems puzzled because she has not lived her life intent on securing a place in the Christian heaven and she still desires this-world happiness (1: 254). Earlier in the novel, she imagines an afterlife in more secular terms as the place of "a joint futurity of endless retribution," perhaps extending the logic of Chillingworth's retributive justice (1: 80). As she witnesses Dimmesdale's death, she asks, "Shall we not meet again?" prodding Dimmesdale to imagine heaven not as a state of transcendence but as an extension of temporal pleasures and relationships (1: 256). If we are to assume that Hester arranged the location of the gravesites, in the manner of Catherine and Heathcliffe in *Wuthering Heights*, we might also assume that she planned them to be the locus of a romantic reunion in death.[48] The narrator of Hawthorne's "Chippings with a Chisel" considers the different ways in which men and women grieve when he explains that men erect monuments to their departed wives because they are "able to reflect upon their lost companions as remembrances apart from themselves," while women "are conscious that a portion of their being has gone with the departed" (9: 412). Hawthorne draws Hester in the image of these women, for her sense of loss and incompleteness without a male is an integral part of her characterization. Being joined with Dimmesdale in death is a way that Hester conceives of extending the power of the self, and this belief may affect her decision to return to Boston in her last years.

Hester's primary task in the final stages of her life is to mourn, remember, and serve. The brief portrait of Hester in the novel's conclusion makes her resemble no one so much as a Victorian widow.[49] Dressed in the gray of a Victorian widow's "half mourning," she returns to Boston and assumes the role of Dimmesdale's chief mourner.[50] The rituals and proscriptives of mourning are designed to provide consolation and healing. The distinctive feature of Hester's grief, however, is that it is ongoing and unrelieved. The end of her life becomes an elegiac refrain because as Hawthorne conceives it suffering and sacrifice are the very essence of Hester's identity. She is a woman whose mourning has prompted her to virtue—witness her wholehearted charity and sympathy for the poor and the women in her community—but it does not bring recovery, and certainly not happiness.

For these reasons, the few metaphors of transcendence associated with Hester are complex and contradictory. At the novel's conclusion, she is remembered as a ghostly woman who "glided shadow-like" back to haunt her own house (1: 261). This unattractive image recalls an even more disturbing metaphor of memory when Hester is described earlier in the novel as a woman of "marble coldness" who in sacrificing her passion has only reconfirmed her materiality (1: 164). In casting Hester as a piece of monumental art, the novel clarifies what the cost of the culture's vision of immortality has been. The beautiful Madonna has been transformed into funerary statuary; her face, "like the frozen calmness of a dead woman's features," a death "mask" (1: 226). The religion of the heart, which, despite Hester's radicalism, Hawthorne defines as her refuge, offers new forms and rituals, but it is clear that it only serves the same basic order. The illusory promise of immortality that devotion to Dimmesdale would bring is but the mirror image of the transcendence of Christian salvation; neither would exempt her from the authority of the patriarchy nor the necessity of female sacrifice.

Ironically, the very nature of woman's suffering, suffering as imagined by the male author, is the reason that the male author finally parts company with his female protagonist. Hester's suffering misleads her; thinking about it only makes her "sad" and brings no new recognition or understanding (1: 165).[51] In a novel in which religious systems are associated with the oppression of women, her appeal to "Heaven's own time" to right women's wrongs becomes only the final proof of the limits of her vision (1: 263). Thus, despite the narrator's identification with Hester in "The Custom-House" when he tries on the letter and feels her pain, despite their similar roles as artists and outsiders, he distances himself from Hester.

Distancing himself from Hester allows him to attribute to her what the novel lacks: a coherent vision of a new social order which would establish the relationships between men and women "on a surer ground of mutual happiness" (1: 263). While feminist critics have acknowledged that Hawthorne has affectingly drawn women's suffering, several call him to account for being unable to offer a vision of an alternative order in which women's—and men's—identities would be cultivated and valued. As Hawthorne imagines it, that failure is Hester's, not the author's. It is she who works for reform without knowing what the nature of reform would be, and she who trusts in conservative consolations of dying, particularly the false consolation of undying romantic love. Hawthorne leaves her at her work, while he calls his readers to meditate among the tombs and to consider last things.

"In That Burial-Ground"

The novel's persistent interest in consolations of dying culminates in its conclusion. *The Scarlet Letter* has shown that in the same way that death "organizes" culture, it organizes the construction of the self; in fact, the novel makes apparent that death organizes culture by organizing the self.[52] Because dying is also gendered, men and women construct different consolations of dying.

The novel leaves us contemplating "a new grave...near an old and sunken one, in that burial-ground beside which King's Chapel has since been built," face to face with death (1: 264). The image of King's Chapel would have had complex resonances for Hawthorne's contemporaries. In Puritan time, Isaac Johnson gave the land on which the chapel was later built to the community as a site for the burial of the dead.[53] Hawthorne has reminded us of this gift at the novel's beginning. Shortly after the Massachusetts Bay Company lost its charter, King James II named Edmund Andros governor of the colony, and he began to build King's Chapel on the site of the old Boston burial ground.[54] A group of influential Puritans strongly contested having this Anglican and Loyalist presence on Puritan soil but to no avail. King's Chapel was built on a corner of the old burying ground and was dedicated on June 30, 1689. In building King's Chapel, Andros displaced the graves of the colony's founding fathers, including those of Isaac Johnson and probably John Winthrop. He had what Blanche Linden-Ward describes as "symbolic reasons" for this action; it "represented forcible imposition of royal political and religious control over the Puritan Commonwealth."[55]

These "symbolic reasons" call into question once again the choice Dimmesdale made when he identified Puritan belief with God's will and personal transcendence. If the power of the Puritan Commonwealth can be displaced by the Anglican, what does this say about the status of the individual who aspires to immortality on the coattails of these seemingly permanent belief systems? The specter of King's Chapel suggests that the beliefs of organized religion are not immutable ideas but cultural productions. Written in the face of death, they may not have the power to sustain the memory of even the most prominent cultural heroes who devoted their lives to upholding and preserving these belief systems. The Puritan community is disappearing and the remains of its heroes and founders, Isaac Johnson and John Winthrop, are not preserved or respected by subsequent generations.

The doubts raised about immortality systems and consolations of dying are redoubled with the final image of the "A" on the grave marker.[56] In discussing the Christian pastoral elegy, Esther Schor concludes that it can have several effects: "it retrieves an image of the deceased, passionately laments an image of the privative present, and celebrates the transcendence of the dead through a visionary evocation of grace." She then considers William Wordsworth's departure from this pattern in a poem of loss, such as the "Intimations Ode," which "replaces Christian transcendence with *descendental* tropes evoking necessity, rather than redemption."[57] The novel's concluding image has an effect that can be compared to that of a "descendental" trope. The "A" on the tombstone awakens memories of the dead but does not "celebrate" their transcendence through grace or love. Instead it simply invites the reader to lament what has been lost: the passion of Hester, the priestly vocation of Dimmesdale, the positive intellectual force of Chillingworth, and the potential for life and happiness of all three. Like Wordsworth's elegies, the conclusion of *The Scarlet Letter* refuses to offer us the consolation of a transcendent image. The "A" is not a "visionary consolation," but a plain and beautiful object that witnesses to the power of the earthly to bring all to the grave. As a "signpost," it does not point to some other "metaphysical place" to which to go but tells us we have come to the last place.[58] The "there" where we have arrived is simply "the end," the final words of the novel.

In the conclusion, Hawthorne retreats and calls us to meditate among the tombs. The subject of our meditations appears to be apolitical: the human situation per se, the reality that human beings are "diminished things" susceptible to death. But what is absent from this final scene may be as significant as what is present. In the face of the grave, Hawthorne does not deny death but leaves us in mourning, a place of loss and longing. He resists speaking moral platitudes and offering conventional consolations. There are no heroes, no new social order, no recognition of the power of absolute justice, undying romantic love, or eternal life to console us. While Dimmesdale thought it a fair bargain to sacrifice Hester for God and male immortality, Hawthorne seems more inclined to sacrifice the transcendental for the natural—the apotheotic "A" in the sky for the "A" on the tomb—a sacrifice which when viewed *sub specie mortis* may have revolutionary implications. Refusing to write his "A" into consolation, Hawthorne closes his valediction encouraging mourning.

"The Custom-House," the Secular Pilgrim, and the Happy Death

In commenting on the representation of death and the pattern of denying death in Shakespeare's plays, James L. Calderwood states that "culture then must not only provide for the survival of the pack but minister to this equally crucial need to live properly and meaningfully."[1] The ethical, moral, philosophical, and religious systems a culture creates to answer death must both relieve the anxiety of personal annihilation and provide the basis for leading a meaningful, even happy, life. It is in this regard that we see the most grievous failure of Puritan Boston's culture. In *The Scarlet Letter*, Dimmesdale never is happy, and certainly Hester is repeatedly described as sad and miserable.

In "The Custom-House" sketch, Hawthorne characterizes himself as an anxious secular man of the modern age who is trying to live a happy life without the psychological consolation garnered from a Christian belief in personal immortality.[2] The sketch is in the familiar form of the spiritual autobiography. Like the pilgrim in these autobiographies, he resembles "an exile and wayfarer in an alien land and the course of his life is a toilsome *peregrinatio* in quest of a better city in another country, which is where he truly belongs."[3] The pilgrim-Hawthorne tells us where he has been, the Old Manse, and explains that, since leaving there, he has lost his way and has no idea of the location of the "better world" (1: 13). His wanderings have brought him to a Custom House where "Neither the front nor the back entrance ... opens on the road to Paradise" (1: 13). It is an alien world that is so unlike where he believes he belongs that his presence in it becomes the source of both humor and somber meditation.

Hawthorne also reassesses some of his contemporaries' conventional assumptions about living and dying as he tries to answer: How does one create a meaningful, even a happy, life without the consolation of the old certitudes? In an ironic inversion of the customary work ethic of the period, he imagines a culture with a strong sleep ethic and equates this idleness and inactivity with decay, revealing the constant presence of death in the business of life. The Custom House is a world of false values—meaningless work, enervated leisure, excessive materialism—which foster self-doubt and an anxious aversion that is so strong that it resembles a sickness unto death. In this essay, Hawthorne represents his own death in a mock-serious tone. With the bookstalls of his contemporaries overflowing with consolation literature written to comfort those who lost a loved one, Hawthorne runs against the grain by penning an essay that mocks death and the afterlife.[4] In the process, he explains the origin of contemporary conditions and offers a primer on the secular way of living and dying.

"Remember Man That Thou Art Dust"

Hawthorne imagines his pilgrimage through life as a journey from the natural, near idyllic world of the Old Manse to the Custom House, a world of suspended existence and infertile decay. This change makes him morbidly retrospective. Back in Salem, he focuses on the past and his dead ancestral fathers whom he links to the dying male patriarch. Their legacy is "dust" (1: 9, 11), a dust which spells his "doom" (1: 12). Describing his legacy from his first American ancestor, he seems fragile and anxious, as if he is anticipating death: "And here his descendants have been born and died, and have mingled their earthy substance with the soil; until no small portion of it must necessarily be akin to the mortal frame wherewith, for a little while, I walk the streets. In part, therefore, the attachment which I speak of is the mere sensuous sympathy of dust for dust" (1: 8–9). His bond with these ancestors is their shared mortality.

The Custom House "patriarchs" with whom Hawthorne spends his days simply heighten his despondency because they have been sorely affected by its atmosphere of enervation and decay. He sees in them a presentiment of his own fate. The Hawthorne persona craves life, not death, and he writes a prescription for holy living—happiness—and defines it as "to live throughout the whole range of his faculties and sensibilities," a seemingly impossible standard to achieve for the

Custom House inhabitants, such as the Permanent Inspector and the Old General (1: 40). He wants nothing less than the affirmation of the whole self, which would validate his capacity for life.

But it is not possible to achieve this wholeness of being because a quadrangle of influences—the Custom House, its patriarchs, Hawthorne's ancestor-fathers, and Salem, coupled with his own temperamental affinity—conspires to create a depression and despair that bring him to the brink of personal disintegration. He feels desperation and "numbness" and his artistic work suffers (1: 35). He imagines the "mirror" of his imagination "tarnished" and his characters "dead corpses" (1: 34). At the point of crisis, he seems to be two selves, and one self, the artist, is "exhaling" its spirit, further jeopardizing the possibility that his identity could be continuous and whole (1: 38).

Hawthorne persistently connects his condition with his culture's. In telling his own story, he provides insight into how people of his time live and work. He writes of the "unprosperous condition" (1: 10) of his contemporaries in a manner reminiscent of Thoreau in Chapter One of *Walden*, and, like him, seems to be asking "whether it is necessary that it be as bad as it is, whether it cannot be improved as well as not."[5] Both Hawthorne and Thoreau envision solutions to the problem of wasted and desperate lives that run counter to those of their contemporaries. The Custom House is Hawthorne's version of Thoreau's Augean stables, and he would agree that the "cost" of earning his daily wages in such a place is too high because he has exchanged "life" for a "pittance of the public gold" (1: 34). Hawthorne might share Thoreau's misgivings about what "most men" would consider happiness: "to glorify God and enjoy him forever." When they come to die, neither wants to "discover that I had not lived."[6]

Hawthorne avoids the righteous and, at times, angry tone of Thoreau's essay and cultivates an offbeat, nonthreatening voice. Instead of confronting his contemporaries' ideas about the nature of happiness directly, he offers them a different perspective on their "condition" by criticizing and belittling himself in a mock-serious voice (1: 34). Feigning deference to gain more control over his narrative, he professes to have few readers and to deserve even fewer. He characterizes himself as woefully misguided when he gives up the Old Manse for the dreary bureaucracy of the Custom House in his search for "public gold" (1: 34). He comes to the Custom House like a lamb to the slaughter, little apprehending the personal cost of the move or the political machinations of the Washington insiders that, he implies, would lead to his firing and political demise. Laying claim to a way of life that few would envy and some, under his tutelage, might even see as a joke, he calls attention to his failure to understand himself or even fully appreciate what was of value in his former life, although he makes it apparent that he has paid the cost in misery for his misjudgments.

Imperceptive, unlucky, ill-used, yet deserving, genial, witty, and seemingly forthright, he endears himself to the reader and preempts his or her challenges. His persona as hapless pilgrim stumbling through life honeys the bitter critical voice that occasionally emerges. By adopting this persona, Hawthorne holds in balance his two purposes: to curry favor and criticize. In this way, when he describes life in Salem and the Custom House as soul-killing, a kind of waiting room for death on life's pilgrimage, he can rest assured that at least a "circle" of faithful readers would be attentive to his diagnosis of the cause and prescription for the remedy (1: 27).

"The Lamb to the Slaughter"

To explain a culture bereft of life and the means to happiness, Hawthorne relies on the logic of sacrifice. The patriarchs, including his ancestors, persecuted women—in the first generation Quaker women and in the next witches. He implies a reason for this persecution when he alludes to the historical "facts" that Surveyor Pue provided in his essay "Main-street" (1: 30). Published in 1849, "Main-street" is actually not particularly fact-based; instead it advances a theory of history with vaguely feminist undercurrents. In the Disney-like audioanimatronic version of American history that the "showman" of "Main-street" presents for his complaining audience, an Indian woman—"majestic and queenly"—is the source of origin, and the white male is the axe-wielding intruder in the wilderness (11: 52, 51). As the white man gains the ascendancy in the social order, the original matriarchy is eclipsed by patriarchy, and the Indian woman and her people are pushed to the culture's margin, only reappearing at intervals in various guises as threatening figures, witches or wolves who hover on the edge of the settlement.

The logic of "Main-street" is duplicated in "The Custom-House." The dynamic equilibrium of the social systems is maintained by a pattern of dominance and submission which necessitates the sacrifice of women and the matriarchy to the claims of the patriarchy. Hawthorne's ancestors enacted a form of female sacrifice of the kind that William Beers in *Women and Sacrifice* links to male immortality rituals.[7] Their actions, while enhancing their sense of themselves as powerful and exempt from personal annihilation, render them vulnerable to the "curse" of the women they have persecuted (1: 10). Furthermore, the consequences extend beyond the personal sphere and result in the "dreary and unprosperous condition of the race" (1: 10).

Hawthorne presents himself both as proof of the existence of the curse and as its cure. While professing to believe "strong traits of their [his ancestors'] nature have intertwined themselves with mine," he imagines that these ancestors would have thought having a writer in the family tree was another manifestation of the curse (1: 10). He wants to free himself from this curse, and he has an even larger hope that he can "hereby take shame upon myself for their sakes, and pray that any curse incurred by them...may be now and henceforth removed" (1: 10). What complicates his perception of the destructive pattern in the matriarchal-patriarchal dynamic cannot completely overcome his complicity in the patriarchy. In trying to balance the opposing claims of the patriarchal and the matriarchal within himself, he struggles to imagine a new kind of man. "The Custom-House" sketch answers the anxiety of death with this new man—Hawthorne himself as artist-hero—at the same time that it exposes the false bravado of this response.

Victor Turner's theory of the stages of social drama clarifies Hawthorne's experiences at the Custom House as they center on the ritual of sacrifice and culminate in his "guillotining." In the sketch, Hawthorne calls attention to symbols and rituals that resemble Turner's "cultural expressions" which "mediate between individual unconscious impulses and intentions and the social processes of the group making for its cohesion and continuity."[8] In this way, Hawthorne can show how his experiences are intertwined with and reflected in the condition of the group, suggesting, as Turner does, the relationship between individual psychology and group dynamic.

In Turner's theory, the social drama that surrounds sacrifice consists of four stages: "*breach,*" "*crisis,*" "*redressive action,*" and either "*reintegration* of the disturbed social group, or of the social recognition and legitimation of *irreparable schism* between the contesting parties."[9] For Turner, the drama begins with the breach that results from breaking the rules "of regular norm-governed social relations."[10] As he does in *The Scarlet Letter,* Hawthorne situates the "breach" in the drama of "The Custom-House" in pre-narrative time, returning to Puritan days to identify the crime against women and the subsequent blood curse as the source of crisis which disrupts the "norm-governed social relations," the status quo of the patriarchal order. Turner equates the crisis phases with liminality.[11]

The "redressive action" stage described in "The Custom-House" is complex; in fact, "The Custom-House" describes two different forms of redression: the presidential election and the firing or "guillotining" of Hawthorne. A presidential election could be considered a social act that provides an opportunity to restore balance to a community because it is an important ritual event enacted by the people and connected to a transfer of power. The election of President Taylor, though, as Hawthorne describes it in "The Custom-House," is a ritual that simply reinscribes the patriarchy. One group of male authorities replaces another, almost identical group of male authorities; stasis, then, a form of morbidity, becomes Hawthorne's unusual manifestation of "disequilibrium." The conditions of decay and lack of prosperity in the Custom House and in Salem are unaffected, and the election process fails to redress any of the real causes of the crisis because the conflict between male and female, patriarchy and matriarchy continues. The election does not affect the essentials of culture: the fictions that the males create to explain themselves to themselves, and the political and social structures that they generate to institutionalize their psychological realities.

Hawthorne's beheading, the second "redressive action," is an individual response that both mirrors and challenges a group response. For a male like Hawthorne, the "breach" has produced a particularly destabilizing loss because, from the perspective of gender, some of the qualities the Hawthorne of this essay clearly values in himself, qualities such as gentleness, passivity, and artistic sensibility, are associated in his culture with the feminine. To some extent, when Hawthorne is disclosing his ancestors' crimes against women, he is linking them to the injustice he has suffered at the hands of these same ancestors and, later, at the hands of the keepers of the political system. What Hawthorne wants is justice or—as Turner might explain it—"meaning," a way to "sift" through all of the "disputes," inconsistencies, and "disparate" narratives of meaning and come to a "set of new ends."[12]

In *Blazing the Trail*, Turner explains that sacrifice often involves an "antinomy" between an "unblemished self" and a "blemished self." In this tension, "two notions of power are contrasted: power based on force, wealth, authority, status, tradition, or competitive achievement; and power released by the dissolution of systemic and structural bonds."[13] The division Hawthorne experiences between his Custom

House self and artist self mirrors this dichotomy between the "blemished self" and "unblemished self," although it is expressed in the vocabulary of the workplace and hints at the tension between the public and private spheres. The Hawthorne persona exists precariously in the tension between these "two notions of power." In the logic of the internal drama of gender, he associates "power based on force" with the public, masculine, "blemished self" and the private, feminine, "unblemished self" with his artist self and his desire to escape from the "systemic and structural bonds" of the Custom House.[14]

Hawthorne, then, describes himself as caught in a curious double bind. He wants power and a way out of the Custom House but dreads slipping into the uncanny space of absence, the world of the "blood curse" and death, in short, the world of women. He fears becoming the beheaded Medusa, at the same time knowing the only way to deal with the claims of the dead mothers is by becoming Medusa's double. A Freudian reader would see the solution of beheading as a form of castration ("the unheimlich"). An anthropological reader influenced by Turner's theories of sacrifice might emphasize "beheading" as a ritual and sacrificial act with "transformative" powers.[15] Hawthorne could be driven to become "the lamb to the slaughter" by an impulse to find a means to control the "dealings of 'man alive' with 'man alive,' and of visible people with the invisible influences that inhere in human actions—the continuing presence of the immediate dead, kinfolk and affines of the living, whose will can still endorse or ban acts contemplated by their descendants."[16]

Like Turner, Hawthorne imagines the presence of the dead as "poles" which "correspond to the dual nature of 'the social,' communitas and structure." These poles exist in tension: "At one pole, self is immolated for the other; at the opposite pole, the other is immolated for self. Between the poles there are many gradations of offering: part of self may be offered for some others; part of the other may be offered for the whole self." Hawthorne complicates this polar tension by making it gendered. He is not beheaded, then, to become woman, or the "unblemished self," nor does he want to remain trapped within the identity of the "blemished self," remaining like the fathers who began the cycle of guilt and retribution because of their cruelty to women. He seems to want to immolate the "structural self...to liberate the antistructural identity."[17]

Hawthorne moves in several directions to explain the nature of this "antistructural identity." He invents a new kind of father, Surveyor Pue, who serves as an intermediary in the polar tension, almost as if to affirm women while protecting himself from his culture's ideas about woman's contamination. This foster father values history and stories, and Hawthorne imagines Pue as having the nineteenth-century female gender characteristics of generosity and sympathy all working in the author's behalf because they inspire him to bequeath to Hawthorne the gift of the scarlet letter. Pue is also linked to death and personal annihilation. Hawthorne remembers that he has read "an account of the digging up of his remains in the little grave-yard" and "nothing" of him was left except his wig (1: 30). He is another displaced patriarch, but in his case Hawthorne creates the consoling fiction of the interested and benevolent ghost, a "majestic" figure doing the King's work with a queenly disposition (1: 30, 33).

"The Realm of Quiet"

But inventing Surveyor Pue is insufficient to satisfy Hawthorne's need for "revolution" (1: 43). He struggles to achieve a new way to define himself that taps cultural sources and has a culturally acceptable logic but moves beyond middle-class conventions of gender and Christianity. Assuming an "antistructural identity" requires imagining a different space: in the metaphor of guillotining/castration, being able to see something similar to what Cixous describes as "what lies on the other side of castration," or in the metaphor of Turner—accomplishing transformation.[18]

In "The Custom-House," Hawthorne leaves his pre-breach state of matriliny, moves on to patriliny at considerable psychic cost because he is wrenched by his conflicting allegiances, and finally narrates a fiction of redression and reintegration in which he imagines himself as residing in both and bounded by neither. Out of the "chaos of positive and negative existence-values," he struggles to find a form of justice for himself. He is able to escape his debt to both his male and female ancestors. Indeed, he eludes any social debt because for Hawthorne the "set of new ends," which Turner envisions as "for the group at large," is for him alone.[19]

The "realm of quiet" where Hawthorne imagines residing after his guillotining resembles Turner's "limen" (1: 44).[20] Like Turner's "threshold people," he "elude[s] or slip[s] through the network of classifications that normally locate states and positions in cultural space. Liminal entities are neither here nor there; they are betwixt and between the positions assigned and arrayed by law, custom, convention, and ceremonial. . . . Thus liminality is frequently likened to death."[21] Neither among the living nor the dead, neither in Salem nor exiled from it, neither aligned with the matriarchs nor the patriarchs, he resides "betwixt and between." Hawthorne's definition of "neutral territory" as a state of "betweenness" extends the implications of liminality, transposing the experience into the basis for an aesthetic theory (1: 36).[22] The artist who can escape the ordinary boundaries of time, space, and condition redefines himself as necessarily "ambiguous," with special powers of immunity from the consequences of "law, custom, convention, and ceremonial."[23]

The hapless pilgrim, then, comes to the Custom House with no apparent program but with one unwavering intent: to deepen his own singularity so that his artistic genius may flourish. Turner uses Wilhelm Dilthey's ideas about the formulation of the nature of value to explain what happens when life is viewed not as a "series of choices between ends" but as a "subsuming of everything to a single end—in the first instance, no unity, no interdependence, can be found in the sequence of alternating choices; in the second, the complexity of life, including its ambiguity and the problem of competing, equally licit choices, is reduced."[24] Hawthorne's "single end"—the achievement of happiness through fiction writing—allows him to make sense of the Custom House experience but, at the same time, does reduce the complexity of the experience. Finally, it is all about Hawthorne. He is removing the curse, not for the sake of the fathers but for himself; he tells the story of the despised women to find justice and redeem a part of himself. He wants to obtain for himself a release from the crisis and tensions he has depicted. In this sketch, Hawthorne seems interested finally not in the way the group reachieves wholeness and equilibrium, but only in the way the exceptional male individual survives. Throughout most of "The Custom-House" the individual's fate and the group's fate seem inextricably bound. The "beheading" brings an almost magical rupture that accomplishes little for the group but means everything for Hawthorne.

Compromised and nearly destroyed by exposure to the world of the Custom House, Hawthorne imagines himself finally able to overcome the effects of this world and resurrect the artistic self. As the beheaded Custom House officer, he assumes the identity of the Medusa, for, like her, he is isolated in the community and experiences a form of hostility.[25] But he does not become woman or identify with her. As several commentators have noted, Hester and Hawthorne are similar—both creative, expressive individuals isolated in communities hostile to their nature—but Hawthorne is careful to draw some important distinctions between them. The "A" is part of Hester's nature. She must return to it (and to Boston), for both the letter and the place define and limit her. With Salem no longer his "destiny," unlimited by time or space, Hawthorne can assume new and different identities (1: 11). He tries on the "A" but lays it aside, refusing to allow it permanently to bound or define him.

Ultimately, Hawthorne achieves his new identity by collapsing two of the culture's most viable—and contradictory—gender myths. He weds Christ to Medusa and assumes the powers of both. No longer the impotent "decapitated" surveyor, he places his head on his shoulders and begins to write (1: 43). He resurrects himself from the grave and ascends into "the realm of quiet" (1: 44), a neutral state where opposition can be controlled and contained or, perhaps more precisely, where opposition can be denied. It is a place beyond the definitional dualities of nineteenth-century culture arrived at by a process similar to what Turner characterizes as "ritual mechanisms." Only the power of ritual could address both the "overt" conflict in which "rational investigation into the motives and actions of the contending parties was obviously possible" and "conflict…at a deeper level," as well as "exorcise familiars or placate ancestral wrath." A power akin to Turner's "religious and magical procedures" accomplishes Hawthorne's liberation from the Custom House.[26]

The depressed artist becomes a new kind of hero, joining the ranks of "transhuman beings"; a metaphysical illness that means a sickness unto death for others has no power over the liberated Hawthorne.[27] Unlike Thoreau, this Hawthorne has no desire to leave a "coat" for his contemporaries to try on and check for proper fit.[28] Despite its astute identification of the gender and social patterns that hinder happiness in the individual and prosperity in the group, "The Custom-House" sketch is a plan of escape, not a scheme of reform. It is a personal, not a political or social "revolution" that Hawthorne wants to accomplish.

There is only one person in *The Scarlet Letter* who rises to the level of heroic individualism. The liberated Hawthorne alone merits being ranked among the worthy dead because, like all true culture heroes, he has challenged death. He has done so by an act of rebellious defiance that emphasizes the power of the individual to circumvent death by freeing the "antistructural identity."[29] But in *The Scarlet Letter* Hawthorne can imagine emancipation only for the Hawthorne persona; not Hester, Arthur, or even Pearl can achieve this liberation and "happy death."

While Hester is driven by a Liebestod fantasy, Hawthorne imagines himself as directed by a resurrection fantasy. The resurrection fantasy often expresses the wish to be happy after death and to maintain the ego or the self intact. Helen K. Gediman distinguishes between the two fantasies in this way: "Liebestod fantasy, in pointing to a primal merger in which the self disappears, is qualitatively different from the resurrection fantasy, which is future-oriented (not primal) and in which the ego is precisely what survives forever."[30] Rather than representing a desire to merge with the other and achieve immortality through identification with the love object, the resurrection fantasy reveals strong narcissistic impulses which push toward "restoration of the self and its perpetuation in immortality."[31] As Hawthorne confers his "blessing" and "forgiveness," he is in a transcendent "neutral" state and seems both totally liberated and disengaged from others (1: 44). He has ascended, ego intact, to a transcendent "realm of quiet," where it seems he could abide forever (1: 44). Refusing to exalt female over male or male over female, he charts a new territory that exists in the space "betwixt and between" the male and the female, life and death.[32] His separate life is its own justification. Achieving his cultural transcendence has required no sacrifice, only a "restoration of the self" as limitless and perpetual. Hawthorne has entered the lists of the literary immortals on his own recognizance.

The "Insult" of Death

In "Fiction, Fair, and Foul I," John Ruskin wrote that it was such a commonplace in late nineteenth-century novels to include a deathbed scene "because the study of it from the living—or dying—model is so easy, and to many has been the most impressive part of their own personal experience."[33] Hawthorne resists this literary commonplace, even though we know that Hawthorne wrote "The Custom-House" and *The Scarlet Letter* during a period of mourning after the death of his mother and, more specifically, after he had witnessed and recorded in his journal her deathbed scene.

For Freud, "the work of mourning" is the work of remembering.[34] In "The Custom-House," Hawthorne revisits the distant past of his ancestors to understand his present pain, using memory as a means of reinvention and a form of control over death. In his study on mourning and loss, John Bowlby explains that in the early months of mourning the bereaved, particularly those who have lost their mothers, are still "searching" for her.[35] Perhaps this "search" may explain an unusual inclusion in Hawthorne's description of the artist's "neutral territory." Hawthorne begins the passage by assuring the reader, and perhaps himself, that "Ghosts might enter here, without affrighting us," and then admits, "It would be too much in keeping with the scene to excite surprise, were we to look about us and discover a form, beloved, but gone hence, now sitting quietly in a streak of this magic moonshine, with an aspect that would make us doubt whether it had returned from afar, or had never once stirred from our fireside" (1: 36). In this liminal space, where the "actual and the imaginary" may meet, where it may be possible to deny the opposition between the living and the dead, he may even be able to recover "beloved" figures "gone hence" (1: 36). Buried in the inmost regions of this space of art is the no longer frightening figure of the dead mother.

In "The Custom-House," Hawthorne imagines himself achieving a modicum of peace, harmony, and power over death that is very unlike the turmoil, self-doubt, and loss of control that the death of his mother actually inspired. His journal entry for July 29, 1849 captures the painful reality of her death. In his description of the domestic scene surrounding his mother's dying, he presents a frankly realistic picture of the pain and isolation of death. He does not draw from the conventional consolation literature, which composed the deathbed scene to emphasize the piety and faith of the dying and her witnesses. Instead of harmonious caregivers, pious witnesses, inspiring last words, and intimations of immortality, his description reveals some disgruntlement and tension among the watchers, no minister in attendance, and a little girl swatting away flies from the body of her grandmother. Hawthorne recounts that when he approached his mother's deathbed, she whispered no words of encouragement about reunion in an afterlife, only a few "indistinct words" that he understood as an "injunction to take care of my sisters." Hawthorne describes himself as weeping inconsolably for a long time at her deathbed and admits, "surely it is the darkest hour I ever lived" (8: 429). After his mother's death, Hawthorne's wife Sophia expressed concern at the extent of her husband's deep mourning for his mother.

The extent of Hawthorne's grief is certainly understandable.[36] His father died when he was nearly four, and throughout childhood Hawthorne depended on his mother for emotional, intellectual, and economic support. As Bowlby explains, children who have lost a parent when they are very young experience a number of characteristic responses that resemble adult mourning.[37] Because very young children are not able to understand the finality of death, for a long time they expect the dead parent to return and are angry, saddened, and disappointed when their expectations are frustrated. This may have been particularly true of young Hawthorne. Since his father had been absent for long periods of time when he was at sea, Hawthorne might have been even more inclined to believe that his father's death was just another one of these long separations and that he would eventually return. The child who has lost a parent also can become very attached to the surviving parent, at some level fearing that she too will die, leaving him orphaned and abandoned. Because of the child's loss and "fear of further loss" he often becomes "anxious and clinging."[38]

These are the symptoms of mourning "when the conditions are favorable," when the child can talk openly of the dead and the cause of death, grieve, and participate in the funeral, and when the widow can express her grief openly, is economically secure, and has a way to conceive of going on with her life without the spouse. Certainly, we know from Hawthorne's biographers that at the time of her husband's death conditions for both Nathaniel and his mother, Elizabeth, were far from favorable: her economic situation was insecure, both the Hawthorne and Manning families were inclined "to veil their feelings," and there was no grave the family could visit to grieve since he was buried abroad.[39]

Neal L. Tolchin's study of the influence on Herman Melville's life and art of his father's death, his mother's mourning, and nineteenth-century mourning practices establishes that the practices of this period placed very strict limits on the expression of grief, and so it was very unlikely that Hawthorne's mother would have had much support or sympathy in her mourning.[40] More likely, she would have suppressed her grief and turned to her children for support, particularly, if Bowlby is correct, to her son.[41] In turn, Hawthorne would have formed a strong, and perhaps anxious, attachment to his mother. There is significant biographical support for this assumption. His letter to her of March 13, 1821 in which he worries about his future choice of profession suggests that when he was young there was a very strong bond and frank communication between them (15: 138). His twelve-year stay at his mother's home after college may further indicate the extent of his attachment to her. Also, he delayed marrying, and his letters suggest he was reluctant to tell her about his marriage plans.[42] Perhaps his strong attachment to her increased his anxiety at separation, further explaining his assessment of their relationship in his notebook: "I love my mother; but there has been, ever since my boyhood, a sort of coldness of intercourse between us, such as is apt to come between persons of strong feelings, if they are not managed rightly" (8: 429). Because of these complex and ambivalent feelings, his pain and grief at the time of her death may well have been extraordinarily strong and the "work" of his mourning great.

Looking again at Hawthorne's description of the scene of his mother's dying, the way Hawthorne tried to cope with this overwhelming sense of loss is revealing. According to his journal, after crying at his mother's bedside, he moves to the window in her room and sees his children playing in the yard. He assumes a stance there that allows him to distance himself somewhat from the pain of his mother's death. At the window, while he negotiates the space between the scene he is so intensely involved in and the scene he observes, he imagines that the observed scene reduplicates the original. In a manner reminiscent of a Jamesian watcher at the window, he has begun the process of transforming observed experience into art. At the window, he has laid claim to a space resembling "neutral territory" that he controls and where he can recover his sense of balance and harmony but not lose sight of his pain. It is in this "territory" where the distance between the living and the dead can be denied and the "beloved" dead figure, who brings both grief and the impetus for art, can be recovered (1: 36).

In this scene, Hawthorne also positions himself as the mediating point between his "poor dying mother" and his daughter Una "so full of spirit and life" (8: 429). When he looks at his dying mother, she brings home to him the fragility of the human condition. He sees in her death the deaths of all human beings and laments, "I looked at my poor dying mother; and seemed to see the whole of human existence at once, standing in the dusty midst of it. Oh what a mockery, if what I saw were all" (8: 429). The word "dust" that so often recurs in *The Scarlet Letter* and "The Custom-House" is a reminder of the biblical description of humans as mere "dust" who will return to "dust." He concludes his notebook passage with a seemingly strong affirmation of a belief in an afterlife. Because it is one of the very few occasions in Hawthorne's letters or notebooks where he expresses his thoughts on human immortality, I will quote it in its entirety: "But God would not have made the close so dark and wretched, if there were nothing beyond; for then it would have been a fiend that created us, and measured out our existence, and not God. It would be something beyond wrong—it would be an insult—to be thrust out of life into annihilation in this miserable way. So, out of the very bitterness of death, I gather the sweet assurance of a better state of being" (8: 429). These are strong words for Hawthorne in their expression of both his anger at the God who would create human beings as mortal and his desire to achieve the consolation of "sweet assurance."

Notice that Hawthorne describes death as an "insult," and, I think that we have to assume here, it is an insult to what William Beers in *Women and Sacrifice* defines as the male sense of the self as powerful and immortal. Hawthorne recognizes that it is possible to suffer what Beers calls a grave narcissistic wound from this "insult." To allow this insult is to accept the self as temporal, finite, merely natural, in short, as capable of experiencing "annihilation" (8: 429). But what is unusual about this passage is that while expressing this fairly radical position, Hawthorne can admit that the experience of his mother's death reawakens his fears about human mortality. In fact, he concludes the passage reemphasizing the doubt by returning to Una. Hawthorne recalls that, as he is reflecting on this proof for the existence of God and eternal life, he hears Una commenting about his mother's death, "'Yes;—she is going to die.'" And he admits, "I wish she had said 'going to God'—which is her idea and usual expression of death; it would have been so hopeful and comforting" (8: 430). But there is no final comfort from Una, and its absence underscores his doubt.[43]

Earlier in the same passage, Hawthorne reflects upon the human condition with another "If...then" proposition. This time he concludes, "Oh what a mockery, if what I saw were all,—let the interval between extreme youth and dying age be filled up with what happiness it might!" (8: 429). The sentiment that Hawthorne expresses here is somewhat similar to that in Philip Freneau's poem "The Wild Honey Suckle" when he contemplates the human condition and writes: "The space between, is but an hour, / The frail duration of a flower."[44] But, in Hawthorne's case, what is absent is Freneau's stoical resignation. Instead Hawthorne seems close to raging against the narcissistic wounding caused by the painful recognition of his own mortality that accompanies the loss of his mother. He cannot negate his doubts completely and finally entertains the possibility that he will have to accept this "wounding" or recognition of "annihilation" of the self as part of the human condition and strive nevertheless to achieve the means to happiness, perhaps without the Christian consolations of dying, a thought which is close to the sentiments of some of the mid- and late-Victorian agnostics.

Reimagining Death

Three to four months later, Hawthorne composed a scene for *The Scarlet Letter* that recalls his description of his mother's death. In "The Leech and His Patient," Dimmesdale and Chillingworth have taken up residence together in Boston near the graveyard. It is a suitable location for the two, one close to death and the other described as a "sexton" who is already "delving into a grave" (1: 129). In this location, they meditate on philosophical issues and moral questions, and they seem drawn to discuss the body-soul dichotomy. Chillingworth, in particular, refers to this doctrine. In his view, it becomes not the basis for belief in the possibility of eternal bliss, but another source of human woe that he will work to grievous consequences for Dimmesdale.

As the two are sitting at home near the graveyard, Dimmesdale questions Chillingworth about some "ugly weeds" that he is examining, and Chillingworth explains that he found them on the grave of a wretched man: "They grew out of his heart, and typify, it may be, some hideous secret that was buried with him, and which he had done better to confess during his lifetime" (1: 131). Chillingworth draws the logical implication of the body-soul dichotomy when he argues, as Jonathan Edwards might, that this weed is simply a natural object testifying to a spiritual fact, challenging Dimmesdale to reattach spirit to body, ideas to things. Dimmesdale understands Chillingworth's point but is unwilling to admit that "secrets," like ideas, necessarily manifest themselves in words or material objects; he attempts to negate completely the value of the material as a source of meaning (1: 131). Dimmesdale's attempt to sever the connection between words and natural facts, nature and symbol, is another example of his struggle to deny the body, the earthly, and the material in his attempt to free himself from temporality and death. Chillingworth's image suggests that Dimmesdale's resistance is an impossible scheme, particularly when viewed from the perspective of the grave.

During this conversation, Dimmesdale has taken a position at the window of his room, a position that mimics Hawthorne's station at the time of his mother's death. This is apparently a familiar place of Dimmesdale's since he is described at the same location in a previous scene. From this mid-position, he can both watch and listen, entertaining Chillingworth's perspective while retaining his distance. He stands precariously between Chillingworth, the "grave" man with his troubling reflections on the human condition, and the graveyard. At the point of crisis in the conversation between the two, when Chillingworth is pressing Dimmesdale to concede that a man who has sinned and not revealed himself as sinner cannot do good work—in fact admitting the inextricable link between spirit and word, thought and thing, and, by implication, soul and body—Dimmesdale looks from the open window and sees Pearl at the graveyard. Like Una in the death scene of Hawthorne's mother, Pearl is an enigma; both what she is and what she does challenge conventional pieties. As "the scarlet letter endowed with life" (1: 102), Pearl should be the perfect commentary on the nature-spirit, word-thing dichotomy, for in her present condition as a child "worthy to have been brought forth in Eden; worthy to have been left there, to be the plaything of the angels" there is no separation between word and thing, nature and spirit (1: 90). She should be perfectly interpretable.

But the problem is, of course, that neither Dimmesdale nor Chillingworth can fathom her meaning. "What, in Heaven's name, is she?" Chillingworth asks, and Dimmesdale cannot answer (1: 134). As they stand at the window and look out at Pearl, these two male protagonists, for the only time in the novel, share a single perspective. Both agree that they cannot comprehend the meaning of the child-woman who is Pearl. When Chillingworth asks, "Hath she any discoverable principle of being?" the irony of Dimmesdale's response is apparent (1: 134). The Christian minister should readily respond "soul" or "spirit," for even Pearl is a child of God capable of redemption. But he tellingly answers, "None,—save the freedom of a broken law" (1: 134). Both these men are frightened by the enigma of Pearl; like her mother, she is to them the unfathomable, the uninterpretable. Her very presence casts everything adrift. Beautiful but "perverse," she seems to them to be a wild principle of anarchy and power without soul (1: 133). Their perspective on her is another manifestation of the way men create "fictions" about women. They invest Pearl with unusual power and then their construction creates a concomitant need to "control the male-perceived power of women."[45] We are witnessing the creation of a myth of origin, one that links women with death and lawlessness and will eventually require redression.

In this scene, Hawthorne links women with death or, more precisely, granted the broader context of its relationship with the description of his own mother's dying, with the truth which is denied about death, and lays the groundwork for a renewed cycle of dominance and violence against women. If, as William Beers asserts, male rituals of sacrifice are designed to control "lines of patrilineal descent," the logic of sacrifice may eventually claim its victim.[46] By the end of the novel, the male order is already asserting its control over Pearl as if to break her bond with Hester and ensure the continuance of male dominance. Chillingworth's fortune and Dimmesdale's kiss propel her into a future apart from Hester that is partly shaped by them.

Still, Pearl is slippery and possibly is capable of eluding their power. The men take the scarlet letter to be her destiny, and, at times, she seems to accept this interpretation of her being as she obsessively fixes her glance on it or plays at trying on the green seaweed "A" (1: 178). But even when her mother offers her another way to "read" the letter, suggesting that it is totally accidental, with "no purport" (1: 178) apart from its wearer, she offers no assent (178). In fact, Pearl's only "thought" that the narrator records comes when, after fashioning the green "A" on herself, Pearl wonders "if mother will ask me what it means," as if she conceives of herself as her own point of definition (1: 178). Pearl is simple, "the scarlet letter endowed with life," yet tests the limits of understanding, the alpha without the omega (1: 102). As Thoreau suggests, no one can comprehend the simple, the new, the first: "I know not the first letter of the alphabet. I have always been regretting that I was not as wise as the day I was born."[47] It is as if in his creation of Pearl Hawthorne is trying to fathom some new creature, a new woman whose link with death does not define her. As the narrator explains in the Dimmesdale-Chillingworth graveyard scene, "skipping, dancing, and frisking fantastically among the hillocks of the dead people," Pearl resembles "a creature that had nothing in common with a bygone and buried generation, nor owned herself akin to it. It was as if she had been made afresh, out of new elements" (1: 134–35).

A year after Emerson's wife died he went to the cemetery, opened her coffin, and stared death in the face. According to Robert D. Richardson, Jr., this event marked a turning point in his life which eventually led him from Boston to Europe where he began an intense period of reflection that laid the groundwork for his philosophical system, one with its roots in Platonism and German idealism.[48] Hawthorne's response to his mother's death is different and yet may proceed from a similar impulse. Like Emerson, he did not seem to be satisfied completely by Christian consolations and sought alternate ways to come to terms with death. He does understand his contemporaries' belief in the power of Christianity to answer death and does not deny its force. The creation of Dimmesdale speaks to this impulse. At the same time, he explores the social, cultural, and ethical implications of the answer that Christian immortality systems provide, particularly the way in which they determine the ideas of males about women and affect women's condition. Like Emerson, he seems to need to entertain doubts, discover new ways of seeing and being, and experiment with responding to death outside of the boundaries of Christian consolations. With his dramatization of his fate in the Custom House, Hawthorne begins to imagine a way to live a life that encompasses "the whole range of his faculties and sensibilities" and promises real happiness (1: 40). To be fully human, yet happy accepting the limits of mortality is the challenge.

But when Pearl enters the discourse, Hawthorne, like his male protagonists, withdraws to the window, not knowing what to make of his new creation whose very existence defies not only the narrow doctrines of Puritan religion but also the conventional pieties of his contemporaries. He plays the same role as he does in the scene of his mother's dying. Taking up his place at the window with his male protagonists, he records, mourns, and mediates, but does not interpret. What Dimmesdale and Chillingworth see from their window is a pictorial rendering of Una's comment at the time of Hawthorne's mother's death. Pearl is in the graveyard below them, and, taking in the full extent of human misery and suffering, she does her version of whistling in the dark as she dances "irreverently" on the graves of her ancestors (1: 133). And it is this defiant dance of death that seems to her father observers to "remove her entirely out of the sphere of sympathy or human contact" to a dangerous and solitary place beyond Christian beliefs and consolation (1: 133).

CHAPTER THREE

"Familial Immortality" and the "Dying of Death" in The House of the Seven Gables

In a lecture given in Boston on January 23, 1839 and in Concord on April 24, Emerson lamented that "history gave no intimation of any society in which despondency came so readily to heart as we see it and feel it in ours." He singled out "grief" and "melancholy" as the defining characteristics of the time and pointed out that these qualities might be even more pervasive among those under thirty years old because "if they fail in their first enterprizes...the rest of life is rock and shallow."[1] In another lecture delivered to the senior class of the Harvard Divinity College only a year before, he expressed concern that "when men die we do not mention them."[2] The two statements taken together evoke a New England middle-class society grieving yet struggling to deny its grief. Where death and failure were concerned, many mid-nineteenth-century New Englanders practiced the policy of avoidance, trying to deny the reality of grief and despondency in their lives.

In characterizing his contemporaries in this way, Emerson may have been one of the earliest to recognize what some cultural historians identify as an emerging phenomenon in nineteenth-century American middle-class culture—"the dying of death."[3] Throughout the century there was a great "concern about death" accompanied by a growing need to shunt it aside.[4] The concern was driven by the demographic reality of high mortality rates, particularly for infants and children. At mid-century, life expectancy was forty years.[5] The possibility that a family would experience the death of one or several of its members within an eighteen-year frame was high. While there has been considerable study of the Evangelical and sentimental traditions which encouraged the display of emotion in bereavement and in memorial remembrances, there has been less attention to the counter impulse linked to the repression of grief and the cultivation of reserve. Less certainty about the nature of the good death, unease about witnessing death, and calls for moderation in mourning and bereavement practices suggest that attitudes about death and dying may have been evolving. Death was becoming less acceptable "as an event" as people became more attached to a worldly, material, and secular view of life.[6]

During this period, Christian beliefs about death and the afterlife were changing.[7] More "varieties of belief" emerged, some of which de-emphasized the idea of hell and consequently fostered less fear of death and less need to focus on the compensatory aspects of heaven.[8] Christian liberals tended to speak of death's didactic value, and new spiritualists downplayed the finality of death, instead stressing the relationship between life and death and the living and the dead.[9] The intense evangelicalism at the beginning of the century may also have indirectly contributed to these shifting perspectives. It inspired belief in God and awakened a popular notion of a millennial Christian era of peace and prosperity on earth, a focus that readjusted the traditional attention on heaven.

With the development of science, some saw death from a more exclusively naturalistic perspective. In "A Discourse on the Burial of the Dead," which included a rationale for the development of a rural cemetery, Jacob Bigelow emphasized that human beings "have natural laws and irresistible affinities which are suspended during the period of life, but which must be obeyed the moment that life is extinct."[10] Others fused nascent evolutionary theory with a faith in progress and speculated that scientific advancement would one day mark the end of disease and accomplish the taming of death.

At the same time that the newly developed rural or suburban cemeteries reduced the "social distance between the living world and the dead world" by encouraging mourners to visit cemeteries and commune with the dead, they also helped them avoid some of the realistic facts of death.[11] Because these cemeteries were so picturesque, they tended to beautify and sanitize death, providing an opportunity for the bereaved to retreat from the unpleasant smells and sights that had assaulted them when they visited the urban church cemetery. The fact that over 2000 people attended the opening ceremony of Mount Auburn Cemetery in Cambridge, Massachusetts in 1831 and for decades Mount Auburn was the second most popular tourist attraction in the New England area testifies to the complex cultural need that cemeteries like this one addressed. Not all came to mourn; many visited simply because in an era before parks Mount Auburn and other cemeteries like it were lovely spots for Sunday outings, carriage rides, and picnics. The rural cemetery movement also included changes that represented the first stage in the commercialization of death which would eventually place the management of death in the hands of professionals and further remove it from the consciousness of the average person.[12]

In this climate of changing ideas about death, Hawthorne writes a tragi-comedy that explores his contemporaries' complex attitudes about the "dying of death." Hawthorne sets *The House of the Seven Gables* in a world in which the Christian idea of eternal life may no longer constitute the single, standard answer to death, and consolations of dying are sometimes framed in more secular terms. Granted the importance of the family in nineteenth-century middle-class life, it is not surprising that some would seek in it the answer to death. Promoting the sanctity and integrity of the family as a property trust was considered a good in itself, and a belief in the family's permanence provided a way for many to face the fearful contingencies of nineteenth-century life. *The House of the Seven Gables*, however, places this particular consolation for dying under intense scrutiny and exposes it as a source of some of the intolerable contradictions that beset middle-class New England life. When viewed in this light, the novel is no paean to middle-class family life but a domestic Gothic horror story that locates the seat of the family in the tomb, not the kitchen or the parlor.

Future Generations

> The love of posterity is a consequence of the necessity of death. If a man were sure of living forever here, he would not care about his offspring.
>
> Hawthorne, *The American Notebooks*

In *Disease, Pain, and Sacrifice*, David Bakan explains the prominent role "familial immortality" plays in the Judeo-Christian tradition as an answer to death. He is especially attentive to the tension between "familial immortality" and the achievement of "individual immortality," and his analysis of this issue helps to open a discussion of the particular manifestation of the conflict that Hawthorne depicts in *The House of the Seven Gables*. Crucial to Bakan's thesis is recognizing the centrality of the Abraham-Isaac story to the Bible and, in turn, to the whole Judeo-Christian culture.[13] To sacrifice one's son at the behest of God is to achieve "individual immortality" at the price of "familial immortality" because obedience to the father becomes the source of self-eternal. From the perspective of the story, the two—cultivation of the self and development of the family—can be understood as working at cross-purposes. The dilemma for the male individual becomes whether he should survive as an adult who kills his child or as a child of the father-God, "deferring to him so that he will not kill one as the 'child.'" By appeasing God, the individual hopes that he might enjoy "endless life," but appeasement also means foregoing "sexuality, reproduction, and one's own fatherhood," in short, the possibility of achieving "familial immortality." Some of the most important psychological work of the Old Testament involves negotiating the space between individual and familial immortality, and it often means the "substitution of familial immortality for individual immortality."[14]

"Roger Malvin's Burial," written in 1832 and published in *Mosses from an Old Manse* in 1846, dramatizes the tension between familial and individual immortality that Bakan describes and can serve as a prelude to a consideration of the tension in *The House of the Seven Gables*. Reuben Bourne and his future father-in-law, Roger Malvin, have both been wounded in battle, and Malvin, assuming he cannot live more than two days, urges the younger Reuben to return to the settlement. Malvin believes that if the wounded Reuben tries to rescue him neither will survive. Reuben, whom Malvin calls "son," is persuaded to leave and promises Malvin he will return to bury him and say a prayer over his grave, a promise he never keeps. Years later, after a life of grief and failure, Reuben Bourne journeys into the wilderness in search of a new homestead. Apparently by chance, his journey takes him, his wife, who is Malvin's daughter, and his son to the place of Malvin's death, and there he accidentally kills his son.

A reading of this tale based on Bakan's thesis would suggest that Reuben Bourne has chosen to heed the "supernatural voice" and defer to the "supernatural power" of the father whom he believes demanded the sacrifice of his son for the expiation of his sin of abandoning the father (10: 356). With this choice he foregoes the opportunity for "familial immortality." The narrator explains that this form of immortality would have come through his children. This tale presents a vision of "what might have been" for Reuben Bourne so detailed and explicit it resembles an encomium to "familial immortality":

> and when hoary age, after long, long years of that pure life, stole on and found him there, it would find him the father of a race, the patriarch of a people, the founder of a mighty nation yet to be. When death, like the sweet sleep which we welcome after a day of happiness, came over him, his far descendants would mourn over the venerated dust. Enveloped by tradition in mysterious attributes, the men of future generations would call him godlike; and remote posterity would see him standing, dimly glorious, far up the valley of a hundred centuries! (10: 352)

Instead of beginning a family line that would continue for a "hundred centuries," Reuben Bourne sacrifices his son and foregoes "future generations." In exchange, he gains what Bakan would describe as "individual immortality," an "endless life" that comes from identification with and subordination to the will of the Father.[15]

In *The House of the Seven Gables*, Hawthorne explores the tension between "familial" and "individual immortality" in ways particularly relevant to the conditions of nineteenth-century middle-class culture. The patriarchal family was the central unit of contemporary New England life, and the culture's emphasis on the family as a property trust enhanced belief in its apparent power to ensure male immortality. On the surface, it would seem there could be no inherent conflict between "familial immortality" and "individual immortality" in nineteenth-century society, particularly because the idea of the family as the locus of "self-culture," particularly male self-culture, had significant appeal.[16] Popular sentiment viewed the family as the ideal place for the development of the male self, and this development seemed compatible with preserving the family and promoting its welfare. But *The House of the Seven Gables* presents a different perspective on the family. Although the family seems to be working in the service of male identity, at the same time its very nature promotes a kind of immaturity and conformity to patriarchal authority that hinders the development of individualism. In short, "familial immortality" and "individual immortality" at times work at cross-purposes. The novel raises questions about injustice to women in the patriarchal family that seem directly connected with the idea of the family as a property trust, and it reveals an alternative source of authority in the family—the matriarchal line. The family drama that plays out in the novel illustrates that familial immortality is purchased at significant cost and ultimately proves to be a sham and a delusion.

Ghosts, Corpses, and Property

In *The House of the Seven Gables*, the family is the traditional patriarchal unit that for generations has assigned all power to the father and implicitly denied power to its other members. The Pyncheon line has bred autocratic fathers who have persecuted their wives and, sometimes, their female children. In this family, it seems that the males who are like the ruling fathers—overbearing, materialistic, unscrupulous, competitive, and self-seeking—repress the males unlike themselves, thus ensuring that their kind will survive. As Hepzibah herself recognizes in explaining Clifford's condition: "they [the Pyncheons] persecuted his mother in him!" (2: 60).

Like gothic stories of ancestral possession, *The House of the Seven Gables* has its horrors and hauntings, but they are often the work of fleshly beings. The dominant Pyncheon males are, if nothing else, men with bodies who are seemingly capable of reproduction apart from women. Because mothers are rarely mentioned, the "original" Pyncheon seems to be cloning male duplicates generation after generation, thus achieving an earthly and "intermittent immortality" (2: 19). After their deaths, the Pyncheon males remain bodies; there is no sense they are transmuted into some higher or spiritual form. They are the undead dead, corrupting corpses that "haunt" their descendents. As the family evolves, the "original" Pyncheon (2: 185) becomes not a glorious benevolent beacon to his posterity but the burden of an "Evil Destiny" (2: 242) that weighs them down, "just as if a young giant were compelled to waste all his strength in carrying about the corpse of the old giant, his grandfather, who died a long while ago, and only needs to be decently buried" (2: 182–83). These descendents mourn the patriarchs not out of a sense of loss but out of fear. The sons are their "slaves," and the dead fathers return to them unbidden to perpetuate this deadly cycle (2: 183).

The traditional center of the family house is usually the fireside or the kitchen, but in *The House of the Seven Gables* it is the corpse of the dead father. The family house resembles a large tomb, and the patriarch's "own dead corpse" is the "broad foundation" on which it rests

(2: 263). This "black depth where a dead corpse lay unseen" is society's "fearful secret," which, if known, would inspire "horror" (2: 291).

James Farrell explains that in the nineteenth century "apprehension" of the loss of property "turned middle class minds to the maintenance of order in the meaning and management of death."[17] Managing the transfer of property promotes the illusion of controlling death. The Pyncheon males' conduct of life rests on a similar premise. For them, the stakes involved in property management are high because a property transfer to male heirs is an immortality preserver; it is a form of "familial immortality." But "familial immortality" is a grotesque cheat because perpetual corporeality brings continual decay without reinvigoration.

Inheriting a house is a source of "misfortune" which brings a fate similar to that of the men described in Thoreau's *Walden* who are "digging their graves as soon as they are born."[18] Property ownership means conspiring to keep the "dead corpse…unseen" (2: 291), thereby promoting the fiction of male immortality, a conspiracy which ensures that the family house becomes a "family tomb."[19]

Father Midas

"The Golden Touch," asked the stranger, "or your own little Marygold, warm, soft, and loving, as she was an hour ago?"

Hawthorne, "The Golden Touch"

The antimaterialistic sentiment that associates property and material goods with death is reiterated in the novel's Midas motif. About two months after the publication of *The House of the Seven Gables*, Hawthorne began work on *A Wonder Book for Girls and Boys*, a collection of myths retold for children. The second entry in the volume is "The Golden Touch," which retells the Midas story with the original addition to the story of a daughter for Midas whom he turns to gold. The Midas story presents in its easy conjunction of fathers, daughters, and gold a revealing parallel to the novel, particularly to its inner narrative, the story of Alice Pyncheon.

The chapter "Alice Pyncheon" reveals the length to which the Pyncheon fathers would go to increase their property and their claim to "familial immortality." To learn the secret of the lost document that would give him vast tracts of land, Gervayse Pyncheon allows Matthew Maule to violate his daughter Alice. After Maule mesmerizes Alice, he gains control over her will and degrades her. Her father knows that his desire for property has implicated his daughter in a fearful struggle against male dominance and possession but does nothing to stop it because he hopes by risking his daughter he will gain the document that will ensure the family fortune. By choosing property over paternal love, Gervayse Pyncheon allows his daughter to be abased and feel like a "worm" (2: 209). After her spiritual violation by Maule, Alice believes she can never marry because she is no longer a free agent who has control over her own actions.

The chapter "Alice Pyncheon," then, recovers the buried story of both *The House of the Seven Gables* and nineteenth-century middle-class domestic culture. The family that the fathers perpetuate is a patriarchal institution that is destructive to mothers and daughters. "Familial immortality" is a male fantasy driven by a wish for continuity of the male line of the family and the male family name. The will of the Pyncheons is made flesh in the Midas touch of dominance and appropriation culminating in acts of suppression of women. The Pyncheon fathers "martyred" their mothers and daughters to ensure their own permanence (2: 208). They might have done it unintentionally, unconsciously, or perhaps regretfully, but nonetheless the pattern is as unrelenting as the Pyncheon iron will. Sometimes this destructive pattern is buried beneath the aristocratic veneer of art, music, and civility, as it is with Gervayse Pyncheon, who has only a tastefully embroidered vest with gold threads to remind us of his link to the Pyncheon Midas touch, or as in the case of Colonel Pyncheon, the Pyncheon patriarch may wear his claim to the Midas touch as openly as if "you had seen him touching the twigs of the Pyncheon-elm, and, Midas-like, transmuting them to gold" (2: 57). In every generation, this repressive "touch" practiced on women is the unspeakable "secret," the decaying corpse buried within this house.

For women to thrive, they must escape the house, both literally and in the metaphorical sense of its meaning in Greek tragedy. Alice Pyncheon could not, despite her trips to Europe, and she was unhappy in it even before the conflict with Maule. She had devoted her life to flowers and music, "although the former were apt to droop, and the melodies were often sad," and found little that would offset the sterile life of New England (2: 192). Judge Pyncheon's wife could not, and it is a struggle over a trivial domestic act, serving a cup of coffee to her husband, that may have precipitated her death. But Hepzibah, a "Pyncheon of to-day," tries (2: 115). In fact, the novel begins with a curious birthing scene. Swimming in the currents of the republican economy, she escapes drowning when she opens the "bar" that had separated her home from the shop, and "Then—as if the only barrier betwixt herself and the world had been thrown down, and a flood of evil consequences would come tumbling through the gap," she is "transformed" from social outcast to shopkeeper (2: 40, 38). Just when it seems as if she were completely dead as every day of her seclusion piled up "another stone against the cavern-door of her hermitage," she is resurrected (2: 39).

Of Brothers and Sisters

> O But I would not have done the forbidden thing
> For my husband or for any son,
> For why? I could have had another husband
> And by him other sons, if one were lost;
> But, father and mother lost, where would I get
> Another brother?...
>
> Sophocles, *Antigone*

In *The House of the Seven Gables*, the patriarchal family is enervated, and the novel offers an alternative model. Hepzibah is at the center of a small matriarchal family unit. It is one devoted to preserving the values of the mother, even when expressed in the males of the family, and centered on brothers, not fathers or sons. It has no conventionally defined structure and can include female cousins displaced by patriarchal families and even like-minded strangers.

Throughout the novel, Hepzibah is capable of courageous acts of resistance against the patriarchal order. In some ways, she resembles Sophocles's Antigone, although her act of defiance against the Creon-like male authority figure, Judge Pyncheon, involves refusing to bury her metaphorically dead brother. It is almost as if the "dragon's teeth" Pearl sowed in *The Scarlet Letter* spring up as the source of the underlying drama in *The House of the Seven Gables*. According to the myth of the dragon's teeth, after a futile search for his kidnapped sister Europa, Cadmus is advised to found a city. On route to the site of the city, he defeats an attacking dragon and cuts out its teeth. Minerva tells him to sow the dragon's teeth, and they are harvested as opposing warriors who battle one another. The five warriors (the Spartoi or the sown) who survive this battle become the heads of the ruling families in the Greek Theban house, the house whose line included Oedipus and Antigone.[20]

The classical stories of Cadmus and of Antigone illustrate the conflict generated when there is a shift from the matriarchal to the patriarchal order. After Oedipus leaves power, his two sons fight over the throne and are killed. Antigone, their sister, believes she must bury her brother Polynices, even though this burial has been forbidden by the edict of Creon, the new ruler. She believes she must honor the blood ties to the mother and bury her brother, and her commitment to the matriarchal line is an important source of the conflict in the tragedy.

Hepzibah's suffering because of her love for her brother and her loyalty to his memory are variations on this theme of loyalty to the blood ties of the mother. Her presence in the family confirms the viability of the female line, even though suppressed and damaged. Luce Irigaray's comments on Hegel's view of history in "Each Sex Must Have Its Own Rights" help to illuminate this family dynamic. In his discussion of the relationship between man and spirit in culture, Hegel offers an analysis of the family and, according to Irigarary, concludes, "the daughter who remains faithful to the laws relating to her mother has to be cast out of the city, out of society." While Irigaray notes that the daughter cannot be "violently killed," she must not be allowed to flourish and instead must be "imprisoned, deprived of liberty, air, light, love, marriage, children." Sophocles's *Antigone*, then, from Irigaray's perspective, tells a primal story to explain a "tragic episode" in culture—the time when the "cultural obligations" to the "mother's blood" are denied and "the passage into patriarchy" is accomplished.[21]

Hepzibah's story is similar to Antigone's. Hepzibah also believes her obligations are to her brother, her mother's blood, and yet because she exists within a patriarchal society her duties to this blood seem, if not unlawful, at least out of the boundaries of normal. Hepzibah and Clifford have been shunted aside from any power in the Pyncheon family line. Judge Pyncheon has framed Clifford for the murder of his uncle and he has been imprisoned. Although a male Pyncheon, Clifford has the recessive personality traits that the dominant male Pyncheons associate with the feminine and want to suppress: he is gentle, delicate, fanciful, and a lover of the beautiful. During his thirty years of incarceration, Hepzibah has cherished his memory and resisted the enticements of the Judge to come over to the patriarchal side.

At the beginning of the novel, the matrilineal family seems on the verge of rejuvenation. Hepzibah has been born to the world of commerce, her brother has returned from prison and she enjoys his companionship, and Phoebe, the young female Pyncheon cousin, joins them at the house. Like Hepzibah when she is reborn in the current of the new economy, Clifford emerges freed from prison as if "risen from a living tomb" (2: 238). Both desire to escape from the house, and, after the death of Judge Pyncheon, they flee its confines. Clifford likens their flight to that of Christian and Hopeful from Despair. But these aging pilgrims never reach the Celestial City, or even the "city of refuge" of Clifford's hopes (2: 265). Instead their "strange expedition" finds them on a train ride to nowhere meditating on the relationship between death, property, and immortality (2: 254).

After the death of Judge Pyncheon should be the time for the matrilineal line to move into the ascendancy, but it is oddly diminished. Hepzibah and Clifford end their journey at a deserted village in such a "dismal state of ruin and decay" that it is another grim reminder of death (2: 266). Their journey has weakened them, and this is particularly apparent in Hepzibah. The narrator seems unwilling to account for these changes, and they make sense only when regarded from the perspective of the tension between the matrilineal and patrilineal lines. When Hepzibah realizes that Judge Pyncheon has died, we might expect her to feel considerable relief and perhaps even empowerment. Instead, she grows passive and is described as a child. After Clifford and she alight from the train and she faces the crumbling church and decaying cottage, she can think of doing nothing but praying: "'Oh God!'—ejaculated poor, gaunt Hepzibah—then paused a moment, to consider what her prayer should be—'Oh, God—our Father—are we not thy children? Have mercy on us!'" (2: 267).

The "should" in this statement is crucial. From the perspective of Bakan's thesis, it may indicate Hepzibah has come to recognize that the only way for her and Clifford to survive is as children acknowledging the bond to the father. At this moment, she defers to what Irigaray would characterize as patriarchal "cultural obligations."[22] Despite its earlier resurgence under her direction, the matriarchal order cannot be restored. Because Hepzibah and Clifford are actually old and are compared to a dying breed of chicken, their progress by rail or in life will inevitably bring them to a destination marked with signs of decay and death. Both for social and moral reasons Hepzibah and Clifford's relationship is at the end of the line.

The breakfast scene in Chapter Seven is suggestive of their fate. In this scene Hepzibah prepares for Clifford one of the only eggs laid by the dying line of hens. By anthropomorphizing the chickens and diminishing the Pyncheon brother and sister, Hawthorne makes the human animal seem little different from other animals. The mother fowl's belief that her egg from this diminished line of fowls would hatch "the one chicken of the world, and as necessary, in fact, to the world's continuance" seems as misguided as Hepzibah's belief that the breakfast egg should be used to sustain her pathetic and wasting brother (2: 151). Unless the sister and brother acknowledge their status as weak "children" (2: 267) who have no claim "as necessary...to the world's continuance" and little value except as progeny, no amount of eggs can preserve them from death (2: 151).

From this perspective, the narrator's taunting and ridiculing of Hepzibah is also more understandable. Of all of the characters in Hawthorne's fiction Hepzibah suffers the greatest disjunction between her words and actions and the narrator's interpretive commentary on them. A reading of the novel that concentrates simply on the words and deeds of Hepzibah makes her seem an extraordinarily resourceful, loving, purposeful, and generous woman. After years of reclusiveness, she bravely sets up a cent shop to support herself and her brother; she is loving and welcoming to Phoebe, and she stands up to Judge Pyncheon. But the narrator seems intent upon discrediting her and making her appear smaller than she is. At one point he characterizes her actions as "overpoweringly ridiculous" (2: 39).

Discrediting Hepzibah may be necessary if the novel is to successfully preserve its happy ending by affirming the preservation of the patriarchal order implied in the union of Holgrave and Phoebe. Having a viable option to the patriarchy would further complicate the meaning of this marriage. In fact, in the patriarch alone must reside the power to circumvent and control death by ensuring the property rights that make male economic independence possible and the control of death necessary. As Irigaray asserts and Hepzibah's situation illustrates, "The daughter is forbidden to respect the blood bonds with her mother," in part because these blood bonds would challenge the customs and laws surrounding male inheritance of real property that were the norm in nineteenth-century New England.[23] It is no accident that Hepzibah's "prayer" forms her penultimate words in the text and after this scene she virtually disappears (267). Once she accepts her role as child to the patriarch, she grows silent as she is passed over by the relegitimation of the patriarchal line.

With this turn of events, the novel apparently lays to rest the possibility of a new family model centered on women. This line has no viable "eggs" that would make reproduction possible. The future seems to reside with Holgrave, the young man whom Hepzibah invites into her house, but who ends up possessing it and assuming control of the line and the future.

Death and Daguerreotype

Holgrave is a perfect representative of those melancholy young men in New England whom Emerson described, young men who perceive themselves as failures and see the remainder of their lives as "rock and shallow."[24] He has been driven to the house by economic necessity, another manifestation of the Midas syndrome. He has had many incarnations in the economic system of mid-century New England. Although he is only twenty-two years old, he has already tried his hand as schoolmaster, newspaper editor, traveling salesman, dentist, lecturer, and bureaucrat on a packet ship. He is the proverbial "Jack of all trades" and, as the brief duration of each of these careers suggests, perhaps "master of none." He has been on his own since he was a boy, probably because of the death or financial exigency of his parents, and is "homeless" until he takes up residence in the house (2: 177). Without financial support to fall back on, Holgrave seems someone susceptible to drowning in the same rough economic waters that threaten to engulf Hepzibah. This fate may be especially worrisome to him since apparently it is the economic legacy of his family, for Holgrave is a Maule, the antagonists of the Pyncheons. Most Maules were "generally poverty-stricken" and came "finally to the alms house, as the natural home of their old age" (2: 25).

Holgrave arrives at the Pyncheon house in his final reincarnation as daguerreotypist and fortune hunter, close to the end of his economic options. He resides in the house to appropriate what is of value in it, although he originally hoped for a kind of metaphysical wealth, knowledge of human nature. Holgrave may be repulsed by the house and its oppressive, death-like atmosphere, but he sees in it the answer to his crisis of despondency and identity. He takes up residence in the house as a borderer, and he attempts to live on the margin between the Pyncheon and Maule lines. He inhabits a remote corner of the house, where it seems he intends to abide in the house of the enemy yet maintain his Mauleness.

He originally sees himself not as Midas but as Jack the Giant Killer. In one of his conversations with Phoebe, the Pyncheon country cousin who is also an economically displaced person, living in the house because there is no room for her in the household of her recently remarried mother, he confesses to his hatred of the burden of the past. He believes "It lies upon the Present like a giant's dead body! In fact, the case is just as if a young giant were compelled to waste all his strength in carrying about the corpse of the old giant, his grandfather" (2: 182). He associates the past with death, and he sees himself initially as the young giant determined to rid himself of this burden or, in another instance, as a Jack perched on the bean-stalk he has recently been hoeing in the Pyncheon garden, poised to do battle with the patriarchal giant.

Holgrave is a revolutionary in the way he conceives of burying the dead corpse of the "old giant." He questions traditions and conventional values, and professes to believe that money and property transmitted from generation to generation are the source of society's ills. As Thoreau does in *Walden*, he associates inherited property and its symbol, the family house, with death. Later in the novel, he finally has the opportunity to confront death in the form of the "old giant," Judge Pyncheon, who is sitting dead in the Pyncheon parlor. And yet, when he meets with death in the form of this patriarchal giant, the giant killer does not bury the corpse, as he planned, but instead takes its picture.

There is something both ominous and magical about this act of picture taking. It can be viewed as a profane act that violates the sacred biblical injunctions neither to make graven images of the father nor to view the patriarch's nakedness. This kind of sight would reveal the father's corporeality and thus expose his temporality. If the father is never reduced to an image, he remains unfathomable, limitless, and omnipotent. Holgrave's picture taking is, then, an act of appropriation that borders on blasphemy, for he has literally captured the image of the dead giant father. But, as is so often the case in Hawthorne's fiction, when individuals intend to do one thing they achieve quite the opposite. As Roland Barthes explains, "every photograph" shows "the return of the dead."[25] While Holgrave's motive in taking the picture seems to be to dominate Judge Pyncheon, he succeeds only in extending his power. Capturing the Pyncheon image assures the Judge's permanence. Although Holgrave tells Phoebe the daguerreotype is "a memorial valuable to myself" (2: 303), she recognizes it for what it is. "This is death!" she states forthrightly when Holgrave shows the daguerreotype to her (2: 302).

Holgrave has succeeded in bringing death out from the darkened chamber into the domestic circle of the "household fire" and continued its prominence in the history of the house (2: 302). What is more surprising, he uses death as the means of wooing Phoebe in a scene reminiscent of another famous wooing scene in Shakespeare's *Richard III*, which also takes place in the presence of a corpse. While Holgrave is certainly not as villainous as Richard III, who woos the Lady Anne after killing her husband Edward, son of Henry VI, the novel shares with the play a concern with family succession, revenge, and legitimacy. There is a sense in both the novel and the play that the male usurper's wooing is motivated, to a greater or lesser degree, by self-interest. Richard has cut himself off from the matriarchal order and judges Queen Elizabeth to be a "Relenting fool, and shallow, changing woman!" (*Richard III.* 4.4.431). Despite his promise to the Queen, "If I did take the kingdom from your sons, / To make amends, I'll give it to your daughter" (*Richard III.* 4.4.294–95), he has only contempt for women.[26] Holgrave is a more benevolent wooer, although, as in Shakespeare's play, the presence of the corpse in this scene pressures Phoebe by reminding her of both the transiency of life and the vulnerability of her situation. The wooer intends to yield no power to the Queen, but to use her to ensure his line.

When Holgrave shows Phoebe the Judge's daguerreotype, he assumes that this death image will prompt her to abandon her independence and agree to wed. Actually, his assumption proves correct; what he does not seem to understand is that they both are diminished by this strategy. They end up feeling lost, afraid, and powerless, "like two children" (2: 305). They cannot master death and the fathers and instead are mastered by them. This failure causes a shift in the dynamics of the couple's relationship, and they revert to the conventional patterns enforced by the patriarch. They are children again obedient to the will of the dead father. Inspired by Phoebe, Holgrave expects to create a "circle of a spell" that will protect him from death, and instead he finds himself subsumed in the identity of dead fathers and determined by his destiny as future father (2: 305).

On a psychological level, then, Holgrave, like Richard III, "kills" the father. Because he "kills" not to lay to rest the power of the Pyncheon patriarch but merely to gain it for himself, he can only perpetuate the cycle. Even though in *The House of the Seven Gables* there is no monarchy, only a family line, Holgrave's actions expose some of the same destructive contradictions found in the fate of kings as told in Greek and Shakespearean tragedies.

While Bakan identifies some basic problems in reconciling what he describes as "familial" and "individual" immortality, he does seem to think that it is possible to reconcile the two. If *The House of the Seven*

Gables followed this line of thinking, the novel would confirm that "individual immortality" and "familial immortality" are compatible. Holgrave's "killing" would have contributed to the maturation of the hero and also created his place within the family with its promise of immortality. But what happens in the novel ultimately seems closer to Luce Irigaray's thinking about the patriarchal family than Bakan's.

In "Each Sex Must Have Its Own Rights," Irigaray describes the family as a small unit of society that perpetuates itself by keeping its members immature and unfulfilled. The family is not a configuration in which "individual differences can be respected and cultivated." As a result, true maturity is impossible within the family. Instead, in the family the "man has transferred that relationship to his wife as mother substitute," and "male and female genealogies are collapsed into a single genealogy: that of the *husband*."[27]

What happens to Holgrave and Phoebe in the novel bears out this thesis. By its conclusion, their identity is defined primarily in terms of relationships; they are children as well as potential fathers and mothers. After the wooing scene, Phoebe, in particular, becomes weaker, more dependent, and more maternal—the perfect paradox, the nineteenth-century girl-mother. At the same time that Holgrave apparently relinquishes his control over Phoebe after telling her the story of Alice Pyncheon, he uses the daguerreotype of the corpse to gain a stronger, if more subtle, hold on her identity. Telling the Alice Pyncheon story may indicate he feels compelled to come to terms with the long neglected part of the Maules' history, the woman's narrative. Different as they are, both Pyncheons and Maules have oppressed women, perhaps the Maules even more relentlessly; women are a totally blank page in the Maules' family narrative. But when Holgrave, now revealed as Matthew Maule, unites with Phoebe, he also betrays a desire to recreate his lost family and his lost mother by "transferring" his future wife to mother and denying her genealogy.[28] He announces his true identity to her in a way that collapses her family genealogy into his: " 'My dearest Phoebe,' said Holgrave, 'how will it please you to assume the name of Maule?' " (2: 316).

Holgrave, then, is playing out his version of the old drama of traditional heterosexual coupling. When he and Phoebe are united, it does seem "a miracle," full of promise for a new beginning (2: 307). What the narrator says about their union is echoed by Luce Irigaray in "Belief Itself" when she explains that the union of all couples, at first, seems to be a miracle: "A couple that will give rise to a new conception of the flesh, to those miracles owed to touch, with or without words, that we know as transfiguration, resurrection, ascension, or assumption? A couple of angels or in which all angels would concentrate their function as mediators—and beyond." The traditional heterosexual relationship has an underlying problem: "But this couple does not appear as such, or at least not according to canonical revelation. She remains only mother and he son, the two obedient to the words of the Father."[29]

In the love scene between Holgrave and Phoebe that takes place in the presence of a corpse, Hawthorne captures the same kind of initial bliss that Irigaray describes. "They transfigured the earth," the narrator intones (2: 307). In fact, to accept that *The House of the Seven Gables* is, indeed, a comedy means believing in the power of love to accomplish this transfiguration or transformation. And, at first, Holgrave and Phoebe's relationship does seem to be a "miracle," but the canonical fiction that the narrator's comments perpetuate is given the lie by the relational configuration that soon is made apparent: she—mother, he—son. The path to "familial immortality" demands assuming the role of child. Holgrave and Phoebe remain subordinate to the father, driven to that position by the grim specter of death: "they were like two children who go hand in hand, pressing closely to one another's side, through a shadow-haunted passage. The image of awful Death, which filled the house, held them united by his stiffened grasp" (2: 305).

Irigaray Meets Freud at *The House* of the Seven Gables

In *The House of the Seven Gables*, Holgrave plays a game of fort-dà that has high personal, emotional, and cultural stakes. In "Beyond the Pleasure Principle" Freud tells a fascinating "story" of a child's game in an effort "to leave the dark and dismal subject of the traumatic neurosis," which in many cases he links to a child's memory of the death of a parent. Freud describes a boy who enjoyed playing a game of throwing out to where he could not see it a wooden reel with a string tied around it, uttering a sound that represented the German word "fort" (gone) and then returning it to himself again, happily saying "dà" (there). The child would play the game of "disappearance and return" repeatedly and with considerable satisfaction. Freud interprets the game as signifying the child's effort to master the painful experience of separation from his mother. He also uses the child's obvious delight in the game as the occasion to ask: "How then does his repetition of this distressing experience as a game fit in with the pleasure principle?"[30]

In "Belief Itself," Irigaray reinterprets Freud's narrative and presents an alternative reading of the game. In her version, the boy "plays symbolically with the mother" because he thinks that "coming into the world, or going out of the world can be made into a game in this way." Acting on the basis of this false assumption, the boy is a "slave to belief" because his fiction of control "authorizes the confusion or substitution of reality and unreality." From Irigaray's perspective, the boy has no real power over the mother's presence or absence, just as he has no or very little control over the "life-death watch."[31]

The House of the Seven Gables rests on Freudian assumptions about the construction of the male subject, which it deeply complicates with something similar to Irigaray's counterarguments about the nature of the male cultural subject. Taken together, Freud's and Irigaray's analyses of the child's game of fort-dà and the related discussion of repetition compulsion and death provide an illuminating context in which to read the relationship between Holgrave and Phoebe, the death of Judge Pyncheon, and the novel's focus, despite its comedic intent, on death.[32]

Particularly in the concluding section of the novel, Hawthorne uses the mother-son paradigm to describe the relationship between Holgrave and Phoebe. Once Holgrave enters fully into the life of the text in Chapter Twelve, "The Daguerreotypist," Phoebe, like the mother in the boy's game, obeys the logic of his compelling psychological needs, appearing and disappearing as if pulled by a string. In a number of important ways Holgrave begins to take over the novel after he tells the story of Alice Pyncheon, and he does not relinquish narrative control until the final paragraphs. After describing the hypnotic effect the story of Alice Pyncheon has on Phoebe, the narrator explains that Holgrave has chosen not to take advantage of her vulnerability and dominate her, as his ancestor had dominated Alice. At the same time, the narrator describes the setting sun, which is usually associated with Phoebe, giving way to the moon "like an ambitious demagogue, who hides his aspiring purpose by assuming the prevalent hue of popular sentiment" (2: 213). This is also a quite apt description of Holgrave's popular Transcendental radicalism that cloaks his economic ambition. The lunar landscape is Holgrave's; in fact, just before Holgrave tells Phoebe the story of Alice she accuses him of being infected with the "lunacy" of the Pyncheons (2: 186).

While Holgrave apparently foregoes overt control over Phoebe, he, at a deeper level, gains mastery over her, the fate of the other characters, and even the plot line of the final third of the novel. After Chapter

Fourteen, often when he expresses a desire, it is later gratified, when he gives an opinion, it proves to be true, and when he guesses an outcome, it happens. He tells Phoebe to leave before they are not friends, and she does. He says he awaits the tragic fifth act of the drama, and it ensues. He calls Clifford and Hepzibah ghosts, and the narrator then describes them in this way. He wishes, "could we but bring him (Clifford) back," and he comes (2: 304). From his vantage point, he controls the outcome of his own story. He allows Phoebe, the woman-embryonic mother to go, or, more accurately, when the difference and conflict between them become apparent, he suggests that she go, and she readily complies. He plays the boy's game of "disappearance and return" in his relationship with Phoebe.[33] He attempts to control and direct her; in fact, before she leaves, he fills her with ideas about her identity that do not conform to her own image of herself but that she ends up accepting.

These ideas reflect Holgrave's "belief" about Phoebe, not, if we were to regard them from Irigaray's perspective, the reality of Phoebe or of her situation.[34] Holgrave regards the feminine other, as the boy does in Freud's game, from a male-centered perspective. He grants her no subject status. Holgrave's masculine desire has seized upon Phoebe as the idealized fulfillment of what he lacks. He refashions working-class Phoebe as his middle-class, gentrified "angel in the house" whom he can control and direct. He wants her life to be circumscribed by the house and tells her she cannot leave because she is indispensable to Clifford and Hepzibah. Overlooking the fact that Hepzibah has survived independently for thirty years, he tries to convince Phoebe that Hepzibah and Clifford are children who "will perish" without her. Assuming the voice of the Victorian father, he burdens her with the responsibility of being the mother of two hapless, helpless "children" who will die without her (2: 216). But the novel also invites a reconsideration of the terms of masculine subjectivity. Phoebe's response to Holgrave implies the construction of the female as a subject in her own right. At times, she seems dissatisfied and maybe a little miffed at Holgrave's interpretation of her role. She anticipates Irigaray's ideas that all the world's a stage and men believe themselves to be the directors of it, when she accuses Holgrave of being the theater manager in this drama of Hepzibah and Clifford and regarding their lives as performed for his amusement. She bluntly asserts, "I am no angel" (2: 221).

The novel hovers uneasily between a Freudian and an Irigarayan view of the construction of the male-female relationship.[35] In "Belief Itself," Irigaray comments on Freud's ideas about the fort-dà game and male mastery with two of the same metaphors Hawthorne uses in this novel—angel and theater. In Freud's version of the game, the boys/ men control and women are drawn along; in Irigaray's revision, the boys/men only *believe* they control. In Hawthorne's version, the boys/ men *believe* they control, and women are still drawn along. In her essay, Irigaray warns that the fort-dà game must be thwarted: "So before the son has perfected his stage set, one can try and steal his veil away from him, take the curtain of his theater, the means or mediator of his *fort-dà*, and loan it or give it back to the *angels*."[36] Phoebe could "take the curtain" of Holgrave's theater because she is sufficiently insightful to distinguish between the appearance and the reality of his power. In this regard, she presents a unique potential threat to the previously male-dominated Maule line. But Holgrave has already "perfected his stage set," and Phoebe is merely his prop, something similar to the boy's wooden reel thrown away and recovered at will; just as she departed when he desired, she returns as if at his bidding, arriving at the perfect moment for him to control her and affect his purposes—marriage into this house and the procurement of a for- tune. In Chapter Twenty, she steps across the threshold of the house, and the door, without any effort on her part, closes rather ominously behind her. Led into the obscurity of the inner rooms, not able to adjust to the transition from the sunshine world, her native element, to the world of shadows, she succumbs to the touch of Holgrave and, as if pulled by the boy's string in Freud's game, she "felt herself drawn along" (2: 300).

The Family Plot

In "Beyond the Pleasure Principle," Freud associates the fort-dà game ultimately with the death wish. He first explains that repeating the game, which is a crucial aspect of it, gives pleasure to the child, and then indirectly links this repetition pattern to the death wish. The game creates tensions in the child that he experiences as pleasure or pain depending on his perceived ability to control the love-object- mother and gain "mastery." The child's behavior illustrates a desire for a reachievement of homeostasis, which in later sections of Freud's essay is linked to the death wish. As Freud explains, "If we are to take it as a truth that knows no exception that everything living dies for *internal* reasons—becomes inorganic once again—then we shall be compelled to say that '*the aim of all life is death.*'" The "organism" desires always to "restore an earlier state of things," a desire that Freud by implication links to the "dà" state of the child's game, to conserve things as they were when the child and the mother were one.[37]

Irigaray would probably also grant the pleasure that this game gives to the male, but her commentary focuses on another aspect of the game which is relevant to our discussion—its ability to delude the player into believing that he exerts control over the woman-mother. Irigaray admits that from the male Freudian perspective, which seems to be very close to the perspective underlying Holgrave's assumptions in the concluding section of the novel, the woman-mother "must be thrown over there, put at a distance, beyond the horizon, so that she can come back to him, back inside him, so that he can take her back, over and over again." And this control over the woman-mother does give the male a sense of mastery. But Irigaray differs from Freud in her emphatic belief that "the disappearance-reappearance, inside-outside, outside-inside" can "no more be mastered than the life-death watch."[38]

Holgrave's desire to master Phoebe and become the master of the house masks a deeper desire to master death by establishing a new family line, but from Irigaray's perspective, and as Judge Pyncheon's death illustrates, no one is death's master and "keeping house" is itself a deadly occupation. Judge Pyncheon has taken the "familiar" route to death; he has led a life full of worldly success that has brought him money and status in the community. He has ensured too that when the dead Pyncheons come out of their graves at night they can see the portrait of the original ancestor still hanging on the wall of the house. The cynically comic tone of the narrator in Chapter Eighteen when he describes the dead family's foray into the world of the living, still together but misguidedly in pursuit of the secret of the ancestral portrait, reemphasizes the folly and futility of their life's purpose.

A custom among middle-class New England families of this period was to be buried together in "family plots."[39] This kind of burial was thought to be a source of consolation for the living because it perpetuated the idea of family unity still intact, even in death. But the procession of grim Pyncheons turns the cultural ideal of family togetherness on its head. Judge Pyncheon has won "familial immortality" and the illusion of the reconstitution and perpetuation of the self through the continuance of the family and the family mansion. And yet, as the narrator observes, the whole idea of dead ancestors concerned about a portrait is "ridiculous," for would even the Pyncheons consider it "worth while to come out of their graves for that?" (2: 279).

Pyncheon has spent his life gaining property and power over others in the hope of incorporating it into himself to render himself invulnerable.

His rage to possess originates in his fear of death. He deludes himself, as Irigaray argues any man does who thinks himself master, into believing he can raise his kinsman from the tomb only for the purpose of torturing a secret from him. He becomes a slave to a belief in his own power, when, in reality, he has none. The final irony in Judge Pyncheon's story reveals the fiction of male mastery, for after sacrificing everything to familial immortality, he dies a "childless man" (2: 312).

So at the same time that Holgrave takes over the discourse of the future, there is a sense in the novel that his motives and methods may not be all that different from those of the Pyncheons of the past. In his earlier life, he tried on different identities, as if he were striving in these reincarnations to bolster his sense of power and continuity. He now decides to give up all of this for the "familial immortality" linked to the role of husband, homeowner, and future father-patriarch. From Irigaray's perspective, he has chosen the inevitable: "All that remains is to pursue this strange continuum, series," the eternal return of himself with himself at the center.[40] There is no escape for this couple from the "masculinist dream of autoproduction."[41]

What is remarkable, though, is that Holgrave affirms Irigaray's idea when he admits that he is bartering his individuality and capability for what may be an illusion. Holgrave knows that houses only give the "*impression* of permanence" (2: 314–15; emphasis mine). But if Holgrave doubts the permanence of family, after the doubt is uttered it is quickly buried, because the fiction of permanence is necessary to protect the male ego from recognition of the surety of annihilation. For the boy, the mother's departure is a serious threat to the integrity of the self. As Freud reminds us, if the boy can't play the game and if the mother really leaves him, he finds a "method of making *himself* disappear."[42] Like Emerson's men who will not mention the names of the dead, Holgrave avoids at all costs the final knowledge of the certainty of personal annihilation.

Conversing with the Dead

In Virgil's *Aeneid*, Aeneas descends into the underworld to meet the shade of his beloved father, Anchises. From this meeting Aeneas hopes to gain the strength to continue his quest and fulfill his heroic destiny. In the concluding section of *The House of the Seven Gables*, Hawthorne alludes to the *Aeneid* and parodies this meeting. In Chapter Eighteen when the corpse of Judge Pyncheon is inside the house, the house is compared to the underworld and the elm-tree branch that overhangs it is "like the golden branch, that gained Aeneas and the Sibyl admittance into Hades" (2: 285). With this allusion, Hawthorne invokes the tradition of "descent poetry" in which the hero undertakes a journey to the underworld to talk with the dead to gain some saving understanding for the living.[43] "Descent poetry" usually has a markedly political quality because the conversation with the dead has significant bearing on the organization of the polis.[44]

Aenea's meeting with his dead father, Anchises, is one of the most affecting scenes in the epic. A deep sense of loss and alienation pervades Aeneas's journey to the underworld as he encounters the suffering shades. Aeneas's meeting with the father helps to dispel his sorrow at this confrontation with death in two ways, for Anchises offers his son the means of both a natural and a preternatural answer to death. His Pythagorean explanation of the transmigration of souls forms part of a spiritual cosmology that includes death as part of a cyclical pattern of regeneration. His further promise that Aeneas's destiny is to be the patriarch who will found a new city also assures him of perpetuity in dynastic succession. The loving patriarch gives to the son the gift of immortality if he will accept this duty and fulfill his high and difficult mission.

Holgrave's meeting with the dead father Pyncheon is closeted, outside of the boundaries of the text, and, as I discussed, involves capturing his image. And yet, while the meeting itself is extra textual, a sense of it is evoked in Chapter Eighteen when the narrator, as Holgrave's stand-in, berates the corpse of Pyncheon.

This encounter between the narrator and the corpse forms the heart of one of the most extraordinary scenes in Hawthorne's fiction and involves an intersection between the living and the dead that breaks many of the conventions regarding the treatment of the dead in nineteenth-century culture. Middle-class society of this period fostered respect for the dead and the dead body.[45] It was during the eighteenth and the nineteenth centuries that the practice of the eulogy was firmly established, and eulogies by their very nature were laudatory. Death bought a certain immunity from criticism, and it was considered bad form then, as it still is today, to speak ill of the dead, a convention that some believe continues because it offers the living the assurance that they too will not be criticized after death. In Chapter Eighteen, though, the narrator violates decorum by taunting and ridiculing the dead Judge Pyncheon. He heaps scorn upon him, as he sits silent in his ancestral chair in the Pyncheon parlor.

Judge Pyncheon says nothing in reply; he cannot justify his own existence and offers no "apologia pro vita sua." In a dramatic reversal of the meeting between Aeneas and his father in the underworld, the dead and the living are totally distant; they cannot communicate. The dead father has no gifts of insight for his living "sons," but only one terrible lingering image of mortality and decay, the fly creeping across the wide open eye of the Judge, and the narrator's ready assent to "give thee up!" (2: 283).

In the "descent" tradition, then, the postmortem encounter with Judge Pyncheon is a dramatic departure from the expected. The meeting between Aeneas and his father proves to him the wisdom of obeying the gods: the rewards in terms of personal honor and the immortality of future glory that attend it. The meeting with Judge Pyncheon seems intended for a different effect; it focuses squarely on the natural facts of death—the decay, passivity, and isolation associated with death. It desacrilizes death and the father and leaves Holgrave bereft. Holgrave has slain the giant of the dead father but cannot be disburdened of his corpse whose image he has perpetuated.

Holgrave fails to imagine a way in his culture not to become the dead father. As a radical thinker, he can envision only tearing down, which would leave a frightening void, not building anew. A traveler in the realms of the dead, he cannot endorse the values of the dead father, nor come to another perspective on the nature of a good life. He can achieve no saving insight into the relationship between past and present. In short, he cannot speak with the dead.

Holgrave's dilemma and his inability ultimately to understand the relationship between the past and present, the living and the dead, are reflected in the novel's competing visions of the patterns of history and its conflicting notions of progress. Critical readings of this aspect of the novel cover a range of views. Those who believe that the novel makes a case for progress tend to interpret the union between Holgrave and Phoebe as a rupture in the pattern of the family history that brings about an abrupt change of direction, one of those unaccountable evolutionary leaps that accomplishes a significant variation in the species that resembles improvement. Others read the novel as making the case for a devolutionary view of history. The fate of the Pyncheon hens illustrates well this pattern. They continue to survive, although they illustrate a commonly held belief that to survive without improvement means to degenerate.

On the other hand, because the male Pyncheon family type with its "Evil Destiny" reappears in each generation, others read the novel as presenting a compelling argument for the cyclical view of history (2: 242). Prior to Chapter Eighteen, the cyclical pattern does seem to dominate the novel. Each day seems much like the last, filled with petty concerns; the lives of the two families measured out in copper coins and gingerbread men. The narrator even taunts the corpse of Judge Pyncheon with thoughts of "Tomorrow! Tomorrow! Tomorrow!" and this line's echo of Shakespeare's *Macbeth* reinforces the impression that this string of days holds little promise that the "petty pace" can or will be altered (2: 276). Instead they will move relentlessly to "dusty death" (*Macbeth* 5.5.19–27).[46] There is no progress, only repetition, which, according to Freud, is another way humans trick themselves into believing that they are avoiding or mastering death.

What may be more significant than Hawthorne's tendency to draw from competing paradigms for his view of history is his avoidance of deferring completely to the increasingly popular theory of progress. At mid-century, even before evolutionary theory added the logic of biological determinacy to the argument, there were pressures from both the religious and secular fronts to believe that the present was an improvement over the past; in fact, to believe the contrary or to accept stasis was a form of admission of defeat and an acceptance of failure.

The liberal Christian model with its emphasis on spirituality and improvement, though, is not apparent in this novel. If there is progress in *The House of the Seven Gables*, it is achieved by natural means, and it seems vulnerable to disruption. Phoebe and Holgrave will prosper, if they prosper, not because they are Christians, but because they are a healthier form of the original type. Phoebe, in particular, is offered as an example of some mutated variation in the genetic line that produced a more resilient and sturdier Pyncheon stock. God has little to do with Phoebe's improvement, and this is in keeping with the novel's unwillingness to involve God or the spiritual in the natural world. In *The House of the Seven Gables* the spiritual world seems to be at a distance from the natural world, and there is little opportunity to bridge the gap. The corpse of Judge Pyncheon has no possibility to "rise," and, while other characters in the novel are on sounder moral ground, "rising up" has not been made an option for them either (2: 276).

The standard of evaluating a life that the novel offers is revealing in this regard. In the nineteenth century, lives of Christians tended to be evaluated *sub specie aeternitate,* from the perspective of eternity. But the novel sets forward a slightly but significantly different measure. The narrator explains: "Death is so genuine a fact that it excludes falsehood, or betrays its emptiness; it is a touch-stone that proves the gold" (2: 310). *Sub specie mortis* becomes the new gold standard. It demands that worth be found in secular values and standards and in this world, not the next. Notice that the narrator taunts the dead corpse of Judge Pyncheon with many things but never with the specter of hell. This omission is in keeping with the climate of Hawthorne's culture where, at least among the Unitarians and intellectuals, damnation is being separated from death. Usually accompanying the loss of hell is also the loss of heaven, and, again, the novel seems to reflect this trend. If Phoebe and Holgrave are a "better" couple, the reward that they will receive must be in this life because the novel has given us no reason to believe there is a next.

"The Final Position"

That is, there is no significant mention of heaven until the final sentence when the narrator reintroduces the memory of "that sweet Alice Pyncheon" who "had given one farewell touch of a spirit's joy upon her harpsichord, as she floated heavenward from the HOUSE OF THE SEVEN GABLES!" (2: 319). Up until this point, reward and punishment have been meted out according to strictly secular standards. But for Alice Pyncheon there is an appeal to a different system, an appeal important to the success of the novel's "happy" ending.

In the novel, the spiritual world as it is known in the Christian tradition seems distant, or even nonexistent. When it is mentioned, it is less a spiritual world than a world of spirits, something akin to a classical land of shades, the home of tormented souls. Rather than achieving eternal bliss or damnation, souls seem to be doomed to haunt, ghost-like, the places with which they have been miserably connected in life.

Consequently, this mention of Alice Pyncheon and heaven is a significant intrusion. If death forms the perspective from which to measure value, Alice Pyncheon has had one of the worst and most unfair lives. She has been punished terribly for a single prideful glance. Dishonored, scorned, and humiliated, she dies repentant, and yet she still must suffer the fate of haunting the house for generations. As an unmarried virgin, she has no family line to perpetuate her; she seems strangely isolated from this family and from this house, yet doomed to be connected to it. In some ways, she represents in an exaggerated form the fate of all the Pyncheon women. They have not perpetrated the crime but they still must suffer. And, as the novel draws to its "happy" conclusion,

Hawthorne does remember the ladies but fails to imagine a way for them to achieve justice in this world. For Alice Pyncheon to receive justice, he must invent a heaven.

The reference to Alice Pyncheon at the novel's conclusion creates a definite blemish on this veneer of earthly happiness. When viewed from the perspective of the Pyncheon and Maule history, the appearance of the ghost of Alice Pyncheon may even create a crisis of social legitimacy. As John E. Seery explains, a social contract fair to all could be created in dialogue with the dead. A journey to the underworld of the kind imagined in "descent poetry" or other literature provides the opportunity to understand the terms of justice for the living, particularly for those in society who have less power—the poor, women, people not of the dominant race or culture.[47] "Intergenerational justice" involves bringing the past to the bargaining table when the claims of conflicting groups or individuals need to be settled, and it is what is done in a most striking fashion with the mention of Alice Pyncheon in these final sentences. It provides the perspective of the "Final Position" and could inspire the reader to raise ethical questions: "What do you say to your other should you meet up with that person in the nether region?"[48] What, in short, do you owe the wronged dead?

The answer that the novel and, to some extent, nineteenth-century culture have provided for the dilemma of death has been the fiction of "familial immortality," one very much in keeping with a Judeo-Christian tradition. But this answer brings its own problems. As it is presented in the novel, the family is not an institution that withstands the *sub specie mortis* test. It creates neither worthy nor happy men and women. It provides no true consolation for dying but seems to work in the service of death. Even if Holgrave and Phoebe are a somewhat improved version of the Maule and Pyncheon lines, their union does not offer any new possibilities outside this paradigm, and there seems little reason to assume that their union will produce a future that is different from the past. The matriarchal family unit is part of an older order; although Hepzibah is noble and heroic, she is not allotted the privilege of rejuvenating the family line. Important questions remain: What will happen to women in this new family line? Will women continue to be expunged from the text? The concept of "intergenerational justice" would demand that the case be made for justice for Alice Pyncheon and a solution be offered for those of her kind.

Framed as the conclusion is with emphasis on Alice's memory, it seems to recognize the validity of her claim and the claims of the matriarchal order; at the same time, it sees no worldly or earthly way to address them. Consequently, the mention of heaven is a necessity that acknowledges the wrong done to women, the strength of their claims, the rightness of reparation, and the equally strong possibility that, granted the current social structure, there will be no justice for the Alice Pyncheons of this world. As in the conclusion of *The Scarlet Letter*, *The House of the Seven Gables* appeals to a supernatural reality to address the wrongs of the past, particularly those done to women, a "heaven" which has no location in the novel's limited geography of gabled house, country house, and poor house.

In a final gesture, then, the novel turns aside from death as a natural phenomenon, the "touchstone" that proves the gold, and toward *sub specie aeternitatis*. And the reader is asked to accept that a shade who was doomed to haunt a house can strike a chord on her harpsichord, become an angel, and float heavenward. There will be no justice for Alice Pyncheon or the women in the house in this life, and no surety of an eternal reward for them in heaven. Consequently, the final paragraph seems to refine the understanding of progress that the novel sets forth. If the angel in this house is the ghost of a wronged woman whose destiny is to haunt this house forever, and the most heroic person in the novel is a woman who must be made less powerful and significant to accomplish the novel's "happy" ending, then has there been progress? In what way is progress related to justice?

For many readers when Aeneas makes his journey to the underworld, his meeting with Dido rivals that with his father. In this meeting, Aeneas tries to explain to "forlorn" Dido why he spurned and brought only death to her, and his reasons make some sense granted the claims of the world.[49] But from the underworldly perspective Dido cannot forgive him for his abandonment of her.[50] Aeneas is somewhat saddened by his meeting with her but readily leaves Dido and death behind in the underworld and continues on his way to be reunited with his father and to make plans to found the city of Rome.

This episode explains from the perspective of the male tradition of classical literature the logic behind the abandonment and mistreatment of women. There is a surety to following the traditional path of fulfilling the father's directive. The wages of feeling and commitment to women are much less certain and involve significant risk. *The House of the Seven Gables* carries forward the story of these competing claims. While the matriarchal order holds promise, it has no future. The price of matriarchy is too high from the male perspective. Women must be abandoned because, as in the *Aeneid*, it is still the male family line that must be protected and the male hero who must fulfill his immortal destiny.

Even if the perpetuation breeds injustice, even if it is a self-defeating enterprise, even if the very fact that it can be perpetuated is called into question, it still must be served because without this fiction the male would have to come face to face with the prospect of annihilation in death. So, on some level, men go forward into the future and women are left in the underworld—or, in Hawthorne's versions, to the house and its haunting, to heaven, or to silence. Men greet the fathers and make plans to fulfill their patriarchal destiny, even when it is recognized as an "Evil Destiny" (2: 242). The destiny of women is different from that of men, even *sub specie mortis*. Death and the afterlife also are gendered.

From Melancholy to Mourning: Death and Politics in The Blithedale Romance

The Scarlet Letter's map of Boston with all locations radiating from the cemetery can be read as an emblem of the tragic implications of the state's control of answers to death.[1] At Blithedale, there is no cemetery, as if to signal that the utopian thinkers of this community have decided to ignore that mortality and the politics of consolation are in the service of patriarchal authority. Just as by joining the commune at Blithedale they have tried to imagine new systems of living, they are also testing new ideas about dying, some of them reflecting emerging ante-bellum attitudes toward death.

At Blithedale, death is dismissed as a "natural" event holding few "terrors" (3: 130). Coverdale professes to believe that "By our sweet, calm way of dying, and the airy elegance out of which we will shape our funeral rites, and the cheerful allegories which we will model into tombstones, the final scene shall lose its terrors; so that, hereafter, it may be happiness to live, and bliss to die" (3: 130). He wants to remake death so it has little to do with decay or pain and everything to do with good cheer, happiness, and "bliss." Coverdale's words echo the sentiments of liberal Christians of New England, some of whom were proponents of the rural cemetery movement who tried to take hellfire, fear, and ugliness out of death.[2] They hoped that by moving the dead body from the center of the urban community to a "rural"—actually suburban— location, they could manage it or, at least, contain it on the margin.[3] In "An Address Delivered On the Dedication of the Cemetery at Mount

Auburn, September 24th, 1831," Chief Justice Joseph Story emphasized that a major reason for founding the rural cemetery was to keep the dead "out of our sight" and thereby to "tranquillize human fears" and "cast a cheerful light over the darkness of the grave."[4] Like these rural cemetery proponents, Coverdale searches for a place of unspoiled natural beauty, a "garden ground" to tranquillize his fear of death (3: 130).[5]

Coverdale's death-defying gestures, though, do little to assuage the anxieties about mortality that seep into his consciousness, and into the narrative, and climax in the spectacle of the "perfect horror" of the dead body of Zenobia (3: 235).[6] The story Coverdale tells, while it speaks of new systems and new orders, is not death denying but continues to inspire the male's anxiety about death because it provides an illustration of the psychological conditions and gender politics that inform the nineteenth-century culture's construction of death's meaning. This "new age" man, who is not particularly religious or particularly moral, works to dispel the angst and depression attached to death, seeking comfort from the collective consolations—utopian schemes, patriarchal aspirations, and romantic love. He tells a story about the founding of a community that should be a myth of origin, a tale of new beginnings. Instead, the story itself becomes a source of heightened anxiety about death and closure.

Admittedly, there are moments in the novel when Coverdale's optimistic sentiments about death seem something more than bravado. At times, the atmosphere of Blithedale resembles that of a forest of Arden where it would be totally inappropriate for death to intrude. The novel associates treachery, delusion, poverty, falsehood, and danger with the city, and by contrast the rural setting of the community seems to portend something better. The two-couple cast of characters prepares us for romance and comic mismatches. At one point, Westervelt even refers to Coverdale as "melancholy Jacques," reminding us of Shakespeare's *As You Like It* (3: 91). Unlike this comedy, however, which begins darkly with autocratic patriarchs issuing death threats but ends in love and romantic union, *The Blithedale Romance* begins promisingly with a beautiful queen extending welcoming invitations but ends at a grave.

Coverdale cannot banish death from this forest of Arden. For Hawthorne's readers particularly attuned to the rural cemetery debate, the references at the beginning of the novel about the need to consider the location of grave sites might have been met with some bemused nods, particularly since Coverdale's journey outside of the city, presumably Boston, to some wooded suburban area within walking distance could have been as likely to bring him in the direction of the outskirts of Cambridge and the site of Mount Auburn Cemetery as to Roxbury, the location of

Brook Farm. Although the imaginative geography of the novel resembles Shakespeare's *As You Like It*, from the start Blithedale's enchanted woods could have seemed divested of their magic to transform death to life. The map of the novel, as Coverdale traces it, promises to return us to a grave, the grave of a woman, as the locus of the new community. The story he tells offers disturbing proof of Luce Irigaray's thesis that "When Freud, notably in *Totem and Taboo*, describes and theorizes about the murder of the father as the founding act for the primal horde, he is forgetting an even more ancient murder, that of the woman-mother, which was necessary to the foundation of a specific order in the city."[7]

Coverdale constructs a myth in the simplest sense of the word: a story that explains why things are the way they are. His narrative must account for failure—both his own and that of the community, their mistakes, misguided passions, and misery. The Blithedale community had hoped to escape the "rusty iron frame-work" of conventional society and to leave behind the patriarchal order (3: 19). Blithedale signified the possibility of a social order conceived on the principles of justice and equality for all. But they end up rewriting the old script of accusation and betrayal of women. Coverdale's narrative recreates the "original matricide" and ultimately locates the origin of the social order in the dead body of a woman.[8] A story that seems to have all of the ingredients of a myth of origin ends up resembling a "terminus myth" which explains the failure of a society to create a social contract written from the perspective of the "Final Position" that promotes justice and happiness for men and women.[9]

The Accused Queen

The Blithedale Romance is nothing less than "the world according to Coverdale." This upper-middle-class New England male tells a story of origin that resonates with the basic narrative elements of the Constance legend or the accused queen narrative of folk and medieval literature.[10] His story shares their plot line: an innocent woman is unjustly accused of a serious wrong and is punished for the crime. This particular story line would have had strong cultural appeal. In the New England region, some of the most powerful oral literature had a similar narrative. The Salem Witch trial accounts and the Anne Hutchinson story have elements of this narrative pattern; Hawthorne's "Grandfather's Chair," which draws from oral tradition and folk narrative sources, includes the account of Anne Hutchinson, who was accused, found guilty, and banished from Massachusetts Bay Colony. In *A Wonder Book for Girls and Boys*, he also included in his version of the myth of Perseus elements of the accused queen motif. Hawthorne, who had a keen eye for a potentially popular subject, had already used this plot line in *The Scarlet Letter* and *The House of the Seven Gables*.

At the core of the plot is the accusation and punishment of the queen, or the extraordinary woman in the community who plays the role of queen. The major variations in this plot center on two important issues: the nature of the accusation and the identity of the accuser.[11] According to Margaret Schlauch's study of the motif in medieval literature, most of the accusations involve serious violations of filial, marital, or maternal relations, and they usually encompass a wide assortment of charges, ranging from infanticide, more common in the folk versions, to infidelity, the usual crime in the medieval romance versions.[12] The identity of the accuser also varies with the form. In the folk versions, the heroine's troubles often begin when she is unjustly persecuted because her father wants to marry her and she refuses.[13] But the medieval romances frequently suppress this plot element and instead substitute as accuser such figures as a mother-in-law (which, according to some analysts, may betray the uneasiness that exists in a culture as it moves toward a more dominantly patriarchal structure) or, in later versions, a rejected lover or ambitious supplanter.[14]

When he used this motif in the earlier novels, Hawthorne followed the pattern of the medieval romance narrative and suppressed the link between the father figure and the queen's accuser and controlled any hint of the incest theme from surfacing. In *The Blithedale Romance*, however, a biological father plays a primary role as the queen's accuser. On the surface, Old Moodie, later revealed to be Zenobia's father, seems harmless enough. In Chapter One, he presents himself as someone in need of help. But a closer look behind his pathetic exterior exposes another Moodie—a manipulative patriarch in quest of authority and power—and reveals he is the source of the accusation that destroys Blithedale's queen, Zenobia.

In Hawthorne's other novels, the early chapters focus on one of the four central characters; the first chapter of *The Blithedale Romance* is entitled "Old Moodie" and introduces the readers immediately to this seemingly peripheral fifth character. Old Moodie is an enigmatic and shadow-like figure. Hawthorne captures his essence with the patch covering his eye, a sparse yet vivid detail that visually fixes in the reader's mind his false and deceptive nature.[15] This seemingly powerless man was once a "man of wealth, and magnificent tastes" whose "home might almost be styled a palace; his habits, . . . princely" (3: 182). At the time of the narrative, he is a deposed monarch, someone who in his former life was named Fauntleroy (literally, "the source of kings"), a person of splendor who "glittered in the eyes of the world" (3: 182).

The Old Moodie who encounters Coverdale in Chapter One is not what he seems to be when he humbly asks, "If you pleased, Mr. Coverdale, . . . you might do me a very great favor" (3: 7). There are many folk tales in which autocratic fathers make the potential suitor's blind obedience to a request the basis for choosing a future son-in-law and successor to the throne. Sometimes the father-king makes winning the daughter a nearly impossible task, demanding that he solve riddles or slay a monster. This "task imposed" motif, like the accused queen narrative of which it is an important corollary, raises the issue of dynastic succession or transfer of power.[16]

In a matrilineal society, when the queen dies the king's right to the throne passes to his daughter's husband, and the "task imposed" is the father-king's attempt to ensure that his daughter never marries or marries someone that he chooses or approves. Old Moodie's request of Coverdale, then, has several implications. Although we later learn that he apparently is asking Coverdale to be his favorite younger daughter Priscilla's sponsor and protector at Blithedale, on another level he appears to be asking him to enter into competition with Hollingsworth for her hand. Old Moodie is trying both to choose Priscilla's suitor and his successor and to ensconce Priscilla at Blithedale, setting her up as a rival sister and potential rival queen to Zenobia.

In Coverdale's version of the myth, Zenobia, an intensely erotic and beautiful woman, reigns over Blithedale. When Coverdale first describes her majesterially ushering guests into the farmhouse, he emphasizes that she "had as much native pride as any queen" (3: 13). Her name and her remarkable beauty underscore her regal status, and the single, brilliant flower that she always wears becomes a token of her queenly office.[17] But from the start she seems to be reigning under threat of a death sentence imposed by her own father who plans to usurp her power. Moodie has no natural affection for Zenobia, only a cold admiration for her beauty and power, while he loves and wants to help his weak and obedient daughter Priscilla. In terms of the plot of a realistic novel, his enmity toward Zenobia is insufficiently and unconvincingly motivated. He supposedly rejects her because of her unkindness to Priscilla. But it is difficult to accept that what he witnesses of Zenobia's behavior toward Priscilla warrants his harsh response, particularly since he has Hollingsworth's testimony that the two relate "like an elder and younger sister" (3: 87). When Moodie observes the sisters together and sees Zenobia put Priscilla aside, he hastily concludes that she mistreats her, and in his wrath "shook his uplifted staff," the symbol of his paternal authority (3: 88).

Although Moodie's angry response to Zenobia seems excessive, if we consider it from the perspective of the accused queen motif, it makes sense. Moodie hates Zenobia because of the threat she poses to his patriarchal status. She has inherited his fortune after the death of her uncle, and although he "shines through her" and professes to be content to do so, it becomes apparent that, like the father in the accused queen narrative, he intends to reassert his control over her (3: 192). In the chapter "Fauntleroy," Coverdale imagines a meeting between Zenobia and her father. Living amid the ruins of the colonial governor's mansion, Moodie seems to be the fallen monarch in disarray, but he still struggles for the mastery in the interview with his daughter. Unaware that this poor man is her father, Zenobia offers him aid, and he responds, rather imperiously, "Keep it—keep all your wealth—until I demand it all, or none!" (3: 191). After the meeting, he menacingly warns, "Yet, let Zenobia take heed!" (3: 193).

Moodie rejects Zenobia and chooses Priscilla, declaring, "I love her best—I love her only!" (3: 193). From the patriarch's perspective, Priscilla is the ideal daughter: she is obedient and passive. Zenobia recognizes that Priscilla is "the type of womanhood, such as man has spent centuries in making it" (3: 122). Schooled in submission by her father, on several occasions in the novel she is described in her characteristic attitude as a silent suppliant at the feet of those in power, gazing beseechingly upward.

Moodie may love Priscilla, but that does not prevent him from being a party to Westervelt's exploitation of her. The two men conspire to "veil" her and transform her into a medium for their voices, a vehicle for their greed. Moodie's confession of his love for Priscilla, a love mingled with "shame," also suggests that he may be capable of a more heinous kind of paternal exploitation (3: 193). In the chapter "Fauntleroy," Coverdale hints at a terrible, unnamed crime in Moodie's first life as Fauntleroy: "just the sort of crime...which society (unless it should change its entire constitution for this man's unworthy sake) neither could nor ought to pardon" (3: 183). Although Coverdale's intimations that Moodie's family attempted to make retribution to those that Moodie wronged might suggest that his crime was one against property, the claim that the crime would change society's whole constitution and its dramatic effect upon Moodie's wife ("his wife perished by the necessity of her innate nobleness, in its alliance with a being so ignoble") hint at incest (3: 183).

These suspicions about Moodie's relationship with his daughter underscore an important issue in the novel: gender and power, and their connection with the death of women. In the folk tales, the king sometimes uses incest to control the throne. The king who fears a successor can circumvent the problem by marrying his own daughter, ensuring that no one else succeeds to the throne. Incest is, then, a dramatic example of the exploitative power of father over daughter. Margaret Schlauch defines incest or its threat as the "opening action" in the accused queen narrative that causes the queen's exile and suffering.[18] Although Moodie's power over Priscilla may not be overtly violent or sexual, it does have incestuous undertones. His intense attachment to her compels him to control her completely and define her to others, directing her life and speaking on her behalf.

It is possible to see some similarities between the sisters—in fact, Hawthorne seems at times to be deliberately blurring the distinctions between them—but there is one marked difference that Zenobia immediately recognizes when she first meets Priscilla. Zenobia is confounded by Priscilla's passive submission and exclaims, "Has she no tongue?" (3: 28). Priscilla has no voice; like the poor maidens in folk and medieval narratives who are victims of sexual violation, often involving incest as well, and whose tongues have been cut out to prevent them from speaking against their tormentors, she is silent and powerless. Zenobia, on the other hand, speaks powerfully and freely. When Coverdale tries to define what makes Zenobia "womanliness incarnated" (3: 44), he emphasizes Zenobia's "free, careless, generous modes of expression" (3: 17). She recoils from the abnegation of the self that Priscilla's silence represents.

To be silenced, from Irigaray's perspective, means to submit to the veil, as, of course, Priscilla does. In Irigaray's analysis of the fort-dà game of Freud in her essay "Belief Itself," she uses the veil as a metaphor to suggest the separation between men and women, a separation that the male both "mourn[s]" and perpetuates. Irigaray explains, "But it seems that from now on he will impose the veil upon her much more than she on him. It is true that she has not begun to speak, that she has her place in the veil." He both longs for and fears the woman, and veiling her expresses his deep need "to master her, reduce her little by little to nothing" in his effort to contain the "all powerful." Veiling the "all powerful" means controlling her sexual force, and with it her power to extend herself in time. This veiling, like the fort-dà game of childhood that Maule tries to master in *The House of the Seven Gables*, takes the place of a relationship with woman that would acknowledge her individuality and selfhood. Behind the veil, she is controlled but lost to him.[19]

Irigaray's thesis helps to explain why Priscilla is the preferred daughter and Zenobia is a serious threat to her father. Zenobia resists the veil and struggles to make others confront her on her terms. She expresses herself in unconventional discourse and her power of articulation allows her to create her own image, while Priscilla waits for men to "veil" or unveil her at will. In short, Zenobia is so dangerous for the patriarchy because she can be who and what she desires. She does not have to remain within the confines of her father's wishes or, more darkly, incestuous desires. When she comes to Blithedale, Zenobia desires freedom and sovereignty, and it is extraordinary, granted the milieu in which she operates, how fully, at first, she seems to have realized her desires. She seems to have escaped the veiled patriarchal order of her contemporaries. She has no last name that binds her to her father; her marital status has no apparent bearing on her social identity. It is not her relationship with men that has determined her estate. Her personal capabilities have sustained the powers that wealth initially conferred.

But in this world of fathers and veils, death invariably annihilates the desiring female self. Zenobia desires to lead many lives; her father returns to force her to play the only role he can imagine for her—submissive woman and daughter, spurned and dead. In Coverdale's story, the most queenly of women is only a bondservant in disguise in the male dominated social order. Several critics have puzzled over what they describe as the insufficiently motivated action of some of the characters of the romance. But the plot's logic is similar to the deeper, but less apparent, logic of a folk tale, particularly when we think about the implications of Moodie's role as father. Zenobia may be a queen, but Moodie is the more powerful king who is determined to choose his own heir. He "murders" Zenobia to seize the future from his victim, and he transfers power to his male heir. Moodie approached Coverdale at the beginning of the story and rejected him, perhaps because Coverdale is somewhat unconventional and less predictable in his behavior and consequently more difficult to control. Moodie chooses instead Hollingsworth, a man, like himself, who is totally comfortable in the male role of dominance and "kingship."

Moodie is the prototype of the unscrupulous, domineering male, and he perpetuates himself in his chosen "son" and heir, Hollingsworth. Zenobia's relationship with Moodie is a rehearsal for the final role that she plays as Hollingsworth's rejected lover. Hollingsworth is Moodie's chosen successor because he embodies the male ideals of competitiveness, autonomy, and power. A strong, overpowering "polar bear" of a man, he comes to Blithedale to pursue a secret, private agenda—to overthrow the community and realize his personal dream of a criminal reformatory that will become a model for the world (3: 26). He has no sympathy with the Blithedale ideal of mutual love and "equal brotherhood and sisterhood" and instead demands personal commitment to his private plans (3: 24). As he tells Coverdale, "Be with me...or be against me! There is no third choice for you" (3: 135).

Hollingsworth has conventional ideas about gender roles. He is disdainful of what he regards as the "aimless beauty" in Coverdale's life and wants to replace it with the "manly" qualities of "strength, courage, immitigable will" (3: 133). In "Eliot's Pulpit," he openly professes his belief in male superiority, asserting that woman without man as her acknowledged "principal" is a "monster" (3: 123). If women were ever to attempt to achieve equal social standing with men, he would feel it was his duty to "call upon my own sex to use its physical force, that unmistakeable evidence of sovereignty, to scourge them back within their proper bounds!" (3: 123). And yet Zenobia loves this man who, like her father, will abandon her and awaken in her deep conflict and self-hatred.

Zenobia's heretical desire for freedom and power challenges the cultural model of womanliness that Hollingsworth and Moodie cherish. But as Coverdale imagines her, to be loved she submits to the patriarchy, and this submission engenders in Zenobia self-hatred and a hatred of her sex that eventually consume her. Zenobia experiences an unresolvable conflict; she wants freedom and power, a "voice" which will some day empower all women to express themselves as they desire (3: 120). In a later scene that also takes place at Eliot's pulpit, she is dismayed by her earlier enthrallment with Hollingsworth and, believing at the moment that she is finally "awake, disenchanted, disenthralled," she realizes that Hollingsworth only desires domination, not love (3: 218). But in her final conversation with Coverdale, trapped between submission and assertion, she is again overwhelmed by self-hatred and hatred of her sex. She accepts total blame for the failure of their relationship and believes that she deserves punishment: "He did well to cast me off" (3: 225). Even the potent Zenobia cannot stand against the climate of antifeminist ideas. She is guilty of love, which in the world of Blithedale leads to submission to the authority of males, conflict, self-hatred, and, finally, death. In Coverdale's version of the accused queen story, it is impossible for a woman like Zenobia to achieve her desires because the patriarchal order represented by Moodie and Hollingsworth is aware of the threat to their power that her desires pose.

The Death of the Queen

In a world where the Moodies are kings, the Zenobias are merely accused queens whom no one will defend. In the final scene at Eliot's pulpit, Zenobia stands accused: "She represented the Oriental princess, by whose name we were accustomed to know her. Her attitude was free and noble, yet, if a queen's, it was not that of a queen triumphant, but dethroned, on trial for her life, or perchance, condemned, already" (3: 213). Because Coverdale arrives too late at the "secret tribunals" where she is condemned "unheard," he can only guess at the charges leveled against her (3: 215). He conjectures that it was "Zenobia's whole character and history; the true nature of her mysterious connection with Westervelt; her late purposes towards Hollingsworth, and, reciprocally, his in reference to her; and, finally, the degree in which Zenobia had been cognizant of the plot against Priscilla, and what, at last, had been the real object of that scheme" (3: 215).

Although there may be some specific charges, Zenobia mainly stands accused of her "whole character and history," of being who she is—a woman who, despite her struggles to repress some of her heretical desires for freedom and power in an attempt to be loved and accepted by her father and Hollingsworth, still is thought to be dangerous because she challenged the cultural norms of womanliness (3: 215). She wants to be totally vindicated for having these desires and believes "any verdict short of acquittal is equivalent to a death-sentence" (3: 215). Before her death she removes the "jewelled flower out of her hair;...as the act of a queen, when worsted in a combat, discrowning herself" and gives the flower to Priscilla, her sister and rival (3: 226). A strong part of Zenobia still believes that she has been "worsted"—but, perhaps significantly, not "bested"—by a "delicate and puny" maiden who is the male's, not her own, ideal of womanliness: silent, passive, and exploitable (3: 226).

The most powerful scene in the novel, and among the most affecting in Hawthorne's fiction, describes the recovery of Zenobia's dead body after her apparent suicide. Her hair, which along with her voice had been the richest token of her sexuality and will, is "streaming down the current" identified with the "Black River of Death" (234). In her death throes, Zenobia's beautifully supple and rounded female form has been transformed into "the marble image of a death-agony" (3: 235). Her dead body is the "perfect horror" of a work of art and becomes the object of the male gaze (3: 235). The male spectators look and seem struck dumb by death.

Zenobia's image invites conflicting readings and, ultimately, may be uninterpretable. Hawthorne directs us to the response of the male spectators, particularly their horror at the posture of her dead body. Her arms "were bent before her, as if she struggled against Providence in never-ending hostility. Her hands! They were clenched in immitigable defiance" (3: 235). The spectators "can't bear to see her looking so," and one of them struggles to refashion her limbs but "they bade him defiance, exactly as before" (3: 236). As would have been customary in a small New England community, Zenobia's dead body is given over to the women "to do their best with her" (3: 236).[20]

In telling his version of the accused queen narrative, Coverdale alters the conventional ending, and Hawthorne exposes the antifeminist sentiments behind these alterations. In the folk and medieval romance versions, the queen is falsely accused, condemned to death, but usually rescued. A radical revision of the narrative might have imagined the accused queen as her own rescuer. But, in Coverdale's version, Zenobia cannot save herself. Neither can she be rescued by the men in the story. Her two potential rescuers have both abandoned her, even if for different reasons. Hollingsworth has rejected her first, and her fate seems to rest with Coverdale. In the meeting between Zenobia and Coverdale that takes place shortly before her suicide, Coverdale asks Zenobia in an almost courtly fashion, "Can I do you any service?" (3: 225), and kisses her hand as a sign of "homage" (3: 227). Despite his expressed devotion, he cannot save her from death since he falls asleep and awakens too late to get help.

Coverdale's impotence in this scene is reminiscent of his powerlessness throughout the novel. Although he professes to be sympathetic to Zenobia's position and even argues that women must not be subordinate to men, he cannot escape the power of prevailing ideas and express his commitment to radical views with action. As a male with androgynous characteristics and someone willing to experiment with change, he might have brought together the strengths of both male and female and affirmed their value. But this resolution of the novel's tensions and competing perspectives is not possible.

Coverdale's inner divisions reveal the way in which the culture operates to shape identity and repress the individual. From the beginning of his stay at Blithedale, his sensibility draws him to Zenobia as the crux of feminine value. But her voice, which he so admires, does not serve as his ultimate guide. Although he shies away from the male competitiveness, assertiveness, and power embodied by Hollingsworth, and both Moodie and Hollingsworth recognize that Coverdale is not stereotypically "manly" and reject him, he wants to identify with them (3: 133). He not only fails to rescue Zenobia but is also complicit in Hollingsworth's "reenactment" of killing what Zenobia represents when he plunges his pole into her submerged breast as they are sounding the pond for her body. Coverdale's denial of the feminine—both within himself and as it was embodied by Zenobia and his devotion to her—culminates in his confession of love for Priscilla and his final allegiance to the patriarchy.

In Coverdale's story of the accused queen, the rejection of the queen is final and unanimous. Crucial to the folk and medieval romance versions of the accused queen narrative is the queen's humble submission to the sufferings inflicted on her by the patriarchy. She triumphs by an abnegation of her will. She does nothing to convince society that her own claims are legitimate. She resignedly awaits the male rescuer's validation of her worth. Implicit in her act of submission is the male author's belief that a woman's moral superiority is contingent upon her patient acceptance of male authority.[21] By the conclusion of the narrative, submissive and silently enduring, she is a paradigm of female virtue as defined by the male order. The accused queen is almost completely under the power of the male. Once an object to be given by her father, later a prize to be won by a suitor, she is now a woman to be judged and found worthy. From the perspective of the male author, the significance of the traditional ending of the folk tales and medieval romance is that it reinforces cultural norms. The accused queen's submission brings about the restoration of order and the affirmation of patriarchal power. Masculine ideas and ideals prevail.

While Coverdale's story resists the conventional ending, its conclusion is devastating in its implications about the possibilities for women and reflects the cultural assumptions of nineteenth-century New England society. Although Zenobia had the potential, she will never become the queen of "bounteous nature" who will "scatter fresh flowers from her hand, and revive ... faded ones by her touch," as Chapter One had promised (3: 21). The power to transform, traditionally identified as the strength of women in romances and legend, is lost. Instead of transforming the world into a place of natural, fresh flowers, Zenobia can only transform herself into the marble rigidity of her death agony. The memory that is the most haunting for Coverdale and, finally, for the reader is not of Zenobia vital and eloquent, defending women's rights at Eliot's pulpit or presiding at the board of Blithedale, but silent and rigid in death. In a bizarre twist, then, Coverdale's narrative of the accused queen ends with a version of the quest to slay the mythical monster. When Zenobia is drawn forth from the water, in a scene reminiscent of that in *Beowulf* when Grendel's mother comes forth from the watery lair, the "heroes," Coverdale and Hollingsworth, know they have wounded Zenobia, not simply because of a personal grievance, but, like all true culture heroes, to fulfill a cultural behest.

Melancholy Coverdale

Since dead women can inspire sympathy, the cultural directive that authorizes this wounding must be sufficiently strong to override or, at least, keep sympathy in check. The cultural drive behind the death of Zenobia is nothing less than the protection of the male identity as superior and powerful. The cultural behest is the perpetuation of the idea of male immortality. In representing the death of Zenobia as tragic, mournful, melodramatic, and farcical, *The Blithedale Romance* evokes a response that encompasses reflection, revulsion, unease, and indignant inquiry. To do this, Hawthorne must make us aware that this narrative is anything but an artless story, that, in fact, the story is a function of the reflecting consciousness, the reflecting male consciousness. As several critics have pointed out, Coverdale is his own subject, and his narrative supplies the link between the living and the dead. His narrative, in short, explains the reasons that the map to the grave of Zenobia is written with the same pen that constructs the male identity.

Coverdale is reminiscent of Jacques in Shakespeare's *As You Like It* whose response to Rosalind and comments about love also indicate a disdain for women, but he also can be thought of as a middle-class New England version of a tragic Shakespearean melancholic, Hamlet. He shares with him a pattern of disabled response to women in which melancholy forms the identity's core or its destructive essence. Like Hamlet's, Coverdale's melancholy seems pathological and his story culminates in the suicide of his love. Freud used Hamlet as the example of the male melancholic in his essay "Mourning and Melancholia," and some of his analysis of the melancholic is particularly relevant to *The Blithedale Romance,* in part because Freud's view is compatible with the perspective of nineteenth-century middle-class culture.

Freud begins the essay distinguishing between melancholia and mourning. In mourning, the nature of the loss to the male is readily definable on the conscious level. In melancholia, the loss is "unknown," difficult to discern, and "puzzling" to the observer. As Freud develops his explanation of the "unknown" loss, it becomes clearer that this loss that is "nameless," or perhaps whose name dare not be spoken, is the loss of the loved object: "An object-choice, an attachment of the libido to a particular person, had at one time existed; then, owing to a real slight or disappointment coming from this loved person, the object-relationship was shattered."[22]

From Freud's perspective, the psychological complexity arises in the way in which the melancholic responds to the loss. The "internal work" that he does in response to loss causes him to privilege loss itself more than the lost object. Freud explains: "Melancholia, therefore, borrows some of its features from mourning, and the others from the process of regression from narcissistic object-choice to narcissism. It is on the one hand, like mourning, a reaction to the real loss of a loved object; but over and above this, it is marked by a determinant which is absent in normal mourning or which, if it is present, transforms the latter into pathological mourning." Freud characterizes this attachment for or "identification with" this lost object as "narcissistic." The ego incorporates this lost love object into itself, but this incorporation creates a tension which splits the ego, creating a "shadow" for the ego, something that resembles the "superego" (a concept Freud at the time of writing this essay had not yet evolved but is here in embryonic form).[23]

In *The Gendering of Melancholia*, Juliana Schiesari offers this clarification of the process: "The melancholic could accordingly be said to be someone who suffers from unrequited love but who then finds satisfaction by abusing part of the self *as if* that part of the self were the disappointing object."[24] This tendency in the melancholic is evident in one of his distinctive traits—his "heightened self criticism," which is manifest in "an insistent communicativeness that finds satisfaction in self-exposure."[25] From this perspective, Coverdale's hypercritical confession is a product of both his self-love and his self-hatred, an identity characteristic peculiarly suited for cultivation in the climate of nineteenth-century New England middle-class society. Freud explains that the melancholic's criticism is actually about someone else, the implication being that it is really about the loved object because he has incorporated it into himself but is critical of it. The melancholic is caught in the narcissistic loop of self-criticism, and having repressed the narcissistic dimension of the process, he begins to experience loss without understanding its basis. As Schiesari explains, "loss itself becomes the dominating feature when the 'content' of loss has been emptied (repressed)." Someone has failed the melancholic, and that someone is a woman. He both wants to preserve her or, if not "her," what her loss represents, hence the impulse to "incorporation," and he wants to deny her, hence the impulse to be critical.[26]

Because he cannot exist in equipoise between these two "dimensions," he strengthens the judging part, making it the dominating trait of his identity, and follows its impulses, which are associated in a patriarchal society, like that of nineteenth-century New England or Germany, with the fathers and male authority figures. At the same time, he denies feminine impulses that direct him to the "lost" and unrecoverable love object. He continually grieves over what has been lost (without being able to define the precise nature of the loss), hence the melancholy. He is inclined to be misogynistic and, even though antisocial, rebellious, and "different," still a voice of the patriarchal establishment. The male's "overestimation" of the shadow, or judging ego, Schiesari explains, is "part of a larger cultural process whereby the feminine or the mother or the woman is devalued in the name of the father."[27]

Coverdale's ultimate devaluation of women is perhaps most apparent in his commentary on the death of Zenobia. Although he is uncertain about the meaning of her death posture, he offers conventionally gendered readings of some key elements of the scene. Hawthorne revised his description of the recovery of Miss Hunt's body from his journal entry of July 9, 1845 to create this scene, and comparing the journal entry with the novel's description highlights what he adds as Coverdale's commentary. The section of the journal in which Hawthorne speculated about the dead woman's interior life has been expanded considerably. Both the journal entry and the novel assume that a woman about to commit suicide would care about her appearance. In the journal entry, speculation is confined to a single sentence: "If she could have foreseen, while she stood, at 5 o'clock that morning, on the bank of the river, how her maiden corpse would have looked, eighteen hours afterwards, and how coarse men would strive with hand and foot to reduce it to a decent aspect, and all in vain—it would surely have saved her from this deed" (8: 264–65).

In the novel, Coverdale is more expansive in developing his assumptions about Zenobia's motives and concerns:

Being the woman that she was, could Zenobia have foreseen all these ugly circumstances of death, how ill it would become her, the altogether unseemly aspect which she must put on,...she would no more have committed the dreadful act, than have exhibited herself to a public assembly in a badly-fitting garment! Zenobia, I have often thought, was not quite simple in her death. She had seen pictures, I suppose, of drowned persons, in lithe and graceful attitudes. And she deemed it well and decorous to die as so many village-maidens have, wronged in their first-love, and seeking peace in the bosom of the old, familiar stream.... But, in Zenobia's case, there was some tint of the Arcadian affectation that had been visible enough in all our lives, for a few months past. (3: 236–37)

These comments may reveal more about Coverdale's ideas about gender than they do about Zenobia. Even in death the woman is imagined as still posing and inauthentic in her desires, thinking of herself as a "village-maiden" and driven by "Arcadian affectation." He further calls into question Zenobia's judgment and character when he says that "she deemed it well and decorous" to choose this death for cosmetic reasons. Coverdale seems intent upon trying to dismiss her as foolish. When he likens her concern about her appearance in a "badly-fitting garment" to her concern about her appearance in death, he undercuts the high seriousness of the entire scene. Up until this point, the reader, following the lead of the spectators, has primarily responded to the death of Zenobia with horror and pity. But to pity a woman shallow enough to reduce her life to an Arcadian performance seems wasted emotion. And yet Coverdale has prefaced this description with this admission: "Were I to describe the perfect horror of the spectacle, the reader might justly reckon it to me for a sin and shame" (3: 235). Ironically, it is his own concern for appearance and the response of others that prompts Coverdale to be not "quite simple" in his description of Zenobia's death.

Earlier in the novel, Coverdale had professed to be a proponent of liberal feminist ideas, but Hawthorne does not base Coverdale's interpretation of Zenobia's suicide on those ideas. In Coverdale and Westervelt's conversation about the reasons for Zenobia's death, even Westervelt seems to take a more liberal view of the subject. He cannot accept that there was any motive that would warrant the suicide of a woman with such talents and promise: "Her [Zenobia's] mind was active, and various in its powers...her heart had a manifold adaptation; her constitution an infinite buoyancy, which (had she possessed only a little patience to await the reflux of her troubles) would have borne her upward, triumphantly, for twenty years to come" (3: 240). Coverdale can only see one major cause: "In all this…there would have been nothing to satisfy her heart" (3: 240).

When Coverdale characterizes Zenobia's suicide as driven by erotomania, a form of extreme satisfaction of the heart, he is drawing upon the romantic convention of the female suicide. His emphasis on her desire for male approval even in death also bespeaks this convention. But there were feminists of the time whose beliefs about suicide ran counter to these. Janet Todd points out that Wollstonecraft, for example, would have been critical of romantic posturing in death: "She [Wollstonecraft] would not have wished guilt and outside authority removed from the act for such effete theatrically to take their place." Wollstonecraft condoned "rational suicide" under certain well-defined circumstances, particularly when it involved no conspicuous "self-display," but condemned the falsely emotional self-murder.[28] Clearly, there were other ideas about female suicide current in the culture that Hawthorne could have had Coverdale draw from, but Coverdale's ideas conform to an antifeminist tradition.

Chapter Fifteen "The Crisis," then, illustrates the crisis that the melancholy man faces as he moves between the impulses of the lost object and the impulses of the "shadow ego," one directing him toward Zenobia, the other leading him toward patriarchal values. In some ways this chapter marks a turning point for Coverdale. Early in the novel, he is drawn to Zenobia's beauty and strength, but her sadness and her complex emotional responses do not conform to his gendered assumptions about woman's nature. On numerous occasions, he characterizes the other males as melancholy but uses this term for Zenobia on only one occasion, in referring to her "melancholy kindness" (3: 169). Female melancholy is not afforded status in the counter culture commune of Blithedale, and in this regard it reflects the world of middle-class New England. In Coverdale's interpretation of Zenobia's despondency, he grants her only disabling and foolish emotions that bring no deeper understanding. He trivializes both her sorrow and her death. At the same time, Coverdale values the brooding sorrow and melancholy of Hollingsworth and interprets it as the sign of a contemplative man.

Coverdale's "Aerial Sepulchre"

The novel explains the way in which even in a newly constituted social order, like that of Blithedale, the fathers reproduce themselves and perpetuate their fictions of identity and immortality. Earlier in the narrative Coverdale had made light of both his and Hollingsworth's aspirations to be the "fathers" of the community. And yet, by the end of the novel, it is apparent that even the seemingly most unconventional of men pay homage to the fathers and their values.

One of the oddest scenes in the novel makes sense when viewed from the perspective of the issue of patriarchy. In Chapter Ten, Moodie sits removed from the others behind some shrubbery while Coverdale and Hollingsworth feed him "like priests offering dainty sacrifice to an enshrined and invisible idol" (3: 83). Old Moodie is their false deity, and they worship at the altar of the patriarchy and aspire to be like the father. After they feed him, Coverdale even experiments with trying on his point of view: "I beheld all these things as through old Moodie's eyes" (3: 84). Although Coverdale professes to agree with some of Zenobia's feminist views, ultimately he identifies with Moodie and Hollingsworth and their ideas about women. He simply does not express these ideas as overtly as they do and may not even entertain them on a conscious level. But this does not alter the fact that he has incorporated the conventional beliefs and laws of the father into himself.

Melancholy Coverdale, then, is a male self-construction born out of an internal need. It is a privileged self, an "idol" fed and fostered by psychic necessity and cultural assumptions. Coverdale has been given cultural dispensation to remove to his melancholy "hermitage" to muse on life's meaning and cultivate his individualism. Zenobia garners no such approval.

Coverdale, Hollingsworth, and Moodie form a trinity of melancholics who have privileged their despondency and reiterated it. They have cultivated their sense of loss and constructed it as a site of important self-recognition, at the same time that they have conspired to devalue and diminish any similar sort of individualism and conspicuous display of the self when manifested in women. Worshipping "idols" is something Coverdale, Moodie, and Hollingsworth hold in common (3: 70). They all have created "idols" that reinforce their sense of themselves as powerful and singular. They deem it holy work to offer sacrifices to these "idols," and, in turn, by these offerings they hope to transcend the limits of personal mortality.

But "The Hermitage" chapter makes it apparent that making an idol of the self and sacrificing everything to its claims does not assuage death anxiety. Coverdale knows that his cloistered bower of the self resembles nothing so much as an above-ground grave or "aerial sepulchre" (3: 98). In this regard, Coverdale is in a peculiarly modern place. His Blithedale scheme involves the "dizzy work" of constructing a self from a hodgepodge of new age ideas that are part of the Blithedale environment (3: 140). This new age self, in foregoing the old certainties of conventional religion and eternal life, finds itself particularly fragile and vulnerable to death anxiety. In response, a man like Coverdale searches for a means to extend or transcend the self, hoping to ensure that the "idol" of the male self—whose value is virtually unquestioned in middle-class New England culture—will remain permanently enshrined.

Despite his self-deluding blather about "sweet, calm" ways of dying and finding beauty in death, Coverdale is preoccupied with last things and intensely anxious about death (3: 130). At the beginning of his adventures at Blithedale he falls ill and acts out his dying. He thinks his state of mind has prepared him for death, and he articulates something close to a death-wish: "Death should take me while I am in the mood" (3: 43). His "mood" is shaped by his belief that he is undertaking an experiment that will allow him to achieve self-transcendence, but the mood is short-lived.

In "The Crisis," Coverdale has resumed his anxious meditation on death. He bemoans that "summer was passing away," and the sense of the transiency of life weighs heavily upon him, causing him to long for "permanent plans" (3: 128). As his time at Blithedale draws to a close, he tries out some of the conventional mid-century consolations of dying to escape the threat to the self posed by death. Intermittently, he grows more conservative, reconceiving the structure of the community as a "great and general family" (3: 128). Like any traditional family, Blithedale needs fathers, and Coverdale imagines: "When we come to be old men...they will call us Uncles, or Fathers—Father Hollingsworth and Uncle Coverdale.... In a century or two, we shall every one of us be mythical personages.... They will have a great public hall, in which your portrait, and mine,...shall be hung up" (3: 129). Despite his apparent radicalism, Coverdale, like the Pyncheon men and Matthew Maule, in a desperate effort to achieve a form of personal immortality seems drawn to the prospect of "familial immortality," and even hopes to enhance his identity to mythic proportions by becoming someone akin to a father of his country.[29]

Coverdale reveals that this quest for permanence is not peculiar to him; many at Blithedale long in one form or another for an "abiding-place" (3: 128). No one, not even radical communitarians, can live with the realization that all is change and flux, particularly when they suspect that their own dissolution is part of this flux. Part of the work of Blithedale is necessarily self-protective and self-delusive: "Altogether, by projecting our minds outward, we had imparted a show of novelty to existence, and contemplated it as hopefully as if the soil, beneath our feet, had not been fathom-deep with the dust of deluded generations, on every one of which, as on ourselves, the world had imposed itself as a hitherto unwedded bride" (3: 128). They hope to establish a permanent utopian community, a plan that provides them with a heroic and self-transcending destiny. In trying to accomplish this plan, they are in the business of the circumvention of death. And yet to carry it off successfully, they must overlook "the dust," Hawthorne's frequently used metonym for death. Their "general brain" (3: 140) must evade death, try to beautify it, or, when all else fails, hope it will be "bliss to die" (3: 130).

Their work is particularly pressing because they see themselves as "pilgrims...whose present bivouac was considerably farther into the waste of chaos than any mortal army of crusaders had ever marched before" (3: 52). Unlike Bunyan's pilgrims who seek the celestial city, or the crusader-pilgrims who journey to recapture the Holy Land, or the Hawthorne-Pilgrim of the Custom House who is looking for a new kind of "road" to "Paradise," these Blithedale pilgrims are marching in another direction "into the waste of chaos" (3: 52). They have a social vision which, at least initially, they believed was the basis for a more perfect union, a New Jerusalem that would bring abiding happiness and a sure means of transcending death. But at some level they realize that in harboring this vision they are "deluded"; the soil beneath their feet is "fathom-deep" (3: 128).

Significantly, they are pilgrims armed with books—"Mr. Emerson's Essays, the Dial, Carlyle's works, George Sand's romances...and other books which one or another of the brethren or sisterhood had brought with them"—books informed by the kind of idealism that forms the philosophical basis for the Blithedalers' reimagining of death (3: 52).[30] In "Experience" when Emerson states, "Grief too will make us idealists," he claims that death will be incapable of touching us and will leave us locked in our private visions and glass houses of perception, confirming our suspicions about the ultimate "insubstantiality" or unreality of nature and experience.[31] These assertions may simply be manifestations of an elaborate defense mechanism that Emerson has established to manage death. He, too, fears death's power to annihilate the male ego, and his idealism provides the philosophical base from which he could reinterpret and downplay death's power. For Emerson, as for many nineteenth-century males of his education and class, what he fears is that death actually has the power to alter him totally—to touch him so profoundly that it will annihilate the self and forever shut the eye/I that forms the center of value and meaning. The Blithedalers follow their philosophical leader by professing to believe in their version of the "phenomenon perfect"—a perfected social order that can perpetuate the position of the privileged male melancholic, left free to shape his fantasy of immortality over the dead body of a woman.[32]

When Coverdale imagines the Blithedalers in the face of death projecting "outward" so that their minds could create a "novelty," he expresses the deep division that this strategy of immortality has created (3: 128). In a parody of the head bathed in "blithe air," feet on the "bare ground" stance of the famous "transparent eye-ball" passage in Emerson's *Nature*, Hawthorne imagines Coverdale and the Blithedalers, their heads bathed in the "novelty" of existence and their feet "fathom-deep" in the dust of death (3: 128). But Hawthorne challenges the basic assumption of Emerson's essay—that this stance brings a sense of "perpetual youth"—by having melancholy Coverdale profess to believe that to focus on the "novelties" is the stuff of delusion.[33] In a telling extended metaphor, Coverdale concludes his statement about their idealistic scheme by linking "dust," "world," and "bride," and this linkage resonates with implications about his understanding of Zenobia, the other unknown bride in the novel (3: 128).

For Coverdale, it all circles back to Zenobia. As much as the dust and the dirt, she poses a challenge to these idealistic schemes. From the beginning, Coverdale is drawn to her body, her erotic power, and he describes her as womanliness incarnated, with "an influence breathing out of her, such as we might suppose to come from Eve, when she was just made" (3: 17). And yet Coverdale would still prefer to have Hollingsworth at his deathbed because he knows how to walk the "unknown path" to death buoyed by "hopeful accents" (3: 42). In Coverdale's eyes, Hollingsworth has lighted upon a sense of purpose "worthy of martyrdom," and any sacrifice it demands only makes him a stronger candidate for eternal life or perpetual self. Union with Zenobia, connected as she is to flawed and finite Eve, would mean the extinction of the male self.

Even before she dies, this vital woman, then, is associated with death. She stands against the force of male transcendence and its underlying idealism. If Hawthorne ever toyed with affirming erotic love in this novel, the presence of the dead body of Zenobia nullifies this option. It also makes impossible any innocence about the blissfulness of death. That her corpse resists the males' attempts to refashion or beautify it only highlights the extent of their illusions about death. In some ways, their attempts are similar to the idealist's efforts to alter nature so that it conforms to the "pure idea in your mind."[34] While Emerson concludes, "Grief too will make us idealists," Hawthorne in *The Blithedale Romance* might counter that "the dead body of a woman can make men materialists."[35] Is any mind capable of transforming the horror of Zenobia's corpse so that it is possible to overlook the corruption of the body? Zenobia's dead body breaks the attachment to mortal eros and fashions a stronger link—that between thanatos and eros. In the process, it shatters the illusion of transcendence and gives the lie to the Blithedale project.

The Restoration

At the conclusion of *The Blithedale Romance*, the queen is dead and the fathers have been returned to their positions of power. The old order has been restored, although the restoration is no cause for celebration. The Blithedalers' desire to create paradise "anew" ends in a pastoral haven which is no Eden. Hollingsworth and Priscilla are married and live together in a rural cottage on the former site of the Blithedale community. Unlike so many novelists of the eighteenth and nineteenth centuries who idealize domestic married life, Hawthorne depicts their union as one that offers little recompense for the Blithedalers' lost dreams of Utopian brotherhood and sisterhood.

On the surface, the ending might appear to be happy. The story concludes with the traditional wedding, and the sexual politics conform to conventional attitudes and expectations about the relationship between the sexes. But is this social arrangement more desirable than that of the Blithedale community? Implicit in Coverdale's story is his version of the stages in the development of the social order: first matriarchy, then a foray into communal living (establishing a tentative equipoise between matriarchy and patriarchy), and finally, a recovery and reassertion of patriarchy centered in the exclusive relationship of the heterosexual couple. The novel, however, does not present this movement as progress.

The rural retreat of Hollingsworth and Priscilla, if conventionally imagined, should be a place of bucolic marital bliss—a patriarchal fantasy of peace and order—but the despondency of the male half of the couple, among other things, highlights its failure. Although the "powerfully built" male figure may still be capable of dwarfing the "slender woman" who walks beside him with a "deep, submissive, unquestioning reverence," he suffers a lack that no woman can fill (3: 242). The cycle is complete: Hollingsworth, in his enervation and despair, resembles no one so much as Old Moodie, and the intense attachment of Priscilla and Hollingsworth, which excludes society and is based on principles of control and submission antithetical to the Blithedale ideal, returns us to a world ruled by the fathers and their ideas about male immortality. By sacrificing women, these men try to appropriate their power of reproduction and extend the self in time, into the future. By inventing a means of male birthing, Moodie and Hollingsworth have usurped from Zenobia the power to reproduce. Moodie has succeeded in replicating himself in his male "sons"—most obviously, Hollingsworth, but even the less conventional and prodigal son, Coverdale.

Moodie's legacy is despondency or, more accurately, a perpetuation of melancholy. Exhibiting the symptoms of melancholy, Coverdale and Hollingsworth are rebellious and antisocial, although ultimately still obedient to the patriarchal establishment. *The Blithedale Romance* explores the logic of melancholy—the attachment to the "lost object," the loss of this "object," and, granted the values of the male culture, the reasons that this loss is necessary and inevitable. The novel also explains the way in which this individual mental disorder forms the basis of a social condition. Implicit in Freud's theory of melancholia is that melancholia tends to be a lasting personality disorder, while it is possible to recover from or, more precisely, to recover *through* mourning. The two differ in their effect; there is no recovery from melancholia because the melancholic does not fully understand or appreciate what has been lost. It is this recognition of the nature of loss and its value that distinguishes mourning from melancholia. Until melancholy becomes mourning, the melancholic is doomed to be unhappy.

The conclusion of *The Blithedale Romance* illustrates the difficulty of recovery when the process of mourning has been aborted by the male culture's devaluation of the "lost" object. Although Moodie, Hollingsworth, and Coverdale form a circle of individuals at the gravesite of Zenobia, there is no diffusion of sympathy, no reparative emotion that ripples from the grave to the rest of society to form the basis of righted social relations in the Blithedale community. These three men are impotent "Titans" who are building stone fences instead of new, viable communal bonds (3: 136). They cultivate melancholy, and, instead of healing, it brings a reproduction of melancholy. In the novel's economy of suffering, there is nothing but waste—aborted emotions.

Returning to Coverdale's response to Zenobia's death, it is revealing how totally devoid of sympathy for Zenobia he is. Even Westervelt, as he wonders what reasons would bring her to suicide, seems more capable of responding to Zenobia as a woman with needs and desires, a subject apart from himself. For Coverdale, Zenobia remains an object upon which he writes the text of his own failures. The death of Zenobia has been transposed into a wounding of his ego that he must avenge and, even more remarkably, a sin of Hollingsworth that he has the power to forgive. Coverdale's final revisioning of Zenobia's death makes blatantly clear that in interpreting her death he has never taken into account her own claims.

From Coverdale's perspective the social relations that are "perpetuated" at the grave of Zenobia must ensure patriarchal values. There is no place in his scheme for Zenobia or what she represents. He wants to forget her, although as the "lost object" she cannot be forgotten until she is recovered. Coverdale's melancholy is a symptom of a narcissism that has rendered him incapable of sympathy and of an imaginative vision that might have brought with it a different outcome to his story. In classical mythology, the Titans are eventually overthrown by Saturn, their cast-off son, who, in turn, is overthrown by his son Jupiter, the supreme deity. In Greek mythology, the Roman god Jupiter is known as Zeus, the god who is the originating principle of Zenobia, a name that literally means "one whose life derives from Zeus."[36] Thus, even Zenobia's name foretells her destiny as originating from and determined by the male "gods" of this narrative. At Blithedale, the god/king/father births, while the goddess/queen/mother dies and is not mourned, a fact that has significant consequences in the formation of the nineteenth-century New England social order.

The Dead Body of Woman and Consensus Politics

One of the most difficult questions the novel raises is what the relationship between the dead body of women and the body politic is.[37] While *The Blithedale Romance* bears out Irigaray's thesis of "original matricide," the question remains, is it undeviatingly so, or can the dead body of a woman ever provide the precipitating force for a diffusion of sympathy that would form the basis of a more perfect social order?[38] Can melancholy lead to reparative mourning and a reconstitution of the state?

Although Blithedale was originally planned without a graveyard, at the end of the novel memory seems to radiate outward from the grave of Zenobia located in the Blithedale "pasture" (3: 238). Even Coverdale's graveside imaginings about the future and his meeting with

Hollingsworth emphasize that, despite his conscious desire to devalue her and diminish her significance, Zenobia herself will be the source of future memories. So powerful is her influence that the "whole soil of our farm, for a long time afterwards, seemed but the sodded earth over her grave" (3: 245).

These lines of memory and grief could form a "magnetic chain of humanity."[39] But Hawthorne controls the response to his accused queen Zenobia differently than the medieval writer did. In the medieval narrative of the accused queen, the dominant note is pathos, which is intended to evoke the piety of its audience.[40] In Chaucer's version of the accused queen, for example, Constance is an exemplum, and her story of suffering is a tale of justice, even if it is the sort of justice that we would expect from a Man of Law.[41] *The Blithedale Romance* complicates the reader's response by adding to pathos feelings of regret, frustration, and longing. This is no feminist tract, but neither does it follow the conservative model of the accused queen story. Also, despite its evocation of *As You Like It*, it is no dark comedy which, in the face of the misogyny and cynicism of its melancholy Jacques, ultimately reasserts the power of love and marriage.

Because the patriarchal order is presented negatively and the novel does not end with a cathartic sense of the restoration of order when the males resume their positions of power, surely no one reading this book would be able to intone, "The queen is dead. Long live the king." Remembering the Blithedale dream that one day men and women would speak with a reciprocal and "living voice," a harmony of thought and expression symbolic of the true equality that would lead to a more perfect union, further complicates the question (3: 120). Writing for a democratic readership raises the problem of how Zenobia will be valuated by the people, for, if there is to be a new social order, it will be built by their consensus of sympathy. The death of an extraordinary individual is frequently the precipitating force for reconstituting society. The death can expose the injustice implicit in the system and sometimes galvanizes the forces for change. The dead body can be a revolutionary force.

In Hawthorne's version of the accused queen narrative, Zenobia has certainly been wronged. Her father has denied her, Hollingsworth has betrayed her, and even her own sister chooses Hollingsworth over her. But are these the kind of wrongs that can galvanize a society for social reform? Also, because her death is a suicide, any ethical questions could be lost in the larger Christian concern about the serious moral wrong. So, would there be any readers, particularly any nineteenth-century readers, who would cry for justice for Zenobia?[42]

In other words, what would be the status of the desiring woman in nineteenth-century society? If she were mistreated and died, would she be mourned? It is a question that is impossible to overlook because of the way in which Hawthorne has structured the novel's concluding section. As he does in the conclusion of *The Scarlet Letter*, he draws readers into the interpretive circle, asking them to write the text that will determine the meaning of a woman's life. According to Sacvan Bercovitch, Hawthorne "compels us" to explain Hester's dramatic change of purpose and belief, and "since, in short, neither author nor characters help us, we must meet the requirement ourselves."[43] In *The Blithedale Romance*, Hawthorne prepares us in a different way for the novel's conclusion. In assessing the meaning of Zenobia's choice, we are inclined to return to her grave and to look to the male characters gathered around it for interpretive "help." But because Coverdale's and Westervelt's interpretations of Zenobia's life and death differ so radically, there seems to be no way to make sense of it.

This scene at the grave site is reminiscent of the scene at Daisy Miller's grave at the conclusion of Henry James's novel. In *Daisy Miller: A Study* the two male protagonists offer radically different readings of a woman's life: she was "the most innocent," says one, while the other responds incredulously.[44] Overwhelmed by grief, the narrator Winterbourne signals that these readings, his own included, are interpretations, and possibly misreadings, when he adds his confession at the novel's close: "I was booked to make a mistake. I have lived too long in foreign parts."[45] In James's *Daisy Miller*, Daisy's death may be the site of conflict and may even be beyond interpretation, but James does present the death as inspiring strong feelings of sympathy.

While the medieval version of the accused queen narrative inspired piety, *The Blithedale Romance* provokes something more like impiety or, at least, discontent and doubt. It fosters a longing for something "other," a society different from Blithedale based upon the principles of sympathy and justice. Because Blithedale was founded upon such high standards of mutual respect and support, the people—and the reader— revisit the grave of Zenobia to see who failed whom. Blithedale's implicit "contract" called for love and ethical behavior, but Coverdale breaks this contract. He lacks sympathy for Zenobia, and his act of censure without compassion brings the downfall of Blithedale. Without sympathy there is little motive for ethical conduct.

In telling his story of Zenobia's death, Coverdale has cloaked the issues of justice in silence. It is no wonder that he would have preferred that she be buried at the base of the huge rock that formed Eliot's pulpit and not in the pasture land. He would prefer that her memory and the "charges" against the accused queen never be made public. After constructing this narrative as a story about a community, he seems to try to deny its communal aspects. His focus on Hollingsworth's retreat to his private guilt suggests that the relationships among these individuals are solely personal or private matters and have no legitimate social or political implications.

But by fashioning the ending of the novel in this way, Hawthorne raises at least one question that Coverdale does not ask: Does drawing the distinction between public and private so rigidly indeed protect women, as some in nineteenth-century society thought?[46] This practice seems to allow no public airings of private wrongs that have grievous public implications. What may be needed at Blithedale, then, is not the guilt of a Hollingsworth, which is counterproductive and brings no good to either himself or the Zenobias of the world, but a healthy dose of shame.[47] Shame springs from the recognition of the public dimension of private acts. It casts private guilt into a public arena and demands a conversation (which includes the claims of both the living and the dead) and consensus about the nature of wrong. After the death of Zenobia, all the men retreat, become private, hidden, concealed. Her father hides behind his handkerchief, Hollingsworth goes into his domestic retreat, and Coverdale grows more obscure and difficult to fathom, self-concealing, as his final confession of "love" for Priscilla confirms. Their guilt renders them obscure and impotent, but with shame might come the possibility of a public airing of Zenobia's position, a recirculation of sympathy, and a redefinition of values by which individuals can live their lives.

"Man versus Men; Woman versus Women"

In the headnote to *Woman in the Nineteenth Century*, Margaret Fuller expressed the longing of society for a new social order conceived in justice when she wrote, "The Earth waits for her Queen." Her vision of the possibility of implementing this order was not naive. Juxtaposed with this headnote was another which read, "Frailty, thy name is WOMAN," and then two more which read, "Frailty, thy name is MAN" and "The Earth waits for its King."[48] It is not that she accepted any one of these as the whole of the story.

One way to think of *The Blithedale Romance* is that Hawthorne wrote it to respond to Fuller's headnotes and test the validity of these juxtaposed assumptions. Fuller's fairly recent death might have been on Hawthorne's mind when he was writing this novel, and the inspiration of Margaret Fuller hovers around it.[49] Hawthorne's bitter comments at her death and his refusal of sympathy are reminiscent of Coverdale's response to the death of Zenobia. Like Coverdale, Hawthorne mocked and undercut Fuller, and he persisted in his reading of her as love-struck and misguided. But he was unable to escape her memory or the impact of her political and feminist ideas. This novel, and the questions it asks about the status of women, like the memory of Zenobia for Coverdale, radiate outward from her grave. It combines the spirit of the bitter and ironic stance of Hawthorne's final comments about Fuller with the sympathetic and almost loving spirit of the description of their meeting at Sleepy Hollow cemetery ten years earlier. With "Margaret lying on the ground, and me sitting by her side," they "talked about Autumn—and about the pleasures of getting lost in the woods—and about the crows, whose voices Margaret had heard—and about the experiences of early childhood, whose influence remains upon the character after the collection of them has passed away—and about the sight of mountains from a distance, and the view from their summits—and about other matters of high and low philosophy" (8: 343). Their meditations among the tombs of Sleepy Hollow were interrupted by the appearance of Emerson. Curiously, Hawthorne concludes this journal entry with a description of the individual's position in the universe that is almost transcendental in spirit but seems more Thoreauvian than Emersonian. On a night with "the most beautiful moonlight that ever hallowed this earthly world," Hawthorne breaks down the boundaries between self and nature and imagines himself wholly calm, immersed in the waters of death: "when I went to bathe in the river, which was as calm as death, it seemed like plunging down into the sky" (8: 344). Anticipating Thoreau's "sky water" in *Walden*, Hawthorne equates death with the deepest intuition: an act of perception that plunges to the "sky."[50]

This passage is unusual in Hawthorne's work because it marks a rare moment of peace, wholeness of consciousness, and unity with nature. More often, the note he strikes is closer to what Fuller characterized on another occasion as "baffled effort." On April 22 and 29 of 1841, Fuller led her conversations on myth for a group of friends and associates, many of whom were transcendentalists, and those on the god Pluto began with Fuller's remarks on "baffled effort," which she argued the Greeks believed was the punishment of Tartarus.[51] At some level, like Hawthorne, she equated failure with death.

In *Woman in the Nineteenth Century*, after Fuller juxtaposes the various quotations, she adds, "frail he is indeed, how frail! how impure," as if to explain the reason that the queen's reign has not come. She acknowledges the possibility of failure, "frailty."[52] But, despite this recognition of "baffled effort," she tended to remain optimistic about the possibility of progress, particularly on the women's question.

Interestingly, her belief in the "promise" of a different future rests on the ability of writers to write stories in which women are imagined differently from their present condition. This promise exists, in part, because writers would be able to imagine new stories in which women play different roles than the conventionally gendered ones. Despite his own misgivings, Hawthorne wrote this kind of new story.

Certeau describes history as a "tale" that involves the "resurgence and denial of the origin." *The Blithedale Romance* is Hawthorne's version of this "tale" and, as such, is "built upon a murder of an originary death." When a Hawthorne story is at its best, as it is in *The Blithedale Romance*, it has a complex effect, one similar to what Certeau characterizes as that of these originary myths. We are consumed with a memory that is "as impossible to recover from as to forget."[53] It is a memory of happiness, of relationships between men and women that were better. We recall, for example, beautiful Queen Zenobia welcoming the newcomers to the fireside at Blithedale, or playfully laughing and talking with Coverdale. These memories come in backward glances, past glimpses, and are often recorded on the consciousness of the male protagonists. But Hawthorne shapes our response to these memories in ways that are arguably different from that of his male protagonist. While Coverdale and Hollingsworth are caught in a gnawing and disabling remorse, we grieve and regret, and "air points of difference."[54] Accompanying our regret at what has been lost is a deep longing for something different, a new system unlike the one that originated the loss, a new Blithedale. This kind of longing comes from the perspective of the "Final Position" and is predicated upon knowledge of the value of the "lost object," knowledge that the novel's male protagonists locked in their solipsistic desire for self eternal are unable to achieve. In this way, Hawthorne can bring us beyond disabling melancholy, the debilitating state where he leaves his male protagonists, to the reparative space of mourning.

"Intimate Equality": Sacrifice and Death in The Marble Faun

In Pierre Bayle's *Historical and Critical Dictionary*, "system" is equated with the organizing principles of thought that define a society and is a term that has a somewhat negative connotation. In *The Writing of History*, Certeau explains that Jean-Francois Delamare saw in Bayle's use of the term some disparagement, for "in religion everything is system."[1] The term system appears several times in Hawthorne's fiction, frequently to describe an ideology closely linked to a set of cultural practices, religious or moral, sometimes in an ironic voice, often in the context of failure. The system usually seems curiously distant from the individuals who inhabit it, as if institutionalized by some force beyond their control, perhaps the "iron men" in authority (1: 197). Hawthorne consistently relies on the metaphor of iron in his novels to characterize the system. Implacable and unyielding, the system rarely works in the individual's favor, and it is more likely to bend him or her to its unalterable purposes.

The Marble Faun returns to the idea of system, and Hawthorne is consistent in his emphasis on its "iron rule" and disregard for the individual (4: 239). The system does not promote human happiness, only misery. In *The Marble Faun*, Hawthorne sometimes uses the term to refer to the beliefs and practices of Roman Catholicism. By directing his criticism at a Christian system that many New Englanders would think alien, connected to an underclass, and influenced by corrupt papal authority, Hawthorne constructs a buffer between himself and his predominately Christian readership reminiscent of what he does in *The Scarlet Letter* by centering his criticism of Christianity on Puritanism.

From this safety zone, he criticizes the deep structure of Christianity and the sociocultural obstacles to an individual's development created by the patriarchal system at its core.

Although *The Marble Faun* has many biblical references, it is not a religious novel.[2] It is more focused on the social than the theological implications of its story. In some ways it follows the logic of the distinction Certeau draws between religious and social history when discussing varying approaches to science and social questions in the nineteenth century. He explains, "a society which is no longer religious imposes *its* rationality, *its* own categories, *its* problems, and *its* type of organization upon religious formulations."[3] While nineteenth-century New England did not qualify as "no longer religious," there was sufficient erosion of the unitary belief system that testing it to see if it would hold might be the legitimate province of a writer prone to skepticism. Whether Hawthorne can be thought of as a believer with doubts or a disbeliever who is a member of the party of the "no longer religious," he is someone who in his fiction articulates his culture's fears and doubts about the old religious certainties. He did not forsake his earlier desire for a "new classification"; it seems to have gone underground, expressing itself in the "explanatory systems" of his fiction. These systems impose their own "rationality" or "type of organization" on experience and, as Certeau argues, are based on a "social model" that involves the "'reemployment' of Christian elements inherited from the past."[4]

The Marble Faun tackles Hawthorne's usual topics—the constitution of the self, male-female relationships, community, and authority—but in this novel he seems to be straining for a deeper and more conclusive exploration of them. Underlying the novel is a theory of civilization that helps to explain the current "organization" of relationships between men and women. The novel also shows the effects of the system's organization on the individuals within it. While presuming to foster and cultivate individuality, the patriarchal system ultimately nullifies the individual's uniqueness and wholeness.

Hawthorne acknowledges the crucial role of Greek and Roman mythology in the creation of Western Christian thought with numerous references to these myths, but the novel's deep structure resonates with allusions to an earlier pre-Hellenic mythology that resurrects ancient female gods and rulers. Echoing the theory of civilization set forth in "Main-street," the novel begins in matriarchy, a golden age of relationship with women and nature, and advances to patriarchy. In this era, the patrilineal family develops with its system of beliefs, and the father displaces the matriarch or queen as head of household and primary progenitor. Many mid-nineteenth-century intellectuals would interpret movement of this sort as progress because they were somewhat reluctant to accept fundamental natural conditions or reconcile themselves to their implications and because they seemed to be inclined to believe that the future invariably brings progress. But Hawthorne's fiction often reveals the underside of progress, the voices of the past silenced by this advancement or buried in the dungeons of the systems that support it.

"Four Individuals"

The first two words of *The Marble Faun* are "Four Individuals," and the implications of these words go beyond the Romantic era's celebration of individuality and the power of free will and self-fashioning (4: 5). As "individuals," the novel's protagonists seem exempt from the defining restrictions of kinship relationships. They are not primarily fathers or mothers, brothers or sisters, husbands or wives, or sons or daughters, crucial relational identities that define and determine the status of many of the protagonists of Hawthorne's earlier novels. Orphanlike, they have tried to create their own network of relationships apart from the Roman system of paternity. And it seems to have given both the men and women remarkable freedom to express themselves, move about, enjoy their leisure, and be productive in their work. For this reason, Miriam's relationship with Donatello, at least in its early stages, is imagined somewhat differently than, for example, Hester's with Dimmesdale or Holgrave's with Phoebe. Within this context, the novel challenges the nineteenth-century notion of individuality, particularly individuality achieved within the kinship system of the heterosexual couple relationship.[5]

The drama of *The Marble Faun* is played out *sub specie mortis*, a perspective that invites redefinitions and altered alliances. Once death intrudes into the narrative, conditions are irreparably changed; beliefs are tested and new allegiances form. Because Donatello committed murder in support of "Queen" Miriam and the matriarchal order, the male culture calls for a form of what Victor Turner would describe as "redressive ritual," a process that involves reeducation into acceptable ideas concerning women and death.[6] Under the tutelage of the New England, Christian, middle-class Kenyon, Donatello exchanges the idea that love of the erotic woman can bring intimations of immortality for a more conventional Christian consolation for dying. By the conclusion of the novel, the wisdom of this substitution has been called into question. Reeducation serves mainly to support the status quo under the guise of defending and sustaining the male "individual."

Donatello and Matriarchy

The story of *The Marble Faun* is told from the perspective of the "deep grave in which old Rome lies buried," and its excavations recover the unfinished narrative of the matriarch buried beneath its surface (4: 17). And yet, while calling into question patriarchal values, and perhaps even subverting the status of the male subject, the matriarchal myth seems unable to sustain a new system of beliefs and consolations. Although the novel begins recalling matriarchy, it devotes much of its energy to attempting to justify the ways of patriarchy to man—and woman.

Donatello is a new creature in Hawthorne's fiction, a male who openly champions matriarchy. In the early stages of the novel, Donatello responds to Miriam free from the determinant of conventional patriarchal kinship bonds. A throwback to an earlier matriarchal era, he somewhat resembles the feral boy of contemporary literature who relies on instinct and lives in harmony with nature. Not governed by the higher law of the state or the church and with no consciousness of an elevated moral purpose, he lives outside of dominant male cultural roles and has little awareness of the rules of social interaction.

Because gender roles are social constructs, he cannot understand them. He loves Miriam because of her essential nature, something almost biological, totally apart from her social role or self-presentation. As he explains, he loves her because "You are yourself, and I am Donatello" (4: 79). This is Hawthorne's version of the naive "Me Tarzan, you Jane" of the primitive as imagined in later popular culture. As a devoted follower of Miriam, Donatello is very "happy," a word used more often in this novel than in any other of Hawthorne's and most often to describe early Donatello (4: 79). But his commitment to his "Queen" Miriam causes him to murder the Monk who persecutes her. Donatello refers to the Monk as a "traitor," presumably because he believes his harassment of Miriam is a blow against the matriarchal order and his own act an assertion of loyalty to his queen (4: 172).

This version of the accused queen myth is the novel's foundation narrative, and while it recalls the happiness of the male and the vitality of the male–female bond in the matriarchal state, it also insists on the necessity, or perhaps inevitability, of moving beyond it. As he often does in his fiction, Hawthorne both invokes and revokes the matriarchal order. As the novel progresses, this order and those aligned with it are viewed as a complex subversive and disruptive force existing within the larger patriarchal system.

In keeping with this shift in perspective, Donatello's "faunness," originally celebrated as a force of naturalness, difference, unconventionality, and freedom, becomes feared and criticized because it defines him as an individual who forms a serious threat to the social consensus established by patriarchal norms. From this altered perspective, his killing is not an act of loyalty to his queen, defending her from a "traitor," but a destabilizing experience that requires "redression."[7]

Hawthorne centers the response to Donatello's deviant behavior in the novel's other male protagonist, Kenyon. Despite some early attraction to Miriam and the matriarchal, Kenyon aligns himself closely with the patriarchal system because it provides him with a meaningful cosmology of death and life. He has linked controlling Donatello to forestalling his own personal disintegration. Faced with the threat of the disruption of the established order, he becomes the primary agent of "redressive action." As the story evolves, he changes dramatically from a creative and expressive artist to a cultural enforcer who promotes the agenda of the status quo.

While Donatello's murder of the Monk is the catalyst for this change, Kenyon's response is not triggered solely by the murder; in fact, it is never completely clear throughout most of the novel that Kenyon actually knows Donatello has committed murder. Kenyon's "redressive action" is more focused on Donatello's relationship with Miriam.

Donatello's Journey of Acculturation

One of the reasons the novel tends to be read conservatively is that a significant portion of its central section could be considered a primer on how to maintain the status quo by educating the "feminized" deviant, the male who aligns with the matriarchy. Donatello and Kenyon represent two modes of being and seeing, two systems of meaning: the matriarchal and the patriarchal. Donatello's profession of love for Miriam because she is "herself" implies that he believes Miriam has her own subjectivity. Set against him is Kenyon, one of Hawthorne's conflicted males who values the powerful sensual woman—witness his sculpting of Cleopatra—but will marry the cultural ideal of womanhood, Hilda, an obedient "daughter of the Puritans" who copies the masters.

As he orchestrates Donatello's journey from his tower in Monte Beni, Kenyon has as his goal nothing less than a radical alteration of Donatello's ideas about women, and he intends to achieve it by indoctrinating him in the normative thinking and behavior of the white, educated, middle and upper class, Christian male culture of mid-nineteenth-century New England. As Kenyon understands it, the properly managed relationship between men and women must be established on a foundation compatible with the principles of Christian idealism, the philosophical base from which he operates. Under his tutelage, two closely linked solutions emerge to what Kenyon would see as the "problem" of women: idealism and sacrifice.

Educating Donatello to appreciate the wisdom of these solutions involves transforming him from materialist to idealist, from a faun-like being who stands "close...to Nature" (4: 83) to someone who has an Emersonian perspective and is capable of seeing "particular natural facts" as "symbols of particular spiritual facts," valuing spirit over nature.[8] When Donatello describes his tower as having a "weary staircase and dismal chambers, and it is very lonesome at the summit," Kenyon interprets it as an image of divine things: "with its difficult steps, and the dark prison-cells you speak of, your tower resembles the spiritual experience of many a sinful soul, which, nevertheless, may struggle upward into the pure air and light of Heaven, at last" (4: 253). At first, Donatello refuses to abandon his materialist perspective. When Donatello's question, "I wonder if the shrub teaches you any good lesson," is turned back to him by Kenyon, Donatello sullenly responds, "It teaches me nothing" (4: 259). But eventually he is influenced by Kenyon's way of thinking, accepting two principles, nature and spirit, body and soul, and agreeing with Kenyon's view that men must not be burdened by the "dead weight of our mortality" but follow the higher impulses of "immortal hopes" (4: 256).

Once Kenyon believes he has grounded Donatello in this philosophical base, he leads him from the tower to undertake his most significant lesson—the interpretation of Miriam and his relationship with her from this Christian idealist perspective. If he is successful in shaping Donatello's perception in this way, he will have altered the template of the heterosexual couple relationship. Initially, it was Miriam's nature that drew Donatello to her. Her voice, her art, and her body inspired his devotion to the material and the earthly—the sensual woman.

But after Donatello's journey with Kenyon, his ideas about her seem to undergo a drastic change. Just as he is no longer capable of enjoying nature for itself, instead looking beyond it for glimpses of "higher" truths, he passes over the material and physical aspects of Miriam. When Kenyon asks him if he recognized Miriam by the wayside, Donatello offers his first gendered assumption: "It was some penitent, perchance. May the Blessed Virgin be the more gracious to the poor soul, because she is a woman!" (299). The woman whom Donatello loved simply because "You are yourself" now exists for him as faceless penitent and symbol of fallen womanhood. Donatello's altered construction of Miriam is more in conformity with cultural norms, what the narrator of *The Scarlet Letter* described as the "long hereditary habit" that Hester believed would need to be "modified" before woman could assume "a fair and suitable position" in the social order (1: 165).

Marriage and "Frozen Passionateness"

That sacrifice and its companion suffering are Kenyon's second solution to Donatello's "eruption" becomes clearer in his direction of Miriam and Donatello's marriage ritual. The social purpose of this ceremony is more apparent when viewed in the context of Turner's thesis of "redressive action" and Kenyon's ideas about the connection between the strife of the couple and the condition of the state. Turner explains that after an "eruption" experience when legal redress fails, "groups may turn to activities which can be described as 'ritualized' whether these 'rituals' are expressly connected with religious beliefs or not."[9]

Under Kenyon's guidance, Donatello's journey culminates in his meeting with Miriam at the statue of Pope Julius, and, in a ceremony that resembles a marriage, Kenyon sanctions a union between them for pain and penitence, not "earthly bliss." Their "marriage" ritual is similar to "redressive ceremonies" whose purpose is to verify publicly that the "eruption" has indeed been put down and the deviant behavior "redressed."[10] Because the ceremony is directed by the conventional Kenyon and takes place in the presence of the statue of a pope, the achievement of this union of suffering and sacrifice is identified with the will of the patriarch and the social good.

This marriage emphasizes the importance of self-sacrifice and suffering in the heterosexual union, reconceptualizing these as marriage's primary purpose. From the Christian idealist's perspective, Donatello and Miriam's relationship must transcend ordinary human love. Erotic love must be refined and elevated, but in this novel love refined is a form of "frozen passionateness"—a bond of sympathy between them forged by "one identical guilt" (4: 282). Despite the unattractiveness of this kind of bond, the novel offers it as a culturally acceptable alternative to unions of mortal passion.

Kenyon believes that strife is at the core of the wrongly managed heterosexual relationship, and this lead to male contamination and unregeneracy, which, in turn, lead to death. Furthermore, this pattern is mirrored in the polis: the strife of the heterosexual couple relationship leads to contamination of the social order, which, if uncontained, would lead to its final rupture and "death." Kenyon's ideas anticipate sociologist and cultural anthropologist John Layard's theory of conflict and gender. Layard links wars to issues of kinship relationships and believes they are "fought almost entirely on questions involving the prestige of one group over against another, in order to maintain the existing order of society by wreaking vengeance on any who seek to disturb it. Now the order of society is based on kinship, and kinship in turn is based on regulations concerning the relations between the sexes." Beers takes Layard's thesis—"the immediate cause of almost all wars is a sexual one"—a step further by arguing that the social drama of war has a psychological basis. It originates in a fear of "matriliny" and a "fear of women."[11]

Kenyon seems particularly susceptible to this fear. From his perspective, eros is a symptom of a serious personal disorder in need of a cure before it becomes a social disease. The history of the tomb of Caecilia Metella, which the narrator mentions, reinforces this theory. The kind of love that inspires Caecilia Metella's husband to attempt to raise an eternal monument to his wife is dangerous, and only serves to make "This tomb of a woman...the nucleus of battles" (4: 420).[12]

Sacrifice and Apotheosis

Without safeguards in place to idealize erotic love, it is the snare standing in the way of the eternal life of the individual and the permanent order of the state. In the Christian tradition, sacrifice is the central transformative act. If Kenyon intends to undo death, he must find the means from within his social and political system to tap the apotheotic power of sacrifice.

The sacrifice and death of Jesus Christ won the redemption of the sinner and the assurance of eternal life. This sacrifice is commemorated on the altar in the Eucharist celebration. By participating in this ritual, Christians reanimate their faith and reconfirm their belief in the efficacy of sacrifice. In the communion ritual, the bread and wine on the altar represent into the body and blood of Christ, and Christians believe by partaking of this food they are demonstrating their place in the corpus dei, the body of Christ, the living Church. When they eat the bread and drink the wine, Christian believers are participating in life eternal.

Sacrifice figures prominently in Hawthorne's tales and novels, particularly in connection with women. But, while placing these acts at the center of his stories, Hawthorne raises questions about them. It is often difficult to understand their meaning and purpose. Beatrice takes the vial before Giovanni in "Rappaccini's Daughter," Georgianna allows herself to become the object of her husband's experiments in "The Birth-mark," and Hester stays in Boston for Dimmesdale's sake, but are these women noble or misguided? Hawthorne returns to this subject in *The Marble Faun* for a final exploration of the role of sacrifice in a patriarchal Christian culture, its relationship to the male's aspiration for transformation and transcendence, and its effect on the female subject's position.

While numerous tales, *The Scarlet Letter*, and *The House of the Seven Gables* trace the familiar pattern of women sacrificing for men, in this final novel Hawthorne complicates matters by creating a complex web of self-sacrificial acts. Donatello sacrifices for Miriam, Miriam for Donatello, Kenyon for Hilda, and Hilda for the old masters. Miriam and Donatello finally sacrifice their union for the union of Hilda and Kenyon. In this novel, Hawthorne raises these individual stories of sacrifice to the level of cultural dramas, playing them out against mythic and legendary models of self-sacrifice, thereby deepening the connection between sacrifice and apotheosis.

But in *The Marble Faun* sacrifice is associated with apotheotic transcendence in such a way that it forces an interrogation of the association. As a ritual that plays a crucial role in the culture's strategies of death denial, it should serve the immediate purposes of the community. But the novel explores what happens when the idea of sacrifice is turned on its head by regarding it from the perspective of the dead, those who sacrificed, and from the perspective of history. By highlighting the historical and personal context of sacrifice, *The Marble Faun* presents the women and men who are sacrificed both as models on which the male has based his hopes for immortality and as transient, time-bound, and perhaps even regretful and misguided victims.

In the first chapter, Donatello is compared to one of the most heroic self-sacrificing figures in the classical tradition—Antinous. When Miriam, Hilda, Kenyon, and Donatello wander through the picture gallery, they observe four antique sculptures, all more or less relevant to the novel's themes. One of these, the Antinous sculpting, depicts the beautiful young man who was the love of the Emperor Hadrian.

According to Anthon's version of the legend of Antinous, when Emperor Hadrian received word that he would die unless someone whom he loved was sacrificed, Antinous willingly drowned himself. After Antinous's death, Hadrian decreed that Antinous be immortalized. Temples were erected to him and a city was built in his honor. Many sculptings were created in his memory, and his image was emblazoned on coins. The cult that grew up around the worship of Antinous was suppressed after Hadrian's death and brought to an end in the Christian era.[13] Hawthorne was probably familiar with the story of Antinous from Anthon. He had a bust of Antinous in his ground-floor room when he lived in Lenox, and this might have made him curious to learn more about the subject. Also, when he saw the bust at the Capitoline Museum, the guides might have told him that it was discovered in Hadrian's tomb.[14] At the beginning of the novel, then, Antinous represents undiminished natural beauty, erotic love, and the nobility of the self-sacrificial act.

As the novel progresses, the meaning of Antinous's sacrifice is complicated by the novel's allusions to Hadrian's tomb. Hadrian's tomb provides the foundation for the Castle of Saint Angelo, the worst prison in Italian history where many who challenged the state's authority, including women and writers, were punished by the Emperor's decree.[15] Even Hilda understands the connection when she imagines St. Michael explaining to the Emperor Hadrian "that where a warlike despot is sown as the seed, a fortress and a prison are the only possible crop!" (4: 370). By reminding the reader of the link between Antinous, the Emperor Hadrian, and the Castle of Saint Angelo, the novel calls into question the value of Antinous's sacrifice because his noble gesture only preserved the "seed" of a corrupt and tyrannical social system that gave rise to the "crop" of decades of dreadful oppression.

The efficacy of sacrifice is a topic of debate in Hilda, Kenyon, and Miriam's conversation about Curtius, the legendary Roman hero. In an act reminiscent of Antinous's, Curtius sacrificed himself to ensure the survival of the Roman state when a group of elders explained that the huge chasm in the Forum would not close until Rome sacrificed what it valued most. While Hilda believes Curtius's sacrifice has "hallowed" this ground, Miriam and Kenyon are more skeptical. Miriam even asks, "Is there such blessed potency in bloodshed?" (4: 163). She withdraws the question quickly because she knows what Hilda's response will be and because she understands the question has serious implications, granted the centrality of sacrifice to the Christian faith of her companions. Christianity has built a redemptive eschatology on the "potency" of sacrifice.

The early Christian martyrs who died at the Coliseum had a special place in the Christian tradition. As types of Christ, these martyrs both recalled Christ's sacrifice and were living testimony to its continuing potency. By evoking Byron's description of the Coliseum at night in *Childe Harold's Pilgrimage*, Hawthorne complicates our response to this holy site and the acts performed there. In his poem, Byron uses the Coliseum to comment on the vicissitudes of time and adds comfortingly: "Oh, Time! the beautifier of the dead, / Adorner of the ruin, comforter / And only healer when the heart hath bled— / Time! the corrector where our judgments err" (Canto 4, stanza 130).[16]

But in *The Marble Faun*, time seems to be the great obliterator. It blurs the lines between opposing forces and threatens to erase moral distinctions, making the meaning of the sacrificial acts associated with the Coliseum almost impossible to determine. Kenyon's response to Hilda's confession of "delightful" pleasure on visiting the Coliseum points to the layers of meaning that an action accumulates over time (4: 156). Unlike T.S. Eliot's idea in "Tradition and the Individual Talent" that "the conscious present is an awareness of the past" greater than "the past's awareness of itself," the conversation between Hilda and Kenyon suggests the difficulty of grasping knowledge of the "conscious present."[17] Competing interpretive frames, in this case the aesthetic and the moral, lead to two different and conflicting readings of the events historically associated with the Coliseum. In response to Hilda's comment about its beauty, Kenyon raises the question of moral perspective as he wonders just how delightful a place those who suffered and died at the Coliseum thought it to be.

Has Hilda's judgment, then, been "corrected" by time or simply rendered more obtuse? Is it proper to "thank" the Emperor Vespasian for the architectural beauty of the Coliseum or condemn him for his bloody sacrifice of the Christian martyrs (4: 156)? Is the aesthetic or the moral response to the Coliseum more valid? This scene invites a reconsideration of the value of sacrifice when the purpose of the action has been forgotten or reinterpreted, when time does not "correct" but erases.

Because the ritual of sacrifice has a public or social purpose as well as a private dimension, the interpretation of the act is a crucial aspect of its meaning.[18] If there is no collective understanding of the meaning of the act, sacrifice has no potency.

Sacrifice and Idealized Love

The imperative of sacrifice also drives the way Hawthorne directs the relationship between the two couples in the novel. The ritual of sacrifice involves substituting an offering of less significant value for a more valuable offering to achieve a higher good. The plot of the novel's conclusion follows the logic of this process. To achieve the novel's happy ending, Donatello and Miriam's union must be sacrificed to ensure the reconciliation of the "higher" couple, Kenyon and Hilda. Donatello and Miriam acquiesce to this substitution because they accept that their relationship has not achieved the perfect state of idealization of that of Kenyon and Hilda.

Kenyon has crafted a relationship between himself and Hilda in the image of the idealized heterosexual union. To create this relationship involves stripping Hilda of any erotic attraction, thereby ensuring his love for her resides on the transcendent level. In the final stage of this process of idealization that transforms Hilda, a spunky and independent New England young woman, into an "unlosable" object, Kenyon refigures her as the resurrected, ideal Hilda who has returned from the heavenly kingdom.[19] During the "mysterious interval" when Hilda disappears for a time from her circle of friends, the narrator imagines that she has journeyed to a "Land of Pictures" where she sees the subject of art in a "better" guise (4: 452). In this transcendent realm, she sees what once "seemed a Woman's face" now transformed to become "divine" (4: 452). To see as Hilda does is to access a power even "higher" than that of the Transfiguration. By marrying Hilda, Kenyon gains access to a form of the Beatific Vision and reaffirms his belief in immortality.

When Kenyon finally encounters the transformed Hilda in one of the novel's final scenes, her pose is reminiscent of the icons of virgin Christian martyrs. As the subject of the public gaze in the carnival scene, she stands apart with an odd expression of pain intermingled with joy on her face. Hilda's expression and the glance of her eyes are similar to those depicted in the icons of the virgin martyr St. Cecelia, who had been mentioned earlier in the novel in connection with Hilda.

The story of St. Cecelia forms a commentary on the story of the novel's other Cecelia, Caecilia Metella. While Caecilia Metella's husband's love for his wife provokes his futile attempts to preserve her bodily remains, St. Cecelia's husband's spiritual love wins for him martyrdom and a heavenly reward. According to legend, when St. Cecelia is betrothed to a pagan, she insists that she will remain a virgin. Her exemplary piety convinces her betrothed to accept her decision and convert to Catholicism, and because of this decision both are martyred by the Romans. Thus, one Caecilia, linked with Miriam, is a source of discord. The other, linked with Hilda, is a force for Christian idealism so powerful that she can convert others to the logic of sacrifice.

But there are ominous undercurrents to this association that call the value of this sacrificial martyrdom into question. When the carnival spectators see Hilda, they throw their tribute of flowers, described as "sweets to the sweet" (4: 453), words which recall Gertrude's farewell to Ophelia in Shakespeare's *Hamlet*: "Sweets to the sweet. Farewell! / I hoped thou shouldst have been my Hamlet's wife, / I thought thy bride bed to have decked, sweet maid, / And not have strewed thy grave" (5.1.229–232).[20] Casting Hilda as a virgin martyr as well as a latter-day Ophelia further complicates the reader's response to this scene because it associates Kenyon's melancholy with Hamlet's and clearly intimates that the problematic union between Hilda and Kenyon, and the sacrifice of Donatello and Miriam for this union, may not bring the desired transformation of this mortal man of sadness.

While Kenyon does not make his decision for Hilda and "higher" or "unlosable" love until the final scene, the way he sculpted his Cleopatra anticipates his choice. This sculpture of Cleopatra has an extraordinary sensual power because Kenyon has an unusual ability, granted his New England middle-class background, to appreciate the erotic woman. Yet in comparing Kenyon's Cleopatra to William Story's sculpture of Cleopatra upon which it is based, we can see that Hawthorne altered one significant detail.[21] William Story's *Cleopatra* had a single breast bared, as if to indicate the accessibility of the female power apparent in the sculpting. There is no such detail in Kenyon's sculpture. He has transformed the erotic Cleopatra into a "magnificent" figure whose power is inaccessible. She is in "repose," seated and clothed (4: 126). From Kenyon's perspective, repose is the ideal state of the female subject. As an artistic term, "repose" suggests a harmony in arrangement; life "repositioned" or refashioned, in this case, by the hand and gaze of the male artist at work on his female subject. The beautiful array that he creates demands quiescence, a state resembling death. By sculpting Cleopatra with covered breasts, he keeps her fierce power concealed and contained.

Reburying Venus

> Venus was only a pretty girl! . . . [Psyche's] story expresses more than that of Venus. It tells not only the story of human love, but represents the pilgrimage of a soul.
>
> Fuller as reported by Dall

When Kenyon unearths the figure of Venus in one of the final scenes of the novel, he takes the measure of the torso of the sculpting and declares it a "rude object" (4: 423). He is relieved to find arms that will cover its private parts. Not until he contemplates the head of Venus does the fragment become "a beautiful Idea," and he begins to feel more comfortable with it (4: 423). Like some of the New England Transcendentalists who were present at Margaret Fuller's conversations on myth, he seems to prefer Psyche's story, representing "the pilgrimage of the soul," to the story of Venus and "human love."[22]

By reburying Venus, Kenyon foregoes the opportunity to acknowledge what she represents as a source of consolation for dying. Hawthorne would have known from Anthon's dictionary that Venus is a rare goddess who represents the procreative force of both the male and the female. The entry on Venus in Anthon's dictionary concludes that "her name is of both genders. Thus we meet with *Deus* and *Dea* Venus."[23] Geoffrey Grigson explains, "the name Venus has been a mystery: a word of neuter form which was feminine, or the name of a goddess which was perversely neuter."[24] Kenyon's discovery of Venus involves the recovery of a procreative force that is compatible with both genders. Venus was born out of the strife between the opposing principles of Gaia and Uranus, Earth and Sky, the original couple in classical mythology. In the version of her origin that Anthon favors, Venus springs forth from the foam in the sea that gathers around the severed genitals of Uranus, who has been mutilated by his son, Saturn, at the request of Gaia (Earth), the mother of Saturn and the mother-wife of Uranus.[25] Consequently, the myth presents the complex nature of Venus. She is a dynamic force that encompasses disharmony and harmony, revealing the procreative potential in this tension.

When Kenyon unearths the statue of Venus, he discovers a source of a union of "intimate equality" different from suffering and sacrifice (4: 283). His sculpting of Cleopatra reveals that he can understand and appreciate the value of this Venus. But, just as he chooses to cover the breast of his powerful Cleopatra, rather than recover Venus, he reburies her. This reburial is the crucial defining act of Kenyon's character.

Like several other Hawthorne males, he chooses what he believes to be the "higher" call of duty over women and immortal longings over mortal love. In the same scene where he discovers the statue of Venus, he is compared to Cadmus, the founder of Thebes who was led by a calf to the spot where the city would stand and where he slays a fierce dragon.[26] Kenyon replays Cadmus's role as founder in curious fashion. By unearthing Venus, he seems to be reaping the harvest of the "dragon's teeth" Cadmus was said to have planted. But because Kenyon fears the strife which is the seed of the harvest, he reburies Venus. His act reverses the birth order and denies the female as a principle of origin, instead reimagining her as a site of death. Kenyon must consign to dust once again the powerfully gendered being who could create the "warriors" who form the basis of a new society. Kenyon and his culture have lost access to this Venus.

With this reburial, Kenyon joins the ranks of Hawthorne's melancholy males. At this moment of crisis when he discovers Venus, he may be capable of recovering knowledge of the cause of his unhappiness. Speaking in Freudian terms, by unearthing Venus, he may be bringing to the surface, to the conscious level, the recognition of the source of his sadness, the loss of the female object. With this recovery, he has the potential to transform melancholy, caused by an unspecified loss, into mourning. But his reburial of Venus suggests something resembling a conscious act of repression. Kenyon both knows and chooses to dis-remember that Venus is the source of his loss. For this reason, he cannot progress. Because he is unable to mourn, Venus remains both a presence and an absence, a loss from which he can never recover.

Hawthorne deviates from the Western tradition of the male melancholic in the way he imagines Kenyon after the reburial. His melancholy does not provide him with a privileged position. It brings him neither new insight nor heightened artistic power. It carries with it only a deeper sense of lack, manifested as diminishment and failure.

From the perspective of the middle-class Christian system, recovering from a loss like Kenyon's involves not returning to the state of origin, union with woman, but reinventing the self as immune from loss, reinventing the self as immortal and perpetual. Kenyon must remain within the Christian system because it offers him the necessary consolation, even if this consolation does not mean happiness. Remaining within the circle of the system may not bring happiness, but it does bring a form of security, the stasis associated with abiding by the conventional norms and beliefs. Thus, with the reburial of Venus Hawthorne associates belief with melancholy and yet makes apparent that belief has its consolations. Kenyon believes because he would not at all be comfortable in his disbelief.

"Will You Share My Tomb with Me?"

Kenyon makes the higher choice for Hilda in keeping with the system of Christian idealization, but his "merry martyrdom" is only worthwhile if it is successful in transforming him (4: 445). In the last sections of this novel, Hawthorne brings together two alternative visions of male success: earthly finite happiness or the happiness of eternal life. Hawthorne makes the litmus test of Kenyon's decision one that is a staple in his fiction: Can this decision bring happiness and allow him to live "throughout the whole range of his faculties and sensibilities" or, if it makes him sad or melancholy, can it tap into such deep powers that it will eventually bring transformation and renewal (1: 40)? In either case, the test of the efficacy of sacrifice is whether it can dispel melancholy.

After Kenyon idealizes Hilda, however, he is left with only a deepened sense of melancholy. He feels lost and alone, longing for Hilda to bring him "home" (4: 461). Earlier in the novel in a conversation with Hilda, Kenyon self-mockingly imagined himself as the founder of a colony of the dead in the cathedrals of Rome. Kenyon envisions that, when a male lover of this colony wants to propose, he would invite his beloved to share a "nuptial home" with the question, "Will you share my tomb with me?" (4: 369).

The conflation of nuptial bed, tomb, and home provides a gloomy foreboding about the future of the heterosexual couple relationship. In this same conversation, Hilda chides Kenyon for his "ridicule" (4: 369) of her feelings about the sanctity of St. Peter's and other cathedrals, while agreeing with him that the "best thing" about St. Peter's is its "equable temperature" (4: 368). The "unchanging climate" that Kenyon wants to find in his marriage to Hilda is expressed in images of the tomb and death, and recalls his overarching desire to separate eros from disharmony or conflict (4: 369). To desire love of this kind is to choose to reside in the "unchanging climate" of the living dead, losing the will to become, achieving neither happiness nor permanence.

At the conclusion of the novel, Kenyon is haunted by the failure of his scheme of transcendence. In the carnival scene his visage is so grim he is compared to a "death's head at a banquet" (4: 445). Earlier in the novel, Kenyon warns Donatello of the dangers of keeping a death skull in his tower as a signifier of death, and in the novel's conclusion

Kenyon himself becomes this signifier. Like Shakespeare's Yorick in *Hamlet*, he reminds the revelers at the carnival "to what base uses we may return" (5.1.224), a comment that casts doubt on his entire scheme of apotheotic idealization.[27]

Ironically, the fiction Kenyon constructs to evade death as the annihilation of the self not only fails to perpetuate individuality but totally erases the individual. In his effort to "change the whole aspect of death," he has dissolved individuality, refashioning Miriam as a figure of self-sacrificing womanhood and Donatello as a type of the Christian repentant sinner (4: 256).

"Arches of Mortality"

The Marble Faun is a *memento mori* that drives home a point that a mid-nineteenth-century reader caught up in the fable of individualism might have found difficult to accept. The novel is not, as promised, about "four individuals" as much as it is about collective experience (4: 5). It studies the way individuals are acculturated to experience themselves from the perspective of their communal social identity, and it identifies the myths and rituals that the culture revises and puts into service to accomplish this important work.

To form a perspective on the idea of the existence of "four individuals" within the Christian patriarchal system, Hawthorne gathers together three of the four protagonists after the death of the Monk and brings them on a field trip to the Church of the Capuchin. In "The Burial Chaunt," the chapter that describes the mourning and burial ritual of the murdered Monk, Hawthorne presents an alternate view of death, one which asks his nineteenth-century reader to reflect on death's link to mortality, bodily corruption, and personal annihilation, not to the more culturally acceptable ideas of eternal life and individual transcendence.

In some of the early references to the Monk he is described as "Miriam's model" with a lower case "m," as if to announce that what he does and who he is are one and the same. What he does is represent the body or, more accurately, the body before it is transformed and reconceived by the culture, before artifice and civilization intervene. In death, he becomes the "Monk," a brother of the Capuchins, a religious order whose main office was attending the dead.

When Donatello sees the dead body of the Monk in the Church of the Capuchins, it is the centerpiece in a Christian ritual commemorating the dead. The scene is built around the tension between death as natural fact and death as cultural construction. The ritual power of the Roman Catholic Church is exercised to present the Monk's death as a transition to eternal life. His dress in the garb of the saintly man, the bier, the candles, and the intonation of the prescribed words of the "De Profundis" (and its promise of "eternal life") are intended to signify the promise of immortality.

And yet the ritual trappings may not be sufficiently powerful to offset a single detail—the blood coming from the Monk's nose, which announces the fact of bodily corruption. The sight of this body and blood fills Donatello with a sense of dread because it suggests defilement and the male's worst fear of personal dissolution. This fear intensifies in the next part of the scene when Donatello, Miriam, and Kenyon learn that the Monk will occupy his space in the burial ground only until another tenant needs it, and then his remains will become part of the altar of the Capuchins.

Philippe Ariès in *The Hour of Our Death* uses the Chapel of the Capuchins to illustrate one of the theses in his history of Western attitudes toward death.[28] According to Ariès's study primarily of French and Italian graveyards and cemeteries, before the eighteenth century most of the dead were buried in mass graves. Because of the lack of space in the graveyards, after a certain period of time, the bones of the dead were unearthed and placed in ossuaries to create room for the more recently dead. The Capuchin Chapel is one of the best known of these ossuaries and is referred to as a "decorative ossuary" because the bones have been fashioned into a work of art. In his history, Ariès describes a similar Capuchin Chapel located in Palermo: "Here the charnel is no longer merely a repository; it is a stage set in which the human bone lends itself to all the convulsions of baroque or rococo art. The skeleton is exhibited as a theatrical prop and itself becomes a spectacle."[29]

This ossuary and the practice of presenting remains of the dead as part of a work of art reflect another position on the spectrum of individuality-communality. As part of this "theater" of death, the dead body has "lost its individuality" and partakes in a "collective life."[30] In the altar arrangement of the Capuchins, the individual has become the property of the Church for the achievement of ritual art.

This arrangement provokes some serious and pointed reflections by the usually complacent narrator of *The Marble Faun*. The narrator notes the loss of identity that attends this burial arrangement: "On some of the skulls there are inscriptions, purporting that such a monk, who formerly made use of that particular head-piece, died on such a day and year; but vastly the greater number are piled up indistinguishably into the architectural design, like the many deaths that make up the one glory of a victory" (4: 193). There is a hint of irony in the reference to "one glory of a victory" achieved by anonymous artists working with "indistinguishable bones." Whose "victory" is it, then, when the individual is reckoned as part of a collectivity? The altar of the Capuchins bears witness to the power of the established authority to shape the individual identity, which parallels the ultimate power of death to annihilate the personal self. For the narrator this altar is a disturbing symbol of mortal limits: "There is no possibility of describing how ugly and grotesque is the effect, combined with a certain artistic merit; nor how much perverted ingenuity has been shown in this queer way; nor what a multitude of dead monks, through how many hundred years, must have contributed their bony frame-work to build up these great arches of mortality!" (4: 193). In this altar no remains are different from any other; individuality has been subsumed to the purpose of the system.

The Roman Catholic rituals of burial may be intended to symbolize that this monk's death is the passage to eternal life, but his remains and the altar of the Capuchins form "arches of *mortality*," not immortality. The narrator concludes: "But the cemetery of the Capuchins is no place to nourish celestial hopes; the soul sinks, forlorn and wretched, under all this burthen of dusty death.... Not here can we feel ourselves immortal, where the very altars, in these chapels of horrible consecration, are heaps of human bones!" (4: 194).

If the system cannot make it possible for those within it to "feel...immortal," then it is at risk. The test of a system's vitality is the consolations for dying it provides. That the Church's ritual fails so utterly to accomplish its purpose may be Hawthorne's way of signaling an important moment of historical transition—from the age of belief to the age of doubt. The novel has articulated a theory of historical movement that reaches from the heathen, matriarchal period, to the patriarchal Christian, to an alternative new society. This society is one of "individuals," friends who could live happy lives apart from the patriarchal kinship systems. But for this new society to succeed it must reconnect with a source of transformation so potent it could reanimate the dead body and resacralize death. It must revise its versions of consolations of dying.

CONCLUSION

In the final sections of the *Phaedo* when Plato described Socrates arguing for the immortality of the soul, he created a myth to make his thesis viable and compelling. He tapped the resources of these powerful narratives when the rhetoric of logic no longer served his purpose. And yet in the *Laws*, Plato linked myths to women and raised questions about the credibility of both: "Who can be calm when he is called upon to prove the existence of the Gods? Who can avoid hating and abhorring the men who are and have been the cause of this argument; I speak of those who will not believe the words which they have heard as babes and sucklings from their mothers and nurses, repeated by them both in jest and earnest." Are mythic tales sacred or profane? Do they express "primitive" prerational thinking or a higher logic? Are they sources of "jest" or "earnest" truth? Plato apparently understood that these stories, which he denigrates as coming with "the breast," were also potential agents of social change so powerful they needed to be controlled by the state.[1]

Hawthorne's contemporaries shared some of this same ambivalence about the nature and purpose of myth. While there was intense interest among intellectuals in classical mythology and in the question of how to interpret and use or "reinvent" the "old" stories, there was little agreement about whether America could create a new mythology and what form this new mythology would take. In "The Age of Fable," for example, Ralph Waldo Emerson wrote admiringly about several stories of Greek mythology, calling them "fine allegory conveying a wise and consistent sense."[2] He seemed to exempt classical stories from his interdiction in "The American Scholar" to avoid the "sere remains of foreign harvests," as if these stories existed in the realm of genius, the common property of any developing nation.[3] In one of Margaret Fuller's conversations, Emerson took the position that America could create its own mythology. Fuller disagreed with Emerson on this point, but had an avid interest in and led a series of subscription conversations on the topic of myth.[4] She felt strongly about the power of myth and, in the final conversation Dall transcribed, was reported to have half-jokingly confessed to an attachment to the old gods that rivaled that to the Christian deity: "when she was first old enough to think about Christianity, she cried out for her dear old Greek gods."[5]

Hawthorne was caught up in his contemporaries' interest in myth, although he was ambivalent about its value and purpose.[6] While he compiled *A Wonder Book for Girls and Boys*, one of the first collections of Greek and Roman classical myths in the English language retold for children, the relative scarcity of direct allusions to myths in three of his four novels might suggest an aesthetic or literary principle directing his decision to limit these references. There is little in the earlier novels that would have prepared Hawthorne's contemporaries for the proliferation of references to myth in *The Marble Faun*, references so extensive their inclusion might suggest he finally succumbed to the "Greekomania" or "mythomania" of his day.[7] Perhaps Hawthorne thought that because the novel was set in Rome myths had a relevance and immediacy they could not have had in a story with an American setting. Various locations throughout Rome are connected with gods and goddesses, and the myths of the divinities associated with these locales enhanced the sense of place.

During his stay in Italy, Hawthorne viewed an extensive number of paintings and sculptures dependent on classical myths for their subjects. Up until then, his exposure to art was largely confined to a few of Sophia's sketches and a limited number of copies and engravings he might have seen at the homes of friends and family, in the books and journals he borrowed from the Salem Athenaeum, and in the exhibits he viewed at the Boston Athenaeum and in London, Manchester, and Liverpool.[8] The masterworks he encountered in Italy seemed to have affected his imagination so strongly that, whatever his prior resolve, they found their way into his art.

But even though references to classical myths proliferate, they are fragmentary. Hawthorne provided the deeper structural unity in *The Marble Faun* with a "new" matriarchal myth. Like all myths that come with "the breast," it invites scrutiny of the patriarchal system. As he had done in *The Scarlet Letter* and *The Blithedale Romance*, Hawthorne connected this myth with a pre-textual time, an era when women were powerful and queenly, and used it to create an undercurrent of tension in his narrative.

The chapter "Myths" in *The Marble Faun* is unusual in Hawthorne's fiction because it provides glimpses of the human condition in the matriarchal era. Positioned at the novel's center, this chapter both evokes the memory of the beauty and happiness of the matriarchal order, linking this order to the state of nature, and tests its potential as a source of transformation.

In this chapter, Donatello tells Kenyon three myths. The first, which he mentions only briefly and in synopsis, is the story of a faun, a forefather of Donatello, who brought to Monte Beni a human maiden whom he loved. Donatello then immediately proceeds to a much fuller rendering of the story of another "progenitor," a "knight" who loved a "fountain-nymph" who had the power to renew and restore him with her kiss (4: 244–45). But when the "knight," Donatello's ancestor, attempts to wash a bloodstain from his hands, he loses forever the comfort of this nymph and spends the remainder of his life in mourning for her. Finally, Donatello tells a personal story of loss. He relates that at one time he enjoyed a communion with nature and was able to call forth from the forest small creatures and animals.

These myths of origin resemble the French "pourquoi" in the way that they explain why things are the way they are. They define the problem of human existence in a manner reminiscent of the philosophy of Ludwig Feuerbach, a radical thinker whose influential work *The Essence of Christianity* (1841) had been translated by George Eliot in 1854 and was causing a stir among intellectuals during the time Hawthorne was in England. From Feuerbach's perspective, because the human essence is material, real, and corporeal, humans can only find happiness in embracing and affirming the natural, "flesh and blood" self. When a human "isolates" himself from nature, either its "visible appearance, or its abstract essence," he becomes a glorious perversion. He assumes a power and importance he does not really possess because he has "convert[ed] himself from a part into the whole, into an absolute essence by himself." This "conversion," according to Feuerbach, is a diminishment because as an isolated "absolute essence" humans are miserable.[9]

Each of Donatello's myths revives the memory of what Feuerbach would describe as a symbiosis between man and nature and in doing so recalls longingly a splendid state of nature. Two of them link this original state with women. The Feuerbachian state of nature is similar to the "happy,...genial,...satisfactory" condition that Donatello enjoyed in the opening "matriarchal" section of the novel. In this wild and natural "faun" state, he existed "just on the verge of Nature, and yet within it" (4: 13). His loss of this original state brings Donatello significant pain.

In *Sexes and Genealogies*, Irigaray asks us to consider what our stories of origin tell us about ourselves. On the most basic level, the story of origin in the "Myths" chapter of *The Marble Faun* explains the reason male humans suffer. Like so many of the men in Hawthorne's fiction, Donatello is miserable and the myths reveal the source of his misery: his separation from women and nature, the matriarchal original state. More importantly, these myths also reveal why in Hawthorne's fiction males *choose* to suffer; why Donatello would choose to continue this separation, why he would, in effect, choose Kenyon's Christian idealism instead of nature and women. And they do so from a philosophical explanatory model remarkably close to Feuerbach's.

As Donatello concludes his narration of the myths, Kenyon asks him a crucial question, "What has happened to you?" and he replies simply, "Death, death!" (4: 249). The reality of death weighs heavily on him, and he desires to deny death by doing precisely what Feuerbach would deem a mistake: securing "the eternity of [his] subjective life."[10] To help him achieve this security, Kenyon instructs him in the principles of Christian idealism, which invests him with "supranaturalistic egoism."[11] In essence, he exchanges his relationship with nature and women to "feel...immortal" (4: 194).

One of the central issues for eighteenth-century mythographers was how to "reconcile the polytheism of ancient religions and their heterodox moralities with the beliefs of Christianity."[12] The chapter "Myths" takes a position on this older debate by revealing what issues are at its core. The ancient religions and Christianity are impossible to reconcile because they are different systems and determine in different ways the culture's construction of identity and the consolations of dying. The male's "choice" is not a simple one between happiness and matriarchy, the materialist "heathen" position, as Feuerbach calls it, or misery and patriarchy, the Christian idealist position. The choice is between forms of consolation and kinds of "potencies," between two possible perspectives on death: the "heathen" or the Christian. Nature and women, "the heathen," will not bring the assurance of an everlasting self. With its indifferent confirmation of generative powers, nature is no place to feed man's immortal aspirations. These myths offer no possibility of transformation that could free men from the fact of the finality of the body's corruption; if anything, they may only heighten awareness of the natural certainty of death. They provide inadequate consolation for dying for nineteenth-century males who have been acculturated to believe in the "eternity of their subjective life."[13]

At the same time, the novel also places in doubt the potency of the Christian answer to death. According to Friedrich W.J. Schelling, a philosopher popular with the Romantic idealists whose position seems almost antithetical to Feuerbach's, the problem of "death, death" is answered by moving through increasingly higher levels of consciousness until human beings achieve a sense of their existence within the divine unity. The consolation of eternal life is based on the assumption that man was "created at the center of this Godhead," and "it is essential for him to remain in that center." To extend his subjectivity into eternity and achieve the final "potency," a Christian idealist must barter his relationship with nature and woman for the higher system of Christianity, his culture's primary form of participating in the "divine unity."[14]

For Hawthorne's predominately Christian readers, the final "potency" and answer to "death, death" were, of course, centered in Jesus Christ. *The Marble Faun*, however, does not rely on the myth of Christ to counter the male's annihilationist fears. In a novel that has so many allusions to Christian art, the absence of references to depictions of Christ suffering is more than puzzling. For readers who are awaiting the coming of the image of Christ suffering to resolve the questions that the novel raises about the efficacy of sacrifice, the reference in Chapter Thirty-Seven to Sodoma's fresco at Siena of Christ bound to a pillar may be somewhat of a letdown. The narrator is tempered in his response to the fresco. While acknowledging the power of this kind of painting, he admits there are few who can appreciate it fully and almost no artist capable of expressing the truth embodied in a complex subject like the scourged Christ. "The Emptiness of Picture-Galleries," the title of the chapter in which the fresco of Sodoma's Christ appears, emphasizes the failing powers of this image of Christ to reconcile the "incongruity" of Christ's two natures, the human and the divine.

Sacrifice has an important performance element; it must create an effect. The presence of this fresco of the suffering Christ, a potentially powerful image, in the midst of a chapter set in the "vast, solitary saloons" of Rome "drearier than the white-washed wall of a prison corridor" (4: 341) and full of "emptiness" undermines the power of the Christian myth to transform (4: 333). The narrator concludes by admitting that the "potency" of Christian art "has no such effect" (4: 340). Like the body of the dead Monk in the ritual performance of death, the fresco of Sodoma's Christ reiterates that sacrifice without transformation is a merely human act; a symptom of loss, not of recovery from loss.

Matriarchy and Race: A Problem

In the chapter "Myths," Hawthorne seems to be asking his readers to ponder the question of human happiness and the human condition from a philosophical perspective. It is in sections of the novel like this chapter that Melville's assessment of Hawthorne in "Hawthorne and His Mosses" as a seeker of absolute truth who asks the metaphysical questions that can lead readers to a "rapt height" seems most valid.[15] But what Richard Brodhead says of Melville is also true of Hawthorne. At the same time that he is asking questions about universal truth, he "eventually gives in to the impulse to look over his shoulder and see how it squares with the texture of actual life."[16] In *The Marble Faun*, this "texture of actual life" includes the idea of race.

Recent critical efforts to revive the "actual" or "real" Hawthorne have focused extensively on the issues of slavery and race.[17] Assuming it would be nearly impossible for a thinking moral man of nineteenth-century New England not to be focused on the central social problem of his day, some argue that underlying the preoccupation with the problem of existential enslavement to despotic authority, in a novel like *The Scarlet Letter*, is an exploration of the particular condition of American chattel slavery. In these readings, Hester's "chain" of connection to her society and Pearl's "mixed" moods make them types of slaves, while the "black man" in the forest and "darkness" or the "blackness" of sin become markers or metaphors for racial difference.

But if there is a concern for slavery in this early novel, unlike the question of gender which is closer to the novel's surface, it is more latent and suppressed, as the issue was for the many in the North in the 1830s and even into the late 1840s. Hawthorne rarely expressed his views on the subject, although when he did his position was decidedly antislavery. He shared with many of his contemporaries, including Emerson, Thoreau, and Fuller, what in the 1830s and 1840s was still considered the moderate position that slavery was an evil that, in time, would disappear. But, unlike theirs, his position changed little as time passed.[18] As late as 1851, when others in New England were aroused to action by the Fugitive Slave Law, he was still somewhat puzzled at the extent of their moral outrage on the subject and wrote, "There are a hundred modes of philanthropy in which I could blaze with intenser zeals. This Fugitive Law is the only thing that could have blown me into any respectable degree of warmth on this great subject of the day—*if it really be the great subject*—a point which another age can determine better than ours."[19] Also, although Hawthorne was antislavery, he was not pro-abolitionism and, in fact, was highly critical of many of the abolitionists. He shared many of the racist attitudes of his contemporaries and, according to Jean Fagan Yellin, might even have been uncertain of the "full humanity of blacks."[20] Perhaps, these perceptions affected his references to blacks in his first three novels. They are virtually absent from these narratives and, when present, play supporting roles in the drama of white middle-class lives. While there might be unconscious adumbrations of the issues of slavery and race relations in the early novels, he does not grant them "direct recognition."[21]

He approached this "direct recognition" in *The Marble Faun*. The reference to the possibility of "one burning drop of African blood" in Miriam's veins brings racism directly into the discourse of the novel (4: 23). Donatello's "faunness," which links him to a primitive and "heathen" era, also hints at racial difference. In his essay "Chiefly about War-matters. By a Peaceable Man," published in 1862 in the *Atlantic Monthly*, Hawthorne connects fauns and slaves overtly when he characterizes the fugitive slaves he sees emerging from the "mysterious depths" of a Virginia forest as "akin to the fauns"; they share with Donatello a "primeval simplicity" and a quality "not altogether human" (23: 419–20). With these allusions, Hawthorne desegregates his usual central cast of four white characters and confounds the problem of gender with the problem of race.

Perhaps it is the heightened conflict in America that is bringing race to the forefront of Hawthorne's consciousness, although, as puzzling as it may seem from our perspective, it may have taken a trip to Europe in the 1850s for him to have been moved to include mixed race individuals as central protagonists in his fiction. Several New England intellectuals had their sympathies fully aroused to the injustices of the institution of slavery and the cause of abolition only when they saw the institution mirrored back to them in the patriarchal despotism of Italy of the 1840s.[22] Being themselves "strangers in a strange land" may have altered their perspective on what even Thoreau in *Walden* characterized as the "somewhat *foreign* form of servitude called Negro Slavery."[23] Intellectuals like Oliver Wendell Holmes and James Russell Lowell began to associate the despotic authority of Italy with the system of slavery and recognized that this system was destroying American democracy.[24] The most articulate of these was Fuller, who in her dispatches from Italy drew the clear connection between the two causes: "I listen to the same arguments against the emancipation of Italy, that are used against the emancipation of our blacks."[25] Against the backdrop of Romish tyranny, she saw more starkly revealed the unfulfilled promise of America, "spoiled by prosperity..., soiled by crime in its willing perpetuation of Slavery, shamed by an unjust war."[26]

The "System" of Slavery

Returning to the word "system" that supplied Hawthorne with a key organizing idea of his novel, it becomes more apparent that for many of his contemporaries one particular association with the word would have been uppermost in their minds: the "system" of slavery. The word "system" appeared frequently in public discussion of American chattel slavery and was almost synonymous with the institution itself. By the 1830s and 1840s, "system" began to appear with regularity in articles in Southern agricultural journals to refer to a complement of practices and behaviors that would ensure the profitable management of the slave population.[27] One slave owner commented in a letter, "No more beautiful picture of human society can be drawn than a well organized plantation.... A regular and systematic plan or operation on the plantation is greatly promotive of easy government. Have, therefore, all matters as far as possible reduced to a system."[28] "Reduce everything to a system," originally a directive to manage the slave population, became a practicing motto of the Southern plantation "perfect society," a system that included both masters and slaves.[29]

Central to the management and perpetuation of the slave system were power and the structure of dominance and submission in social networks this power promoted. In *Narrative of the Life*, Frederick Douglass exposed the ways in which slavery spun out a "whole system of fraud and inhumanity" designed to manage every aspect of the life of the slaves and deny them an identity and status.[30] He understood that this dynamic of "irresponsible power" affected both slaves and masters, and extended into the polis.[31] In his speech "Northern Ballots and the Election of 1852: An Address Delivered in Ithaca, New York, on 14 October, 1852," Douglass refers to the political threat of "slave power" and brings to this term, used primarily by Northern republicans to characterize the power of the slaveholding class, a special understanding of the nature of the power dynamic.[32] Southern "slave power" was generally represented as patriarchal, aristocratic, arbitrary, despotic, alien, and conspiratorial; it was, in short, totally antithetical to the values that the North associated with American republicanism.[33] In his speech, Douglass notes these qualities and emphasizes as well the way in which power works to extend its corrupting influence.

Voracious in its appetite for new conquests, it operates on the principle of expansion to ensure perpetuation. According to Douglass, "It [slave power] needs endless, limitless fields over which to pour its poisonous and blasting influence."[34] While the present system claimed slaves as its victims, if it was not destroyed, "slave power" would extend into the North and destroy the liberties of all.

The language and descriptors used in *The Marble Faun* to characterize the system of the Roman church and state are similar to those used by Douglass for the system of slavery and its corollary "slave power." The system is "arbitrary" (4: 264), "corrupt" (4: 375, 387), and "despotic" (4: 456, 465); the Italian revolutionaries did not weaken it but perhaps only forced it to become more covert. Its hierarchical structure seldom works in favor of the individual. Innocent Hilda's detainment in the Convent of the Sacre Coeur illustrates well that in this system individual rights are totally subordinated to the preservation of patriarchal authority.

Hawthorne relies on the image of Miriam enchained to explore the full effects of this system on the individual. In one of the novel's early scenes, when Kenyon sees Miriam and the Monk together—he standing, she kneeling nearby—he describes them this way: "Marvellous it was, to see the hopelessness with which—being naturally of so courageous a spirit—she resigned herself to the thraldom in which he held her. That iron chain, of which some of the massive links were round her feminine waist, and the others in his ruthless hand…must have been forged in some such unhallowed furnace as is only kindled by evil passions and fed by evil deeds" (4: 93).

To construct this scene, Hawthorne drew from the pictorial tradition of the female captive, a popular image of woman in the mid-nineteenth century.[35] Miriam's terrible "thraldom" is reminiscent of the attitude of Harriet Hosmer's sculpting of Zenobia, the clay version of which Hawthorne had seen in Hosmer's studio in March of 1859.[36] Many of Hawthorne's contemporaries would have identified this group of sculptures as a class that included subjects that crossed various racial lines. Although the poses and attitudes of the subject are determined, at least to some extent, by race, the subject's suffering and vulnerability remain a constant.[37] In this tradition, women are depicted as both captive slaves and accused queens whose power is restrained. Miriam is described as "fettered and shackled more cruelly than any captive queen of yore, following in an Emperour's triumph" (4: 108).

Hawthorne's description of enchained Miriam differs from Hosmer's sculpture of Zenobia in at least one important detail. Her Zenobia is presented as "grasping it [her chain] with 'impatience,' gathering it up in her left hand while letting her right hang down under its weight."[38] Miriam submits to the massive chain about her waist that the Model holds, but, despite her apparent submission, this relationship creates resistance and resentment. The Monk exerts a terrible power over Miriam, and her "thraldom" inspires hatred and breeds ongoing strife.

With this scene in *The Marble Faun*, Hawthorne has written himself into a difficult place. He has linked women with slaves, a connection he may have hinted at in other novels when, for example, in *The Blithedale Romance* Priscilla is described as a "bond-slave" to Hollingsworth or Hollingsworth says he would "scourge" and drive back into their place women who challenge men, but he had not made the association explicit (3: 55, 123). With Miriam's "drop of African blood," slavery is connected with race, thereby shifting slavery itself from the realm of the metaphysical into the vexed arena of contemporary social and political issues surrounding the system of American chattel slavery (4: 23). Also, he has identified the destructive pattern of dominance and submission at the system's core and the dynamic that ensures its perpetuation. Finally, he has linked violence against oppressed women and slaves with a representative of Christianity. In aligning the pattern of dominance and submission in the system of slavery with that of patriarchal Christianity, however, he has made it more difficult to resolve the problems of race, gender, and slavery that he has raised in a way that would resonate with his Christian readers.

Reformation and the "System"

The Marble Faun evokes the issue of slavery and despotism and evades it or, at least, evades answering what was to be done about it and the conflict it promised to bring. Hawthorne seems to have anticipated his deferral of a resolution simply by setting his novel in the time period in which he did: after the fall of the Roman republic, after the hopes for the overthrow of the "Papal despotism" had faded (4: 109). Although this novel tells the story of Donatello's revolutionary defiance against probably one of the most widely recognized literary symbols of patriarchal abuse, a monk, and his initial alignment with the new matriarchal order, ultimately Hawthorne frames Donatello and Miriam's story as one of loss, strife, and suffering without recuperation. Fuller's dispatches from Italy are brimming with hope for a new social order both for Italy and by extension for all parts of the world, including

America, where despotic patriarchs hold sway. She envisions the decaying body of America reanimated, while Hawthorne, relying on the same metaphor to characterize the Roman body politic—"the dead corpse of a giant"—leaves it dead (4: 110).[39]

The basis for Fuller's hope is similar to Harriet Beecher Stowe's in *Uncle Tom's Cabin*—Christianity. In one of her Italian dispatches, she wrote, "As in the time of Jesus, the multitude has been long enslaved beneath a cumbrous ritual," and Jesus has the power to break the chains of the enslaved and raise the dead, transforming the body politic.[40] Jeffrey Steele explains that "The corrupt social body she [Margaret Fuller] diagnosed in New York is now dead and buried, waiting (like the entombed Christ) the moment of resurrection."[41] The degenerate patriarchal order can be transformed through the evocation of the suffering and death of Jesus Christ. In *Uncle Tom's Cabin*, Stowe was extraordinarily successful in tapping into the redemptive force of the suffering of Jesus Christ to answer the problem of slavery. The forces of white, despotic "slave power" are put down by the suffering and sacrifice of Uncle Tom. As we have seen, *The Marble Faun* alludes to many sacrificial victims and Christ figures, but they cannot enkindle hearts, minds, or wills, as Uncle Tom does in the novel's concluding scene when, as he is whipped by Simon Legree, he recalls Christ scourged, submitting to his suffering, forgiving his oppressors, educating the good thief, and finally dying and going home to his heavenly father. Hawthorne's wariness of patriarchal Christianity and religious zealotry may have caused him to write a novel that thwarts sympathy and blocks apotheosis, leaving his Christ scourged as the god that failed.

The Marble Faun presents Christianity as a source of the problem, not as its answer, and the reason for this is at least twofold: Christianity is a patriarchal religion with an authoritarian structure and it is a sacrificial religion.[42] Hawthorne was certainly not the first American writer to expose the vexed relationship between slavery, authority, and Christianity. In *Narrative of the Life*, for example, Douglass stated unequivocally: "For of all slaveholders with whom I have ever met, religious slaveholders are the worst."[43] These slaveholders are particularly dangerous because they believe it is their prerogative to replicate in the slave system they control the structure of dominance and submission that is inherent to patriarchal Christianity. As fathers, they sacrifice their slave victims for their own aggrandizement, essentially to extend their power.

But while Douglass in *Narrative of the Life* could work through the dilemma of writing a slave narrative that criticized the religion of his primary audience by identifying and recovering two Christianities, the "Christianity of this land," a fallen and depraved form that feeds on brutal power and domination, and the benevolent "Christianity of Christ," Hawthorne can imagine only one Christianity.[44] The Christianity of *The Marble Faun* follows Douglass's model of the "Christianity of this land" in its willingness to dominate and "sacrifice, but seldom to show mercy."[45]

When Hawthorne draws distinctions between religions, as he does at the conclusion of *The Marble Faun*, it is not between two Christianities but between two markedly distinct religious systems: the patriarchal Christian and the matriarchal "heathen" (4: 456). In a single page of the novel's final scene, he returns to this novel's usual associations with Christianity: "despotic government," "power," "secrecy," "barbarism," and "inscrutable tyranny" (4: 456). But the alternative heathen matriarchal system is certainly not viable, nor can it be the source of the "qualitative leap" that could bring change.[46] Associated in this final scene with nature, sunlight, animals, and Miriam, "heathenism" is radically "unlike" Christian "civilization" but still no better able to form the basis of a new social order (4: 457). Just as it was imagined in the chapter "Myths," this heathen or primitive matriarchal era, linked in this novel to "faunness" and ambiguous racial identity, is in the past and unrecoverable. At base, there is no way either can affect transformation and answer the problem of slavery.

Twin Legacies

In "Chiefly about War-matters. By a Peaceable Man," Hawthorne describes the Mayflower as a "fated womb" that sent forth into the new world twin offspring: "a brood of Pilgrims upon Plymouth Rock" and "Slaves upon the southern soil" (23: 420). Just as in *Moby-Dick* Ishmael and Queequeg are joined by the "Siamese ligature" of the monkey-rope for "better or worse," the "kindred" bond created by this birth from the mother Mayflower joins the fates of black and white, "even at the cost of blood and ruin" (23: 420).[47] This twin legacy is the logical extension of the system's dynamic, as Hawthorne understood it. Because the system cannot be transformed, it simply perpetuates itself in the same patterns of dominance and submission, creating diametrically opposed forces. The Mayflower's twin legacy was its curse, producing two offspring in conflict, one doomed to be subordinate to the other, united yet divided.

The two couples, Miriam and Donatello, Kenyon and Hilda, resemble the twin legacies of the Mayflower. Originally of equal status, "four individuals," they meet quite different fates (4: 5). Around his white New England couple, Kenyon and Hilda, Hawthorne plots a love story that concludes in a union, while Miriam and Donatello are classic star-crossed lovers doomed to separation. More to the point, the reunion of Kenyon and Hilda seems contingent upon the misery of Miriam and Donatello, as if one couple has been sacrificed for the other. Hawthorne reiterates this pattern in the "Postscript" in which he imagines that he is simply deferring to Kenyon and Hilda's superior knowledge of his story. It is as if his master couple is writing the final draft of the history of Miriam and Donatello, in effect controlling their fate from a privileged position "remote in the upper air" at the "top of St. Peter's," a position resembling *sub specie aeternitate* (4: 464).

The novel's original final chapter emphasizes the different status of the two couples. While its title is "Miriam, Hilda, Kenyon, and Donatello," the four are no longer "together," as they were described earlier in the novel (4: 24). The chapter's focus is on Hilda and Kenyon and how they see or, more precisely, cannot see Miriam. To them, she is "invisible" (4: 459). In this scene, she is granted no subjectivity and hence no power to challenge Hilda's final assessment that she simply "cannot be" (4: 459). Donatello's status is equally troubling. He is literally "invisible," absent from this final scene and reduced to a question: "And where was Donatello?" (4: 462).

This question is significant because it reminds us that by the novel's conclusion both Miriam and Donatello have no place and no social claim.[48] In Kenyon and Hilda's perception of them the distinctions between the living and the dead blur. It is as if they have suffered a "social death" similar to what Orlando Patterson describes as the condition of "natal alienation" endured by the enslaved.[49] Miriam is a wanderer with no right to any homeland or, at least, not to Kenyon and Hilda's America, since when they see her in the Pantheon, they "suffered her to glide out of the portal," as if this portal marked the boundaries of their natal space (4: 461). The differences between them are perceived as so vast that she is on "the other side of a fathomless abyss" (4: 461). Donatello's status as "natally alienated" is perhaps more puzzling because, unlike Miriam who had a complex and ambiguous national and racial history, Donatello is an Italian. It is almost as if what defines him by the novel's conclusion is some primitive natural essence associated with his "faunness," a racial difference that trumps nationality. Despite his acculturation by Kenyon and his seeming "improvement," he is still a faun and as such a danger to the social order. He too cannot claim the social rights of a homeland and, like Miriam, must be kept at a distance in a separate, but unequal, space.

The uncertain prospects and subordinate status of Miriam and Donatello in the novel's conclusion presage the future Hawthorne imagined for the freed slaves in "Chiefly about War-matters. By a Peaceable Man." Their fate may be exclusion. When he sees a band of faun-like slaves coming from the forest and characterizes them as a "token of a social system thoroughly disturbed," he states that he feels "most kindly" toward the slaves but also wonders whether there is a place for them in his homeland, which he describes from the slave's perspective as a "stranger's land" (23: 419, 420). He admits he "knew not precisely what to wish in their behalf" because a "wish" implies the promise of a future and these freed slaves, like Miriam and Donatello, seem to have no prospects. As strangers in a "stranger's land," they reside in the space of difference, something resembling the land Hawthorne imagines at the end of *The Marble Faun* as "between two countries," whose inhabitants endure the status of "none at all" (4: 461). It is a state resembling death, and Hawthorne connects it with the "little space" of the grave (4: 461).

Early in the novel, on one of the two couples' first "rambles" in Rome, Hilda, Miriam, Kenyon, and Donatello have a conversation that brings together some of the novel's central issues. As they regard the Trevi Fountain, Kenyon imagines that, if he were given a commission to carve the "one-and-thirty...sister-States," he would have them pouring water into a basin that represents the "grand reservoir of national prosperity" (4: 146). But an English observer responds wryly to Kenyon's comment: "you could set those same one-and-thirty States to cleansing the national flag of any stains it may have incurred" (4: 146). Since the thirty-first state in the union was California, one of the states gained from the Mexican War, Hawthorne, as Fuller had in her dispatches, might be referring to the national stain associated with this combat.

No one responds directly to the Englishman's controversial comment, but as the conversation rambles on it becomes more apparent that this comment about the blood on the flag has gone underground to determine the thematic flow of their subsequent observations. Miriam mentions Corinne, Madame de Stael's heroine associated with Italy and women's emancipation, and she further complicates this allusion by linking it with race. Staring into the fountain in a gesture imitative of Corinne, Miriam sees the image of herself, Donatello, and the Monk as three "separate shadows, all so black," intertwined as they lie on the bottom of the basin, "as if all three were drowned together," regardless of their differing roles as oppressor or oppressed (4: 147). This trinity of unhealthy relationship is identified as the source of the disease of the "sickly" Roman body polis, and the dust and decay accumulating over it are the soil over the grave (4: 149). Buried in this soil is the ruin of past monuments, including the Emperor Trajan's Forum, and these ruins form a stepping-stone for Miriam, Hilda, and Kenyon's comments that link problems of women and gender with questions about human transiency and the ethics of immortality strategies.

At this point, the four talk directly about a central issue of this novel: What is the cost of feeding immortal hopes? How much suffering can be weighed in the balance to sustain the possibility of eternal self? In Emperor Trajan's case his immortality strategy was constructed on the "base" of "bloody warfare" (4: 151). Miriam sees no consolation in the ruins of Trajan and instead defines the only consolation as recognizing and accepting mortality. She asks the group to consider: "would you sacrifice this greatest mortal consolation, which we derive from the transitoriness of all things—from the right of saying, in every conjuncture, 'This, too, will pass away'...!" (4: 150). But there are those in Rome who value permanence. In the background are the voices of those who remember the glory of Trajan and call him from the dead to contemplate his grand monument to immortal hopes. But Kenyon understands that the Emperor would receive no consolation from viewing his monument because, if called back, he would view it from a different perspective, one resembling *sub specie mortis*. From the perspective of the grave, he would understand that the "bloody warfare" and sacrifice enacted to achieve it are "but an ugly spectacle for his ghostly eyes" (4: 151). In this scene, Hawthorne imagines Kenyon understanding what he spends the rest of the novel trying to forget: the ethical imperative of immortality strategies. The immorality of feeding immortal longings with sacrifice, blood, and strife is not preached from the pulpit but forms the texts of, what Hilda characterizes as, "sermons in stones" (4: 151).

Coda: The Death of the "Cultural Structure of a Lifetime"

In 1948 the psychoanalyst Heinz Kohut wrote an analysis of Thomas Mann's novel *Death in Venice* that explains its psychological dynamic from the perspective of narcissism, sublimation, and repression. According to

Kohut, *Death in Venice* originated in the conflicts Mann experienced because of living in the repressive bourgeois society of Germany. When Mann wrote *Death in Venice*, he was at a time of crisis. His sister had committed suicide, and his wife had been hospitalized with tuberculosis. Mann feared the loss of his creative powers and the disintegration of the self he thought might come with his loss. Despite the fact that he was living a conventional middle-class existence as a husband and father of several children, his sublimated desires—particularly his latent homoerotic tendencies—created "profound conflicts" that he expressed in the condition of his central protagonist, Ascenbach, an artist and writer. In *Death in Venice*, Ascenbach longs for a forbidden relationship with the child Tadzio even though he knows it will destroy him, because he desires the renewal and revitalization he associates with it. He has idealized the relationship and thereby voided it of any erotic content, perceiving it as a necessary antidote to his stultifying and deadly bourgeois existence.[50]

Kohut theorized that Mann's creation of Ascenbach and his crisis suggested he was in danger of bringing from the preconscious or unconscious to the conscious level his own repressed desires and fantasies. Mann was beginning to recognize the way in which management of these desires was connected with death, repetition, and loss of creative power. Since, from Kohut's perspective, two processes are crucial for a writer's success, sublimating his own desires and idealizing, the struggles of Ascenbach mirror Mann's. To die in Venice, then, means not to lose access to knowledge of the self but to gain access to this sublimated knowledge, an access that means the death of the artist.

A more appropriate title for Hawthorne's final novel might have been "Death in Rome" because this novel deals with some of the same questions of repression and desire that form the center of Mann's novel. Like Ascenbach, Kenyon seems deeply divided, both drawn to conventional middle-class life and values and repelled by them, just as he is both drawn to and repelled by Donatello and Miriam. One part of Kenyon enforces the culture's work of inhibition and exclusion on the two, and another loves them and wishes them to unite "forever" (4: 323).

Like Mann, Hawthorne was at a point of crisis when he wrote this final novel. His daughter Una's recent serious illness may have awakened his memories of his mother's death and the intense annihilationist anxiety he experienced at the time. For someone who did not seem to adjust particularly well to change, completing his tenure as U.S. Consul in Liverpool and returning to America to uncertain prospects and a tense social and political climate could have threatened his sense of self. He had not written a novel in several years, and his journal entries suggest he was having more difficulty than usual making good progress on *The Marble Faun*.

Kohut might also see in Hawthorne's family background the basis for unresolved gender identity issues. He evidenced what Kohut defined as one of the artistic personality's primary characteristics, "identification with the mother and ambivalently passive attitude toward the father."[51] Since Kohut believed that the attachment to the mother is "more strongly repressed and seems to evoke even deeper guilt than the ambivalent attitude toward the father,"[52] he would probably consider it particularly revealing that when Hawthorne published *A Wonder Book for Girls and Boys* he chose as the myth of origin the story of Perseus and included in his version the important opening event: Perseus and his mother's journey on the sea to escape the tyrannical father. The mother in the myth is the daughter of a king—thus the prototype of the accused queens in Hawthorne's fiction—although the identity of the accuser and the nature of the accusation are suppressed from this version of the myth.

Following Kohut's lead, if we were to read Hawthorne's final novel's pivotal act, Kenyon's reburial of Venus, from the perspective of what the scene may suggest about the emotional life of its creator, it becomes particularly complex. When Hawthorne has Kenyon rebury Venus, he has brought both himself and his male protagonist to a crossroads. Reburying Venus might protect Kenyon from the emotional turmoil and dissolution of the kind that Ascenbach suffered, but what did imagining this scene accomplish for Hawthorne? Perhaps being able to write this scene suggests that Hawthorne was beginning to understand the dynamic of repression, including the way acts of repression are necessary if we are to be able to continue to live successfully within our culture's systems of meaning. Not to rebury and to be aware of the significance of not doing so would mean suffering what Kohut described as the loss of the "whole cultural structure of a lifetime," a loss that could spell the disintegration of the self.[53] Being disconnected from the moorings of the cultural system, particularly its means and measures to answer death and write the fiction of a perpetual self, would make fierce demands on the writer's resources to construct meaning. It would necessitate doing more than putting out a call to mourning; it would require that the author structure a new system and inhabit it.

Perhaps for this reason Hawthorne's self-presentation is somewhat different in this last novel. Hawthorne intrudes in a way that asks we focus more directly on him and his quest for permanence. The metaphor of veiling the Hawthorne reader is accustomed to honoring in the reader-writer relationship gives way to the metaphor of "peeping" as the author begins to insinuate himself more aggressively and perhaps even a bit perversely into the text. There is a curious joking quality to some of his self-references; for example, when Hawthorne is talking about what makes New England better than Rome, he speaks of mosses. The faithful little band of Hawthorne readers, as he refers to them in the preface, cannot help but think this clever allusion is an insider reference to his earlier collection. Characteristically, though, Hawthorne accompanies this compliment with a slight, reminding his readers of their mortality and his prospects for immortality. He grows increasingly distant from them and ironical, as he promises he will outlast them, becoming the moss on their grave.

In the novel's "Postscript," Hawthorne professes to take as proof of his novel's "failure" the fact that he had to add this section. But the new conclusion did little to change the mixed reviews readers and critics gave the book, and even today, when readers do not agree with Hawthorne's own estimation, the novel is usually regarded as, at best, a partial success. There are various reasons for this assessment, but several of them can be distilled into one complaint—its failure in originality. Rather than a celebration of the transformative power of art and myth, the novel, with its extended sections "copied" from Hawthorne's notebooks and long, sometimes tedious descriptions of works of art and Roman tourist sites, becomes a commentary on the failure of art to originate. It only repeats, and the repetition extends and defers the inevitable—the novel's end or death. For Hawthorne, "to die in Rome," then, might be similar to what Kohut believed it meant for Mann "to die in Venice": to gain access to what has been sublimated, a knowledge that could cause the loss of the "cultural structure" and put the artist at risk of personal disintegration. Kohut theorized Mann did not "die" in Venice because telling the story of the dissolution of his protagonist Ascenbach allowed him "to spare himself, to live and to work, because they [his characters] suffer in his stead."[54] Kenyon was "spared" but Hawthorne granted himself no such reprieve.

What follows *The Marble Faun* in Hawthorne's career as a writer of fiction is a series of uncompleted novels. The three uncompleted novels of his last project, *The Elixir of Life Manuscripts*, repeat essentially the familiar story of a male's abortive efforts to find a cure for annihilationist anxiety. The *Septimius Felton* and *Septimius Norton* drafts of this project center on the quest of a younger man for immortality and include several "mixed race" characters and plot lines connected with their race (13: 512). The central protagonist, Septimius, has a "wild, mixed nature, the monstrousness that had grown out of his hybrid race" that in a later version seems to be at the root of his problems (13: 40). But the extensive notes for revision accompanying the drafts indicate Hawthorne was having difficulties managing his material.[55] His willingness to include multiple plot possibilities had proved fruitful in previous novels, but they now seemed disabling. The different racial identities for his main characters and his multiplication of divergent plot lines spun out of his control and only offered a seemingly endless series of unresolvable issues. But in *The Dolliver Romance*, the last fragment Hawthorne worked on before his death, he seemed more in control as he struggled to disentangle the quest for immortality from the problems of women or race. The immortality narrative is more conventionally rendered as a quest for something magical, an elixir of life that would "cure" death, and the primary male and female relationship in the novel is a white New England great-grandfather and his great-granddaughter, apparently more neutral and safer ground for his conventional plot.[56]

But male anxiety about death intrudes even into this relationship and plot line. In a scene oddly evocative of one in *The Scarlet Letter* in which Dimmesdale and Chillingworth watch wonderingly from their window as Pearl dances in the graveyard, Dr. Dolliver, an elderly man, comes to an area near a graveyard to tend the vegetation with Pansie, his Pearl-like sprightly great-granddaughter. Despite his warning that it is "poison...poison" (13: 476), Pansie becomes fixed on a wretched weed, curiously similar to the weed growing out of a dead man's bosom whose meaning Dimmesdale and Chillingworth ponder in *The Scarlet Letter*. She plucks it and runs with it to the graveyard. Dolliver pursues her, stumbles, and narrowly escapes falling into an open grave, "ready to receive its tenant" (13: 477). When he asks his great-granddaughter what she would have done without him if he had fallen, she replies laughingly, "Make the grass grow over grandpapa" (13: 476–77).

The presentiment of the open grave marks the point of origin of Hawthorne's final plot and of Dolliver's journey from age to youth, for Dolliver does find the elixir of "deathless" life, and it is a potion concocted from a "recipe for immortality" (13: 508). In this final fragment, the male protagonist finally discovers an unequivocal answer to death. But after providing him with his answer, Hawthorne had trouble imagining a purpose for Dolliver's life. He writes almost as an aside to himself in his notes to this uncompleted novel, "The difficulty is to know what he wants to live for" (13: 536). There may be several reasons Hawthorne struggled with this "difficulty," including his changing economic fortunes, the war strife in his home country, and his diminishing health. Aesthetically, there is also the difficulty of writing a novel under the plot constraints he had set for himself with this early graveyard scene. What are the consequences of being able to imagine a young girl imagining an old man dead, when he indeed is an immortal, and she is left "running as if to escape time or death" (13: 477)? It is almost as if finding the elixir of life means losing the will to come to grips with anything outside the self, any impulse to understand what has come before or shape what comes after. Writing the fragments of this final novel into consolation from this point of origin might have carried Hawthorne so far beyond his "cultural structures" to have taxed even his myth-making powers.

NOTES

Introduction

1. Emily Dickinson, *The Poems of Emily Dickinson*, ed. R.W. Franklin (Cambridge, Mass. and London: Belknap Press, 1999), 352. This phrase is from poem F789.
2. All references to Hawthorne's works are to *The Centenary Edition of the Works of Nathaniel Hawthorne*, ed. William Charvat, Roy Harvey Pearce, Claude M. Simpson, and Thomas Woodson (Columbus: Ohio State University Press, 1962–97), vols. 1–23 and are noted parenthetically in the text by volume and page number.
3. Michel de Certeau, *The Writing of History*, trans. Tom Conley (New York: Columbia University Press, 1988), 5. In the "Introduction" to *Death and Representation* (Baltimore: Johns Hopkins University Press, 1993), Sarah Webster Goodwin and Elisabeth Bronfen write, "much of what we call culture comes together around the collective response to death" (3).
4. Alexis de Tocqueville, *Democracy in America*, trans. Henry Reeve, rev. Francis Bowen, ed. Phillips Bradley (New York: A.A. Knopf, 1987), 2: 20–21.
5. John Greenleaf Adams, *The Christian Victor: or, Mortality and Immortality; Including Happy Death Scenes* (Boston: A. Tompkins, 1851), 69.
6. According to William M. Newman and Peter L. Halvorson in the *Atlas of American Religion: The Denominational Era, 1776–1990* (Walnut Creek, California: AltaMira Press, 2000), by the 1850s several new religious movements had developed that challenged the four major denominations existing in the colonies in 1776: Congregational, Presbyterian, Episcopal, and Baptist (18). Also, by mid-century these four "old" denominations had experienced "a process of fragmenting" caused primarily by "internal" forces, such as theological disputes, contention over the slavery issue and Western migration, and, to a lesser extent, the external factor of immigration (26–29).
7. Edgar Allan Poe, *Tales and Sketches*, ed. Thomas Ollive Mabbott (Urbana and Chicago: University of Illinois Press, 2000), 2: 1243.
8. Jacob Bigelow, "A Discourse on the Burial of the Dead," *A History of the Cemetery of Mount Auburn*, 1860. Reprint (Cambridge: Applewood Books, 1988), 177.
9. For a discussion of the rural cemetery movement in New England, see Blanche Linden-Ward, *Silent City on a Hill: Landscapes of Memory and Boston's Mount Auburn Cemetery* (Columbus: Ohio State University Press, 1989); David Charles Sloane, *The Last Great Necessity: Cemeteries in American History* (Baltimore: Johns Hopkins University Press, 1991); David E. Stannard, ed. *Death in America* (Philadelphia: University of Pennsylvania Press, 1975); James J. Farrell, *Inventing the American Way of Death, 1830–1920* (Philadelphia: Temple University Press, 1980); and Gary Laderman, *The Sacred Remains: American Attitudes Toward Death, 1799–1883* (New Haven: Yale University Press, 1996).

10. After observing American society of the 1830s, Tocqueville writes, "Christianity has therefore retained a strong hold on the public mind in America; and I would more particularly remark that its sway is not only that of a philosophical doctrine which has been adopted upon inquiry, but of a religion which is believed without discussion" (*Democracy in America* 2: 6). While Christianity had a "strong hold," actual church membership figures were relatively modest. In 1776 approximately 10 percent of the estimated population of 2.5 million in the colonies were church members (Newman and Halvorson, *Atlas of American Religion*, 16). By the 1850s the percentage had increased markedly: "with about three in every ten Americans identified as adherents the nation had become far more 'churched' than at its founding" (29).

    For discussions of Hawthorne's Christianity, see John T. Frederick, *The Darkened Sky: Nineteenth-Century American Novelists and Religion* (Notre Dame, Ind.: University of Notre Dame Press, 1969); Randall Stewart, *American Literature and Christian Doctrine* (Baton Rouge: Louisiana State University Press, 1958); and T. Walter Herbert, *Dearest Beloved: The Hawthornes and the Making of the Middle-Class Family* (Berkeley: University of California Press, 1993). Frederick describes Hawthorne as a conservative Unitarian (29), while granting that there has been "an astonishing conflict in interpretations of Hawthorne's own religious position" and acknowledging Hawthorne's aversion to institutional religion (27–28). Stewart concludes, "It was Hawthorne's dilemma, as well as Melville's, to find it difficult either to believe or to be comfortable in unbelief" (78). Herbert discusses the deep conflicts in Hawthorne's life and art related, in part, to the "fundamental transformation" in American Christianity manifest in the culture's "sacralization of womanhood" and reverence of the "domestic angel" (74).

11. Philippe Ariès, *The Hour of Our Death: The Classic History of Western Attitudes Toward Death Over the Last One Thousand Years*, trans. Helen Weaver (New York: Barnes and Noble Books, 2000), 442. For discussions of changing attitudes toward death in America, see Farrell, *Inventing the American Way of Death*; Stannard, *Death in America*; Lewis O. Saum, "Death in the Popular Mind of Pre–Civil War America," in *Passing: The Vision of Death in America*, ed. Charles O. Jackson (Westport, Conn.: Greenwood Press, 1977), 65–90; Thomas G. Connors, "The Romantic Landscape: Washington Irving, Sleepy Hollow, and the Rural Cemetery Movement," in *Mortal Remains: Death in Early America*, ed. Nancy Isenberg and Andrew Burstein (Philadelphia: University of Pennsylvania Press, 2003), 187–203; and Laderman, *The Sacred Remains*.

12. Nina Baym, "Review of *Dearest Beloved*, by T. Walter Herbert," *JEGP* 93 (April 1994): 272.

13. Goodwin and Bronfen, *Death and Representation*, 4.

14. Ibid.

15. Ernest Becker in *The Denial of Death* (New York: Free Press, 1973) popularized the theory of the "denial of death." He argues that, while fear of death is a universal experience, each society "answers" (or denies) death with its culture-specific "hero system" (5). "Denial of death" directs human activity: "the idea of death, the fear of it, haunts the human animal like nothing else; it is a mainspring of human activity—activity designed largely to avoid the fatality of death, to overcome it by denying in some way that it is the final destiny for man" (ix). James L. Calderwood in *Shakespeare and the Denial of Death* (Amherst: University of Massachusetts Press, 1987), Kirby Farrell in *Play, Death, and Heroism in Shakespeare* (Chapel Hill: University of North Carolina Press, 1989), and Robert N. Watson in *The Rest Is Silence: Death as Annihilation in the English Renaissance* (Berkeley: University of California Press, 1994) have approached Renaissance literature from the perspective of Becker's thesis, although in each case Becker's thesis is simply the inspiration for complex explorations of Renaissance ideas about death, dying, and annihilation. My approach to Hawthorne's novels has been influenced by all of these excellent studies. Watson's important distinction between fear of death and fear of annihilation has proved particularly helpful.

Becker considers the "narcissism" at the core of death denial as a quality of "human nature" (7), not a gender-specific characteristic. See William Beers in *Women and Sacrifice: Male Narcissism and the Psychology of Religion* (Detroit: Wayne State University Press, 1992) and Ilene Philipson in "Gender and Narcissism," *Psychology of Women Quarterly* 9 (1985): 213–28 for a discussion of the thesis that narcissism "denotes a way of being in the world that is primarily if not exclusively experienced by men" ("Gender and Narcissism," 215). In Hawthorne's fiction, death denial tends to be a male gender–specific activity.

16. John E. Seery, *Political Theory for Mortals: Shades of Justice, Images of Death* (Ithaca: Cornell University Press, 1996), 41.

17. Hélène Cixous, "The Laugh of the Medusa," trans. Keith Cohen and Paula Cohen, *Signs* 1 (1976): 885.

18. Herman Melville, "Hawthorne and His Mosses," in *The Portable Melville*, ed. Jay Leyda (New York: Viking Press, 1952), 405.

19. David Bakan, *Disease, Pain, and Sacrifice: Toward a Psychology of Suffering* (Chicago: University of Chicago Press, 1968), 119.

20. Luce Irigaray, "Body Against Body: In Relation to the Mother," in *Sexes and Genealogies*, trans. Gillian C. Gill (New York: Columbia University Press, 1993), 11.

21. Ibid.

22. In Chapter 16, "On the Edge of a Precipice," Miriam, Hilda, and Kenyon discuss the "chasm" that "lies beneath us, everywhere" and the dangers of falling through the "thin crust" of happiness overspreading it (4: 161–63).

23. In *The English Notebooks*, Hawthorne quotes Melville as saying he had "pretty much made up his mind to be annihilated," and he adds, "He can neither believe, nor be comfortable in his unbelief" (22: 163).

24. Heinz Kohut, "*Death in Venice* by Thomas Mann: A Story About the Disintegration of Artistic Sublimation," in *The Search For the Self: Selected Writings of Heinz Kohut, 1950–1978*, ed. Paul H. Ornstein (New York: International Universities Press, 1978), 1: 107–30.

25. Ibid., 118, 126.

26. Cixous, "The Laugh of the Medusa," 885. See also Elisabeth Bronfen in *Over Her Dead Body: Death, Femininity and the Aesthetic* (New York: Routledge, 1992), for an investigation of the relationship between femininity and death that considers an impressive range of representations of female death, both visual and narrative, from the eighteenth to the twentieth centuries. She focuses on the representations of the dead body of women primarily from Lacanian, Freudian, and feminist perspectives and tends to emphasize the objectifying male gaze and the relationship between the "corpse and textuality" (7).

While my book also considers the relationship between women and death, my focus is not on the aesthetics of the female corpse but on the male's search for consolations of dying because this issue tends to provide a nuanced picture of a culture's moral and ethical systems. My book is tightly focused on the fiction of a single mid-nineteenth-century New England writer, and, unlike Bronfen's primary interest in the aesthetic, central to my discussion is the culture's systems of belief, particularly the Christian model that was a dominant cultural force even for writers such as Hawthorne who contested it in some respects.

27. See T. Walter Herbert, *Sexual Violence and American Manhood* (Cambridge, Mass.: Harvard University Press, 2002), for a discussion of a range of texts, including Hawthorne's *The Scarlet Letter*, which illustrate the thesis that the American concept of "competitive self-reliant manhood" has contributed to male on female sexual violence and male "self-war" (93). See Leland S. Person, "Hawthorne's Early Tales: Male Authorship, Domestic Violence, and Female Readers" in Millicent Bell, ed. *Hawthorne and the Real: Bicentennial Essays* (Columbus: Ohio State University Press, 2005). Person argues that Hawthorne "played with female readers by manipulating their emotions, violently disrupting the domestic order with which they identified, and deliberately causing them pain through their identification with the

female characters he disappointed or shocked" (127–28). Person acknowledges that he would agree with David Leverenz in *Manhood and the American Renaissance* (Ithaca: Cornell University Press, 1989) who argues that Hawthorne's fiction "presents conventional manliness as aggressive, insensitive, and murderously dominant" (Leverenz as cited in Person, "Hawthorne's Early Tales," 127). In *Manhood and the American Renaissance*, Leverenz emphasizes that Hawthorne's fiction often dramatizes the effects his culture's "ideology of manhood" has on men's relationships with other men, rather than on their relationships with women (90, 93). He considers Hawthorne's "secret subject" to be "the drama of one man trying to invade and possess another's soul" (93).

28. See Richard H. Millington's introduction to *The Cambridge Companion to Nathaniel Hawthorne* (Cambridge: Cambridge University Press, 2004), for a thought-provoking discussion of the "Hawthorne that continues to matter" (9). As Millington explains, there are a range of perspectives among Hawthorne scholars and readers about the "use" of Hawthorne's fiction and the ways in which he does or does not "continue to matter." He concludes that Hawthorne is "a writer made acute by the conflicts of meaning and value emerging all around him, whose articulate discomfort makes him…crucially of use" (9).

29. Dennis Berthold, "Review of *Gothic America: Narrative, History, and Nation* by Teresa A. Goddu." http://www.rc.umd.edu/reviews/back/goddu.html.

One   Unholy Dying in *The Scarlet Letter*

1. Certeau, *The Writing of History*, 5. Certeau makes this point in the context of his consideration of changing conceptions of the writing of history, but his more general idea that cultural practices and productions have their origin in mourning and loss is relevant to this discussion.

2. Some of Hawthorne's contemporary reviewers did find fault with the way Christianity was presented in *The Scarlet Letter*. An anonymous reviewer notes, "The author nowhere recognizes the transforming and redeeming power of that Christian faith through which the spiritually dead may yet live and the lost be restored.…The remedial character of his religion is not understood." "The Scarlet Letter," *Christian Register*, April 13, 1850, 38; reprinted in *The Critical Response to Nathaniel Hawthorne's "The Scarlet Letter,"* ed. Gary Scharnhorst (New York: Greenwood Press, 1992), 28. Orestes Brownson points out that the novel is "full of mistakes…, in those portions where the author really means to speak like a Christian, and therefore we are obliged to condemn it"; yet, even this conservative Christian reviewer still concludes, "we acquit him [Hawthorne] of all unchristian intention." "Literary Notices and Criticism," *Brownson's Quarterly*, NS4 (October 1850): 528–32; reprinted in *The Critical Response*, ed. Scharnhorst, 38.

3. F.O. Matthiessen's position in *The American Renaissance: Art and Expression in the Age of Emerson and Whitman* (London: Oxford University Press, 1941) that Hawthorne shared Milton's "accurate reading of human nature" (312) influenced the scholarship of critics in the 1950s and 1960s, particularly R.W.B. Lewis's *The American Adam: Innocence, Tragedy and Tradition in the Nineteenth Century* (Chicago: University of Chicago Press, 1955), Hyatt H. Waggoner's *Hawthorne: A Critical Study* rev. ed. (Cambridge, Mass.: Belknap Press, 1963), and Roy R. Male's *Hawthorne's Tragic Vision* (New York: Norton, 1964). Matthiessen also acknowledges the influence of Bunyan on Hawthorne's fiction (312), as have Robert Stanton in "Hawthorne, Bunyan, and the American Romances," *PMLA* 71 (1956): 155–65 and David E. Smith in "Bunyan and Hawthorne," *John Bunyan in America* (Bloomington: Indiana University Press, 1966). Carol Bensick raises questions about whether Hawthorne tried to imitate either Bunyan's "method" or his "audience" in "Hawthorne and His Bunyan," *Nathaniel Hawthorne Review* 19.1 (Spring 1993): 2.

4. Jeremy Taylor, a seventeenth-century divine, was a particular favorite of Hawthorne, as well as of Emerson and a number of the British Romantics, including Coleridge, Lamb, and Hazlitt. See P.G. Stanwood, ed. "General Introduction," *Holy Living and Holy Dying* (Oxford: Clarendon Press, 1989), 1: lvi–lvii).

5. Ibid., 2: 22.

6. John Milton, *Paradise Lost*, ed. Merritt Y. Hughes (New York: Odyssey Press, 1935), 348.

7. In mid-nineteenth-century New England, there was a strong taste for biography, and ministerial biography was a popular form of the genre. Some of the ministerial biographies published between 1825 and 1850 first appeared in religious magazines and newspapers, and many were reviewed there. Frank Luther Mott in *A History of American Magazines, 1741–1850* (Cambridge, Mass.: Harvard University Press, 1939) explains that these Christian publications were extremely popular and "a large share of the talent and effort of most of the leading churches went into publishing channels" (1: 369). By 1828, there were more than twenty-one religious monthlies and seventy-three weekly newspapers (136). Christian periodicals, such as *Christian Examiner, Spirit of the Pilgrims*, and the *Christian Parlor Magazine*, included biographical sketches of ministers.

   From Ann Douglas's perspective, the proliferation of ministerial biographies would be interpreted as another sign of the clergy's efforts to shore up their position in the face of diminishing authority and status, particularly among the Unitarian and Congregational sects in New England. See "Heaven Our Home: Consolation Literature in the Northern United States, 1830–1880," in *Death in America*, ed. Stannard, 51–52. Douglas notes the predominance of "the ministerial-feminine 'memoir,'" a type of biography characterized by "exercises in necrophilia" in *The Feminization of American Culture* (New York: A.A. Knopf, 1977), 198, 200.

   George M. Marsden in *The Evangelical Mind and the New School Presbyterian Experience: A Case Study of Thought and Theology in Nineteenth-Century America* (New Haven: Yale University Press, 1970) does not see the authority of Christian ministers as waning during this period. He argues, "Protestant clergymen still maintained leadership in nearly every area of learning," and emphasizes the significant impact of the evangelical movement on American intellectual life (106). The budget for evangelical organizations "easily rivaled the major expenditures of the federal government," and much of this money was directed to fund various publication projects, such as magazines, newspapers, and tracts, several of which published biographical sketches of ministers (16). See Karin E. Gedge, *Without Benefit of Clergy: Women and the Pastoral Relationship in Nineteenth-Century American Culture* (Oxford: Oxford University Press, 2003), for a brief discussion of *The Scarlet Letter* as a novel that illustrates Gedge's thesis that the efficacy of the clergy was weakened by the "tenuous position" that it occupied "somewhere between the two gendered spaces, neither comfortable nor effective in either" (105). Despite this problem, she concludes, "Victorian culture continued to rely, albeit with less confidence, on religion as the source of moral order and authority" (105).

8. Mary Bushnell Cheney, *Life and Letters of Horace Bushnell* (New York: Arno Press, 1969), 357.

9. Oliver W.B. Peabody, "Memoir," in *Sermons By the Late William B.O. Peabody, D.D. With a Memoir, By His Brother* (Boston: Benjamin H. Greene, 1849), 44.

10. Elisabeth Jay in *The Religion of the Heart: Anglican Evangelicalism and the Nineteenth-Century Novel* (Oxford: Clarendon Press, 1979) presents an extensive discussion of the importance of the death scene in nineteenth-century literature (154–68). Pat Jalland in *Death in the Victorian Family* (Oxford: Oxford University Press, 1996) discusses the central role of death in the Evangelical Movement, the Christian tradition whose ideas strongly influenced Victorian concepts of dying, explaining that "The Evangelical model of the good Christian death was widely disseminated through Evangelical journals and tracts, which were intended primarily to provide spiritual edification and example—to save souls by showing people how to live and die well" (21). Although Jalland and Jay are focused on the ideas of Evangelicalism

and dying in England, the influence of the Evangelical Movement in the production of the ministerial biographies, the nature of their appeal, and the importance of religious magazines in their dissemination seem similar on both sides of the Atlantic. See Farrell, *Inventing the American Way of Death,* for a discussion of the role of the American Evangelical movement in affecting attitudes toward death and for a brief discussion of the significance of the deathbed scene (39–40).

Deathbed scenes were so popular during this period that they were excerpted and reprinted separately. See, for example, Adams, *The Christian Victor;* approximately one-third of the "happy death scenes" included in this volume describe the deaths of ministers.

11. Bettie Anne Doebler describes the *ars moriendi* as a "set of ideas and values" that fifteenth-, sixteenth-, and seventeenth-century believers used to organize the experience of death and to understand the relationship between the living and the dead, in *"Rooted Sorrow": Dying in Early Modern England* (Rutherford, N.J.: Fairleigh Dickinson University Press, 1994), 22. The *ars moriendi* tradition reflects conservative Christian attitudes toward death (19). For additional explanations of *ars moriendi,* see Peter C. Jupp and Clare Gittings, eds. *Death in England: An Illustrated History* (New Brunswick, N.J.: Rutgers University Press, 2000); Nancy Lee Beaty, ed. *The Craft of Dying: A Study in the Literary Tradition of the Ars Moriendi in England* (New Haven: Yale University Press, 1970); David William Atkinson, *The English Ars Moriendi* (New York: Peter Lang, 1992); and Sister Mary Catharine O'Connor, *The Art of Dying Well: The Development of the Ars Moriendi* (New York: Columbia University Press, 1942). Erik R. Seeman in *Pious Persuasions: Laity and Clergy in Eighteenth-Century New England* (Baltimore: Johns Hopkins University Press, 1999) describes the eighteenth-century New England clergyman's version of the *ars moriendi*: "resignation to God's will, a well-grounded (but not overly confident) hope that one was saved, and temperately offered final counsels" (44).

Sister Mary Catharine O'Connor notes that there was some uncertainty about the efficacy of dying confessions, which would further complicate the response to the scene of dying. Augustine, the "chief authority" on the issue, was somewhat ambiguous because "overstress on the mercy of God might lead men to presume; on His justice, to despair" (39). Jeremy Taylor in *Holy Dying* also raises questions about the efficacy of deathbed repentance.

12. Jay in *The Religion of the Heart* draws a distinction between a High Church and a Protestant response to the scene of dying that may be helpful in understanding the response of Hawthorne's contemporaries to this scene: "The High Church tends to concentrate upon the dying person whereas Protestantism throws greater emphasis upon the effect made upon the bystanders" (157). Saum in "Death in the Popular Mind" places the focus in descriptions of scenes of dying on both the departed and "the gathered circle" who hoped to receive inspiration "by witnessing a calm, clear-eyed death" (in *Passing,* ed. Jackson, 79). See Jane Tompkins, *Sensational Designs: The Cultural Work of American Fiction, 1790–1860* (New York: Oxford University Press, 1985), for a discussion of Little Eva's death scene in Stowe's *Uncle Tom's Cabin* that emphasizes its power as rhetorical performance to redeem and revitalize the bystanders (127–34). Julia Stern in "The Politics of Tears: Death in the Early American Novel" in *Mortal Remains,* ed. Isenberg and Burstein considers the way representations of death, dying, and funerals in early American fiction "reveal the reprobation of certain forms of emotion and the manipulation of collective affect that could be—and was—exploited for political purposes" (118–19). Colleen McDannell in *The Christian Home in Victorian America, 1840–1900* (Bloomington: Indiana University Press, 1994) emphasizes that the American Victorian family controlled the "life cycle" rituals in the home and that "the heightened domestic drama" of these events "far surpassed the church funeral for eliciting emotion, creating social bonds, and making statements about the 'quality' of the family" (98–99)

13. Eliza Lee Cabot Follen, *The Life of Charles Follen,* vol. 1 of *The Works of Charles Follen, With a Memoir of His Life* (Boston: Hilliard, Gray, and Company, 1841–1842), 581.

14. Dimmesdale compares the dying Winthrop to a "triumphant pilgrim" en route to the celestial city, as if Winthrop has overcome his battle with death and ended his journey gloriously. His metaphor of triumph is particularly revealing when it is compared to Cotton Mather's depiction of Winthrop's dying in *Magnalia Christi Americana Books I and II*, ed. Kenneth B. Murdock (Cambridge, Mass.: Belknap Press, 1977). Mather stressed that on his deathbed Winthrop "was Buffeted with the Disconsolate Thoughts of Black and Sore Desertions" and confessed, "I stand trembling before the tribunal" (227). In *Parentator*, Cotton Mather described the death of his father, Increase, in a similar fashion as a time of "Fear and Trembling," concluding "That going to Heaven in the way of Repentance, is much safer and surer than going in the way of Extasy"; see *Two Mather Biographies: Life and Death and Parentator*, ed. William J. Scheick (Bethlehem, Pa.: Lehigh University Press, 1989), 195.

15. Milton, *Paradise Lost*, 295.

16. Goodwin and Bronfen, eds. *Death and Representation*, 8–9.

17. For discussions of the novel as love story, see Martin Cronin, "Hawthorne on Romantic Love," *PMLA* 69 (1954): 89–98; Ernest Sandeen, "*The Scarlet Letter* as a Love Story," *PMLA* 77 (1962): 425–35; and Brook Thomas, "Love and Politics, Sympathy and Justice in *The Scarlet Letter*," in *The Cambridge Companion to Nathaniel Hawthorne*, ed. Millington, 162–85. Cronin believes that Hawthorne tests and finds wanting the Romantic assumption that one should give all for love; only when "no moral impediment is destined to confound their love" is Hawthorne able to describe the "emotions they experience in fine Romantic fashion" (96). Sandeen considers the novel a tale of "disastrous" love that destroys any possibility for happiness for Hester and Arthur but "matures them morally and spiritually" (425). Thomas discusses the novel as a love story with strong "political implications" (163). Anthony Trollope was among the earliest critics to raise questions about the novel as love story when he characterized it as a complex tale in which hatred "revel[s]" (in *The Critical Response*, ed. Scharnhorst, 73). Henry James in *Hawthorne* (New York: AMS Press, 1968) concludes "no story of love was surely ever less of a 'love story'" (112). Monika Elbert describes the story as a "marriage drama" which puts "on trial…the institution of marriage" in "Hester on the Scaffold, Dimmesdale in the Closet: Hawthorne's Seven-Year Itch," *Essays in Literature* 16.2 (Fall 1989): 234. Herbert in *Sexual Violence and American Manhood* states that the novel "draws the reader into a hall of mirrors that endlessly replicates the intramale drama of masculine on feminine sexual cruelty" (97). Critics have also noted that the various kinds of love the novel explores are expressed in the tension between the heterosexual and homosexual love plots. Sandra Tomc refers to the novel as a "heterosexual love story" that diverges to "dwell defiantly on the illicit, unmasculine erotic interaction" between Dimmesdale and Chillingworth in "A Change of Art: Hester, Hawthorne, and the Service of Love," *Nineteenth Century Literature* 56 (March 2002): 483. In the latter stages of the novel Hawthorne severs his identification with Hester in part to distance his "romance" from those other tales of romance, confirming that his "supremacy as an artist lies in his ability to marshal sympathy and love, feeling and pain, without in the least succumbing to their effects" (468, 487). Scott S. Derrick argues that the homosexual plot is able to "alter forever" the heterosexual plot and "reconnecting Dimmesdale to this [Hester's] passion will be the chief task of the second half of the text" in "'A Curious Subject of Observation and Inquiry': Homoeroticism, the Body, and Authorship in Hawthorne's *The Scarlet Letter*," *Novel* 28 (1995): 323. The novel's "representations of both hetero- and homosexuality are shaped in crucial ways by the nature of the novel or romance, and by what it means for a novelist or romancer to write one" (317).

18. Plato, *The Dialogues of Plato*, trans. Benjamin Jowett (Oxford: Clarendon Press, 1875), 1: 456.

19. Augustine, "The Free Choice of the Will," *The Teacher. The Free Choice of the Will. Grace and Free Will*, vol. 59 of *The Fathers of the Church*, trans. Robert P. Russell (Washington, D.C.: Catholic University Press, 1968), 80.

20. Henry Staten in *Eros in Mourning: Homer to Lacan* (Baltimore and London: Johns Hopkins University Press, 1995) considers the way in which the "Platonic-Stoic-Christian" traditions of Western thought "caution that no object that may be lost is to be loved in an unreserved fashion—that only a limited or conditional libidinal flow toward such objects is to be allowed" (10). His approach has influenced my discussion of object love and eros. He uses the Augustine quotation (from a different translation) to help develop his thesis (11).

21. Beth Ann Bassein, *Women and Death: Linkages in Western Thought and Literature* (Westport, Conn.: Greenwood Press, 1984), 20.

22. See Dickran and Ann Tashjian, *Memorials for Children of Change: The Art of Early New England Stonecarving* (Middletown, Conn.: Wesleyan University Press, 1974), 27–29; Gordon E. Geddes, *Welcome Joy: Death in Puritan New England* (Ann Arbor, Mich: UMI Research Press, 1981), 120–21; David E. Stannard, *The Puritan Way of Death: A Study in Religion, Culture, and Social Change* (New York: Oxford University Press, 1977), 112.

23. In 1852, Hawthorne placed the story of Medusa and Perseus first in the collection of myths he published for children. Several critics have noted that Hawthorne finds this myth compelling. Hugo McPherson in *Hawthorne as Myth-Maker: A Study in Imagination* (Toronto: University of Toronto Press, 1969) identifies the Perseus myth as a recurring pattern in Hawthorne's fiction and points out that in *A Wonder Book for Girls and Boys* Hawthorne concentrates the story of Perseus on one adventure: his quest for the head of the Gorgon Medusa (16–19; 47). Joel Pfister in *The Production of Personal Life: Class, Gender, and the Psychological in Hawthorne's Fiction* (Stanford: Stanford University Press, 1991) considers Hawthorne's use of the Perseus myth in *A Wonder Book* (93; 99–100). He also discusses Hester as Medusa and concludes: "A dread of Medusa let out of the bag…moves Hawthorne to disqualify his puritan woman of vision, Hester Prynne, as the ideal reformer" (101). He adds, "Medusa stands for cultural revolution as opposed to feminine evolution," a prospect that "petrifies" Hawthorne (102).

24. See Tobin Siebers, *The Mirror of Medusa* (Berkeley: University of California Press, 1983), 30, for a detailed discussion of the Medusa figure and its relationship to the fascinator.

25. For a discussion of the relationship between the evil eye and the Medusa, see Siebers, *The Mirror of Medusa*, Clarence Maloney, ed. *The Evil Eye* (New York: Columbia University Press, 1976), and Alan Dundes, ed. *The Evil Eye: A Casebook* (Madison, Wis.: University of Wisconsin Press, 1992).

26. Probably the most influential thesis about woman's role in Hawthorne's fiction has been Nina Baym's assertion that "'woman' stands for a set of qualities which the male denies within himself and rejects in others" ("Hawthorne's Women: The Tyranny of Social Myths," *Centennial Review* 15.3 [1971]: 250); see also her essay, "Thwarted Nature: Nathaniel Hawthorne as Feminist," in *American Novelists Revisited: Essays in Feminist Criticism*, ed. Fritz Fleischmann (Boston: G.K. Hall, 1982), 58–77. Baym points out: "Yet how victimized woman was to go about freeing not only herself but the male from his misapprehensions— misapprehensions of such psychological comfort to him—Hawthorne could not begin to imagine" ("Hawthorne's Women," 272). Baym makes a compelling case for "Hawthorne as a feminist writer from *The Scarlet Letter* onward" in "Revisiting Hawthorne's Feminism," *Nathaniel Hawthorne Review* 30.1 and 2 (2004): 32–55.

    A major activity for the past generation of Hawthorne scholars has been defining the nature of what Baym called male "misapprehensions" and offering reasons they exist. Lauren Berlant in *The Anatomy of National Fantasy: Hawthorne, Utopia, and Everyday Life* (Chicago: University of Chicago Press, 1991) adds a political dimension to the question, noting that Hawthorne's women are "fantasy projections of patriarchal fear about the imminent end of male hegemony within the political public sphere" (9). From my perspective, *The Scarlet Letter* investigates the ways in which Christian ideas about holy living and holy dying shaped the "misapprehensions" and "fantasy projections."

    For a discussion of a range of issues focused on Hawthorne's relationships with and ideas about women, see John L. Idol, Jr. and Melinda M. Ponder, eds. *Hawthorne and*

Women: Engendering and Expanding the Hawthorne Tradition (Amherst: University of Massachusetts Press, 1999). See Louise DeSalvo, *Nathaniel Hawthorne* (Atlantic Highlands, N.J.: Humanities Press International, 1987), for a review of various feminist approaches to the novel. See Alison Easton, "Hawthorne and the Question of Women" in *The Cambridge Companion to Nathaniel Hawthorne,* ed. Millington, for a survey of the women characters in Hawthorne's fiction considered in light of the "inconsistencies and shifts in attitudes" (82) on gender and class issues over the period of Hawthorne's career. For a discussion of women's scholarship on the novel and its reception, see Jamie Barlowe, *The Scarlet Mob of Scribblers: Rereading Hester Prynne* (Carbondale: Southern Illinois University Press, 2000).

27. Cixous, "The Laugh of the Medusa," 885.

  Shari Benstock in "*The Scarlet Letter* (a)dorée, or the Female Body Embroidered" approaches the novel from the perspective of French feminist theory, particularly that of Julia Kristeva, and concludes that the novel "works not to exploit oppositional structures of sexual-textual difference but rather to expose the fictional nature of these modes, revealing absolute sexual difference as a fantasy of patriarchal oppositional and hierarchical logic" (290). In the introduction to this volume, Ross C. Murfin states that Benstock positions Hawthorne as a "precursor of French feminist theory" (284). *The Scarlet Letter,* ed. Ross C. Murfin (Boston: Bedford Books of St. Martin's Press, 1991).

28. Beers, *Women and Sacrifice,* 11.

29. Ibid., 12.

30. Ibid., 130.

31. Kohut, *The Restoration of the Self* (New York: International Universities Press, 1977), 171–73. Kohut's theories prove helpful in understanding Hawthorne's fiction because they seem based on similar assumptions about the nature of women and the role of the mother. When describing the failed self/self-object relationship, Kohut links the woman/mother to the Medusa figure: "behind the head of the Medusa lies the supposedly castrated genital of the woman" (189).

32. Ibid., 174.

33. Ibid.

34. Kohut, *The Search For the Self* 1: 433.

35. Kohut, *Restoration,* 49, 177–79.

36. Ibid., 104–5, 171–74.

37. Kohut, *The Analysis of the Self: A Systematic Approach to the Psychoanalytic Treatment of Narcissistic Personality Disorders* (New York: International Universities Press, 1971), 152.

38. Ibid., 153. Also cited in Beers, *Women and Sacrifice,* 129.

39. Kohut, *Restoration,* 7–8, note on 208. While I am speaking of these reactions to "faulty" mirroring or "faulty or disrupted empathy" (Kohut, *Restoration,* 8) as if they were separate and unrelated, they are part of a whole continuum of responses, often experienced simultaneously.

40. Beers, *Women and Sacrifice,* 49, 117–18.

41. Beers explains, "The male anxiety about women, which fuels the change from matriliny to patriliny . . . and which is embodied in ritual blood sacrifice, is anxiety about esteem, power, and differentiation. The anxiety is narcissistic. And narcissism fuels the religious symbols and rituals that address that anxiety" (117). For Beers, unlike Kohut, narcissism is a male gender-specific characteristic. Consequently, men "do not sacrifice in order to give the power from women (mothers) to other women. They sacrifice to exclude women from this power. . . . [T]he role of gender in the development of gender-specific anxiety is crucial to understanding sacrifice" (101).

42. Bakan, *Disease, Pain, and Sacrifice,* 79. Beers cites Bakan to establish that Bakan's theory of the psychology of suffering is relevant to a theory of sacrifice (10).

43. My discussion of the way the pre-Christian and pre-Platonic man would experience death has been influenced by Staten's perceptive analysis of death and mourning in *The Iliad* (*Eros in Mourning,* 21–46).

44. Ibid., 21.

45. Ibid., 25.

46. Helen K. Gediman, *Fantasies of Love and Death in Life and Art: A Psychoanalytic Study of the Normal and the Pathological* (New York: New York University Press, 1995), 6.

47. Richard H. Brodhead in *Hawthorne, Melville, and the Novel* (Chicago: University of Chicago Press, 1973) may have defined most succinctly the "conflict" revealed in this final scene: "a dogmatic and theological and a secular and humanistic imagination come into passionate conflict one last time" (65).

48. From Gediman's perspective in *Fantasies of Love and Death*, this kind of wish for reunion in death may be a form of a Liebestod fantasy in which the desire to die together includes "hopes of resurrecting the love relationship after death" (90). This wish for reunion can extend along a "normal-pathological continuum" (7). Gediman explains, "Pathology occurs when a lover fails to resolve the conflicting desires for separateness and oneness" (7).

49. See Elbert in "Hester on the Scaffold" for a discussion of the way Hester is able to "escape categorization" and thus gain "freedom" because of her "uncertain status" in the community "as a widow or as a separated/divorced woman" (250).

50. Jalland, *Death in the Victorian Family*, 300.

51. Juliana Schiesari in *The Gendering of Melancholia: Feminism, Psychoanalysis, and the Symbolics of Loss in Renaissance Literature* (Ithaca: Cornell University Press, 1992) makes the important distinction that when males write of melancholia in males it is frequently imagined as an experience that enhances self-understanding. But when the condition is described in females, it is seen as limiting and often is linked to depression. Hawthorne seems within this tradition when he portrays the sadness of Hester.

52. Certeau, *The Writing of History*, 5.

53. The narrator of Hawthorne's "Grandfather's Chair" in *The Whole History of Grandfather's Chair* tells the story of Lady Arbella Johnson who brought grandfather's chair to the colonies. She died one month after her arrival, and her grave—located on land given by her husband Isaac Johnson—became the site on which "a city had sprung up, . . . [and] a church of stone was built upon the spot" (*True Stories From History and Biography* 6:18). Isaac Johnson died a month after his wife and was buried in the same location; following his death many requested to be buried near him and "so the field became the first burial ground in Boston" (6: 19). In *The Scarlet Letter* Hawthorne describes Johnson's grave and lot as forming the "nucleus" from which came "all the congregated sepulchers in the old church-yard of King's Chapel" (1: 47).

54. Henry Wilder Foote in *Annals of King's Chapel: From the Puritan Age of New England to the Present Day*, vol. 1 (Boston and Cambridge: Little, Brown, and Company, 1882) explains that Edmund Andros initiated the plans for its construction shortly after the death of his wife and, "tradition reports," because "she may well have desired to be laid near the spot destined for the house of prayer of her own people" (75).

55. Linden-Ward, *Silent City on a Hill*, 25.

56. The simple "A" as a grave marker would have seemed unusual to Hawthorne's contemporaries, who would have been familiar with the style of the images on New England graves. Dickran and Ann Tashjian in *Memorials for Children of Change* explain that the images on the gravestones in New England change over time from death's-head (seventeenth and early eighteenth centuries) to cherub (second quarter of the eighteenth century) to portraiture (post–mid-eighteenth century) (57). Max Cavitch in "Interiority and Artifact: Death and Self-Inscription in Thomas Smith's Self Portrait," *Early American Literature* 37 (2002) notes that "heart shapes" and "stylized breasts" also appeared on seventeenth-century New England tombstones (104). For a discussion of the Puritan grave markers, see also Stannard, *The Puritan Way of Death*, 116–21.

57. Esther Schor, *Bearing the Dead: The British Culture of Mourning from the Enlightenment to Victoria* (Princeton: Princeton University Press, 1994), 126–27.

58. David Ferry in *The Limits of Mortality; An Essay on Wordsworth's Major Poems* (Middletown, Conn.: Wesleyan University Press, 1959) describes the way the Romantic poet uses natural objects as "'signposts' to that metaphysical place to which he wants to go," and, as signposts, "if they tell us the way to get there, they also tell us that we have not gotten there yet" (10–11). I am drawing a distinction between this way of using natural objects and Hawthorne's. He seems to be simply calling attention to the "A" as a beautiful natural object, not a transcendental sign.

Two "The Custom-House," the Secular Pilgrim, and the Happy Death

1. Calderwood, *Shakespeare and the Denial of Death*, 5.

2. Nina Baym in "The Romantic *Malgre Lui*: Hawthorne in the Custom House," *ESQ* 40 (1973): 14–25 and Paul John Eakin in "Hawthorne's Imagination and the Structure of 'The Custom-House,'" *American Literature* 43.3 (1971): 346–58 were among the first critics to emphasize the complex form of Hawthorne's autobiographical sketch. Baym described "The Custom-House" as an "autobiographical romance" (14), and Eakin called it a "fiction" (353). Both descriptions suggest that the "Hawthorne" of this sketch is a persona Hawthorne created for complex personal and rhetorical purposes.

3. M.H. Abrams, *Natural Supernaturalism: Tradition and Revolution in Romantic Literature* (New York: W.W. Norton, 1971), 165.

4. Ann Douglas in *The Feminization of American Culture* discusses the popularity of consolation literature during the period from 1820 to 1875 and offers some reasons for the "magnification of mourning" in note 6 (371–72).

5. Henry David Thoreau, *Walden: A Fully Annotated Edition*, ed. Jeffrey S. Cramer (New Haven: Yale University Press, 2004), 2. See James R. Mellow, *Nathaniel Hawthorne in His Times* (Boston: Houghton Mifflin, 1980), and Raymond Adams, "Hawthorne and a Glimpse of Walden," *Essex Institute Historical Collections* 94 (July 1958): 191–93, for a discussion of the Hawthorne-Thoreau relationship and the content of *Walden* Hawthorne might have "glimpsed." On November 22, 1848, Thoreau lectured at the Salem Lyceum at the invitation of Hawthorne, who served as manager and corresponding secretary. His lecture topic was "Student Life in New England: Its Economy," which later "formed part" of *Walden* (Mellow, *Nathaniel Hawthorne in His Times*, 289). Thoreau lectured at the Lyceum again at Hawthorne's invitation on February 28, 1849, reading portions of the second chapter of *Walden* (Adams, "Hawthorne and a Glimpse," 191–93).

6. Thoreau, *Walden*, 88.

7. Beers, *Women and Sacrifice*, 24. Beers explains, "Patriarchy does not exist simply because of man's social and logical systems. These social structures and the cultures they contain are woven by actual, living weavers. Blood sacrifice reflects something deep within men's psyches—be they memories, dreams, fantasies, ideals, and feelings (conscious or unconscious)—and anyone seeking to explain human thought and action would be hard pressed to avoid the realization that there is something psychologically internal to cultural thought and action" (24).

8. Victor Turner, *On the Edge of the Bush: Anthropology as Experience* (Tucson: University of Arizona Press, 1985), 126.

9. Ibid., 180 (italics in the original).

10. Ibid., 180, 215.
11. Ibid., 180.
12. Ibid., 218.
13. Victor Turner, *Blazing the Trail: Way Marks in the Exploration of Symbols*, ed. Edith Turner (Tucson: University of Arizona Press, 1992), 111. In this work, Turner gives a somewhat more complex reading of the nature of sacrifice, seeing in it antithetical forces, some of which draw toward cohesion and social continuity, while others support the "antistructural identity" (110–11).
14. Hawthorne's assumptions about gender in this essay seem similar to those informing his novels. He accepts, as a basic premise, an essentialist and biological based theory of gender. At the same time, the characters he imagines suggest that he would tend to agree with Margaret Fuller that "There is no wholly masculine man, no purely feminine woman." Margaret Fuller, *Woman in the Nineteenth Century*, ed. Larry J. Reynolds (New York: W.W. Norton, 1998), 69. Thus, the Hawthorne men, such as Dimmesdale and Coverdale, have in varying degrees feminine traits, and the Hawthorne women, such as Hester and Zenobia, have masculine traits. Usually having these traits puts these characters at risk for both inner and outer conflict and unhappiness. In "The Custom-House" sketch, Hawthorne imagines the Hawthorne of the essay as trying to come to terms with sometimes competing masculine and feminine gender characteristics, a struggle that also creates tension, pain, and anxiety, and yet provides the potential for personal growth and new insight. Unlike several of his protagonists, the Hawthorne of this essay triumphantly succeeds in his struggle. He does not succeed by becoming an androgynous figure, however, but by transcending and moving to the gender "neutral territory" of the "realm of quiet" (1: 36, 44). For a helpful summary of some important discussions of issues of gender in Hawthorne's fiction and an explanation of the use of the terms man and woman and their distinction from male and female or masculine and feminine, see Herbert, *Dearest Beloved*, 299 (note 8). Baym in "Revisiting Hawthorne's Feminism" argues that Hawthorne believes in "essential differences between human nature in the two sexes" (44). Herbert in "Hawthorne and American Masculinity" in *The Cambridge Companion to Nathaniel Hawthorne*, ed. Millington agrees that Hawthorne subscribes to "the theory that manhood and womanhood are established by nature" (62). Baym does not see Hawthorne using "these essentialist beliefs as conservative excuses to keep women down" (45). While acknowledging that Hawthorne's fiction illustrates that these essentialist theories "stunt the lives of women" (77), Herbert emphasizes that Hawthorne's focus is more on the theories' effects on men, particularly on himself. Because the "reigning model of manhood...violated his own temperament," Hawthorne "insisted on the right to fulfill that temperament in defiance of conventional prohibitions" ("Hawthorne and American Masculinity," 76). Herbert concludes that "Hawthorne portrayed that defiance in Hester" ("Hawthorne and American Masculinity," 76).
15. Turner, *Blazing the Trail*, 94–95.
16. Ibid., 100.
17. Ibid., 110, 110–11, 111.
18. Cixous, "Fiction and Its Phantoms," *New Literary History* 7 (1975): 536.
19. Turner, *On the Edge of the Bush*, 218.
20. See Robert Daly's "Liminality and Fiction in Cooper, Hawthorne, Cather, and Fitzgerald," in *Victor Turner and the Construction of Cultural Criticism: Between Literature and Anthropology*, ed. Kathleen Ashley (Bloomington, Ind.: Indiana University Press, 1990), 70–85, for a discussion of the role of liminality in Hawthorne's fiction.
21. Turner, *The Ritual Process: Structure and Anti-Structure* (Chicago: Aldine Publishing Company, 1969), 95.

22. Hawthorne's idea of "neutral territory" makes it resemble a "safe house" for art, a space where the author can seek protection from the barbs of criticism and immunity from prosecution when considering difficult or controversial issues and subjects. Baym explains that Hawthorne "put himself forward as an author whose work declined engagement with issues of public moment." He did this at the same time that he was engaging these issues. Baym, "Again and Again, the Scribbling Women," in *Hawthorne and Women*, ed. Idol and Ponder, 32. See Richard H. Millington, *Practicing Romance: Narrative Form and Cultural Engagement in Hawthorne's Fiction* (Princeton: Princeton University Press, 1992), for his idea that "neutral territory," the space of romance, is a "conceptual place" where "boundaries are blurred and the capacity to resee the mind—and by that reseeing to revise it—is recovered" (53, 54).
23. Turner, *The Ritual Process*, 95.
24. Turner, *On the Edge of the Bush*, 216–17.
25. Siebers in *The Mirror of Medusa* explains that Medusa figures are those perceived to be different, the "so-called outsider within the community," and the community unites in opposition against him or her (89–90).
26. Turner, *On the Edge of the Bush*, 218.
27. Ibid.
28. Thoreau, *Walden*, 2.
29. Turner, *Blazing the Trail*, 111.
30. Gediman, *Fantasies of Love and Death*, 9. Gediman explains that the two fantasies can interact, and when they do not "we are not dealing with an expression of a wish for a certain type of object love in merger but primarily with a wish for narcissistically continuing the self without particular reference to an object" (92).
31. Ibid., 9.
32. Turner, *On the Edge of the Bush*, 180.
33. John Ruskin, *The Works of John Ruskin*, ed. E.T. Cook and Alexander Wedderburn (London: Longmans, Green and Co., 1908), 34: 274.
34. Sigmund Freud, "Mourning and Melancholia," in *The Standard Edition of the Complete Psychological Works of Sigmund Freud*, ed. and trans. James Strachey (London: Hogarth Press, 1974), 14: 245.
35. John Bowlby, *Loss: Sadness and Depression*, vol. 3 of *Attachment and Loss* (New York: Harper Collins, 1980), 277.
36. Hawthorne biographers and critics treat Hawthorne's relationship with his mother and this event in different ways. For example, Edwin Haviland Miller in *Salem Is My Dwelling Place* (Iowa City: University of Iowa Press, 1991) emphasizes the unspoken and repressed nature of the love of mother and son (272, 298). Brenda Wineapple in *Hawthorne: A Life* (New York: A.A. Knopf, 2003) concludes after discussing the scene: "In some ways, mother and son remained afraid of one another after all these years, or at least of the intensity of their feelings" (207). Mellow in *Nathaniel Hawthorne in His Times* describes Hawthorne's mother's death as Hawthorne's "psychological nadir" but does not emphasize that his relationship with his mother, or his grief, was abnormal (297). Herbert in *Dearest Beloved* characterizes Hawthorne as "psychically dependent on his mother" and discusses the scene as a complex rendering of the "anguish" of his unresolved "maternal fixation" (148, 167). Gloria Erlich in *Family Themes and Hawthorne's Fiction: The Tenacious Web* (New Brunswick, N.J.: Rutgers University Press, 1984) describes Hawthorne's mother as "loving" but passive, and notes that her lack of confidence made her unable to instill in her son what the psychologist Erik H. Erikson defined as "basic trust" (65). Her death affected Hawthorne with "a powerful perception of his place in the cycle of life" (21).
37. Bowlby, *Loss*, 276–77.

38. Ibid., 277, 288. The child sometimes develops a form of separation anxiety that can be characterized by symptoms such as those experienced when Hawthorne was living in his mother's home in Salem after college. While the portrait of reclusive Hawthorne is exaggerated, it does seem as if he tended to stay close to home and, particularly during certain periods of his life, suffered from a form of agoraphobia and social anxiety.

39. See Miller in *Salem Is My Dwelling Place*, for a consideration of the emotional life of the Mannings and Hawthornes and a discussion of the effect on Hawthorne of the death of his father. Miller describes two incidents that Hawthorne's sister Elizabeth remembers from Hawthorne's childhood. The earliest stories Hawthorne told to entertain his family were written in the first person and ended with him standing on the seashore declaring, "And I'm never coming home again." The second incident that Miller characterizes as "deeply significant" and fraught with "unconscious reverberations" is young Hawthorne's habit of reciting the lines from *Richard III*: "Stand back, my Lord, and let the coffin pass" (26). This play-acting may be similar to the behavior of young children who make up games that involve death and mourning as a way to gain mastery over the death of a parent.

40. Neal L. Tolchin, *Mourning, Gender, and Creativity in the Art of Herman Melville* (New Haven: Yale University Press, 1988), 13. Tolchin emphasizes that "the codes of Christianity and gentility conspired to regulate and formalize bereavement," and the emotions of antebellum American mourners were "kept within strict bounds" (13). Hawthorne's mother, Elizabeth, like Melville's mother, Maria, mourned for an extended period after the death of her husband. In his biography of his father, Julian Hawthorne referred to his grandmother's life-long mourning as characterized by an "exaggerated, almost Hindoo-like construction of the law of seclusion which the public taste of that day imposed upon widows" (1: 4–5). Julian Hawthorne, *Nathaniel Hawthorne and His Wife: A Biography* (Boston: Houghton Mifflin, 1884), 1: 4–5. Baym dispels the legend of the morbidly melancholy and reclusive mother in "Nathaniel Hawthorne and His Mother: A Biographical Speculation," *American Literature* 54 (March 1982) in which she considers the novel to be a "complex memorial" to Hawthorne's mother (23). Erlich argues that "contemporaneous opinions show disagreement about the reclusiveness of mother and son" and asserts that Hawthorne's mother sought varying degrees of privacy during the different stages of her life (*Family Themes*, 65, 67).

41. Bowlby, *Loss*, 314.

42. On February 27, 1842, Hawthorne wrote to Sophia Peabody: "Belovedest, I have thought much of thy parting injunction to tell my mother and sisters that thou art her daughter and their sister. I do not think thou canst estimate what a difficult task thou didst propose to me" (*The Letters, 1813–1843* 15: 611). Hawthorne's sister Elizabeth wrote to Sophia Peabody on May 23, 1842 that her brother had kept his mother and sisters "so long in ignorance" of their impending marriage (15: 627 note).

43. In his study of Melville's Calvinism, *"Moby-Dick" and Calvinism: A World Dismantled* (New Brunswick, N.J.: Rutgers University Press, 1977), T. Walter Herbert considers Hawthorne's thoughts on "annihilation," made at the time of his mother's death, and concludes, "But Hawthorne's is scarcely a positive faith; his assertion of religious hope is animated essentially by his horrified recoil from the prospect of conceiving existence as an insult measured out by a transcendent fiend" (16).

44. Philip Freneau, *Poems of Freneau*, ed. Harry Hayden Clark (New York: Harcourt, Brace and Company, 1929), 341.

45. Beers, *Women and Sacrifice*, 12.

46. Beers cites Nancy Jay that sacrifice "works as evidence of, and therefore as a means for constituting, lines of patrilineal descent" (*Women and Sacrifice*, 11).

47. Thoreau, *Walden*, 96.

48. Robert D. Richardson, Jr., *Emerson: The Mind on Fire* (Berkeley: University of California Press, 1995), 121.

Three   "Familial Immortality" and the "Dying of Death" in *The House of the Seven Gables*

1. Emerson, "Tragedy," in Robert E. Spiller and Wallace E. Williams, eds. *The Early Lectures of Ralph Waldo Emerson* (Cambridge, Mass.: Belknap Press, 1972), 3: 104.

2. Emerson, "The Divinity School Address," in Robert W. Spiller and Alfred R. Ferguson, eds. *The Collected Works of Ralph Waldo Emerson* (Cambridge, Mass.: Belknap Press, 1971), 1: 89.

3. Farrell, *Inventing the American Way of Death*, 4. Farrell explains that the phrase "the dying of death" was first used in 1899 by an English author to identify a phenomenon in the American conception of death between 1830 and 1920 (4). The "dying of death" does not refer to the "banishment of biological death, but the cultural circumvention of dread of death" (4–5).

   For another perspective on this question, see Watson, *The Rest Is Silence*. Watson believes that the Jacobean period in England produced literature that "often reverts from its surface narrative to repressed anxieties about death as eternal annihilation" (3), and, although this pattern may be more pronounced in this period, it is not unique or new to this era. He argues that cultural critics "have underestimated the continuity of human anxieties about death partly because they underestimate the continuity of selfhood assumed in earlier cultures. The fact that the invention of individuality always seems to occur during the period in which the investigator specializes should give some pause" (326). He would grant that in various historical periods certain historical and cultural events did shape responses to death, but also that death denial is natural and the "dying of death" is a phenomenon apparent in varying degrees in any time period or culture (4).

4. Jackson, ed. *Passing*, 61.

5. Ibid.

6. Ibid.

7. Ariès in *The Hour of Our Death* argues that there was a world-wide shift in attitudes toward death at the beginning of the nineteenth century (442). For other studies of changing attitudes toward death in America, see note 11 in my "Introduction."

8. See William James, *The Varieties of Religious Experience: A Study in Human Nature* (New York: Collier Books, 1961), for his characterization of the liberal "variety" of religion: "The advance of liberalism, so-called, in Christianity, during the past fifty years, may fairly be called a victory of healthy-mindedness within the church over the morbidness with which the old hell-fire theology was more harmoniously related. We have now whole congregations whose preachers, far from magnifying our consciousness of sin, seem devoted rather to making little of it. They ignore, or even deny, eternal punishment, and insist on the dignity rather than the depravity of man" (87–88).

9. Farrell in *Inventing the American Way of Death* explains that as early as the 1820s Unitarianism affected attitudes toward death, although the full force of religious liberalism, which crossed the lines of several Protestant denominations, was not completely apparent until mid-century (28–30; 74–75).

10. Bigelow, *A History of the Cemetery of Mount Auburn*, 176.

11. Jackson, *Passing*, 61.

12. By the middle of the century, the number of rural cemeteries in America had grown to sixty, and the expanded role of cemeteries in nineteenth-century cultural life led to the development of several death-related industries, including cemetery horticulturalists and monument artisans and marketers. Peggy McDowell and Richard E. Meyer, *The Revival Styles in American Memorial Art* (Bowling Green, Ohio: Bowling Green University Press, 1994), 14. A core group of the founders of Mount Auburn Cemetery were horticulturalists who proposed that professionally tended grounds and graves should form an integral part of the cemetery. The grounds of the rural cemetery became the prototypes of the recreational urban and suburban park (Linden-Ward, *Silent City*, 296).

13. Bakan, *Disease, Pain, and Sacrifice*, 116–20.
14. Ibid., 119.
15. Ibid.
16. See Pfister, *The Production of Personal Life*, and Herbert, *Dearest Beloved*, for a discussion of the complex relationship between male identity and the middle-class family and the way this relationship is expressed in Hawthorne's life and art.

    See Alison Easton, *The Making of the Hawthorne Subject* (Columbia: University of Missouri Press, 1996), for a thorough analysis of the developmental patterns of image and idea that cluster around the concept of the human subject in Hawthorne's fiction. Her approach to subjectivity does not focus as singly as Pfister's or Herbert's on issues of class or gender. She argues that in Hawthorne's fiction the "locus of reality" is the "individual consciousness," but this consciousness rarely can "originate its own meaning," and "subjectivity becomes the far more common site on which many conflicting, mainly socially derived views struggle for primacy" (7).
17. Farrell, *Inventing the American Way of Death*, 11.
18. Thoreau, *Walden*, 3.
19. Ibid., 36.
20. Hawthorne's version of the myth of the dragon's teeth is based on Charles Anthon's in *A Classical Dictionary* (New York: Harper, 1857), 278. According to McPherson, Anthon's dictionary is Hawthorne's primary source for information about myth (14). "The Dragon's Teeth," Hawthorne's version of the Cadmus story written for children, is included in *Tanglewood Tales For Girls and Boys Being A Second Wonder Book* (1853).
21. Irigaray, "Each Sex Must Have Its Own Rights," in *Sexes and Genealogies*, 1–2.
22. Ibid., 2.
23. Ibid.
24. Emerson, "Tragedy," in *The Early Lectures* 3:104.
25. Roland Barthes, *Camera Lucida: Reflections on Photography*, trans. Richard Howard (New York: Hill and Wang, 1981), 9. See Jay Ruby, *Secure the Shadow: Death and Photography in America* (Cambridge: MIT Press, 1995), for an interesting review of the practices of post-mortem daguerreotypists in the antebellum period. The most common practice was to capture the image of the dead at peace, in "'the last sleep' pose" (72). Because the corpse of Judge Pyncheon is described as "still seated" after the daguerreotype is taken, Holgrave took a rarer, although not unheard of, seated portrait of dead Pyncheon, a pose entitled "alive, yet dead" (72).
26. William Shakespeare, *Major Plays and the Sonnets*, ed. G.B. Harrison (New York: Harcourt, Brace and Company, 1948), 144, 142.
27. Irigaray, "Each Sex Must Have Its Own Rights,' in *Sexes and Genealogies*, 4, 2 (italics in the original).
28. Irigaray believes that in the "patriarchal regime" a woman must devote herself to her husband and children, while "there seems little indication that man has sublimated the natural immediacy of his relationship to the mother. Rather, man has transferred that relationship to his wife as mother substitute" (ibid., 2).
29. Irigaray, "Belief Itself," in *Sexes and Genealogies*, 39.
30. Freud, "Beyond the Pleasure Principle," in *The Standard Edition* 18: 14–15.
31. Irigaray, "Belief Itself," in *Sexes and Genealogies*, 31–32.
32. See Frederick Crews, *Sins of the Fathers: Hawthorne's Psychological Themes* (New York: Oxford University Press, 1966), for an influential Freudian reading of Hawthorne's fiction that he later called into question in *Skeptical Engagements* (Oxford: Oxford University Press, 1986). Pfister in *The Production of Personal Life* offers an insightful explanation of the relevance of Freudian theory to Hawthorne's fiction (50–52). Some of Irigaray's ideas about the nature of the family and the construction of the male subject are grounded in Freud's theory, although they critique this theory. Combining Freud's and Irigaray's theories makes more

apparent the complex and nuanced way in which Hawthorne imagined the male-female relationship.

33. Freud, "Beyond the Pleasure Principle," in *The Standard Edition* 18: 15.
34. Irigaray, "Belief Itself," in *Sexes and Genealogies*, 27.
35. In *Irigaray and Deleuze: Experiments in Visceral Philosophy* (Ithaca and London: Cornell University Press, 1999), Tamsin Lorraine distinguishes four versions of the Irigarayan female subject: "In addition to depicting the feminine other as seen by the masculine subject, Irigaray depicts the feminine other co-opted by masculine subjectivity (that is, the feminine other who buys into the way the masculine subject views her), the feminine other of the masculine subject as she is apart from the masculine subject's perspective, and the feminine other in the process of articulating herself as a subject and thus providing an alternative paradigm for subjectivity that may not yet be actualized" (16). In "Beyond the Pleasure Principle," Freud confines his portrayal of the feminine other to the first category. In *The House of the Seven Gables*, Hawthorne ranges among these various ideas about the feminine other in his depiction of both Hepzibah and Phoebe. In his portrayal of Hepzibah, he provides glimpses of "an alternative paradigm for subjectivity," but, finally, he presents both Hepzibah and Phoebe as "co-opted by masculine subjectivity."
36. Irigaray, "Belief Itself," in *Sexes and Genealogies*, 35 (italics in the original).
37. Freud, "Beyond the Pleasure Principle," in *The Standard Edition* 18: 16, 38, 41 (italics in the original).
38. Irigaray, "Belief Itself," in *Sexes and Genealogies*, 31.
39. See Stanley French, "The Cemetery as Cultural Institution: The Establishment of Mount Auburn and the 'Rural Cemetery' Movement," in *Death in America*, ed. Stannard, 83–84; Farrell, *Inventing the American Way of Death*, 106–7, 113; Sloane, *The Last Great Necessity*, 70–71, and Linden-Ward, *Silent City*, 217, 226–27, for discussions of the significance of the family plot in nineteenth-century New England rural cemeteries. During this period family plots in cemeteries became more popular, promoting the idea that the family could be together forever. Fences around family grave-sites also became more common, as if the plot of land they enclosed was the exclusive property of the family-dead. The upkeep of these plots was entrusted to professionals to ensure "perpetual control" (Linden-Ward, *Silent City*, 212). Linden-Ward concludes, "Mount Auburn provided for a private cult of ancestors enshrined in carefully defined family burial lots even more than for a cult of heroes meriting public fame" (226).
40. Irigaray, "Belief Itself," in *Sexes and Genealogies*, 41.
41. Lorraine, *Irigaray and Deleuze*, 61.
42. Freud, "Beyond the Pleasure Principle," in *The Standard Edition* 18: 15 (italics in the original).
43. Seery, *Political Theory for Mortals*, 157.
44. Ibid., 156–62.
45. Laderman in *The Sacred Remains* identifies "four trends" in mid-nineteenth-century New England Protestant attitudes toward death: "valorization of the affections of the survivors, memorialization of the dead, augmentation of the spiritual possibilities in the next world, and domestication of the corpse" (55). This scene with dead Judge Pyncheon runs counter to the spirit of these "attitudes" because it avoids any inference of affection for dead Judge Pyncheon by his family, includes as his only memorial the photograph taken by Holgrave, and refuses to offer hope of heaven. Although the scene occurs in the house, the position of the corpse, seated rigidly in the parlor, and the disturbing reference to the emblem of decay, the fly, thwart "domestication."
46. Shakespeare, *Major Plays and the Sonnets*, 860.
47. Seery, *Political Theory for Mortals*, 182. Seery sets forth a political theory of death that involves writing a social contract from the perspective of the dead. This kind of social contract is not "written from the state of nature, it is written from the land of Hades; rather than an origin myth, it might be called a terminus myth" (159). The perspective of the "Final Position" involves "a collapse of all boundaries between public and private" (161).

See Russ Castronovo, *Necro Citizenship: Death, Eroticism, and the Public Sphere in the Nineteenth Century United States* (Durham and London: Duke University Press, 2001), for another perspective on the role of the dead in the American polis. Castronovo believes that the antebellum political system was structured to encourage "dead" citizenship (not only were certain citizens "dead" to the polis, but the system encouraged all, even the dominant white males, to assume the stance of death). While Seery believes it is possible that the dead can be considered an active political force, Castronovo views nineteenth-century United States citizens as immune to the political energy of the dead. He concludes, "The dead speak: the question is whether the living will hear a story about the ways in which belonging, incorporation, and other processes of democratic community produce social corpses" (149).

48. Seery, *Political Theory for Mortals*, 162.
49. Virgil, *The Aeneid*, trans. Robert Fitzgerald (New York: Random House, 1983), 457.
50. Seery discusses this scene in *Political Theory for Mortals*, 156–57.

Four From Melancholy to Mourning: Death and Politics in *The Blithedale Romance*

1. This chapter is a revised and considerably expanded version of my essay, "Tyrant King and Accused Queen: Father and Daughter in Nathaniel Hawthorne's *The Blithedale Romance*," *ATQ* 6.1 (March 1992): 31–45. This essay focuses on the novel as the story of a plot to overthrow the accused queen Zenobia by her father/king, which brings death to the queen and impotence to her male usurpers. Zenobia's death is the source of the downfall of the Blithedale state (31–45).

2. Farrell in *Inventing the American Way of Death* states that religious liberalism "affected the established forms of religious funeral practice" (99). He also notes that in New England liberal ideas were important to the "first stage" (1830–55) in the development of the modern cemetery, the "rural" or "garden" cemetery (99). Laderman in *The Sacred Remains* uses the rural cemetery movement in New England to illustrate his thesis that the culture was undergoing a "gradual process of 'dechristianization' that led to reconceptualizations of the meaning of the corpse and of death in general" (10).

3. Mount Auburn Cemetery is located on the outskirts of Cambridge, Massachusetts and was referred to as "rural" probably because of the way in which the principles behind its founding drew from the "rural" or pastoral tradition, rather than because of its actual location. See Linden-Ward, *Silent City*, for a thorough discussion of the social and cultural forces that affected the establishment of Mount Auburn Cemetery. See Thomas G. Connors, "The Romantic Landscape: Washington Irving, Sleepy Hollow, and the Rural Cemetery Movement" in *Mortal Remains*, ed. Isenburg and Burstein, who credits Washington Irving's "romantic tastes" with shaping the ideas and conceptions of the rural cemetery movement (187).

4. Chief Justice Joseph Story, "An Address," in *A History of the Cemetery of Mount Auburn*, ed. Bigelow, 144, 160.

5. See Linden-Ward, *Silent City*, for a discussion of the important emphasis on gardens in the original plans for Mount Auburn Cemetery (197–203). In one of the earliest reports to the original subscribers of Mount Auburn, several of whom were members of the Massachusetts Horticultural Society, General Dearborn referred to Mount Auburn as a "Garden of Experiment and Cemetery." See "General Dearborn's Report," in *The Picturesque Pocket Companion, and Visitor's Guide, Through Mount Auburn; Illustrated With Upwards of Sixty Engravings on Wood* (Boston: Otis, Broaders and Company, 1839), 40.

6. In a brief discussion of *The Blithedale Romance* (241–49), Elisabeth Bronfen in *Over Her Dead Body* focuses on the function of the dead body of Zenobia in the text, using Walter

Benjamin's analogy between allegory and ruin (242). She explains that even as Coverdale "tries to find a way to recuperate a sense of univocality, harmony and identity disrupted by this corpse, any allegorisation leads him inevitably to notions of disjunction between signifier and intended signified, to notions of difference and failure as part of what is signified and to a plurality of readings that offer no peace" (244–45).

7. Irigaray, "Body Against Body: In Relation to the Mother," in *Sexes and Genealogies*, 11. Irigaray explains, "One thing is plain, not only in everyday events but in the whole social scene: our society and our culture operate on the basis of an original matricide" (11).

8. Ibid.

9. Seery in *Political Theory for Mortals* describes a social contract written *"among the dead"* from the perspective of the "Final Position" (159; italics in the original).

10. Margaret Schlauch's identification and analysis in *Chaucer's Constance and Accused Queens* (New York: New York University Press, 1927) of several key narrative patterns of the story of the accused queen inform my discussion.

11. Ibid., 8.

12. Ibid., 9–11.

13. Ibid., 5, 43–45.

14. Ibid., 9.

15. In *Hawthorne as Myth-Maker*, McPherson discusses the Greek mythic patterns in *The Blithedale Romance*. He sees Fauntleroy-Moodie as central to the romance because he is a "kind of god" (151).

16. Schlauch, *Chaucer's Constance and Accused Queens*, 45, 60.

17. John C. Hirsh in "Zenobia as Queen: The Background Sources to Hawthorne's *The Blithedale Romance*," *The Nathaniel Hawthorne Journal 1971*, ed. C.E. Frazer Clark, Jr. (Englewood, Colo.: Microcard Editions, 1971) explains that Zenobia was a "third-century queen of Palmyra who defied the Roman empire itself and was ultimately crushed for her disobedience" (182).

18. Schlauch, *Chaucer's Constance and Accused Queens*, 5.

19. Irigaray, "Belief Itself," in *Sexes and Genealogies*, 33–34.

20. In the early nineteenth century in New England, the preparation of the dead body for burial would have been the province of the women in the community. See Farrell, *The American Way of Death*, 147; and Colleen McDannell, *The Christian Home in Victorian America, 1840–1900*, 98. The care of the dead body in America was not consigned to professionals until the time of the Civil War, and it was not a practice that became common among the middle class until the concluding decades of the century (Farrell, *The American Way of Death*, 148–49; Laderman, *Sacred Remains*, 8).

21. Jennifer Waelti-Walters, *Fairy Tales and the Female Imagination* (Montreal: Eden Press, 1982), 11.

22. Freud, "Mourning and Melancholia," in *The Standard Edition* 14: 245–46; 248–49.

23. Ibid., 249–50.

24. Schiesari, *The Gendering of Melancholia*, 47. My reading of Coverdale's melancholy is indebted to Schiesari's discussion of Freud's theory of melancholia.

25. Freud, "Mourning and Melancholia," in *The Standard Edition* 14: 246–47.

26. Schiesari, *The Gendering of Melancholia*, 47.

27. Ibid., 54.

28. Janet Todd, *Gender, Art, and Death* (New York: Continuum, 1993), 113.

29. Bakan, *Disease, Pain, and Sacrifice*, 119.

30. For a discussion of the novel as a response to Hawthorne's experiences in Concord from 1842 to 1845, including his relationships with Emerson and Fuller, see Larry J. Reynolds's "Hawthorne's Labors in Concord" in *The Cambridge Companion to Nathaniel Hawthorne*, ed. Millington, 10–34. Reynolds sees Hollingsworth as "a subtle partial portrait of Emerson, at least as he was perceived by Hawthorne" (11).

31. Emerson, "Experience," in *The Collected Works* 3: 29.
32. Emerson, "Nature," in *The Collected Works* 1: 44.
33. Ibid., 10.
34. Ibid., 44–45.
35. Emerson, "Experience," in *The Collected Works* 3: 29.
36. Peter B. Murray, "Mythopoesis in *The Blithedale Romance*," *PMLA* 75 (1960): 591–96. See Anthon's *A Classical Dictionary* for this version of the Titan myth.
37. See Castronovo, *Necro Citizenship*, for an interesting reading of the complex role of the dead body of Zenobia in the polis. Castronovo explains: "Zenobia's living corpse argues, however, that as equality and liberty appear in public, they are already imbued with death because exclusion and forgotten privilege precede—and enable—the human actor's entrance into the public sphere and underwrite his or her freedom" (150). See Gail Holst-Warhaft, *The Cue for Passion: Grief and Its Political Uses* (Cambridge, Mass.: Harvard University Press, 2000), for a discussion of grief's potential to "be manipulated for political ends" or to be "positively harnessed as a means to effect political change" (5). She discusses the way in which women particularly have been "inspired by the passion of grief" to threaten an oppressive regime or state (123).
38. Irigaray, "Body Against Body In Relation to the Mother," in *Sexes and Genealogies*, 11.
39. "Ethan Brand," in *The Snow-Image and Uncollected Tales* 11: 99.
40. Winthrop Wetherbee, "Constance and the World in Chaucer and Gower," in *John Gower, Recent Readings: Papers Presented at the Meetings of the John Gower Society at the International Congress on Medieval Studies, Western Michigan University, 1983–1988*, ed. Robert F. Yeager (Kalamazoo, Mich.: Medieval Institute Publications, Western Michigan University, 1989), 69.
41. Joseph E. Grennen, "Chaucer's Man of Law and the Constancy of Justice," *JEGP* 84 (1985): 498.
42. See Mary Suzanne Schrieber, "Justice to Zenobia," *New England Quarterly* 56.1 (March 1982): 61–78, for a somewhat different perspective on the achievement of justice for Zenobia. Because Coverdale is an unreliable narrator, he has misinterpreted the meaning and motivation behind Zenobia's death. Schrieber concludes that Zenobia's death is either "accidental" or a suicide motivated by a "despair of woman's lot and future prospects" (62). While critics disagree about the extent of Coverdale's unreliability, most recent critics agree that he is at least somewhat unreliable. Schrieber's interpretation assumes that he is unreliable both for the facts and for his interpretation of the facts. My assumption about Coverdale's reliability is probably closer to Richard H. Brodhead's assessment in *Hawthorne, Melville, and the Novel*: "He is not generally unreliable either in his information or even in his surmises—the guesses he makes about the other characters' secrets are usually remarkably accurate—but he is unreliable in explaining his own motives" (101). Brodhead adds that Hawthorne's relationship with his narrator is not "consistent" and at times Coverdale "exhibits a moral obtuseness that makes him seem to be the object of Hawthorne's scorn" (100).
43. Sacvan Bercovitch, "Hawthorne's A-Morality of Compromise," in *The Scarlet Letter*, ed. Ross C. Murfin (Boston: Bedford Books of St. Martin's Press, 1991), 345.
44. Henry James, *The Tales of Henry James*, ed. Maqbool Aziz (Oxford: Clarendon Press, 1984), 3: 201.
45. Ibid., 202.
46. See Barbara Welter, *Dimity Convictions: The American Woman in the Nineteenth Century* (Athens: Ohio University Press, 1976) and Nancy F. Cott, *The Bonds of Womanhood: "Woman's Sphere" in New England, 1780–1835*, 2nd ed. (New Haven: Yale University Press, 1997), for an explanation of the thesis of separate spheres. Alison Easton in "Hawthorne and the Question of Women" in *The Cambridge Companion to Nathaniel Hawthorne*, ed. Millington makes the important point that "Although ideological efforts

were made to contain the question of women through the concept of separate gendered 'spheres' of existence, men's and women's lives were, of course, inextricably intertwined" (81). She explains that Hawthorne could not have been "unaffected" by the understanding of such women as Margaret Fuller that "women were not insulated from the public realm, nor were men detached from the domestic, but that all inhabited a common world, albeit differently" (81). Other studies, such as Cathy N. Davidson and Jessamyn Hather, eds. *No More Separate Spheres!* (Durham: Duke University Press, 2002) and Monika Elbert, ed. *Separate Spheres No More: Gender Convergence in American Literature, 1830–1930* (Tuscaloosa: University of Alabama Press, 2000), challenge the metaphor of separate spheres as an exclusive conceptual model for understanding nineteenth-century gender roles. In *Men Beyond Desire: Manhood, Sex, and Violation in American Literature* (New York: Palgrave Macmillan, 2005), David Greven expresses his important concern that these studies, while valuable, have the potential to "obscure" the "experiential realities—such as compulsory homosociality" of nineteenth-century society (253, note 2).

47. Seery emphasizes the importance of shame in initiating the process of writing a new and more just "social contract, to be debated and negotiated, written and performed *among the dead*" (*Political Theory for Mortals*, 159; italics in the original).

48. Fuller, *Woman in the Nineteenth Century*, 7.

49. Thomas R. Mitchell in *Hawthorne's Fuller Mystery* (Amherst: University of Massachusetts Press, 1998) sees Hawthorne and *The Blithedale Romance* as haunted by "two Fuller ghosts…, the Fuller of his memory at Concord and the Fuller of his imagination at Rome" (209). He also discusses the meeting between Fuller and Hawthorne that took place in the woods of Sleepy Hollow in 1842 (72–77). Larry J. Reynolds in "Hawthorne's Labors in Concord" in *The Cambridge Companion to Nathaniel Hawthorne*, ed. Millington comments that the scene "suggests the unusual openness Hawthorne displayed in his relations with Fuller" (22).

50. Thoreau, *Walden*, 182.

51. In *Margaret and Her Friends: Or, Ten Conversations with Margaret Fuller upon the Mythology of the Greeks and Its Expression in Art* (New York: Arno Press, 1972), Caroline W. Healy Dall reported that in Fuller's conversation on the myth of Pluto and Tartarus she used the term "baffled effort" to describe the "penalty" least endurable to the Greeks (124).

52. Fuller, *Woman in the Nineteenth Century*, 7.

53. Certeau, *The Writing of History*, 47.

54. Seery, *Political Theory for Mortals*, 161.

Five   "Intimate Equality": Sacrifice and Death in *The Marble Faun*

1. Certeau comments on the significance of the word "system" in note 22 in *The Writing of History*, 193.

2. Roy R. Male explains, "The biblical allusions in *The Marble Faun* should not tempt us into reading it as scripture or theology.…Hawthorne's position, to use R.W.B. Lewis' phrase, was an 'offbeat traditionalism'" (117). See Roy R. Male, "The Transfiguration of Figures: *The Marble Faun*," in *The Merrill Studies in "The Marble Faun,"* ed. David B. Kesterson (Columbus: Charles E. Merrill Publishing Co., 1971), 103–18.

3. Certeau, *The Writing of History*, 141 (italics in the original).

4. Ibid.

5. Baym states that Hawthorne is "preoccupied with the heterosexual couple and the obstacles that make of a supposedly fulfilling social form something so fraught with misery" ("Revisiting Hawthorne's Feminism," 42). Recent discussions of the Hawthorne

heterosexual couple tend to assume that Hawthorne's "formulations of the feminine" are complex and frequently involve dismantling "the culturally conventional binary of pure woman/fallen woman" (Easton, "Hawthorne and the Question of Women," in *The Cambridge Companion to Nathaniel Hawthorne*, ed. Millington, 96). This thesis raises questions about previous approaches to the novel based on the assumption that Hilda is the fair innocent and marriage to her is an unquestioned good. For essays on the novel that call into question this assumption, see, for example, Emily Schiller, "The Choice of Innocence: Hilda in *The Marble Faun*," *Studies in the Novel* 26.4 (Winter 1994): 372–91. Schiller argues that Hilda's innocence is dangerous and deeply problematic. After asking whether we are to assume that whoever marries in Hawthorne's fiction is right, she characterizes the courtship of Hilda and Kenyon as a "ritual banishing of uncomfortable, ambiguous thought" (388). See also Emily Miller Budick, "Perplexity, Sympathy, and the Question of the Human: A Reading of *The Marble Faun*" in *The Cambridge Companion to Nathaniel Hawthorne*, ed. Millington, 230–50. Budick argues that the subject of the novel is simple—the failure of sympathy or relationship—but the "perplexing" questions the subject raises about ethical and moral choices have a "complicated answer" that has to do with moving beyond formulaic binaries into "the self-conscious knowledge of the undecidability of physical phenomena and therefore the subjectivity of all human perception" (232). Hilda is characterized as a "stone" dove who "preserves her innocence at the expense of her goodness," and Kenyon's union with her and journey to home become a "Banishment from the only reality that matters: the perplexed and perplexing world of innocence and evil" (248).

6. Turner, *On the Edge of the Bush*, 232. See Robert S. Friedman, *Hawthorne's Romances: Social Drama and the Metaphor of Geometry* (Amsterdam: Harwood Academic Publishers, 2000), for a reading of Hawthorne's *The Marble Faun* through the "liminal lens" of Turner that comes to different conclusions (xiii). Friedman regards Donatello's liminal journey as offering "hope," and the novel as "a new fiction that investigates the meaning of sin and the power of the past" (167, 142).

7. Turner, *On the Edge of the Bush*, 232.

8. Emerson, "Nature," in *The Collected Works* 1: 17.

9. Turner, *On the Edge of the Bush*, 197.

10. Ibid., 197–98.

11. John Layard, *Stone Men of Malekula: Vao* (London: Chatto and Windus, 1942), 588. This quotation is also cited in Beers, *Women and Sacrifice* (with the omission of "in turn") to confirm Beers's thesis that links male sacrifice and "fear of women" (158–59). From Beers's perspective, it is important that when Layard undertook his study of the social life of the Malekula and their rituals of sacrifice the region of Malekula was "undergoing many serious social and cultural changes, . . . not the least of which was, . . . an apparent changeover from a system of matrilineal descent to that of patrilineal descent" (149). Layard describes this changeover as the source of "high tragedy" in the community because tribe members "were forced to outrage all personal feeling" in turning from allegiance to their matriarchal kin to the "new principle of overt patrilineal descent" (606–7).

12. This pattern of strife or conflict centering on the site of a woman's place of burial is similar to what Hawthorne alludes to in *The Scarlet Letter*. Sir Edmund Andros was influential in having King's Chapel erected "on a corner of the old [Johnson] burial-ground" (1: 82) as a memorial to his late wife, Lady Andros, who had been buried on this site about a decade earlier. As I discuss in the conclusion of chapter one, this church, the first Anglican place of worship in the colonies, was a source of controversy and contention between the Separatists and the Non-Separatists in Puritan New England for several years. See Foote, *Annals of King's Chapel*, vol. 1, for the early history of King's Chapel.

13. Anthon, *A Classical Dictionary*, 143. Anthon emphasizes the excessiveness of Hadrian's response to Antinous's sacrifice (143).

14. Gail Coffler, "Classical Iconography in the Aesthetics of *Billy Budd, Sailor*," in *Savage Eye: Melville and the Visual Arts,* ed. Christopher Sten (Kent, Ohio: Kent State University Press, 1991), 258–59.

15. Hawthorne discusses Hadrian's tomb and its relation to the Castle of Saint Angelo in *The French and Italian Notebooks* 14: 142–43.

16. Lord Byron, *The Complete Poetical Works*, ed. Jerome J. McGann (Oxford: Clarendon Press, 1980), 2: 167.

17. T.S. Eliot, "Tradition and the Individual Talent," *Selected Essays* (New York: Harcourt, Brace and Company, 1950), 6.

18. One of the major theological controversies of Hawthorne's day centered on the doctrine of Christ's sacrifice, particularly on the vexing question of the purpose of vicarious sacrifice. See Gary Dorrien, *The Making of American Liberal Theology: Imagining Progressive Religion, 1805–1900* (Louisville: Westminster John Knox Press, 2001). While Hawthorne seemed to have had little interest in doctrinal debates and belonged to no organized religion, his emphasis on the natural and social consequences of sacrifice places him in the "subjectivist moral influence tradition" of Coleridge, Wycliffe, Locke, and Kant, and anticipates Horace Bushnell's conclusion in his major work *Vicarious Sacrifice, Grounded in Principles of Universal Obligation* (New York: Charles Scribner and Company, 1866) that "It [sacrifice] is made for impression and in that has its end" (as cited in Dorrien, *The Making of American Liberal Theology*, 167).

19. According to Staten in *Eros in Mourning*, the "strategies of idealization and transcendence" (21) transform "losable objects" (14) into unlimited, permanent libidinal investments, and in this way the male tries to master automourning (16). From the perspective of the tradition of Western literature, immortal "objects" are worthier "objects" of love (xii–xiii).

20. Shakespeare, *Major Plays and the Sonnets*, 648.

21. Joy S. Kasson in *Marble Queens and Captives: Women in Nineteenth Century American Sculpture* (New Haven: Yale University Press, 1990) describes William Story's *Cleopatra*: "sunk in reverie, sitting in a chair with her feet outstretched and her arm resting on the chair's back, her body turned slightly to the side, her head leaning on her hand. As in Guido's painting, the bare breast suggests vulnerability....However, the firm breast and the smooth curve of the exposed shoulder also served as a reminder of Cleopatra's famous beauty, offering a carefully controlled allusion to her sensual, erotic powers" (210–11).

22. Dall, *Margaret and Her Friends*, 97. According to Dall, Fuller interpreted the conflict between Venus and Psyche in the myth as instigated by Venus's "jealousy" of Psyche. Venus's jealousy was understandable as an emotion that "the good must always feel toward the better which is to supercede it" (97).

23. Anthon, *A Classical Dictionary*, 1377.

24. Geoffrey Grigson, *The Goddess of Love: The Birth, Triumph, Death, and Return of Aphrodite* (London: Constable, 1976), 217.

25. Anthon, *A Classical Dictionary*, 1376. Anthon cites Hesiod's version as his source for the story of Venus's origin.

26. Ibid., 278.

27. Shakespeare, *Major Plays and the Sonnets*, 647.

28. Ariès, *The Hour of Our Death*, 383.

29. Ibid., 383–84. Ariès argues that the "attitude of anonymity in death" declined after the twelfth century, although, among the poor, mass graves or unmarked graves persisted until the eighteenth century: "One of the major differences between the rich, or the less poor, and the real poor is that the first group tended increasingly to have individual tombs to preserve the memory of their bodies, while the second group had nothing" (207).

30. Ibid., 384.

Conclusion

1. Plato, *The Dialogues of Plato*, 5: 456. In *The Creation of Mythology*, trans. Margaret Cook (Chicago: University of Chicago Press, 1986), Marcel Detienne uses this reference to Plato's *Laws* to support his thesis that Plato both looked down on these "myths" as "primitive"— and connected with women—and recognized myths can possess significant social and political impact (84). (Detienne's translation of this passage differs in an important way from Jowett's, the translation I cited; Detienne uses the term "myths" for Jowett's "words.") Detienne also argues that there should be no attempt to distinguish between the rational and the imaginative, the civilized and the primitive, when considering the origins and interpretations of myth because myths exist "two-headed" in a realm beyond the binaries (103, 121–23).
2. Emerson, "The Age of Fable," in *The Early Lectures* 1: 257.
3. Emerson, "The American Scholar," in *The Collected Works* 1: 52.
4. Dall, *Margaret and Her Friends*, 45. Dall reported a spirited exchange between Fuller and Emerson on the subject of the creation of an American mythology. Fuller argued, *"We could not create a Mythology"* because "ours was the age of Analysis," and Emerson retorted, "Why not? We had still better material" (45; italics in the original).
5. Ibid., 161–62.
6. For extensive discussions of Hawthorne's use of myth, see McPherson, *Hawthorne as Myth-Maker* and Nina da Vinci Nichols, *Ariadne's Lives* (Madison, N.J.: Fairleigh Dickinson University Press, 1995). Nichols's approach to myth in Hawthorne's fiction, like McPherson's, is shaped by Northrop Frye's ideas about the "bumps and hollows" hiding beneath the surface of a text that, when mapped, reveal a good deal about the underground imagination of its author (*Ariadne's Lives*, 11). While McPherson identifies a broad range of mythical character types in Hawthorne's fiction, such as "iron men, Dark Ladies, mercurial heroes, and frail princesses" (17), Nichols concentrates her study of Hawthorne's use of myth on the figure of Ariadne.

   According to Coffler in "Classical Iconography" in *Savage Eye*, ed. Sten, "the Greco-Roman heritage was the strongest cultural force in America, influencing both structure and image in government, law, education, architecture, and sculpture" (258). Most educated men of Hawthorne's day followed in this tradition and studied ancient history and classical Latin and Greek. Hawthorne's career at Bowdoin College included "a heavy concentration in Greek and Latin." Mellow, *Nathaniel Hawthorne in His Times*, 29. Thomas Woodson in "Hawthorne and the Author's Immortal Fame," *Nathaniel Hawthorne Review* 30.1 and 2 (2004) explains that "we know little" about what specific classical texts Hawthorne read and studied while at Bowdoin (62).
7. Burton Feldman uses the terms "Greekomania" and "mythomania" to describe the strong interest in myth among the Romantics. See "German Romanticism and Myth" in Burton Feldman and Robert D. Richardson, eds. *The Rise of Modern Mythology 1680–1860* (Bloomington: Indiana University Press, 1972), 302. He explains that "Greekomania" was used originally in a satirical poem of Johann C.F. Schiller (302).
8. For an informative discussion of Hawthorne's knowledge of art, see Rita K. Gollin and John L. Idol, Jr., *Prophetic Pictures: Nathaniel Hawthorne's Knowledge and Uses of the Visual Arts* (New York: Greenwood Press, 1991). See Rita K. Gollin, "Hawthorne and the Visual Arts," in *A Historical Guide to Nathaniel Hawthorne*, ed. Larry J. Reynolds (New York: Oxford University Press, 2001), 109–33, for a more extensive discussion of Hawthorne's ideas about meaning and value in art.
9. Ludwig Feuerbach, *The Essence of Christianity*, trans. George Eliot (New York: Harper and Brothers, 1957), 91, 107.
10. Ibid., 150.

11. Ibid., 270.
12. J.B. Bullen, ed. "Introduction," *The Sun Is God: Painting, Literature, and Mythology in the Nineteenth Century* (Oxford: Clarendon Press, 1989), 5.
13. Feuerbach, *The Essence of Christianity*, 150. Feuerbach believed that Christians "secured the eternity of their subjective life only by annihilating,...the opposite of subjectivity—Nature" (150).
14. Schelling, "Introduction to the Philosophy of Mythology," in *The Rise of Modern Mythology*, ed. Feldman and Richardson, 326.
15. Melville, *The Portable Melville*, 405.
16. Brodhead, *Hawthorne, Melville, and the Novel*, 132.
17. See Jennifer Fleischner, "Hawthorne and the Politics of Slavery," *Studies in the Novel* 23 (1991): 96–106; Teresa A. Goddu, "Letters Turned to Gold: Hawthorne, Authorship, and Slavery," *Studies in American Fiction* 29 (2001): 49–76; Jay Grossman, "'A' is for Abolition?: Race, Authorship, *The Scarlet Letter*," *Textual Practices* 7 (1993): 13–30; Deborah L. Madsen, "'A for Abolition': Hawthorne's Bond-Servant and the Shadow of Slavery," *Journal of American Studies* 25.2 (1991): 255–59; Larry J. Reynolds, "'Strangely Ajar with the Human Race': Hawthorne, Slavery, and the Question of Moral Responsibility" in *Hawthorne and the Real: Bicentennial Essays*, ed. Millicent Bell (Columbus: Ohio State University Press, 2005), 40–69; Leland S. Person, "The Dark Labyrinth of Mind: Hawthorne, Hester, and the Ironies of Racial Mothering," *Studies in American Fiction* 29.1 (2001): 33–48; and Jean Fagan Yellin, "Hawthorne and the Slavery Question" in *A Historical Guide to Nathaniel Hawthorne*, ed. Reynolds, for discussions of the issues of slavery and race.
18. In his balanced account of Hawthorne's position on slavery, Reynolds in "Strangely Ajar with the Human Race" in *Hawthorne and the Real*, ed. Bell explains that in the 1830s and 1840s several of the Transcendentalists feared the radicalism of the abolitionist movement, and Hawthorne "shared their early political quietism built on a belief in an innate moral sense and the presence of a beneficent tendency at work in the world" that would eventually bring the end of slavery (47–48). While they moved beyond these "gradualist sentiments," Hawthorne did not (48, and note 19 on 67).
19. Hawthorne to Longfellow, May 8, 1851 in *The Letters, 1843–1853* 16: 431 (emphasis mine).
20. In her thorough review of Hawthorne's notebooks, letters, journal entries, and sketches, Yellin in *A Historical Guide,* ed. Reynolds, states: "Hawthorne became intimately acquainted with the essential facts of chattel slavery, as well as with the debate raging around it" (135). Her conclusion about Hawthorne's position is based primarily on his entries in *The American Notebooks*, the essay "Chiefly About War-matters," and his comments in a letter to Horatio Bridge in which he writes: "A civilized and educated man must feel somewhat like a fool, methinks, when he has staked his own life against that of a black savage, and lost the game. In the sight of God, one life may be as valuable as another; but in our view, the stakes are very unequal" (Hawthorne to Horatio Bridge, April 1, 1844 in *The Letters, 1843–1853* 16: 26; also cited in Yellin, 151).
21. Ibid., 157.
22. Francis E. Kearns, "Margaret Fuller and the Abolition Movement," *Journal of the History of Ideas* 25 (1964): 122.
23. Thoreau, *Walden*, 6 (emphasis mine).
24. Kearns, "Margaret Fuller and the Abolition Movement," 122.
25. Margaret Fuller, *"These Sad But Glorious Days": Dispatches from Europe, 1846–1850,* ed. Larry J. Reynolds and Susan Belasco Smith (New Haven: Yale University Press, 1991), 165.
26. Ibid., 230.
27. Michael Mullin, ed. *American Negro Slavery: A Documentary History* (Columbia: University of South Carolina Press, 1976), 151–53.
28. No author, as cited in Mullin, ed. *American Negro Slavery,* 152.

29. Ibid., 151.
30. Frederick Douglass, *Narrative of the Life of Frederick Douglass, An American Slave, Written by Himself*, ed. Benjamin Quarles (Cambridge, Mass.: Belknap Press, 1960), 108.
31. Ibid., 63.
32. Frederick Douglass, "Northern Ballots and the Election of 1852: An Address Delivered in Ithaca, New York, On October 14, 1852," in *The Frederick Douglass Papers*, ed. John W. Blassingame (New Haven: Yale University Press, 1982), 2: 404.
33. William E. Gienapp, "The Republican Party and the Slave Power," in *New Perspectives on Race and Slavery in America: Essays in Honor of Kenneth M. Stampp*, ed. Robert H. Abzug and Stephen E. Maizlish (Lexington: University Press of Kentucky, 1986), 57.
34. Frederick Douglass, "Northern Ballots," in *The Frederick Douglass Papers,* ed. Blassingame, 2: 404.
35. Kasson, *Marble Queens and Captives*, 73.
36. Ibid., 154. For discussions of Hawthorne's response to Hosmer's Zenobia, see also Gollin and Idol, *Prophetic Pictures*, 96, and John L. Idol, Jr., "Nathaniel Hawthorne and Harriet Hosmer," *Nathaniel Hawthorne Journal* 6 (1976): 123–25.
37. Teresa A. Goddu in *Gothic America: Narrative, History, and Nation* (New York: Columbia University Press, 1997) emphasizes the difference between the black and white subject: "As a white body, the Greek slave represents the veil of femininity, but when refigured as a black body in 'The Virginian Slave'. . . , she explicitly symbolizes the market that buys and sells female flesh" (100).
38. Kasson, *Marble Queens and Captives*, 154. Kasson emphasizes that, despite the fact that Hosmer portrays Zenobia as enchained, she is no "acquiescent victim," and with this depiction Hosmer "took a cautious step toward the celebration of woman's power" (154, 155).
39. Jeffrey Steele in *Transfiguring America: Myth, Ideology, and Mourning in Margaret Fuller's Writing* (Columbia: University of Missouri Press, 2001) discusses Fuller's representation of the state as a corrupt body politic in several of her dispatches from Rome published in 1847 (269).
40. Fuller, *"These Sad But Glorious Days,"* 250.
41. Steele, *Transfiguring America*, 291.
42. In *Rituals of Blood: Consequences of Slavery in Two American Centuries* (Washington, D.C.: Civitas Counterpoint, 1998), Orlando Patterson explains: "Christianity is quintessentially a sacrificial creed" (xv). He emphasizes the central role the idea of sacrifice played in the "rituals of the lynch mob" in the post–Civil War South (xiii). Just as Beers in *Women and Sacrifice* links violence enacted against women with the idea of sacrifice in Christianity, Patterson argues that the lynch mob's "sacrificial murder" has Christian "religious significance" (208).
43. Douglass, *Narrative of the Life*, 110.
44. Ibid., 155.
45. Ibid., 159.
46. Mary Daly in *Beyond God the Father: Toward a Philosophy of Women's Liberation* (Boston: Beacon Press, 1985) argues that because of the entrenched power of the rigidly patriarchal structure of religion a change in the status of women demands imagining a "qualitative leap" in human evolution (xxiii).
47. Herman Melville, *Moby-Dick; or the Whale* (New York: W.W. Norton, 1976), 318.
48. For a different perspective on the fate of Miriam and Donatello, see Budick's "Perplexity, Sympathy and the Question of the Human" in *The Cambridge Companion to Nathaniel Hawthorne,* ed. Millington. Budick concludes that the reader sees Kenyon and Hilda's return to America as a "final banishment from the only reality that matters: the perplexed and perplexing world of innocence and evil" (248).
49. In *Slavery and Social Death: A Comparative Study* (Cambridge, Mass.: Harvard University Press, 1982), Orlando Patterson explains, "On the cognitive or mythic level, one dominant

theme emerges, which lends an unusually loaded meaning to the act of natal alienation: this is the social death of the slave" (38).

50. Kohut, "Death in Venice by Thomas Mann," in *The Search For the Self* 1: 107–130.
51. Ibid., 127.
52. Ibid.
53. Ibid., 118, 126.
54. Ibid., 130.
55. See the "Historical Commentary" and "Ancillary Documents" sections of *The Elixir of Life Manuscripts,* vol. 13 of *The Centenary Edition,* for a thorough discussion of the fragments.
56. Pansie is referred to in the manuscript as both "granddaughter" and "great-granddaughter."

BIBLIOGRAPHY

Abrams, M.H. *Natural Supernaturalism: Tradition and Revolution in Romantic Literature*. New York: W.W. Norton, 1971.

Abzug, Robert H. and Stephen E. Maizlish, eds. *New Perspectives on Race and Slavery in America: Essays in Honor of Kenneth M. Stampp*. Lexington: University Press of Kentucky, 1986.

Adams, John Greenleaf. *The Christian Victor: or, Mortality and Immortality; Including Happy Death Scenes*. Boston: A. Tompkins, 1851.

Adams, Raymond. "Hawthorne and a Glimpse of Walden." *Essex Institute Historical Collections* 94 (July 1958): 191–93.

Anthon, Charles. *A Classical Dictionary*. New York: Harper, 1857.

Ariès, Philippe. *The Hour of Our Death: The Classic History of Western Attitudes Toward Death Over the Last One Thousand Years*. Translated by Helen Weaver. New York: Barnes and Noble Books, 2000.

Atkinson, David William. *The English Ars Moriendi*. New York: Peter Lang, 1992.

Augustine, Saint. *The Teacher. The Free Choice of the Will. Grace and Free Will*. Vol. 59. *The Fathers of the Church*. Translated by Robert P. Russell. Washington, D.C.: Catholic University Press, 1968.

Bakan, David. *Disease, Pain, and Sacrifice: Toward a Psychology of Suffering*. Chicago: University of Chicago Press, 1968.

Barlowe, Jamie. *The Scarlet Mob of Scribblers: Rereading Hester Prynne*. Carbondale: Southern Illinois University Press, 2000.

Barthes, Roland. *Camera Lucida: Reflections on Photography*. Translated by Richard Howard. New York: Hill and Wang, 1981.

Bassein, Beth Ann. *Women and Death: Linkages in Western Thought and Literature*. Westport, Conn.: Greenwood Press, 1984.

Baym, Nina. "Again and Again, the Scribbling Women." In *Hawthorne and Women: Engendering and Expanding the Hawthorne Tradition*, ed. John L. Idol, Jr., and Melinda M. Ponder, 20–36.

———. "Hawthorne's Women: The Tyranny of Social Myths." *Centennial Review* 15.3 (1971): 250–72.

———. "Nathaniel Hawthorne and His Mother: A Biographical Speculation." *American Literature* 54 (March 1982): 1–27.

———. "Review of *Dearest Beloved: The Hawthornes and the Making of the Middle Class Family*, by T. Walter Herbert." *JEGP* 93 (April 1994): 271–75.

———. "Revisiting Hawthorne's Feminism." *Nathaniel Hawthorne Review* 30.1 and 2 (2004): 32–55.

Baym, Nina. "The Romantic *Malgre Lui*: Hawthorne in the Custom House." *ESQ* 40 (1973): 14–25.

———. *The Shape of Hawthorne's Career*. Ithaca and London: Cornell University Press, 1976.

———. "Thwarted Nature: Nathaniel Hawthorne as Feminist." In *American Novelists Revisited: Essays in Feminist Criticism*, ed. Fritz Fleischmann, 58–77. Boston: G.K. Hall, 1982.

Beaty, Nancy Lee, ed. *The Craft of Dying: A Study in the Literary Tradition of the Ars Moriendi in England*. New Haven: Yale University Press, 1970.

Becker, Ernest. *The Denial of Death*. New York: Free Press, 1973.

Beers, William. *Women and Sacrifice: Male Narcissism and the Psychology of Religion*. Detroit: Wayne State University Press, 1992.

Bell, Millicent, ed. *Hawthorne and the Real: Bicentennial Essays*. Columbus: Ohio State University Press, 2005.

Bensick, Carol. "Hawthorne and His Bunyan." *Nathaniel Hawthorne Review* 19.1 (Spring 1993): 1–10.

Benstock, Shari. "*The Scarlet Letter* (a)dorée, or the Female Body Embroidered." In *The Scarlet Letter*, ed. Ross C. Murfin, 288–303.

Bercovitch, Sacvan. "Hawthorne's A-Morality of Compromise." In *The Scarlet Letter*, ed. Ross C. Murfin, 344–58. Boston: Bedford Books of St. Martin's Press, 1991.

Berlant, Lauren. *The Anatomy of National Fantasy: Hawthorne, Utopia, and Everyday Life*. Chicago: University of Chicago Press, 1991.

Berthold, Dennis. "Hawthorne, Ruskin, and the Gothic Revival: Transcendent Gothic in *The Marble Faun*." *ESQ* 20 (1974): 15–32.

———. "Review of *Gothic America: Narrative, History, and Nation* by Teresa A. Goddu." *Romantic Circles*. Ed. Jeffrey N. Cox. June 2, 2005. *www.rc.umd.edu/reviews/back/goddu.html*

Bigelow, Jacob. *A History of the Cemetery of Mount Auburn*. 1860. Reprint. Cambridge: Applewood Books, 1988.

Bowlby, John. *Loss: Sadness and Depression*. Vol. 3 of *Attachment and Loss*. New York: Harper Collins, 1980.

Brodhead, Richard H. *Hawthorne, Melville, and the Novel*. Chicago: University of Chicago Press, 1973.

Bronfen, Elisabeth. *Over Her Dead Body: Death, Femininity and the Aesthetic*. New York: Routledge, 1992.

Brownson, Orestes. "Literary Notices and Criticism." In *The Critical Response to Nathaniel Hawthorne's "The Scarlet Letter,"* ed. Gary Scharnhorst, 34–39.

Budick, Emily Miller. "Perplexity, Sympathy, and the Question of the Human: A Reading of *The Marble Faun*." In *The Cambridge Companion to Nathaniel Hawthorne*, ed. Richard H. Millington, 230–35.

Bullen, J.B., ed. *The Sun Is God: Painting, Literature, and Mythology in the Nineteenth Century*. Oxford: Clarendon Press, 1989.

Byron, Lord. *The Complete Poetical Works*. Vol. 2. Edited by Jerome J. McGann. Oxford: Clarendon Press, 1980.

Calderwood, James L. *Shakespeare and the Denial of Death*. Amherst: University of Massachusetts Press, 1987.

Castronovo, Russ. *Necro Citizenship: Death, Eroticism, and the Public Sphere in the Nineteenth Century United States*. Durham and London: Duke University Press, 2001.

Cavitch, Max. "Interiority and Artifact: Death and Self-Inscription in Thomas Smith's Self Portrait." *Early American Literature* 37 (2002): 89–117.

de Certeau, Michel. *The Writing of History*. Translated by Tom Conley. New York: Columbia University Press, 1988.

Cheney, Mary Bushnell. *Life and Letters of Horace Bushnell.* New York: Arno Press, 1969.

Cixous, Hélène. "Fiction and Its Phantoms." *New Literary History* 7 (1975): 525–48.

———. "The Laugh of the Medusa." Translated by Keith Cohen and Paula Cohen. *Signs* 1 (1976): 875–93.

Coffler, Gail. "Classical Iconography in the Aesthetics of *Billy Budd, Sailor.*" In *Savage Eye: Melville and the Visual Arts,* ed. Christopher Sten, 257–76. Kent, Ohio: Kent State University Press, 1991.

Connors, Thomas G. "The Romantic Landscape: Washington Irving, Sleepy Hollow, and the Rural Cemetery Movement." In *Mortal Remains: Death in Early America,* ed. Nancy Isenberg and Andrew Burstein, 187–203. Philadelphia: University of Pennsylvania Press, 2003.

Cott, Nancy F. *The Bonds of Womanhood: "Woman's Sphere" in New England, 1780–1835.* 2nd ed. New Haven: Yale University Press, 1997.

Crews, Frederick. *Sins of the Fathers: Hawthorne's Psychological Themes.* New York: Oxford University Press, 1966.

———. *Skeptical Engagements.* Oxford: Oxford University Press, 1986.

Cronin, Martin. "Hawthorne on Romantic Love." *PMLA* 69 (1954): 89–98.

[Dall], Caroline W. Healy. *Margaret and Her Friends: Or, Ten Conversations with Margaret Fuller upon the Mythology of the Greeks and Its Expression in Art.* New York: Arno Press, 1972.

Daly, Mary. *Beyond God the Father: Toward a Philosophy of Women's Liberation.* Boston: Beacon Press, 1985.

Daly, Robert. "Liminality and Fiction in Cooper, Hawthorne, Cather, and Fitzgerald." In *Victor Turner and the Construction of Cultural Criticism: Between Literature and Anthropology,* ed. Kathleen Ashley, 70–85. Bloomington, Ind.: Indiana University Press, 1990.

Davidson, Cathy N., and Jessamyn Hather, eds. *No More Separate Spheres!* Durham: Duke University Press, 2002.

Derrick, Scott S. "'A Curious Subject of Observation and Inquiry': Homoeroticism, the Body, and Authorship in Hawthorne's *The Scarlet Letter.*" *Novel* 28 (1995): 308–26.

DeSalvo, Louise. *Nathaniel Hawthorne.* Atlantic Highlands, N.J.: Humanities Press International, 1987.

Detienne, Marcel. *The Creation of Mythology.* Translated by Margaret Cook. Chicago: University of Chicago Press, 1986.

Dickinson, Emily. *The Poems of Emily Dickinson.* Edited by R.W. Franklin. Cambridge, Mass. and London: Belknap Press, 1999.

Doebler, Bettie Anne. *"Rooted Sorrow": Dying in Early Modern England.* Rutherford, N.J.: Fairleigh Dickinson University Press, 1994.

Dorrien, Gary. *The Making of American Liberal Theology: Imagining Progressive Religion, 1805–1900.* Louisville: Westminster John Knox Press, 2001.

Douglas, Ann. *The Feminization of American Culture.* New York: A.A. Knopf, 1977.

———. "Heaven Our Home: Consolation Literature in the Northern United States, 1830–1880." In *Death in America,* ed. David E. Stannard, 49–68.

Douglass, Frederick. *Narrative of the Life of Frederick Douglass, An American Slave, Written by Himself.* Edited by Benjamin Quarles. Cambridge, Mass.: Belknap Press, 1960.

———. "Northern Ballots and the Election of 1852: An Address Delivered in Ithaca, New York, On October 14, 1852." *The Frederick Douglass Papers.* Vol. 2. Edited by John W. Blassingame, 397–420. New Haven: Yale University Press, 1982.

Dundes, Alan, ed. *The Evil Eye: A Casebook.* Madison, Wis.: University of Wisconsin Press, 1992.

Eakin, Paul John. "Hawthorne's Imagination and the Structure of 'The Custom-House.'" *American Literature* 43.3 (1971): 346–58.

Easton, Alison. "Hawthorne and the Question of Women." In *The Cambridge Companion to Nathaniel Hawthorne*, ed. Richard H. Millington, 79–98.

———. *The Making of the Hawthorne Subject*. Columbia: University of Missouri Press, 1996.

Elbert, Monika. "Hester on the Scaffold, Dimmesdale in the Closet: Hawthorne's Seven-Year Itch." *Essays in Literature* 16.2 (Fall 1989): 234–55.

———, ed. *Separate Spheres No More: Gender Convergence in American Literature, 1830–1930*. Tuscaloosa: University of Alabama Press, 2000.

Eliot, T.S. *Selected Essays*. New York: Harcourt, Brace and Company, 1950.

Emerson, Ralph Waldo. *The Collected Works of Ralph Waldo Emerson*. Vol. 1. Edited by Robert E. Spiller and Alfred R. Ferguson. Cambridge, Mass.: Belknap Press, 1971.

———. *The Early Lectures of Ralph Waldo Emerson*. Vol. 3. Edited by Robert E. Spiller and Wallace E. Williams. Cambridge, Mass.: Belknap Press, 1972.

Erlich, Gloria. *Family Themes and Hawthorne's Fiction: The Tenacious Web*. New Brunswick, N.J.: Rutgers University Press, 1984.

Farrell, James J. *Inventing the American Way of Death, 1830–1920*. Philadelphia: Temple University Press, 1980.

Farrell, Kirby. *Play, Death, and Heroism in Shakespeare*. Chapel Hill: University of North Carolina Press, 1989.

Feldman, Burton, and Robert D. Richardson, eds. *The Rise of Modern Mythology 1680–1860*. Bloomington: Indiana University Press, 1972.

Ferry, David. *The Limits of Mortality; An Essay on Wordsworth's Major Poems*. Middletown, Conn.: Wesleyan University Press, 1959.

Feuerbach, Ludwig. *The Essence of Christianity*. Translated by George Eliot. New York: Harper and Brothers, 1957.

Fleischner, Jennifer. "Hawthorne and the Politics of Slavery." *Studies in the Novel* 23 (1991): 96–106.

Foote, Henry Wilder. *Annals of King's Chapel: From the Puritan Age of New England to the Present Day*. Vol. 1. Boston and Cambridge: Little, Brown, and Company, 1882.

Follen, Eliza Lee Cabot. *The Life of Charles Follen*. Vol. 1. *The Works of Charles Follen, With a Memoir of His Life*. Boston: Hilliard, Gray, and Company, 1841–1842.

Frederick, John T. *The Darkened Sky: Nineteenth-Century American Novelists and Religion*. Notre Dame, Ind.: University of Notre Dame Press, 1969.

French, Stanley. "The Cemetery as Cultural Institution: The Establishment of Mount Auburn and the 'Rural Cemetery' Movement." In *Death in America*, ed. David E. Stannard, 69–91.

Freneau, Philip. *Poems of Freneau*. Edited by Harry Hayden Clark. New York: Harcourt, Brace and Company, 1929.

Freud, Sigmund. *The Standard Edition of the Complete Psychological Works of Sigmund Freud*. Vols. 14 and 18. Translated and Edited by James Strachey. London: Hogarth Press, 1974.

Friedman, Robert S. *Hawthorne's Romances: Social Drama and the Metaphor of Geometry*. Amsterdam: Harwood Academic Publishers, 2000.

Fuller, Margaret. *"These Sad But Glorious Days": Dispatches from Europe, 1846–1850*. Edited by Larry J. Reynolds and Susan Belasco Smith. New Haven: Yale University Press, 1991.

———. *Woman in the Nineteenth Century*. Edited by Larry J. Reynolds. New York: W.W. Norton, 1998.

Geddes, Gordon E. *Welcome Joy: Death in Puritan New England*. Ann Arbor, Mich.: UMI Research Press, 1981.

Gedge, Karin E. *Without Benefit of Clergy: Women and the Pastoral Relationship in Nineteenth-Century American Culture*. Oxford: Oxford University Press, 2003.

Gediman, Helen K. *Fantasies of Love and Death in Life and Art: A Psychoanalytic Study of the Normal and the Pathological*. New York: New York University Press, 1995.

Gienapp, William E., "The Republican Party and the Slave Power." In *New Perspectives on Race and Slavery in America: Essays in Honor of Kenneth M. Stampp*, ed. Robert H. Abzug and Stephen E. Maizlish, 51–78.

Goddu, Teresa A. *Gothic America: Narrative, History, and Nation*. New York: Columbia University Press, 1997.

———. "Letters Turned to Gold: Hawthorne, Authorship, and Slavery." *Studies in American Fiction* 29 (2001): 49–76.

Gollin, Rita K. "Hawthorne and the Visual Arts." In *A Historical Guide to Nathaniel Hawthorne*, ed. Larry J. Reynolds, 109–33.

Gollin, Rita K., and John L. Idol, Jr. *Prophetic Pictures: Nathaniel Hawthorne's Knowledge and Uses of the Visual Arts*. New York: Greenwood Press, 1991.

Goodwin, Sarah Webster, and Elisabeth Bronfen, eds. *Death and Representation*. Baltimore: Johns Hopkins University Press, 1993.

Grennen, Joseph E. "Chaucer's Man of Law and the Constancy of Justice." *JEGP* 84 (1985): 489–514.

Greven, David. *Men Beyond Desire: Manhood, Sex, and Violation in American Literature*. New York: Palgrave Macmillan, 2005.

Grigson, Geoffrey. *The Goddess of Love: The Birth, Triumph, Death, and Return of Aphrodite*. London: Constable, 1976.

Gross, Rita M., ed. *Beyond Androcentrism: New Essays on Women and Religion*. Missoula, Montana: Scholars Press for the American Academy of Religion, 1977.

Grossman, Jay. "'A' is for Abolition?: Race, Authorship, *The Scarlet Letter*." *Textual Practices* 7 (1993): 13–30.

Hawthorne, Julian. *Nathaniel Hawthorne and His Wife: A Biography*. 2 vols. Boston: Houghton Mifflin, 1884.

Hawthorne, Nathaniel. *The American Notebooks*. Edited by Claude M. Simpson. *The Centenary Edition of the Works of Nathaniel Hawthorne*. Vol. 8. Columbus: Ohio State University Press, 1972.

———. *The Blithedale Romance and Fanshawe*. Edited by Fredson Bowers, Matthew J. Bruccoli, and J. Neal Smith. *The Centenary Edition of the Works of Nathaniel Hawthorne*. Vol. 3. Columbus: Ohio State University Press, 1964.

———. *The Elixir of Life Manuscripts: Septimius Felton, Septimius Norton, The Dolliver Romance*. Edited by Edward H. Davidson, Claude M. Simpson, and L. Neal Smith. *The Centenary Edition of the Works of Nathaniel Hawthorne*. Vol. 13. Columbus: Ohio State University Press, 1977.

———. *The English Notebooks, 1853–1856*. Edited by Thomas Woodson and Bill Ellis. *The Centenary Edition of the Works of Nathaniel Hawthorne*. Vol. 21. Columbus: Ohio State University Press, 1997.

———. *The English Notebooks, 1856–1860*. Edited by Thomas Woodson and Bill Ellis. *The Centenary Edition of the Works of Nathaniel Hawthorne*. Vol. 22. Columbus: Ohio State University Press, 1997.

———. *The French and Italian Notebooks*. Edited by Thomas Woodson. *The Centenary Edition of the Works of Nathaniel Hawthorne*. Vol. 14. Columbus: Ohio State University Press, 1980.

———. *The House of the Seven Gables*. Edited by Fredson Bowers, Matthew J. Bruccoli, and L. Neal Smith. *The Centenary Edition of the Works of Nathaniel Hawthorne*. Vol. 2. Columbus: Ohio State University Press, 1965.

———. *The Letters, 1813–1843*. Edited by Thomas Woodson, L. Neal Smith, and Norman Holmes Pearson. *The Centenary Edition of the Works of Nathaniel Hawthorne*. Vol. 15. Columbus: Ohio State University Press, 1984.

Hawthorne, Nathaniel. *The Letters, 1843–1853.* Edited by Thomas Woodson, L. Neal Smith, and Norman Holmes Pearson. *The Centenary Edition of the Works of Nathaniel Hawthorne.* Vol. 16. Columbus: Ohio State University Press, 1985.

———. *The Letters, 1857–1864.* Edited by Thomas Woodson, James A. Rubino, L. Neal Smith, and Norman Holmes Pearson. *The Centenary Edition of the Works of Nathaniel Hawthorne.* Vol. 18. Columbus: Ohio State University Press, 1987.

———. *The Marble Faun; Or the Romance of Monte Beni.* Edited by Fredson Bowers and L. Neal Smith. *The Centenary Edition of the Works of Nathaniel Hawthorne.* Vol. 4. Columbus: Ohio State University Press, 1968.

———. *Miscellaneous Prose and Verse.* Edited by Thomas Woodson, Claude M. Simpson, and L. Neal Smith. *The Centenary Edition of the Works of Nathaniel Hawthorne.* Vol. 23. Columbus: Ohio State University Press, 1994.

———. *Mosses from an Old Manse.* Edited by Fredson Bowers, L. Neal Smith, John Manning, and J. Donald Crowley. *The Centenary Edition of the Works of Nathaniel Hawthorne.* Vol. 10. Columbus: Ohio State University Press, 1974.

———. *The Scarlet Letter.* Edited by Fredson Bowers and Matthew J. Bruccoli. *The Centenary Edition of the Works of Nathaniel Hawthorne.* Vol. 1. Columbus: Ohio State University Press, 1962.

———. *The Snow Image and Uncollected Tales.* Edited by Fredson Bowers, L. Neal Smith, John Manning, and J. Donald Crowley. *The Centenary Edition of the Works of Nathaniel Hawthorne.* Vol. 11. Columbus: Ohio State University Press, 1974.

———. *True Stories From History and Biography.* Edited by Fredson Bowers, L. Neal Smith, and John Manning. *The Centenary Edition of the Works of Nathaniel Hawthorne.* Vol. 6. Columbus: Ohio State University Press, 1972.

———. *Twice-told Tales.* Edited by Fredson Bowers, L. Neal Smith, John Manning, and J. Donald Crowley. *The Centenary Edition of the Works of Nathaniel Hawthorne.* Vol. 9. Columbus: Ohio State University Press, 1974.

———. *A Wonder Book for Girls and Boys and Tanglewood Tales.* Edited by Fredson Bowers, L. Neal Smith, and John Manning. *The Centenary Edition of the Works of Nathaniel Hawthorne.* Vol. 7. Columbus: Ohio State University Press, 1972.

Herbert, T. Walter. *Dearest Beloved: The Hawthornes and the Making of the Middle-Class Family.* Berkeley: University of California Press, 1993.

———. "Hawthorne and American Masculinity." In *The Cambridge Companion to Nathaniel Hawthorne,* ed. Richard H. Millington, 60–78.

———. *"Moby-Dick" and Calvinism: A World Dismantled.* New Brunswick, N.J.: Rutgers University Press, 1977.

———. *Sexual Violence and American Manhood.* Cambridge, Mass.: Harvard University Press, 2002.

Hirsh, John C. "Zenobia as Queen: The Background Sources to Hawthorne's *The Blithedale Romance.*" In *The Nathaniel Hawthorne Journal 1971,* edited by C.E. Frazer Clark, Jr., 182–91. Englewood, Colo.: Microcard Editions, 1971.

Holst-Warhaft, Gail. *The Cue for Passion: Grief and Its Political Uses.* Cambridge, Mass.: Harvard University Press, 2000.

Homer. *The Illiad of Homer.* Translated by Richmond Lattimore. Chicago and London: University of Chicago Press, 1961.

Idol, John L., Jr., "Nathaniel Hawthorne and Harriet Hosmer." *Nathaniel Hawthorne Journal* 6 (1976): 120–28.

Idol, John L., Jr., and Melinda M. Ponder, eds. *Hawthorne and Women: Engendering and Expanding the Hawthorne Tradition.* Amherst: University of Massachusetts Press, 1999.

Irigaray, Luce. *Sexes and Genealogies.* Translated by Gillian C. Gill. New York: Columbia University Press, 1993.

Isenberg, Nancy, and Andrew Burstein, eds. *Mortal Remains: Death in Early America*. Philadelphia: University of Pennsylvania Press, 2003.

Jackson, Charles O., ed. *Passing: The Vision of Death in America*. Westport, Conn.: Greenwood Press, 1977.

Jalland, Pat. *Death in the Victorian Family*. Oxford: Oxford University Press, 1996.

James, Henry. *Hawthorne*. New York: AMS Press, 1968.

———. *The Tales of Henry James*. Vol. 3. Edited by Maqbool Aziz. Oxford: Clarendon Press, 1984.

James, William. *The Varieties of Religious Experience: A Study in Human Nature*. New York: Collier Books, 1961.

Jay, Elisabeth. *The Religion of the Heart: Anglican Evangelicalism and the Nineteenth-Century Novel*. Oxford: Clarendon Press, 1979.

Jupp, Peter C., and Clare Gittings, eds. *Death in England: An Illustrated History*. New Brunswick, N.J.: Rutgers University Press, 2000.

Kasson, Joy S. *Marble Queens and Captives: Women in Nineteenth Century American Sculpture*. New Haven: Yale University Press, 1990.

Kearns, Francis E. "Margaret Fuller and the Abolition Movement." *Journal of the History of Ideas* 25 (1964): 120–27.

Kesselring, Marion Louise. *Hawthorne's Reading, 1828–1850*. New York: New York Public Library, 1949.

Kesterson, David B., ed. *The Merrill Studies in "The Marble Faun."* Columbus: Charles E. Merrill Publishing Co., 1971.

Kohut, Heinz. *The Analysis of the Self: A Systematic Approach to the Psychoanalytic Treatment of Narcissistic Personality Disorders*. New York: International Universities Press, 1971.

———. *The Restoration of the Self*. New York: International Universities Press, 1977.

———. *The Search For the Self: Selected Writings of Heinz Kohut, 1950–1978*. Edited by Paul H. Ornstein. 2 vols. New York: International Universities Press, 1978.

Laderman, Gary. *The Sacred Remains: American Attitudes Toward Death, 1799–1883*. New Haven: Yale University Press, 1996.

Lambert, Royston. *Beloved and God: The Story of Hadrian and Antinous*. New York: Viking, 1984.

Layard, John. *Stone Men of Malekula: Vao*. London: Chatto and Windus, 1942.

Leverenz, David. *Manhood and the American Renaissance*. Ithaca: Cornell University Press, 1989.

Lewis, R.W.B. *The American Adam: Innocence, Tragedy and Tradition in the Nineteenth Century*. Chicago: University of Chicago Press, 1955.

Linden-Ward, Blanche. *Silent City on a Hill: Landscapes of Memory and Boston's Mount Auburn Cemetery*. Columbus: Ohio State University Press, 1989.

Lorraine, Tamsin. *Irigaray and Deleuze: Experiments in Visceral Philosophy*. Ithaca and London: Cornell University Press, 1999.

Madsen, Deborah L. "'A for Abolition': Hawthorne's Bond-Servant and the Shadow of Slavery." *Journal of American Studies* 25.2 (1991): 255–59.

Male, Roy R. *Hawthorne's Tragic Vision*. New York: Norton, 1964.

———. "The Transfiguration of Figures: *The Marble Faun*." In *The Merrill Studies in "The Marble Faun,"* ed. David B. Kesterson, 103–18. Columbus: Charles E. Merrill Publishing Co., 1971.

Maloney, Clarence, ed. *The Evil Eye*. New York: Columbia University Press, 1976.

Marsden, George M. *The Evangelical Mind and the New School Presbyterian Experience: A Case Study of Thought and Theology in Nineteenth-Century America*. New Haven: Yale University Press, 1970.

Mather, Cotton. *Magnalia Christi Americana Books I and II*. Edited by Kenneth B. Murdock. Cambridge, Mass.: Belknap Press, 1977.

———. *Two Mather Biographies: Life and Death and Parentator*. Edited by William J. Scheick. Bethlehem, Pa.: Lehigh University Press, 1989.

Matthiessen, F.O. *The American Renaissance: Art and Expression in the Age of Emerson and Whitman*. London: Oxford University Press, 1941.

McDannell, Colleen. *The Christian Home in Victorian America, 1840–1900*. Bloomington: Indiana University Press, 1994.

McDowell, Peggy, and Richard E. Meyer. *The Revival Styles in American Memorial Art*. Bowling Green, Ohio: Bowling Green University Press, 1994.

McPherson, Hugo. *Hawthorne as Myth-Maker: A Study in Imagination*. Toronto: University of Toronto Press, 1969.

Mellow, James R. *Nathaniel Hawthorne in His Times*. Boston: Houghton Mifflin, 1980.

Melville, Herman. *Moby-Dick; or the Whale*. New York: W.W. Norton, 1976.

———. *The Portable Melville*. Edited by Jay Leyda. New York: Viking Press, 1952.

Miller, Edwin Haviland. *Salem Is My Dwelling Place*. Iowa City: University of Iowa Press, 1991.

Millington, Richard H., ed. *The Cambridge Companion to Nathaniel Hawthorne*. Cambridge: Cambridge University Press, 2004.

———. *Practicing Romance: Narrative Form and Cultural Engagement in Hawthorne's Fiction*. Princeton: Princeton University Press, 1992.

Milton, John. *Paradise Lost*. Edited by Merritt Y. Hughes. New York: Odyssey Press, 1935.

Mitchell, Thomas R. *Hawthorne's Fuller Mystery*. Amherst: University of Massachusetts Press, 1998.

Mott, Frank Luther. *A History of American Magazines, 1741–1850*. Vol. 1. Cambridge, Mass.: Harvard University Press, 1939.

Mullin, Michael, ed. *American Negro Slavery: A Documentary History*. Columbia: University of South Carolina Press, 1976.

Murfin, Ross C., ed. *The Scarlet Letter*. Boston: Bedford Books of St. Martin's Press, 1991.

Murray, Alexander S. *Manual of Mythology: Greek and Roman, Norse and Old German, Hindoo and Egyptian Mythology*. Philadelphia: David McKay, 1895.

Murray, Peter B. "Mythopoesis in *The Blithedale Romance*." *PMLA* 75 (1960): 591–96.

Newman, William M., and Peter L. Halvorson. *Atlas of American Religion: The Denominational Era, 1776–1900*. Walnut Creek, Calif.: AltaMira Press, 2000.

Nichols, Nina da Vinci. *Ariadne's Lives*. Madison, N.J.: Fairleigh Dickinson University Press, 1995.

O'Connor, Mary Catharine, Sister. *The Art of Dying Well: The Development of the Ars Moriendi*. New York: Columbia University Press, 1942.

Patterson, Orlando. *Rituals of Blood: Consequences of Slavery in Two American Centuries*. Washington, D.C.: Civitas Counterpoint, 1998.

———. *Slavery and Social Death: A Comparative Study*. Cambridge, Mass.: Harvard University Press, 1982.

Peabody, Oliver W.B. "Memoir." In *Sermons By the Late William B.O. Peabody, D.D. With a Memoir, By His Brother*, ed. William B.O. Peabody, 1–110. Boston: Benjamin H. Greene, 1849.

Pease, Donald, ed. *National Identities and Post-Americanist Narratives*. Durham and London: Duke University Press, 1994.

Person, Leland S. "The Dark Labyrinth of Mind: Hawthorne, Hester, and the Ironies of Racial Mothering." *Studies in American Fiction* 29.1 (2001): 33–48.

———. "Hawthorne's Early Tales, Male Authorship, Domestic Violence, and Female Readers." In *Hawthorne and the Real: Bicentennial Essays*, ed. Millicent Bell, 125–43.

Pfister, Joel. *The Production of Personal Life: Class, Gender, and the Psychological in Hawthorne's Fiction.* Stanford: Stanford University Press, 1991.

Philipson, Ilene. "Gender and Narcissism." *Psychology of Women Quarterly* 9 (1985): 213–28.

The Picturesque Pocket Companion, and Visitor's Guide, Through Mount Auburn; Illustrated With Upwards of Sixty Engravings on Wood. Boston: Otis, Broaders and Company, 1839.

Plato. *The Dialogues of Plato.* Vols. 1 and 5. Translated by Benjamin Jowett. Oxford: Clarendon Press, 1875.

Poe, Edgar Allan. *Tales and Sketches.* Edited by Thomas Ollive Mabbott. Urbana and Chicago: University of Illinois Press, 2000.

Porte, Joel. *The Romance in America: Studies in Cooper, Poe, Hawthorne, Melville, and James.* Middletown, Conn.: Wesleyan Press. 1969.

Reynolds, David S. *Beneath the American Renaissance: The Subversive Imagination in the Age of Emerson and Melville.* New York: A.A. Knopf, 1988.

Reynolds, Larry J. "Hawthorne's Labors in Concord." In *The Cambridge Companion to Nathaniel Hawthorne,* ed. Richard H. Millington, 10–34.

———, ed. *A Historical Guide to Nathaniel Hawthorne.* New York: Oxford University Press, 2001.

———. "'Strangely Ajar with the Human Race': Hawthorne, Slavery, and the Question of Moral Responsibility." In *Hawthorne and the Real,* ed. Millicent Bell, 40–69.

Richardson, Robert D., Jr. *Emerson: The Mind on Fire.* Berkeley: University of California Press, 1995.

Ruby, Jay. *Secure the Shadow: Death and Photography in America.* Cambridge: MIT Press, 1995.

Ruskin, John. *The Works of John Ruskin.* Vol. 34. Edited by E.T. Cook and Alexander Wedderburn. London: Longmans, Green and Co., 1908.

Sandeen, Ernest. "*The Scarlet Letter* as a Love Story." *PMLA* 77 (1962): 425–35.

Saum, Lewis O. "Death in the Popular Mind of Pre–Civil War America." In *Passing: The Vision of Death in America,* ed. Charles O. Jackson, 65–90.

"The Scarlet Letter." In *The Critical Response to Nathaniel Hawthorne's "The Scarlet Letter,"* ed. Gary Scharnhorst, 25–28.

Scharnhorst, Gary, ed. *The Critical Response to Nathaniel Hawthorne's "The Scarlet Letter."* New York: Greenwood Press, 1992.

Schiesari, Juliana. *The Gendering of Melancholia: Feminism, Psychoanalysis, and the Symbolics of Loss in Renaissance Literature.* Ithaca: Cornell University Press, 1992.

Schiller, Emily. "The Choice of Innocence: Hilda in *The Marble Faun.*" *Studies in the Novel* 26.4 (Winter 1994): 372–91.

Schlauch, Margaret. *Chaucer's Constance and Accused Queens.* New York: New York University Press, 1927.

Schor, Esther. *Bearing the Dead: The British Culture of Mourning from the Enlightenment to Victoria.* Princeton: Princeton University Press, 1994.

Schrieber, Mary Suzanne. "Justice to Zenobia," *New England Quarterly* 56.1 (March 1982): 61–78.

Seeman, Erik R. *Pious Persuasions: Laity and Clergy in Eighteenth-Century New England.* Baltimore: Johns Hopkins University Press, 1999.

Seery, John E. *Political Theory for Mortals: Shades of Justice, Images of Death.* Ithaca: Cornell University Press, 1996.

Shakespeare, William. *Major Plays and the Sonnets.* Edited by G.B. Harrison. New York: Harcourt, Brace and Company, 1948.

Siebers, Tobin. *The Mirror of Medusa.* Berkeley: University of California Press, 1983.

Sloane, David Charles. *The Last Great Necessity: Cemeteries in American History.* Baltimore: Johns Hopkins University Press, 1991.

Smith, David E. "Bunyan and Hawthorne." *John Bunyan in America*. Bloomington, Ind.: Indiana University Press, 1966.

Sophocles. *The Theban Plays*. Translated by E. F. Watling. London: Penguin, 1947.

Stannard, David E., ed. *Death in America*. [Philadelphia]: University of Pennsylvania Press, 1975.

———. *The Puritan Way of Death: A Study in Religion, Culture, and Social Change*. New York: Oxford University Press, 1977.

Stanton, Robert. "Hawthorne, Bunyan, and the American Romances." *PMLA* 71 (1956): 155–65.

Staten, Henry. *Eros in Mourning: Homer to Lacan*. Baltimore and London: Johns Hopkins University Press, 1995.

Steele, Jeffrey. *Transfiguring America: Myth, Ideology, and Mourning in Margaret Fuller's Writing*. Columbia: University of Missouri Press, 2001.

Stern, Julia. "The Politics of Tears: Death in the Early American Novel." In *Mortal Remains: Death in Early America*, ed. Nancy Isenberg and Andrew Burstein, 108–19.

Stern, Madeleine B. *The Life of Margaret Fuller: A Revised, Second Edition*. New York: Greenwood Press, 1991.

Stewart, Randall. *American Literature and Christian Doctrine*. Baton Rouge: Louisiana State University Press, 1958.

Taft, Lorado. *The History of American Sculpture*. New York: Macmillan, 1930.

Tashjian, Dickran, and Ann Tashjian. *Memorials for Children of Change: The Art of Early New England Stonecarving*. Middletown, Conn.: Wesleyan University Press, 1974.

Taylor, Jeremy. *Holy Living and Holy Dying*. 2 vols. Edited by P.G. Stanwood. Oxford: Clarendon Press, 1989.

Thomas, Brook. "Love and Politics, Sympathy and Justice in *The Scarlet Letter*." In *The Cambridge Companion to Nathaniel Hawthorne*, ed. Richard H. Millington, 162–85.

Thoreau, Henry David. *Walden: A Fully Annotated Edition*. Edited by Jeffrey S. Cramer. New Haven: Yale University Press, 2004.

de Tocqueville, Alexis. *Democracy in America*. Vol. 2. Translated by Henry Reeves, revised by Francis Bowen, edited by Phillips Bradley. New York: A.A. Knopf, 1987.

Todd, Janet. *Gender, Art, and Death*. New York: Continuum, 1993.

Tolchin, Neal L. *Mourning, Gender, and Creativity in the Art of Herman Melville*. New Haven: Yale University Press, 1988.

Tomc, Sandra. "A Change of Art: Hester, Hawthorne, and the Service of Love." *Nineteenth Century Literature* 56 (March 2002): 466–94.

Tompkins, Jane. *Sensational Designs: The Cultural Work of American Fiction, 1790–1860*. New York: Oxford University Press, 1985.

Trollope, Anthony. "The Genius of Nathaniel Hawthorne." In *The Critical Response to Nathaniel Hawthorne's "The Scarlet Letter,"* ed. Gary Scharnhorst, 70–75.

Turner, Victor. *Blazing the Trail: Way Marks in the Exploration of Symbols*. Edited by Edith Turner. Tucson: University of Arizona Press, 1992.

———. *On the Edge of the Bush: Anthropology as Experience*. Tucson: University of Arizona Press, 1985.

———. *The Ritual Process: Structure and Anti-Structure*. Chicago: Aldine Publishing Company, 1969.

Virgil. *The Aeneid*. Translated by Robert Fitzgerald. New York: Random House, 1983.

Waelti-Walters, Jennifer. *Fairy Tales and the Female Imagination*. Montreal: Eden Press, 1982.

Waggoner, Hyatt H. *Hawthorne: A Critical Study*. rev. ed. Cambridge, Mass.: Belknap Press, 1963.

Watson, Robert N. *The Rest Is Silence: Death as Annihilation in the English Renaissance*. Berkeley: University of California Press, 1994.

Weldon, Roberta F. "Tyrant King and Accused Queen: Father and Daughter in Nathaniel Hawthorne's *The Blithedale Romance*." *ATQ* 6.1 (March 1992): 31–45.

Welter, Barbara. *Dimity Convictions: The American Woman in the Nineteenth Century*. Athens: Ohio University Press, 1976.

Wetherbee, Winthrop. "Constance and the World in Chaucer and Gower." In *John Gower, Recent Readings: Papers Presented at the Meetings of the John Gower Society at the International Congress on Medieval Studies, Western Michigan University, 1983–1988*, ed. Robert F. Yeager, 65–94. Kalamazoo, Mich.: Medieval Institute Publications, Western Michigan University, 1989.

Wineapple, Brenda. *Hawthorne: A Life*. New York: A.A. Knopf, 2003.

Woodson, Thomas. "Hawthorne and the Author's Immortal Fame." *Nathaniel Hawthorne Review* 30.1 and 2 (2004): 56–91.

Yellin, Jean Fagan. "Hawthorne and the Slavery Question." In *A Historical Guide to Nathaniel Hawthorne*, ed. Larry J. Reynolds, 135–65.

INDEX

9 780230 602908